THE CREW

GOD DUST SAGA
BOOK 1

SADIR S. SAMIR

Copyright © 2022 by Sadir S. Samir

All rights reserved.

No part of this book may be reproduced in any form or by any electronic or mechanical means, including information storage and retrieval systems, without written permission from the author, except for the use of brief quotations in a book review.

Cover Illustration & Cover Design: Love Gunnarson

Editor: Sarah Chorn

For my Father, who gave me enough of his crazy DNA to turn me into an Author just like himself.

CHAPTER ONE

Before the killing began, Varcade wanted to enjoy a glass of iced milk sweetened with honey. He licked his lips, drumming his fingers on the counter as the bartender poured the drink in a clay cup, then set it before Varcade. "There. Happy now?"

Varcade flipped a copper coin to the woman. "You bet," he said with a smile before downing it in one swig. He exhaled and wiped the milk from his upper lip. "Alright, with that out of the way, it's time for me to kill a guy. I'm looking for someone by the name of—"

"You what?" the bartender interrupted. "Kill a man? Here?"

"Yup." Varcade nodded. "That's the job I've been paid for. Why else would I be somewhere like this? No offence, but we're in the middle of the desert. You couldn't have chosen a livelier place for your tavern?"

"Are you bloody stupid?" the woman said. "You can't come to my establishment and tell me you're gonna kill someone. I'm trying to make a living here."

"You do you, and I'll do me. How 'bout that?" Varcade turned away from the bartender and leapt on the nearest table, knocking over their drinks and food to the dismay of the patrons sitting around it.

Now he had everyone's attention. Behind him, he heard the bartender shouting something about guards.

"I'm looking for a guy calling himself Frying Pan Pete," Varcade said. "I've been told he likes coming here. Just point me in the right direction and I'll be gone before you know it."

The man seated by the table tugged on Varcade's leg. "You really don't wanna be messin' with Frying Pan Pete, man," he whispered. "Trust me."

"Is that so?" Varcade said, a tingle of excitement running up his spine.

"Yeah, he and his gang are bad news. Don't get me wrong, I'd love to see that bastard taken care of, but—and no offence—you don't exactly look like the guy to do it. I do like your red coat, though. Where'd you get it?"

The door to the bar slammed open, and a group of rowdy men and women entered. The group wasn't exactly looking to hide their thuggish natures. They were dressed in mixed pieces of leather armour, though they left plenty of skin bare, likely due to the scorching desert of the Harrah region. They were armed with a variety of crude weapons meant for causing pain. The man in front of the pack was tall and lanky, but his face was round like a . . .

Ah. Now I get it.

The man who, without a doubt, must've been Frying Pan Pete barked his drink order at the bartender. He turned and leaned against the counter, resting his elbows on it like a proper asshole. His eyes widened, fixing on Varcade, who was standing on the table waving at him and smiling.

"What the?"

Varcade liberated the two swords strapped to his back and pointed one of them at his target. "I've been paid good coin to end your frying days, Pete. You can make this easy and come with me now or we can do it the fun way. Please choose the fun way. I beg you."

Frying Pan Pete's gang drew their weapons. The patrons in the bar took that as their exit cue and scampered out the door.

"Kill this stupid bastard," Frying Pan Pete ordered. "And where's my goddamn beer?" he said to the anxious bartender who had beads of sweat adorning her brow.

The thugs rushed Varcade. The first to reach him was a woman with brown hair and a nose ring. She growled and swung her axe at his legs, but Varcade deflected it with ease, using his other sword to deliver a fatal slice across her throat.

He leapt over two other thugs, landing behind them. He kicked the closest one in the back, making the man crash into a table, his butt an open target. A quick in-and-out with the blade where the sun doesn't shine, and the man was no more.

Varcade grunted as a bolt burst from his chest. He pulled it out before dropping it on the floor, blood gushing from the wound. "Oh, come on . . . Really?"

He turned and faced the remaining thugs; one was still aiming his crossbow at Varcade. The man's mouth was frozen in an O. "What? How're you still alive?"

"Wouldn't you like to know," Varcade said, inspecting the tear in his coat. "I'm so gonna kill you for that."

"Don't stand around like idiots, you idiots!" Frying Pan Pete growled from across the room. "Kill him!"

Before the remaining thugs could act, Varcade dashed forward and decapitated the one who shot him with the crossbow. Before the headless body sagged to the ground, Varcade had already engaged two other thugs. They swung at him wildly, one armed with a spiked club, the other with an axe, but Varcade's footwork was superior, and they couldn't touch him. In a matter of seconds, both were felled by Varcade's blades.

"Are you bloody kiddin' me," Frying Pan Pete growled. "How's he moving like that!"

Varcade jumped on another table, sheathing his swords on his back. "Have to say I'm pretty damn disappointed. I was expecting this to be a challenge based on how much the guild is paying me. You all suck, man. Like, really."

Another thug made a feeble attempt at grabbing his legs, but Varcade stepped to the side and kicked her in the face, knocking her out cold.

"Oh yeah?" Frying Pan Pete said. "You want some fun, that it? I'll show you a good time, tough guy." He snatched a small glass vial hanging around his neck on a leather cord, and carefully poured a white line on top of his other hand.

"You're so gonna get it now," a thug added, his face that of a weasel. "You've made him mad, mister."

God Dust? Varcade thought, his eyes narrowing on the white powder.

Frying Pan Pete brought his hand up to his nose and snorted the line in one go. In seconds, blue energy glowed around his fists, sparking and crackling as Frying Pan Pete rolled his shoulders and got into a boxing stance. "Come on, then. Let's do this."

"Oooh, we've got a Duster on our hands!" Varcade said with a big smile. "What's your power? Pulling snakes out of your ass? This is so exciting!"

Frying Pan Pete frowned. "What? No! Why the hell would *that* be my power? You can *clearly* see the lightning around my hands! I'm gonna fry you up good, boy."

"Fair point, I guess," Varcade said, then added, "Say, how did loser like you get your hands on God Dust?"

"Shut up!"

Varcade shook his head. "There's no chance in hell *you* found that stuff on your own. You obviously don't have the chops to get it yourselves. You stole it, didn't you?"

"So what if I did? I'm still gonna kill you."

Varcade had a dilemma. He wanted to see the power of this Duster in action, but he wasn't exactly eager to be the test subject himself. Frying Pan Pete on his own wouldn't be much of a problem but sniffing up the bones of dead gods could make anyone a serious threat, even for a former Educator like himself.

"What the hell are you waiting for? Come get some!" Frying Pan Pete barked.

"Can you give me a damn second to think?" Varcade snapped, scratching the back of his head as he contemplated the situation.

"For *what*?"

"How 'bout this? You hit that weasel-faced friend of yours instead and I'll leave."

"Are you for real?"

Varcade nodded.

Frying Pan Pete bit his lip. "I have your word that you'll leave and not come back for me?"

"I swear. You'll never see me again, and you can get on with your thuggish lifestyle and all it entails."

The weasel-faced thug swallowed, his eyes darting back and forth between Frying Pan Pete and Varcade. "Boss?"

After a few seconds Frying Pan Pete said, "Okay, we have a deal. Get over here, Midgy."

"Please don't, boss . . ."

"Shut up and take it like a man."

"Yeah, take it like a man," Varcade added.

Midgy dragged his feet as he made his way to his boss, his eyes on the floor. "Will it kill me?"

"I don't think so," Frying Pan Pete said. "I'll hit you in the stomach, alright?"

"I appreciate that," Midgy said. "If things go sideways, at least we had a good run, didn't we, boss?"

"We did. I'll make sure your family's taken care of, so don't worry 'bout that."

Say what you will about weasel faced Midgy, no one can ever question that man's loyalty, Varcade thought.

Midgy closed his eyes.

Frying Pan Pete drew back his arm.

Varcade clapped his hands excitedly.

Frying Pan Pete's energised fist slammed into Midgy's gut and sent the thug flying with amazing force. He crashed into the wall before landing face-first on the floor.

"Ouch . . ." Varcade said, watching Midgy's limp, smoking body. "That guy's dead, man. I can't believe you did that."

"You told me to!" Frying Pan Pete stuttered, his eyes darting between Varcade and Midgy's corpse.

Varcade clicked his tongue. "So what? I didn't force you, did I? This is all on you Pete. You killed your friend. That's messed up."

"Oh my god," Pete muttered and unsteadily walked over to Midgy before sinking to his knees. "I didn't mean to kill—"

Frying Pan Pete choked on his words as Varcade's blade entered his back. The thug looked down at the bloody sword sticking out through his gut. "Huh," he moaned before falling onto his side with a thud.

Varcade pulled out his sword and wiped the nasty bits off on the man's clothes before sheathing it on his back. He snatched the vial of God Dust and then grabbed Pete's foot and started dragging the body toward the door.

"You're a bad, bad man," the bartender muttered, half her face sticking up from behind the counter. She wiggled a finger in the air. "Very bad."

Varcade's head turned towards her with a shrug before he walked out.

Most people in the Harrah region didn't travel anywhere by foot. If the blistering sun and sandstorms weren't enough, there were always bands of marauders on the prowl ready to take advantage of easy prey.

Luckily, for a couple of coins, people could get between the city-states by way of armoured caravans. Those monstrous constructions were your best shot of making it alive from one point to another. Varcade had travelled to the bar using one and paid the driver extra to wait until he was done.

Varcade dropped Pete's leg and wiped some sweat from his brow and glared at the corpse. "You're heavier than you look, you big ol' bastard."

The caravan driver had his back turned on Varcade, busy feeding the two massive six-legged insects that pulled the caravan. Their pincers were the size of a man's legs, and at a first glance, they could be quite scary. However, the beasts had a rather kind nature, and only rarely snapped their drivers in half using said pincers. They might not look the part, but those creatures moved liked the wind even at their slowest pace.

"You ready to go?" the driver said over his shoulder. "I picked up another guy who's headed to Razula."

"Whatever, I don't care." Varcade was more focused on the fact he had to spend the next couple of hours inside the caravan. The advantages heavily outweighed the disadvantages, but the negatives still sucked.

Sure, it was an easy way to travel since all you needed to do was lounge about, but the quarters were cramped and hot and reeked from unwashed people. Very yucky.

Right before Varcade got onboard, he stopped and looked around. For the second time in two days, he couldn't shake the feeling someone was watching him. But if someone was, they were doing a damn fine job of hiding, because Varcade couldn't spot anything out of the ordinary.

Shaking his head, Varcade got on board, huffing, and puffing as he pushed Frying Pan Pete's body inside the caravan. He dropped the dead man and sank onto one of the benches lining the wall.

The other passenger, seated on the opposite bench looked at Varcade with a smirk and scoffed, then crossed his arms before looking away, shaking his head. "Yup, I see what you're trying to do, don't think I don't."

Varcade gave the man a questioning look. "Huh, what's that?"

The man snorted. "Like you don't know. Come on, give me a break."

"I genuinely don't have a clue what you're on about. I don't even know why you're talkin' to me."

"What, I'm supposed to just ignore *that*?" The man said, nodding at Frying Pan Pete's corpse; not with disgust or fear, but rather like a sweet raspberry pie you'd been told not to touch.

"I don't care if you ignore it or not. Stop talking to me."

"Fine, fine," the man said, holding up his hands in mock surrender. "Doesn't matter. I don't tangle with those type of *urges* anymore. Back in the day, sure, I would indulge like there was no tomorrow. But again, I'm done with that life. I stay away from the forbidden candy."

The caravan finally started moving.

"But there's nothing wrong with looking, am I right?" the man continued, licking his lips, eyes locked on the corpse.

Varcade frowned. "Why'd you do that thing with your mouth when you said that?"

The man's eyes were still on the body as he replied. "Huh, what's that?"

"You licked your lips, you weirdo."

The man shot Varcade an angry look. "Well excuse me for getting a bit peckish when you present it like that."

"That's a dead man," Varcade snapped. "Not food. Stop acting like it's edible. What's wrong with you?"

"Fine, fine, hey listen," the man said in hushed voice. "I'll trade you for it. I'm a merchant, right? I've got some damn fine treasures in here." He opened the large sack in front of him.

"If I don't deliver this body, I'm not getting paid. I doubt you have anything–hey, what's that?"

The man held up a small cube with a rotating handle on the side. "Oh this? It's a Mr. Flabby. Magical stuff. Only like three or four of 'em exist. The Supreme who used to make 'em is dead."

"Supreme, eh?" Varcade said. "That's those who can wield magic without the use of God Dust, right?"

The man nodded. "That's right. People of the Old Blood. Rare individuals. You'll never find another one of these beauties *anywhere*, that much I can tell ya."

Varcade was still trying to get his head around all this God Dust business. It was a resource unique to the Harrah region since it had been the final battleground where the Old Ones had been killed by mankind with the aid of the Primordial Jinns.

"So, you're saying one of these Supremes created this?"

"That's exactly what I'm saying." The man looked Varcade up and down. "Are you thick in the head?"

"Do I *look* like I'm from around these parts? What the hell do I know?"

The man shrugged. "Guess not. I figured you had dyed your hair or somethin' just to stick out."

"Nope, it's all natural, so shut up about it." Varcade leaned closer. "What does this Mr. Flabby do?"

"Here, just turn the handle a couple o' times and you'll see. Go on."

Varcade placed the box on his lap and did as he was told. At first, nothing happened, then the lid flew open and a tiny, pudgy potato-looking creature stood up.

"Whatever you say to it, Mr. Flabby will repeat mimicking your exact voice. Give it a go."

Varcade grinned. "My name is Varcade."

"My name is Varcade," Mr. Flabby repeated.

Varcade's mind was blown. "Amazing!"

"Amazing!" Again, the strange creature repeated.

Before Varcade had a chance to say anything else, the man snatched it back from him. "Good stuff, right? Give me the body and I'll give it to you."

"Fine, take the stupid corpse, I don't care. Give me back my Mr. Flabby."

"Excellent," the man said with wolfish eyes.

"One thing," Varcade said, grabbing the man by the collar of his shirt. "You don't eat him while we're traveling, got it?"

"But—"

"No."

"Fine . . ." The man leaned back, pouting.

"Good. I'm gonna grab some shuteye now. If I wake up and find you're snacking, we're gonna have some problems, got it?" Varcade clasped his hands behind his head and closed his eyes.

CHAPTER TWO

A wet and disgusting sound startled Varcade from his sleep. He blinked a couple of times, rubbing his eyes. *You've got to be bloody kidding me?*

The stranger was gnawing and nibbling on Frying Pan Pete's pinkie finger, barely any flesh left on the bone.

"Hey!" Varcade shouted, shooting out his hand and grabbing the man by the ear. "What did I tell you? I was clear, wasn't I?"

"I'm sorry!" the man said, licking blood from his lips. "I couldn't stop myself, man. Y-you don't understand how tasty it is . . ."

Still holding him in an iron-grip, Varcade used his other hand and pounded on the metal wall separating the driver and passenger section of the caravan. "We need to make a quick stop," he said.

The caravan came to a halt and Varcade slid the heavy doors open. He threw the cannibal out headfirst and then shoved out Frying Pan Pete's body after him.

"You can't do this!" the stranger said. "I've paid to be taken all the way to Razula!"

"Too bad for you," Varcade said grabbing the door handle and slamming it shut.

He signalled the driver to continue their journey.

Varcade woke as the doors to the caravan slid open, a burst of sunlight streaming in.

"We're here," the driver said, leaning his head inside. "Pay up and get out."

"What a rude way to wake someone up . . ." Varcade muttered and yawned, scratching his head. He took his new possession, the Mr Flabby, under his arm and stepped outside and paid the driver.

The caravan took off again, leaving a billowing cloud of dust behind. Varcade brushed himself off, squinting from the bright light as he walked towards his destination.

The guildhall was commonly known as the Nest by those people in the trade, and it was a run-down building that no ordinary person would ever give any passing thoughts to. But for any sellsword in the city-state of Razula, this was *the* place where all sorts of shady business was conducted. The secret guild did not accept just anyone, and being a member was considered not only a privilege but also a testament to one's ability to complete the work they were hired to do.

Varcade pushed the doors open with unnecessary force and strode inside like he owned the place. "I'm back," he said. "Did you miss me?"

Many of the sellswords of the guild usually hung out at the Nest between jobs, kicking it and enjoying a few dozen drinks. The scattered group of people inside grunted and snorted in response to Varcade's question.

The moment the doors swung shut, the locale was once again shrouded in a gloomy but cosy darkness. The windows were boarded shut, but here and there, beams of sunlight made their way through a crack or gap, revealing specks of dust swirling in the air.

In the centre of the room was a horseshoe formed counter. Behind it stood Shamil, a bald man with the tiniest of moustache above his upper lip. Shamil was the so-called bartender in the joint, but in truth he was more of do-everything-around-here kinda guy.

"Tough crowd today, eh?" Varcade said, planting his butt on one of the stools before the counter.

"They're itching for work, sir. It is rather dry at the moment," Shamil said, rubbing a mug with a white cloth. "If you don't mind me saying, I don't see a dead body with you, sir. That's not good. Not good at all."

Varcade waved it off with a grin. "Don't you worry your shiny head 'bout that and fix me my drink, please. It's been a long trip and a guy needs his milk."

Varcade suddenly felt a looming presence. That along with the smell. "Oh, if it isn't my least favourite person in the world. What do you want, Bosco?" he said without turning around.

Bosco was a Wormian, a race of extremely muscular humanoids with slim worm-like heads, big bulbous eyes, and a large mouth. "You botched the gig, didn't you?"

Varcade took a sip from his milk and honey drink. "So, what if I did? None of your concern, worm-head."

Bosco turned to the other sellswords in the room theatrically. "Surprise, surprise, Varcade failed, once again."

Some sellswords cheered whilst other complained as coins changed hands.

Bosco returned his attention to Varcade and leaned close, his reeking breath assaulting Varcade's nostrils. "Listen, we don't like foreigners like you coming to our part of the world and taking our jobs; especially when you screw it up. I've had enough of you."

Varcade spun around on the stool, facing the foul-mouthed wormian. "Maybe if you were better at your job, Patches wouldn't give me the contract to begin with. Ever think about that?"

"The old man has a soft spot for you for some reason," Bosco growled. "You're the definition of a hit-and-miss. You fail half of the contracts you take on. Contracts that could've gone to us instead."

"That's life for ya. Work harder or somethin', stop bugging me about your shortcomings."

"You little bastard. I could snap your neck like a twig."

Varcade stood. "Really? Please, by all means, give it a go." Bosco clenched his fists but that was all he did. "Yeah, didn't think so, wormy. Now get the hell outta my face."

"This isn't over," Bosco said between clenched teeth before walking away.

Varcade emptied his drink and smacked his lips. "All talk but no show, like usual."

"You seem determined to make as many enemies in the guild as possible," Shamil said, already preparing another drink for Varcade.

"It is what it is, my friend." Varcade smiled. "Some folks just don't get along."

A door at the far end of the room opened and a burly man wearing oddly shaped yellow goggles stomped towards Varcade. It was fair to say he looked like a mixture of a porcupine and a barrel.

"I thought I heard your voice," Patches said, stopping before Varcade, looking him up and down and all around.

When Patches got upset he tended to grind his teeth and huff and puff like a rutting boar. "Where's the damn body? I don't see it, why don't I see it?"

"Mr. Flabby!" Varcade said with a grin, holding up the magical box like a child showing their parents an ugly thing they'd made and now wanted to receive praise for. "Come on, turn the handle!"

"Varcade, I swear to the Golden King, if you messed up this job, that's it. You'll be out on your ass—"

"Forget about that. Just turn the handle, you big oaf."

"Damn you, boy," Patches grunted, grabbing the box, and turning the handle.

Patches was not impressed with Mr. Flabby, as evidenced by the box crashing into the wall.

"Mr. Flabby!" Varcade shrieked, running to pick up the box.

"My quarters. Now."

"That wasn't very nice," Varcade muttered as he followed Patches into the room.

Patches rubbed the bridge of his nose, exhaling loudly. "I can't keep doing this, Varcade."

The two of them sat in Patches' cramped quarters, the guild boss behind a massive desk and Varcade on a chair opposite him.

"Don't be dramatic, boss-man," Varcade said, his attention focused on the tear in his coat he'd received during the fight with Frying Pan Pete's thugs. "It wasn't that big of a contract to begin with. And you saw Mr. Flabby—"

"Enough about that stupid thing," Patches erupted, before bringing his voice down again like it'd never happened. "I know you don't *care* about things like coin or failing and succeeding, but I'm tryin' to run a business here, boy. I can't keep sticking my neck out for you. The other sellswords are getting antsy, if you can't tell."

"Sure, but they're—"

"Shut up and let me finish. This is real talk now. The moment I learned you were a rogue Educator, I took pity on you, sure, but I also knew what a man of your skills could bring to this guild."

The second Patches mentioned the Educators, Varcade tensed. He stopped fiddling with his coat and crossed his arms. Just thinking about his past filled him with an unparalleled rage; like there was a great slumbering beast within just waiting to break free and wreak havoc.

"Listen," Patches continued, "the other swords have nothin' on you. You're better than they could ever be. I've heard the rumours of what those zealot freaks do to the kids they take. The experiments an' all."

"Don't go there," Varcade said, his tone making it clear that the topic was off-limits.

"Fine, I won't, but whatever was done to you, you got out. Broke free, made your escape. I applaud you for that. I'm just sayin', you could use the skills you gained to become the best sword in Harrah. Use it as a gift instead of a curse." Patches sucked in a deep breath. "You're special, boy. Those killers in that room, like Bosco, don't have anything else goin' for 'em. You get what I'm saying? You can do more with your life. You just need to put in the effort."

Varcade knew what Patches was trying to accomplish with this talk, and a part of him found it commendable, but he hadn't asked for the man's guidance. Instead of surrendering to his anger, he put on a smile. "Listen, Patches, if you're gonna kick me out of the guild then do it. No harsh feelings, I swear, but I did not sign up for some heart-to-heart talk."

Patches sighed, shaking his head. "You're the most stubborn sonuvabitch I've ever met."

"You're good people, but I am who I am. I ain't changin' for no one."

"That's no way of living, boy. You need to find peace and move on from the things that were done to you. Otherwise, you'll spend your whole life runnin'."

"The world's a big place, bunch of stuff to see and experience."

"You're impossible," Patches rubbed his brow.

Varcade stood. "So, is this it then, boss-man? I'm out?"

Patches looked at him. A few moments passed before he let out a long sigh. "You're not out. I'll give you one more chance."

Varcade would never admit it, but hearing that made him feel something. It might even have been happiness. "Sweet, then I'll stick around for a while. Hey, before I forget," he said and placed the vial of God Dust on the table. "Snatched it from Frying Pan Pete, who turned out to be a Duster. Figured you could sell it for a pretty penny."

Patches broke out into a huge grin. "Why didn't you show me this immediately, you fool. This's worth ten times more than the contract. See, this is why I keep you around." He met Varcade's eyes. "You didn't use any yourself, did you?"

"Yeah, right. Like I'd allow a dead god to crawl up my ass–or nose–and take over my mind and body. Pass on that, thank you very much."

Varcade had heard that if one consumed too much God Dust, their bodies turned into an Anchor, a physical connection to the mortal plane that the Old Ones could use to take over. Become one of the Taken.

"Okay, good. This crap is worth a lot of money, but it's dangerous stuff. You'd think the Bone Lords would be better at keeping it safe in their vaults."

"Who says it was necessarily stolen from a Bone Lord's vault? Frying Pan Pete could've gotten it from one of those Bone Hunters sneaking into the Blight?"

The Blight was the strip of landmass in Harrah where most of the Old Ones had been killed, their corpses left to rot. It was said that the blood seeping into the soil was the reason the flora and fauna had forever been altered, turning the whole area into an unstable and volatile location unlike any other place in the known world.

"Perhaps. There are still more bones to be mined in the Blight and the God Bones Consortium don't catch all the Bone Hunters. Some of 'em make it out alive."

The God Bones Consortium was an ancient organisation tasked with overseeing all mining operations in the Blight and allocating the God Dust to each of the seven city-states.

"It's funny, you go on about how dangerous God Dust is, but you have no issue selling it to whoever can pay the most."

Patches grunted. "I don't have to like it; I just sell it. I'm a businessman."

"Whatever," Varcade said, not really interested in going deeper into the topic. "So, got a new contract for me or what?"

Patches was back to inspecting the white powder in the vial. "Nope, not at the moment. You're gonna have to sit back and wait like everyone else."

Varcade exhaled dramatically. "I don't wanna do that . . . You gotta have somethin', man?"

Patches shrugged. "Tough luck. Deal with it."

"Fine," Varcade sighed. "You better have a new job when I come back."

Varcade had not been in the mood to sit around the bar with the other sellswords, so he retreated to his room on the upper floor of the Nest. The modest living quarters Patches arranged for him weren't fancy: a small room with a small bed and a small window; just the bare necessities needed between jobs.

His room back in the Educator Temple had been similar, the only difference being that one had always been damp and cold, while everything in Harrah was hot and dry.

Varcade had tried and failed to get some shuteye for the past hour or two, but instead of being welcomed by the sweet embrace of sleep, he'd kept shifting and turning, unable to let his body and mind relax. The mattress was itchy, and the room was too hot. With a loud grunt, he finally admitted defeat and sat up on the edge of the bed.

Parts of the conversation with Patches still clung to him like a bad stink. It was as if Varcade had fallen into a pile of shit and now had a swarm of Patches-faced flies buzzing around his head.

Varcade hadn't joined the guild of sellswords to be judged and lectured about his lifestyle and what choices he'd made. That had been his life as an Educator, and he'd be damned to let anyone decide things for him again. *Screw them all*, he thought and started getting dressed. *Telling me what to do and how to live my life.*

Varcade decided to get out of the Nest and get something sweet to chew on to take his mind off things. He threw on his red coat–an Educator coat turned inside out–and strapped his two swords on his back before going down the stairs and outside.

Razula was one of the smaller city-states in the desert region of

Harrah, but still enormous compared to what Varcade was used to. Karkan—known as the Land of Mountains—where Varcade was from, was mostly speckled with smaller villages and a few cities across the great mountain range. The empire known as the World Authority controlled the majority of that region, but across the sea, here in Harrah, things were different. Seven city-states dominated the Harrah region, each one with their own ruler titled Bone Lord.

The seven city-states all functioned autonomously with their own laws, but a fickle alliance called the Seven had been formed to stand against an impending invasion from the World Authority. The World Authority was technically more advanced and had the support of the Educator order, but Harrah had God Dust and that made the empire think twice before engaging in a military conflict.

As Varcade made his way through the narrow and sprawling streets, he couldn't help but feel like he was being followed, the hair in the nape of his neck standing up. *This is getting on my nerves*, Varcade thought, looking around. But just like it had been the previous days, he was unable to see any evidence of the fact.

Deciding to ignore it, Varcade made his way to the bazaar where a variety of vendors were selling delicious treats of all kinds. The marketplace was packed with people, and if you were someone who got easily claustrophobic, this would be hell. Luckily for Varcade he couldn't care less, and made his way through the crowd with ease, arriving before a small sun-coloured tent.

The vendor was a big woman with a welcoming smile, and a part of Varcade wanted her to hug him. Her warm presence reminded him of a neighbour from his childhood who used to bake all sorts of treats and bring them over to their house. Varcade and his older brother had called her auntie even though they weren't really related.

He watched as she rolled small dough balls in the palm of her hand and dropped them in hot oil, one by one. "Welcome to Belkquiz's Sweets," she said, wiping her brow then resting her hands on her hips while the dough balls fried. "What can I get you, my boy?"

Varcade leaned over the finished donuts displayed on a platter. The crust was beautifully golden, and they were sprinkled with different coloured sugar. "I'd like five of the ones with green sugar and five of the ones with pink," he said, licking his lips, saliva pooling in his mouth.

"Of course," the woman said and began placing the donuts on a napkin.

"Add two of the purple ones," a voice said behind Varcade.

He turned and saw a man wearing a hooded, black robe. He wasn't old, a few years older than Varcade, but his face told the tale of someone who'd been through some shit in his days. His hair and black beard were rugged, but his dark eyes were sharp as steel. "This man's treat," the stranger added.

"You're weird," Varcade said to the stranger with a shrug then nodded at the woman to signal it was okay. Coins and treats exchanged hands, and Varcade thanked the woman. *I wish you were my mother*, he thought for a split second.

"Thank you," the stranger said, picking out the purple donuts he'd requested. "Appreciate it."

"No big deal," Varcade said, taking a big bite from his own donut. "So, you're the one who's been following me, eh?"

The stranger raised an eyebrow. "What makes you say that?"

"Your smell. It's not bad or anythin', but distinct." Varcade sniffed the air a few times. "Lavender oil, right? Fancy stuff. You're no commoner."

The stranger nodded. "Impressive. Is that an Educator trick?"

Varcade froze, but only for a second. In a breath, his hands gripped the sword handles strapped on his back. "Think carefully before uttering your next words," Varcade said. "They spell the difference between your life and death."

If the stranger felt any distress, he did a great job hiding it. "I am not your enemy."

Varcade's eyes narrowed to slits, locking eyes with the stranger. "The Educators sent you?"

"No. I have no relation to the Order. I swear."

The Educators were rarely subtle in their dealings. If they sent someone after him, Varcade would know. He released the grip of his swords. "Fine, I believe you. Now what do you want?"

"I'd like to talk, but not here. Too many eyes and ears. Let's go to the Nest. Patches is expecting me."

"Huh," Varcade said, picking his teeth with no regard to how savage it looked. "So, this is about a contract?"

"It is," the stranger said, a slight hesitation in his voice that Varcade picked up on.

Varcade crossed his arms, looking the man up and down. "Then what was this about? You could've gone straight to the Nest. You clearly know about the guild and Patches. Why go through the trouble of following me around?"

"I wanted to see you in person. I needed to see a rogue Educator with my own eyes before taking things further."

"Should I be flattered?"

"I do not care if you are flattered or not," the stranger said in a hushed but agitated tone. "I heard the rumours of your existence the moment you set foot on my side of the world. I've been keeping track of your whereabouts since."

"You're tellin' me you've been following me for years? Yeah, this is gettin' a bit creepy . . ." Varcade said.

The stranger shook his head. "Not in person, no. I have–I *used to* have a network of spies all over Harrah. It was my job to identify potential security threats. A wildcard like yourself, with the skills you possess, ticked all the boxes."

"Who the hell are you, man?" Varcade scratched the back of his head.

"You'll get the full story once we head back to the Nest." The stranger took a deep breath and met Varcade's eyes, clearly forcing himself to utter the words. "My name is Edghar, and I plan to kill the ruling Bone Lord of Akrab."

CHAPTER THREE

Edghar sat at the counter, his drink untouched before him. It was a strange atmosphere inside the Nest. Six months ago, being in a wretched hive of scum and villainy like this would've been unthinkable; sharing the same space with killers and other crooked individuals. But, of course, that was before Edghar had been branded a traitor to the throne by the Bone Lord of Akrab herself.

The guild leader, Patches, had wanted a moment with the rogue Educator before they went over the contract and the details. Waiting was playing a number on Edghar's nerves.

What the hell am I doing here? he thought, stopping his foot from tapping on the floor like a nervous child. He sighed, rubbing his eyes. *How the hell did it all come to this?*

"Hey," came a gruff voice.

Edghar looked up at the huge wormian that had strolled up to him.

"If you want a job done right, that fool in there isn't the guy to do it. Trust me on that one. You want someone like me," he said, sticking his thumb to his muscular chest. "My track record speaks for itself."

"I'm well aware who you are, Bosco the Vandal," Edghar said, returning his attention to his untouched drink. "I know what you do, and I want no part in it."

"What the hell is that supposed to mean?" Bosco said, placing one hand on the counter and leaning close to Edghar's face.

"You're not just a sellsword. You'd kill for free. Not interested."

Bosco growled and leaned in even closer. They were practically kissing at this point. "You have the guts to come in *here* and pass judgement? I could rip your head off, little man, and no one would bat an eye."

"While that might be true, dear Bosco, the boss doesn't take too kindly to guild members killing potential clients," the bald man behind the bar said, his tone bored like he'd seen the same thing play out countless times. "I suggest you leave the man alone."

"Fuck off, Shamil," Bosco said, still staring daggers into Edghar's eyes. "Don't you have a bathroom to clean or somethin'?"

"This is getting tedious," Edghar said.

Bosco roared and drew back his neck to deliver a head-butt, but Edghar shifted to the side making the wormian smash his face into the back of the chair instead. The big sellsword pressed a ham-sized hand to his non-existent nose (worms don't have noses).

Edghar slid out from his seat and positioned himself before the wormian. Bosco would surely punch a hole through his skull if he landed a hit, so the key was to make him miss and then counter the attack.

Bosco huffed and puffed, pumping himself up for another charge. Edghar stayed loose on his feet, swaying slightly side-to-side, ready to turn the attack around. The wormian ran at him head-on in an attempt to grab Edghar in a crushing bearhug, but Edghar ducked under the massive arms and tripped the big sellsword who crashed face-first to the floor.

Before Bosco could get up, Edghar leapt on his back, pressing his knee down to keep him in place, while pulling the wormian's arm up in a painful angle. "You make another move and I break your arm. Your choice."

"Fine," Bosco hissed, "get off me, shithead."

Edghar applied more pressure on the man's arm, producing a high-pitched wail from the sellsword. "You will behave now, correct?"

"Yes, yes, let go of my arm," Bosco growled.

Edghar released his grip and stood, dusting himself off. It'd been a while since he'd been in a tussle. It felt good to get the blood pumping and took his mind off his nerves.

Bosco got to his feet and shot Edghar a glare before going to the table in the corner to sulk.

"Impressive, sir," the bald bartender said. "Let me offer you another drink as a thank you."

Edghar waved the bartender off. "Not all good deeds need compensation."

The bartender seemed to consider that for a moment before saying, "You're right. I guess I have been in this kind of work for a tad bit too long. Nothing happens here without gain."

"I would not mind some water," Edghar said, resuming his seat at the counter.

"Certainly." The bartender poured him a glass from a ceramic jug. The bald man had a curious look on his face as he slid the glass over, like he wanted to say something but was hesitating.

"Something on your mind?" Edghar said, after gulping down the water.

"If I may," the bartender said, lowering his voice to a whisper. "How was it working with her? The Bone Lord of Akrab, that is."

"Complicated." The words escaped Edghar's lips without thought, surprising himself. *Huh, I guess that sums it up quite well.* "So, you know who I am?"

The bartender chuckled, but in a polite way. "Please, sir, this is a professional operation. We don't even consider taking on a client without doing our own research first."

"You wouldn't think that was the case by the looks of this building, or what's inside of it for that matter," Edghar said.

"It is all calculated. Our location, the run-down building, the boarded windows. Our profession requires us to operate from the shadows. We are not meant to be known or seen."

"What about that rogue Educator? He is not a subtle man. I've been following him for quite some time."

"Varcade is . . . a special case, one could say. Normally someone like him would never be a member of the guild, but his unique circumstances make him a great asset. But I'm sure you're well aware of that, since you've specifically requested him for the contract you have in mind."

Edghar nodded, scratching his scruffy beard that was a new look for him. "I never imagined seeing an Educator with my own eyes, or rather a rogue Educator. There were rumours, long ago, about an Educator who came to Akrab, but I believe she was killed by an angry mob. My people did not appreciate having the Teachings shoved down their throats."

"I am not surprised to hear that," Shamil said. "Our part of the world is a much different place, after all. No place for the World Authority or the Educators here."

"Then why did the guild accept him?" Edghar said.

"Our guild boss, Patches, sees unlimited potential in Varcade." The bartender sighed. "The horrendous experiments done to him as a boy made him something more than human. It was done to turn him into an Educator, a living tool of justice. The scars may not be visible on his skin, but they're still there, in his mind."

"I have heard some of the stories," Edghar said. "Rumour has it the children are given to the Educators by their parents. Supposedly it's considered a tremendous honour to have your child chosen by the Order."

"In truth, I know almost nothing about Varcade's past. It's impossible to get him to talk about it. If what you say is true, it's even worse than I thought."

The door to the room in the back opened and Patches motioned for Edghar to join him.

Edghar stepped inside the cramped room and took a seat next to Varcade. Patches sat behind a sturdy desk, his thick and hairy arms resting on the table. Varcade leaned back on a chair pressed against the wall to Edghar's right, his hands clasped behind his head.

The walls were lined with racks upon racks displaying countless bottles of wine. A quick glance at their labels told Edghar this was high quality—he would know, having lived most of his life in the Bone Lord's ziggurat in Akrab, where only the finest things were served.

"Admiring the collection, eh?" Patches chuckled, his round belly jiggling.

"Indeed," Edghar said, "and also thinking that crime does pay after all."

"It sure does," Patches said with a grin. "It sure does."

Edghar's hands were sweaty, and his heart thumped loudly in his ears, but he refused to let it show. *Keep it together*, he thought, steadying his breath. *Clea must be stopped. I won't allow her to destroy the city.*

"Eh, are you gonna say somethin' or. . ." Varcade said.

Edghar snapped back to reality. He studied the sellsword. Everything about him made him stand out and Edghar was confident it was not by chance. The silvery/grey hair cemented him as a foreigner, something he could easily have addressed to blend in. And the ridiculously stylish red coat took it even further. He stuck out like a sore thumb wherever he went.

"Umm, hello?" Varcade said. "You're looking at me weird. Stop it."

Edghar sat straighter. "My apologies. I have a lot on my mind."

"That's fine," Patches said, scratching his big beard. "Let's talk business, shall we?"

"Yeah, spill it," Varcade said. "What's the job? You mentioned somethin' about assassinating the Bone Lord of Akrab, right?"

Edghar tried to suppress the nauseous feeling in his gut. "Yes. That is the job."

Patches blew out a long breath. "Damn, that's . . . Big. Huge. Massive. You're talking about killing one of the Seven."

"I am aware," Edghar said. "I would not be here if I thought there was another way."

"Why you want her dead?" Varcade said, loudly biting into an apple that hadn't been in his hand a second ago.

Where to even begin?

"The city-state of Akrab is on the verge of a civil war. The Bone Lord is a young, reckless woman, but when I was by her side, I could always make her see reason; make her think before acting on her impulses. It was never the steadiest of ships, but together we made it work."

"When you were by her side?" Varcade said, scratching his non-existent beard.

"Yes. I'm the Bone Lord's former Spymaster." It felt strange uttering the words, a mix of both pride and shame.

"And now you want her killed? That's a bit backstabby," Varcade said.

"It's not a matter of *me* wanting her dead," Edghar said, locking eyes with the sellsword. "Something happened to her. She has changed. She no longer sees reason, and her actions are going to lead the city to destruction. I can't allow that to happen."

Patches leaned forward. "What happens after she's gone? Are you going to be the new Bone Lord of Akrab?"

"If I must, then I must. I will do what is needed for the people of Akrab."

The guild leader grunted. "What's this civil war you mentioned? What's happening?"

Edghar sighed. "A conflict between the demon and human population in the city has been brewing for years. We have had several riots break out, but now, in more recent times, many of the demons have turned more hostile than ever, seemingly attacking human citizens without provocation. To solve this, Clea began funding the Alchemy Guild to develop new experimental weaponry to be used against the demons. Together, they established a new security force to take control of the city."

Patches grunted again. "That doesn't sound like the best idea, if you ask me, but what the hell do I know."

"I would be inclined to agree," Edghar said. "And if that was not enough, she has also hired a group of Dusters as her new private protection. She's allowing those vile people to live in the ziggurat itself, amongst the regular staff."

Patches leaned back in his chair, clasping his hands. "Well, you came to the right place, my friend. You want the Bone Lord dead, and we can help with that. But first, let's talk payment. I don't think I need to stress how big a job like this is. We would need—"

"God Dust." Edghar said. "Once the Bone Lord is gone and we take over the ziggurat, I will have access to the vaults. You will be paid."

Patches laughed. "I do like the sound of that!" The guild boss turned his attention to the sellsword with a greedy grin. "Well, boy? What do you say? Wanna get rich?"

The rogue Educator stretched and let out a big yawn. "Boring. All this political stuff is makin' me sleepy. Pass."

"*Pass?*" Patches said, his eyelids fluttering like the rapid beating of a bug's wings.

"You heard me," Varcade said. "I've no interest in getting involved in stuff like this. Too much, too big. Gives me a headache. Pass."

"Now, just wait a minute, Varcade—" Patches began.

"Give me a contract to kill a thug here or some other bastard there, something fun. Not this stuff."

"You don't finish half the contracts I give you because you grow bored or get distracted," Patches said, slamming his fist on the table. "You always complain things are too easy and not challenging enough. Now you get a job that's bigger than anything you've ever done, and you say you're bored and don't want it?"

Varcade shrugged. "What can I tell ya, boss-man, not feelin' this one. I don't see the big deal. You've got a room out there full of other swords that'd be glad to take the job. Give it to one of 'em."

"You make it sound like you have a choice in the matter."

Varcade and Patches snapped their attention to Edghar who had remained silent until this point.

"What the hell is that supposed to mean?" Varcade said.

"It means exactly what I said. I did not come here *asking*. You will do this job because I require it, or I will have this whole guild shut down and the lot of you thrown in the dungeons."

Patches grunted. "Hey now, if you think you can threaten—"

"I may not officially carry my title of a Spymaster these days, but I still know many powerful people. People who owe me. If you want to keep this guild going, you will do what I say."

"I don't care. Shut it down. I'll be long gone before anyone throws me in any dungeon."

"Boy," Patches said, looking at Varcade. "This is my livelihood. I can't lose the guild. Too many people depend on me."

"What if I straight up kill you right here?" Varcade said to Edghar, placing one hand on the sword hilt sticking up from his back. "How would you like that?"

"You believe I walked in here without a plan? Who do you take me for? Anything happens to me, and this guild is history."

"Varcade, don't," Patches said with a sigh. "Please. For once just do what I tell you."

The rogue Educator looked like he wanted to argue, but his boss's pleading put an end to it. "Whatever. I'm not saying I'll do it, but I'll think about it," Varcade said and left the room.

CHAPTER FOUR

Varcade sat on the ledge of the massive, fortified wall that went all around the city. The sun was slowly making its descent, giving the sky a beautiful purple and orange glow.

The chilly evening breeze felt nice, his legs dangling down the wall. There was nothing but desert and dunes as far as the eye could see. Varcade rarely enjoyed silence or even sitting still, but the few instances he did, he'd found he enjoyed coming up here.

Two guards from the city watch on either side of him lined the walls, positioned there to keep an eye out for any potential threat to the city-state. Varcade wasn't really allowed to be up there with them, but the guards enjoyed his company so they didn't make a fuss about it.

Varcade tried to convince himself he wouldn't care if Edghar shut down the guild, but truth of the matter was, he did. He hadn't expected to feel such a bond to Patches when he began working for him as a sellsword; but the boss had treated him almost like a son, something Varcade had never imagined would happen. *Perhaps taking on this job won't be so bad . . . I'll get the God Dust and help the old boar retire. He deserves it.*

"You're awfully quiet tonight," one of the guards said. His name was either Biggs or Wedge. Varcade had a hard time telling them apart; it felt like they looked different every time he saw them.

"Yeah, that's no fun," the other one said. "You're supposed to liven things up when you come here."

"Sorry, boys, not feeling it," Varcade said, his eyes still focused on the landscape stretching out before him. "Just up here to enjoy the scenery tonight."

"It's a bloody desert," one of the guards chuckled. "Not much to see. Sand, sand, and more sand. Gets boring fast."

"I like it," Varcade said. "No deserts where I come from. A whole lot o' mountains though."

The other guard took off his helmet and held it under his arm, clearly welcoming the chill in the air. "What's it like back in Karkan? I hear it's very different from Harrah."

"Definitely," Varcade said. "Never saw a whole lot of it though. I grew up in a small village before being taken to the Temple in the mountains. Never got around much. When I left, I jumped on the first ship I could find and it took me straight here to Harrah."

"Huh," one of the guards said. "That eager to get away?"

"Yup," Varcade said.

And you'd be too if you had lived in a place where your every move was judged as incorrect by a group of mad people controlling everything and everyone.

"Say," the other guard said, tilting his head and observing Varcade like he was an exotic creature. "Is it true the Educators have special abilities and stuff? Like, unique to the Order and no one else?"

Varcade nodded once. "Yes. We—they—can harness the powers of the Saints who bless them with certain abilities." He sucked in a deep breath and exhaled then added, "That's all I'll say about it. If you wanna know more go read a book or somethin'."

After a minute or two of silence, one of the guards whispered something to the other one, which developed into a hushed argument.

"I'm not a trained monkey who performs tricks," Varcade said, making both guards abruptly stop their bickering. "I can hear what you're saying."

One of the guards scratched the back of his head, an awkward grin on his face. "You can't blame a fella for being curious, eh?"

"Come on, man, we're friends, aren't we? We just wanna know what you can do, that's all. Please?"

Varcade rolled his eyes. "Fine. I'm faster and stronger than any regular ol' human, and my bones are also hollow, making me lighter and more athletic. A trained acrobat has nothin' on me. My senses are also more heightened; I can smell stuff from far away and see in the dark. Things like that."

"Really? That's wicked—"

"But I can't do any of the Saints stuff. I left the Temple before reaching that stage of training."

The guards stared at him, mouths gaping like children. It actually made Varcade brighten a bit, so he decided to properly blow their minds.

"Alright, I'm feeling generous tonight, boys. You wanna a show, I'll give you a show. One of you draw your sword and stab me right in the heart. Go on."

"What? I'm not doing that."

"Me neither, you crazy?"

"Stop being babies and just do it. I don't have a death-wish. I'll be fine. Trust me."

"You do it then," one said to the other.

"Hell no. You do it."

"Do it now or the show's over," Varcade said, spreading his arms out wide. "Right in the heart. Go on."

"Shit, okay," one of them said, fumbling with the sheath as he drew his blade. "You're sure? Like, for real?"

Varcade nodded.

The guard sucked in a breath and rammed his blade right into

Varcade's chest. Varcade's hands gripped the protruding hilt, blood trickling from the wound. He made a groaning sound and fell to his knees. "You . . . killed me . . . Why?"

The guard who had stabbed him shrieked. "I didn't mean to! You told me to do it!" He turned to the other guard. "You heard him say it, too!"

"I thought we were friends . . ." Varcade stuttered, falling over on the side. "Why would you do this . . ."

"The guild's gonna come after me now," the guard-killer stuttered. "You don't mess with one of theirs and get away with it. I'm gonna have a target on my back for the rest of my life." Panic was written on the man's face, his eyes almost popping from their sockets. "Aw, man, I'm screwed—"

"Surprise!" Varcade said and leapt to his feet, his knuckles resting on his hips, the sword still sticking out from his chest. "I'm back from the dead."

The killer-guard shrieked again and tripped over his own feet, falling on his ass. The other one's face was whiter than bone.

Varcade pulled out the bloody sword and offered it to the guard on the ground. "I believe this is yours."

"How," the killer-guard stuttered. "How is it possible? I stabbed you in the heart. It doesn't make sense."

Varcade nodded in a way a teacher would when hearing a question from a student. "I can see why you'd think that, but the fact of the matter is, you didn't."

"Huh?"

Varcade smirked. If someone else had looked the way he looked right now, he would've wanted to punch them on the mouth. "I shifted the position of my heart right before the blade went in. I can do that with most of my organs without even thinking about it. Neat, right?"

"That's messed up," the white-faced guard said. "It shouldn't be possible."

"But it is," Varcade agreed. "It can come in handy at times."

"I don't think I want to play anymore," the not-really-a-killer guard muttered, standing on wobbly legs. "This isn't fun."

"Fine with me," Varcade said, feeling satisfied from seeing the two guards scared and confused. *They wanted a show and I gave them one.*

The two guards moved down the wall and left Varcade to his solitude. He sat again and observed the desert. His chest hurt a little, but the wound would heal in minutes.

Most people would probably have wished they had the abilities he had, but Varcade never had a choice in the matter, and that made all the difference. These abilities were forced on him; his body violated by strangers when he'd been only a child. Cutting and sawing through his flesh and bones with invisible instruments forged by the hands of the god-like beings known as the Saints. No, he would never wish anyone to go through the things he had endured back in the Educator Temple.

Varcade was just about to call it a night when something on the horizon caught his eye. An ordinary person wouldn't have been able to see it, but nothing about Varcade was ordinary.

A train of people were making their way across the desert. Around thirty of them. Both adults and children. They seemed to be carrying their belongings with them, or rather, dragging them on the ground, since they all looked deadly exhausted.

What the hell are they doing traveling by foot? Varcade thought, standing. *Don't they know–*

That's when he saw what he was fearing.

Shit, marauders.

"Hey," Varcade called to the guards. "Trouble outside the wall. You need to help those folks before that band of marauders gets them."

One of the guards scoffed, taking a look with his spyglass. "Yeah, that's not happenin'. Ain't our problem."

"Don't sweat it, Varcade. Just a bunch of refugees. They die out in the desert all the time. They never learn."

"There are children there with them," Varcade said, his tone holding no humour. "You're really not gonna do anything?"

"Give it a rest, man. Razula doesn't accept refugees from the other city-states. If they can't handle their problems, then that's their issue. We're under strict order from the Bone Lord to deny them entrance. If the marauders don't get 'em, then the desert beasts will, come nightfall."

Varcade contemplated kicking both guards off the wall for a moment, but then decided against it.

"Can't believe I ever liked either of you," Varcade said. "Cowards."

"Come on, don't be like that," one of the guards said as Varcade brushed past him. "We're just following our bloody orders, man."

"That's right," the other one said. "We'd lose our jobs if we disobeyed the Bone Lord's orders."

"Whatever," Varcade said, stopping at the ledge, the wind blowing hard around him.

Guess it's up to me to help those people then.

Varcade leapt from the wall like a bird taking flight, but with the difference that he wasn't a bird and didn't have wings. But who needed that when your body was unnaturally light. The instant his feet touched the sand he used the momentum to roll forward, then took off at a sprint, all in one motion.

The refugees had now realised the marauders were coming for them, and panic spread amongst them like a shockwave. The marauders were biting at their ankles, armed with long spears, and mounted on large mantis-like creatures known as kankers.

The creatures were armed with a hard, sandy-yellow exoskeleton, standing twice as tall as most men on their powerful hind legs.

The grownups desperately pushed the smaller children in front of them, urging them to run towards the gate of the city for safety—a safety the ruling powers had deemed was *not* for them.

Those farthest back in the train were the old and slow, making them easy pickings for the marauders who skewered them with their spears as they rode past, howling and cheering like wild animals.

Varcade ran as fast as his legs could carry him, which was faster than any normal person, but there was still a lot of distance to cover. He could only watch in anger as the savage scene unfolded before his eyes.

The men and women tried to fight back, hurling their belongings at the marauders. But the mantis-creatures were not only hard to hit because of their speed, they also used their four, spiked raptorial limbs to deflect any incoming objects.

Two brave women threw themselves at one of the creatures, grabbing hold of one of the hind-legs. Their combined pull made the kanker lose balance and topple over, pinning the marauder beneath its bulk. The women leapt at the marauder, showering him with kicks and punches.

One of the marauders, dressed in a desert wolf's pelt, broke free from the rest of the band, his eyes fixed on the running children. The savage had madness in his eyes and a twisted snarl on his lips. He kicked his kanker into a full sprint, standing in the saddle with his spear raised high.

One of the kids was a bit chunkier than the others, his short legs not optimal for running from a killer coming after you with a spear. The boy allowed himself a quick glance over his shoulder to see the impending doom baring down on him.

Varcade pushed himself to his absolute limit and leapt up high in the air. He soared past the heavy-set boy and drew his two swords mid-air, flipping their grip and planting both blades into the marauder's chest.

The marauder died instantly, but Varcade now dangled awkwardly down the side of the kanker who was still charging. His grip on the swords was the only thing allowing him to hold on. The dead marauder's body went limp, causing him to slowly sag sideways from the saddle. Varcade pushed himself up and rotated his body, pulling out the swords and taking the marauder's seat as the corpse toppled over.

"Keep runnin', boys and girls," Varcade shouted, forcing the kanker to a halt by pulling the reigns hard. He forced the creature around and kicked it into a sprint, turning back towards the remaining refugees.

There were still six marauders assaulting the innocent people, and many of the refugees had already been killed as Varcade arrived.

Varcade leapt from the saddle and drop-kicked the marauder closest to him. Both his feet smashed into the savage's face with a satisfying crunch as bones shattered. Varcade got back on his feet in a blink and hurled one of his swords. The blade struck another marauder between the shoulder blades.

The remaining four marauders now turned their attention on him, spreading out before him in the shape of a half-moon. The savages wore mixed pieces of armour they'd likely ripped from past victims at some point and were draped in different leathers and pelts from a variety of desert beasts.

"Not so fun when someone actually fights back, is it?" Varcade said, his sword resting on his shoulder. "I'm no saint, but you fellas are some real cowardly scum."

"Back off," one of the marauders snarled. "This doesn't concern you."

Varcade nodded. "True, true, but I just can't stand you bastards."

"We'll share the loot with you," another marauder said. "Come on."

"Really?" Varcade said. "Why didn't you say that earlier? Do they have any good stuff?"

The marauders looked at each other, confused. "Didn't think you'd actually say yes," one said, scratching his chin. "One of 'em carried a pot that looked kinda nice. You can take that?"

Varcade scoffed. "A pot? What am I supposed to do with that?"

"You sell it or trade it."

"Nah, doesn't interest me. What else?"

Those refugees who were still alive were frozen in place, their eyes darting between Varcade and the marauders.

A marauder sat down her hunches, rummaging through a sack. "Got some dried meat here," she said, sniffing the food. "Smells good."

"I can eat," Varcade said and walked up to her, holding out his hand.

The marauder gave him a strip of meat. Varcade took a big bite. "A bit chewy, but otherwise good. Good seasoning."

"What's happening?" he heard one of the refugees whisper. "I thought he was saving—"

"Just keep quiet and pretend you're not here," the other one replied in a hushed tone.

"You satisfied now?" One of the marauders said, staring at Varcade, more attitude in his tone.

Varcade swallowed with a big gulp. "Makes you kinda thirsty. Anything to drink around here?"

The female marauder nodded. "Yeah, got some—"

"Shut the fuck up! Stop giving him things," the marauder with the attitude growled. "He's playing us for fools."

"*Finally*," Varcade exclaimed. "Holy shit, I thought we were gonna go on forever."

"KILL HIM!"

The marauders all swarmed him at once, thrusting their spears with deadly intention. Varcade slid between the pointed heads with the grace of a dancer. The good thing about the spear was the range. The bad thing was the time it took to make another thrust, and those few seconds was enough time for Varcade to close the distance and deal out his own attack.

Varcade's first swing sliced one of the marauders from their belly to their throat. Another marauder tried stabbing him in the back, but Varcade cartwheeled out of the way on one hand.

One of the marauders used all his force for his next thrust. Varcade waited for the exact moment to stomp down hard on the shaft, making the marauder stumble forward. His foot still holding the spear in place, Varcade chopped the savage's head off, sending it flying. For some reason one of the refugees–a young man with a turban–grabbed the head mid-air and held it up with a big smile like he'd won a prize.

Two marauders were still alive, but one of them decided to turn tail and make a run for it. Before she made her escape, one of the refugees tripped her. Feeling the tide had now turned, the prey become the hunter, and the refugees jumped on the downed marauder like hyenas. Varcade could swear one of them was even biting her–the same one who'd grabbed the head.

"Just you and me, big guy," Varcade said to the last marauder, the one with the attitude. "You gonna put up a fight or go down like the rest?"

The savage dropped his spear and pulled a large stone-axe from his back. "The others were weak. Not me. My axe will taste your blood."

"Alright, lessgo," Varcade motioned with his hand. "Come at me—"

One of the refugees leapt on the marauder's back and sank his teeth into the savage's neck.

What's up with the all the biting, my guy? Varcade thought with a raised eyebrow.

Blood spurted from the missing chunk of flesh on the marauder's neck, and the Biter had wrapped his limbs around the savage's body, holding him in place.

"I guess I'm done here, then?" Varcade said, looking around.

The marauder's eyes rolled back in his head as his body went limp and crashed to the ground.

The Biter walked up to Varcade, his bloodied mouth and frantic eyes making him look like a demon. "We did it, my friend," he said with a huge smile. "You saved us."

Why is he still holding on to the head?

"Yeah, sure, no problem," Varcade said, leaning back a bit.

"I am bound to you now. Wherever you go, I will come with you."

"That's really not necessary," Varcade frowned.

The Biter licked blood from his lips. "No, I *must*. That is the way of my kind. There can be no discussion. My life is bound to yours."

His kind? What does that even mean?

"Not sure what I should say," Varcade muttered, rubbing his neck. "Fine, I guess?"

Another refugee ran toward him, bringing Varcade's sword, which had been stuck in one of the marauder's backs. "Thank you, thank you," the woman said, panting for air. "I thought we were going to die. I really did."

Another one grabbed Varcade's hands and shook them. "Thank you, kind stranger. How can we repay you? Anything I have is yours."

"It's all good," Varcade said, gently taking possession of his own hands again. "Don't need anything."

The Biter sat down and crossed his legs, the severed head resting in his lap. "We come from Akrab. We have been travelling for twelve days. When we set out, there were more than eighty of us, but many died on the way."

Varcade swallowed. "I'm sorry to hear that. That's terrible. You should all probably—"

"Things are terrible in Akrab," one of the refugees said, his eyes tearing up. "The Bone Lord's new military unit and their fire weapons are causing so much death and destruction. Countless bodies burning. The stench is sickening. We couldn't stay there. Our children . . ." The man's voice broke, and no more words came out.

Varcade shifted, rubbed his neck, and stared at his feet. He didn't want to think about it, but his mind betrayed him, conjuring up images of children being taken by the Educators; children like him and his brother, whom Varcade had turned his back on when he escaped. Instead of helping them, he had fled across the known world.

Even worse, these poor bastards weren't going to be let into the city based on what the two guards had told him. He couldn't bear the thought of telling them that after everything they had been through getting here.

I can't just leave them here and turn my back on them. I won't.

"Okay, listen up: gather everyone and follow me. I have an idea."

CHAPTER FIVE

A couple of hours had passed since the meeting with Varcade and Patches. It was now dark and Edghar was frustrated by simply sitting around and waiting in the Nest.

All the months since Edghar had been branded a traitor by the Bone Lord of Akrab had led to this point, and he had counted on things going differently once he presented the job to the rogue Educator. You offer a sellsword a hefty payment—which he had in form of God Dust—and you move on to the planning stage. Unfortunately, Varcade did not fit the mould.

I knew the man was erratic and unpredictable, but turning down a job because it sounded boring? I did not expect that . . . He had no moral qualms about threatening to shut the guild down, but the uncertainty of the situation was still gnawing on him.

"I would welcome something of the stronger kind, Shamil," Edghar said to the bartender.

"Certainly, sir," Shamil said. "If I may say, you look quite upset, so let's bring out something from the better stock." The bald man grabbed a bottle with a golden-honey liquid and poured him a glass. "On the house."

Edghar mustered a smile and took a sip. The drink burned his throat and tickled his tongue in a way he found comforting. He couldn't help but imagine how he must have looked at this exact moment and chuckled at the miserable sight.

"Do you ever consider the unexpected turns one's life can take without warning, at any moment?" Edghar said, taking another sip. "You believe you know exactly where you are going and what you need to do, but then, unexpectedly, *something* happens that brings you to your knees?"

"No, not really," the bartender said, wiping the counter with his rag. "What is life if not a series of events that you can't control?"

"Fair point," Edghar said. "But we wish to *believe* we are in control, do we not? It brings comfort."

"Of course, sir. You would lose your mind if you obsessed about all the random moments that could alter your life in the blink of an eye. Those things that you can never prepare for however much you wanted to. Nothing good comes from thinking about those things in my opinion."

Edghar leaned back, gently swirling the golden liquid in his glass. "That is life for you, is that what you're saying? Shit happens, take it in and deal with it then move on?"

"Something along those lines," the bartender said and offered a kind smile. "The past is the past. Focus on the future."

Edghar snorted. "I can tell you're used to having conversations like these with other drunken bastards."

The bartender's smile faded. "Sir, do you think most of the people in our guild wanted this life? When they were youngsters, do you think they dreamed of spending their time taking coin to hurt other people?"

"I'll be honest and say I never gave it much consideration. Perhaps I should have, but no. I guess not," Edghar said.

"Well, they did not. The people here are all lost souls in one way or another, each with their own story that led them to this life. Some were their fault, of course, bad decisions and so forth, but some were struck by that exact randomness we just talked about. Something that turned their lives completely upside down. Much like yourself, If I may say."

Edghar's first instinct was to argue that statement, but his sensible side took control. *Well, he's not wrong,* Edghar thought with a depressing realisation. *In my mind I'm nothing like these people. But that isn't true, is it? Perhaps before all of this happened, but not now. I'm sitting here planning to overthrow a whole regime. One could argue I might even be worse than them ...*

The sound of a bottle sliding across the counter jolted Edghar from his thoughts.

"Here," the bartender said. "I have some tasks to attend to, but I'll leave the bottle. You are welcome to hang around as long as you'd like."

Edghar offered a thank-you nod but resisted the urge to fill his glass. Sure, he could down the whole bottle and momentarily forget about everything, let himself surrender to a blissful existence for a time being, but that was no solution to his problems. While he sat in the Nest feeling sorry for himself, his city was being torn apart. *No, I don't get to have the luxury of drinking my problems away.*

"Still here, eh?" Edghar shot a lazy glance over his shoulder and saw Patches crossing the room. The guild boss pulled out a chair and sank his heavy frame into it. "And looks like Shamil is taking good care of you. That's the good stuff," Patches said, nodding at the bottle.

"Aye, he's a good man," Edghar said.

Patches smiled. "Don't I know it. Much too good for a place like this, if I'm being honest." After a long moment of tense silence, he said, "I've got plenty of other capable swords here in the Nest who're itching for work."

"I don't doubt that," Edghar said, "but that will not work. I told you, the Bone Lord has a band of powerful Dusters working for her. I'm not after good, I'm after the *best*."

Patches exhaled. "Aye, I get that. I'm not going to sit here and tell ya Varcade isn't the best, because he is. He's a rogue Educator. The crap those folks can do isn't comparable."

Edghar shrugged. "Then you understand. I will not be able to accomplish what I'm about to do without someone like him."

"Believe me, I wish the guy was right in the head," Patches said. "A successful job like this means I could probably retire. But if there's one thing I've learned about Varcade, it's that *no one* can force him to do anything he doesn't want to do. I know he cares for the guild, but even your threats might not even be enough to change his mind."

"I will admit, I had not expected him to turn it down in such a blatant way. I thought the promised payment in God Dust would make any sellsword jump at the opportunity to get rich beyond their wildest dreams. It's like saving Akrab from a mad Bone Lord didn't seem to interest him. The fool was bloody yawning when I told him the state of the city."

"Aye," Patches said. "Tugging at Varcade's heart won't do the trick. There's not much left of it after everything those zealot Educator bastards did to him."

Feeling agitated, Edghar reached for the bottle and refilled his glass. Patches poured himself one as well.

"What was the final straw?" Patches said after a minute or two of silence. "Between you and the Bone Lord, I mean. What led to this point?"

Edghar took a deep breath and exhaled slowly. "It was not simply one thing. Clea had always depended on my council in the everyday affairs of ruling the city. She needed what I was glad to give. But as the conflict between the demon and human population escalated, so did Clea's patience.

She demanded simple solutions to complex problems; in her mind and those around her, it should be as easy as putting out fires with buckets of water. Fine, that's one part of it, but what about the reasons for why the fires got started in the first place?"

Patches grunted. "I think I understand. Like, maybe there's something wrong with the construction material that needs to be looked over, to prevent fires from flaring up in the first place?"

"That's right," Edghar said. "But that's not what she wanted to hear from me." He shook his head. "By bringing up these points it turned *me* into a thorn in her side. With each passing day I found myself more and more excluded from the regular council meetings; my council was no longer needed it was said. She began avoiding me, claiming she was too tired or not feeling well. Aye, the stress was getting to her, I do not deny that. The times I laid eyes on her she looked exhausted; the colour drained from her face."

"Heavy is the head that wears the crown as they say," Patches said. "Just running this guild has almost ruined me."

"You asked what the final straw was?" Edghar said. "She branded me a traitor in front of everyone in her close council and ordered me executed."

"That'll do it," Patches said.

"One day I surrendered to the anger and frustration that had been building for months. I stormed into one of the council meetings and laid the truth bare. My claims that she had lost her ways and was spiralling out of control made her blaze with righteous indignation." Edghar sighed. "My mistake was doing it in front of everyone in the close council . . . I should have known Clea's pride wouldn't allow anyone to openly challenge her. But I lost it. And she retaliated. And that was that."

That was that. What a damn joke.

Clea broke his heart that day. Edghar had known and loved her all his life. He would have willingly died a thousand times over if it had meant protecting her. And she loved him too. Or at least she had, he was sure of it. But all that was in the past now. This was bigger than his relationship with another person. Edghar's ultimate loyalty was towards the innocent people of Akrab. They deserved better, and he would do whatever he could to make it right.

The silence in the room was broken when the doors to the Nest suddenly opened, making both Edghar and Patches look over their shoulders.

Varcade held the doors open as a large group of dirty people shuffled inside, confused expressions and trepidation in their steps.

"Come on, hurry up, hurry up," Varcade said, shutting the door as the last one made it inside.

Edghar looked at Shamil, who was back tending the bar. He shrugged in a way that said he wasn't surprised.

"Patches!" Varcade shouted. "Get your ass over here."

The burly man stood, his neck snapping left and right at the group Varcade had brought with him. "Who are all these people?"

"Just some folks I saved from a band of marauders outside the city," Varcade said, plopping down on a stool at the counter. "Refugees from Akrab."

"Why'd you bring them here?" Patches said, spreading his thick arms. "How'd you even get them into the city?"

"I snuck 'em in." Varcade tapped the counter. "Be a darling and fix me a drink, Shamil. I'm parched."

One of the refugees, a young man with a turban and blood around his mouth appeared next to Edghar, standing awkwardly close. "Hello," he said, gently placing his hand on top of Edghar's hand.

Edghar slowly pulled his hand away but didn't know what to say, so he said nothing.

"What am I supposed to do with a group of refugees?" Patches said.

"They live here now," Varcade said. "Figured they can do work around the bar an' stuff. Help ol' Shamil or somethin'. Figure it out, I've done my part."

Patches started saying something then closed his mouth.

Varcade looked at Edghar like he just noticed he was there. "So, you're still here? Good."

"Why's that good?" Edghar said, his eyes narrowing.

"That job you had? I'm in. Not because of your little threats or whatever."

Edghar was taken aback. "Then why? What made you change your mind?"

Varcade downed his drink in one swallow. "These poor sonuvabitches told me about the situation over in Akrab. That's some messed up stuff happening there. I feel I should do something about it. It could be fun and challenging."

"I *know* about the situation in my city," Edghar hissed. "I told you all about it."

"You did?"

Edghar looked around in disbelief. "Are you playing me for a fool?"

"Man, you went *on* and *on* in there. You expected me to take it all in? Who do you think I am?"

Edghar dragged a hand through his black hair. "I appear to not have a clue, it seems . . ."

"And you're paying us in God Dust, right? A lot of it. I want the boss man to be able to retire after this. He deserves it."

"So that part you heard," Edghar muttered, before speaking up, "Aye, that's the deal."

"Good. Then it's settled."

One of the refugees grabbed a broom and started sweeping the floor. Patches made a half-hearted attempt to stop him, but then his shoulders slumped in surrender. "Whatever," he muttered. "I give up."

Edghar observed Varcade as he chatted away with Shamil, all smiles and high in spirit. He seemed so different from how he had behaved merely hours ago.

You took out a band of marauders all on your own, huh? Edghar thought, sneaking another look at Varcade who was trying to grab something from behind the counter, Shamil pushing him back. *If I can just steer this man in the right direction and concentrate, we can really save Akrab. It's worth the headache. Big question is, how well will he play with the others I need for the crew . . .*

CHAPTER SIX

The Bone Lord of Akrab was not happy. But to be fair, she hadn't felt an inkling of joy for quite some time, so this was her regular reality these days. Her mood was fouled even further by the yapping voice of Berenberg, the Keeper of the Royal Seal.

She slouched in her throne, face resting on her arm. Berenberg's nasally voice made her blood boil. He kept going on and on about the state income and the increasingly depleting state treasury, but all she could think of was taking off her bone crown and shoving one of the sharp edges into his eye.

"So, as I was saying," the treasurer continued, adjusting his eyeglasses, "we are alarmingly close to being broke. The Bone Lord of Nuzz has offered us a loan, but he has some specific conditions that need to be met before we can come to an agreement."

How can a man be so utterly boring and live with himself? He looks like a person that would make flowers wither if he passed them by, sucking out whatever source of life they had. The Bone Lord studied the man's lifeless grey eyes, devoid of any emotion, his pale, waxy skin with a yellow hint to it. *Is he even human?* she contemplated. *He can't be.*

"Your Excellency?"

"Yes, just do it," she sneered. "We need the coin."

Berenberg cleared his throat. "But I haven't informed you of the Bone Lord's conditions. They're quite excessive and detailed, but I have them right here with me." He reached inside his suit and took out a rolled parchment.

Khanon, the Army General met her eyes, and apparently murder was written on Clea's face because the man spoke up immediately. "I think that's fine for the moment, Berenberg," he said. "It can surely wait. We have some other, more pressing matters to attend to."

"Very well." The treasurer returned the roll inside his suit. "We'll discuss it at a later time then."

"What's next?" Clea barked, closing her eyes and rubbing her temples. She was getting another migraine. The pulsating sensation wrapped itself around her head and squished her brain. "Where is Tarkus?"

"The Vizier is on his way as we speak," Erikz, the Royal Guard Captain said. "He's bringing those . . . Dusters with him."

"You have something you want to say, Erikz?" Clea said. "Well? Go on, out with it."

The Royal Guard Captain shifted, not meeting Clea's eyes. Like always, the young man donned his pristine golden plate armour, his helmet resting in the fold of his arm. "I'm sorry, Your Excellency, but I'm still not convinced it's a good idea working with a band of Dusters."

"Well, thankfully, you don't have to worry your pretty head about that," Clea said. "I'm the one in charge. If anything needs to be stabbed, I'll let you know. Does that sound good to you?"

The Royal Guard Captain looked away. "Yes, Your Highness. My apologies."

"With all due respect, My Lord," Khanon the Army General said, "Erikz is not wrong in his assessment. Those Dusters are criminals. At any other time we would bring them to justice and have them executed for their crimes."

Clea looked at the older man, and he met her stare with confidence. The grizzled veteran had served her parents before they had been tragically assassinated, and he'd known Clea from the moment she'd been born.

"You say that, but perhaps their presence within the ziggurat is a testament to your utter incompetence in doing your jobs?" Clea said, her eyes staring daggers. "You think I *enjoy* having those freaks here? But desperate times call for desperate measures, and those Dusters and their skills are undeniable."

"As you say, Your Highness," Khanon said. "We merely shared our opinion on the matter."

"Next time keep it to yourselves," Clea said.

The atmosphere in the throne room was pressed and uncomfortable. Clea hated admitting it, but ever since Edghar betrayed her and fled the ziggurat, she hadn't laughed or smiled once. She hadn't realised how much of a vacuum his absence would leave behind. He'd been the only one she could relax with, where she could be *Clea* for a while instead of *The Bone Lord of Akrab*. But one pivotal moment had changed all of that.

Kill him.

Those two words had repeated in her mind over and over again, always when she prepared for bed. During the day she was too busy with all the responsibilities that came with being a ruler, but the moment she could have a moment to herself and relax, they would be there, echoing.

The look Edghar had given her when she gave the order was burned in her retina. She had never kicked a puppy, but if she had, she imagined it would have given her the same look.

Damn you, traitor, for forcing me to do that. I will never forgive you for making me feel this way.

The double doors to the throne room swung open and Tarkus was the first one through. The Vizier was a bald and pudgy man, dressed in several layers of different coloured rags that together formed the semblance of robe.

"Your Excellency," Tarkus said with his honey smoothed voice, shuffling up to the throne, his bare feet on the carpet. The man always bore a large closed-mouthed smile that went from ear to ear, giving him almost a comical look, and his eyes were rarely fully opened.

"Tarkus," Clea said, feeling herself relax. Something about the Vizier had a soothing effect on her; like all her troubles could be solved and anything was possible.

"How are you, my dear? You look tired." The Vizier said, taking a jar from one of the hidden pockets in his robe. He plopped the lid off and dug two fingers into the creamy substance within, then rubbed his hands together. He then proceeded to rub the lotion all over his arms, legs, and face; the wet and squishy sound making Clea wince.

"Must you do that right in front of me?" Clea said.

The Vizier grinned. "My apologies, Your Highness, but you know how sensitive my skin is."

"Fine," Clea said. "Whatever. Bring the Dusters in. It's about time I meet them properly."

The Vizier turned and beckoned for the guards at the door.

The moment the Dusters set foot in the throne room the atmosphere changed. Clea had had almost no interaction with the group to this point; it was mainly Vizier Tarkus who dealt with them. Clea leaned back in the throne, instinctively feeling she wanted even more distance from them—and that was before the group of Dusters stood before her.

These weren't just criminals, but *something* else entirely; everything about them was wrong. Consuming God Dust was a crime across Harrah. Only the Bone Lords themselves could grant permission for the dust to be used, and only in the case of war–though not against another city-state, but against the World Authority, should they ever invade. If the need ever arose, the Bone Lords would open their vaults and allow their soldiers to snort the stuff. It would turn them into magically enhanced beings unrivalled on the plains of a battlefield.

THE CREW

The lead Duster, a man named Hangman-Daddy, was taller than most men and wore a long, tattered coat and a wide hat. Thin, white hair ran down to his lips, obscuring his face, and he carried a large, dirty old sack slung over his shoulder.

Hangman-Daddy strolled down the carpeted path to the throne, casually glancing at the tapestries of ancient battles then up at the enormous painting in the dome. He stopped before Clea and looked up at her. "Get in my sack?"

"Quiet, Hangman," Vizier Tarkus said to the Duster, a big smile on his face.

Duster or not, Clea refused to be intimidated by the likes of this man. "Why is there an animal inside my throne room?" She said, observing a dog coming up behind Hangman-Daddy. The muscular white canine was medium sized with a wide head and an underbite.

"That is Dog Man," Vizier Tarkus said. "Latest addition to the group. He is a tracker. Brought him onboard for Edghar specifically."

"How'r ya?" the dog said, scratching his head with his hind leg.

THE DOG TALKS? Clea couldn't keep her eyes from widening in surprise, but at least she held her tongue and didn't blurt it out.

"Hi," a boy said.

Oh no, not that creep . . . Clea thought, remembering seeing him stalking the hallways at times. The boy was Gloomy Glen and looked to be ten years old, but his face was much older. He was pale and had wet short hair parted down the middle. Something about his presence made Clea deeply uncomfortable; like life lost all its meaning. She had to physically look away to fight off the sense of drowning.

Thankfully, Vizier Tarkus noticed Clea's distress. "That's good, Gloomy Glen. You can go stand in the back now. Oh, and that's Bonky-Bonk over there," Tarkus said, gesturing at a massive figure standing behind the others. "She doesn't speak much."

The Duster was covered in heavy armour from top to bottom and held a huge hammer. Her round face-helmet was in the shape of a smiling child.

These people are worse than I thought, Clea shuddered. *How much of their humanity even remains at this point?* She forced herself to sit in a more fitting position for a Bone Lord.

"Well, go on, properly introduce yourself," Vizier Tarkus said. "Don't just stand there."

"My pleasure," said a thin, pale man with an angular face and a receding hairline. He wore a black coat ending below the knees. "I'm the Baker." The Duster had what looked to be a ball of dough in each of his hands.

Before Clea could even reply to the one calling himself the Baker, the last Duster suddenly startled her, shouting a barrage of incoherent words. The man was ancient, barely any skin left on his bones. The reason Clea could see that was because he was stark naked, his long white beard the only thing obstructing his manhood. For some reason he also carried a steel bucket that stunk of fish?

"Shut up, Nimbus," Vizier Tarkus said with a forced chuckle. "That's quite enough from you."

Is that a Duster or a random crazy person they found out in the streets? It was impossible to tell.

Vizier Tarkus cleared his throat. "So, with all the formalities officially out of the way, let us speak properly about the plan going forward."

Clea took a deep breath. She was having a hard time stringing her thoughts together. A part of her felt it was utter madness to employ these Dusters, but for some reason she found herself unable to speak against it. Her headache was getting more intense by the minute. Not only that, lately it had felt as if spiders or other insects were crawling around her brain, whispering things that made it impossible for Clea to think.

"Your Highness?" Tarkus said. "Is it those head pains again? We can do this at a later time, but things are growing more dire with each passing day–"

"Go on," Clea gestured with a wave of her hand, closing her eyes. "I can handle it."

"Very well," Vizier Tarkus said. "The Alchemy Guild is doing impressive work training our soldiers on how to handle their new weaponry. They are already patrolling deeper and deeper into the demon-infested areas of the city."

"Infested?" The Army General said. "Is that the language we have started to use?"

The Vizier smiled at Khanon. "What do you wish to call it, dear General? Have they not proven to be a sickness to our great city?"

"No," Khanon said. "They are not. Clea's parents opened the gates of Akrab to provide a home for the demons after the First Contact War. We were meant to be living together side by side."

Vizier Tarkus scoffed. "And how has that worked out, old friend? Hmm? Face it, they need to learn their place or we will rid them from all of Akrab. We have a duty to the people who were here first."

The army general clenched his teeth, turning his attention to Clea. "Your Highness? Is this really–"

"The city's close to breaking out in a civil war, you fool," Clea snapped. "Something must be done. I trust the Vizier to handle this."

Tarkus nodded. "I thank you for your trust, Your Excellency–"

"I don't care, get this over with." Clea's head was close to exploding. She wanted this council to be over so she could get some rest.

"Of course," Vizier Tarkus said. "Gloomy Glen here will work together with the Alchemy Guild and the newly trained soldiers. Together, they will crush the demon riots and bring order back to our city."

"If I may add," came Berenberg's nasally voice, "there is also the financial situation—"

"Silence," Clea said, not even looking at the man. "Why are you still here? Travel to Nuzz and get us a loan from that fat Bone Lord of theirs!"

"Very well," the treasurer slid back and once more merged as one with the decor in the room.

"And what about Edghar?" Clea said, rubbing the bridge of her nose. "I *know* he's out there, plotting against me. What's being done about that?"

"Do not worry about that," Vizier Tarkus said. "I have ordered the other Dusters to focus fully on finding our former Spymaster. It is only a question of time at this point."

An image of Edghar suddenly flashed before Clea's eyes. The picture her subconscious conjured was of her former spymaster, disapproval in his eyes. She hated when he looked at her with disappointment. Grabbing that strain of anger, she said, "Fine, send the Dusters after Edghar. They better not fail."

"As you wish, My Lord," Vizier Tarkus nodded.

"When it comes to Edghar, I'd prefer to have him brought here alive," Clea said, then hesitantly added, "But it's not a requirement."

"What does he look like?" the talking dog said.

Again, an image of Edghar invaded Clea's mind; this time he had a smile on his lips. She forced it away and replaced the image with the man who had openly defied her that day.

"Average built, black hair." After a pause. "Good looking. Strong jawline. He might have a beard now."

"Wow, he's really one of a kind then," Dog Man said. "We're gonna need somethin' more'n that."

Clea hesitated. "He . . . has a tattoo on his right shoulder."

"Can you write this down?" the dog barked at Nimbus. "It's not like my paws can do it."

Nimbus started screaming something impossible to decipher, while waving his bucket high in the air.

The State Treasurer Berenberg cleared his throat, approaching the two Dusters with a cocky stride. "I've taken the liberty of drawing up these wanted posters of the former Spymaster," he said with a satisfied smirk, handing them over. "I've always had a somewhat artistic vein, I've been told."

Dog Man and Nimbus shared a quick glance with each other before the dog answered. "Ah, these're great." The look on the dog's face, however, indicated the opposite. "Don't you have something old of his?" the dog said to Clea, ignoring Berenberg. "All I really need is to get a whiff of his scent. If he's in Akrab I'll find him."

Clea was sick at the idea of giving the Dusters something that had been Edgar's, but she needed to let go of the past. The man was a traitor. She motioned for one of the guards and told the woman to retrieve a shirt from Edgar's old quarters.

"Is that all?" Clea said, rubbing her temples. "I need to rest."

"You heard her," Vizier Tarkus said. "We know what to do."

CHAPTER SEVEN

The next morning, Edghar had demanded they had another sit-down and talk things through before taking off to Akrab. Varcade had reluctantly agreed.

He and Edghar sat outside in the run-down patio behind the Nest. A couple of sad plants surrounded them. The unsteady chairs were ready to break at any moment. Shamil had brought out some bread, cheese, fruits, and tea for the two of them to break their fast.

Varcade was surprised at the tingling in his body. He was excited, he realised, to go after the Bone Lord of Akrab. Not because he had any personal stake in the matter, but rather because of the challenge it presented. This was bigger than anything he'd ever taken on before.

He noticed Edghar sneaking glimpses at him from the corner of his eyes. "What?" Varcade said. "Something on my face?"

Edghar looked thoughtful. "No, nothing like that."

"Then what?"

"I'm just thinking. All this time I imagined the Educators to be a certain way, but now that I have met you, it has become clear you're . . . *different*. And younger."

Varcade laughed. "So, what *did* you imagine, eh?" He popped a grape in his mouth.

"Well," Edghar began, "From everything I have heard about the Order, I initially expected a serious, never-smiling person who's unable to relax. Of course, the more I heard about *you* specifically, it became clear you didn't fit that description at all."

"Sorry to disappoint you, I guess?" Varcade said with a grin. "I am who I am."

Edghar shrugged. "It doesn't really matter. As long as you are as good as I believe you are, then we have a real chance of succeeding."

Of course, Varcade knew his past as an Educator carried certain expectations with it, so Edghar's confusion wasn't surprising. But Varcade had never fit with the Order. He was always making a fool of himself, making the other kids laugh and drawing the Masters' ire.

Varcade leaned back in his chair, hands clasped behind his head. The warm touch of the rising sun lingered on his face, and the gentle morning breeze kept the heat to a pleasant degree. But something in the back of his mind bothered him, making him unable to fully relax in the moment. He had tried to ignore it, but the thought refused to go away.

"Why are you doing this?" Varcade said, staring up at the grey-blue sky slowly turning bright and yellow.

"I already went over it," Edghar said, a slight flare up in his voice. "The Bone Lord is out of control and must be stopped. Thousands of innocent people—"

"Not that," Varcade interrupted. "Why *you*?"

"What do you mean?"

Varcade sat up, his hands on his knees. *What do I mean?*

He had never asked Patches for the reasons behind a client's contract, but this was different. The stakes were much higher. Varcade's actions could potentially lead to the downfall of a whole regime. The city-state Akrab could change forever.

"I guess what I'm saying is that I've killed plenty of people for a bag of coins. One bastard dying here and there isn't exactly world-altering business," Varcade said, scratching his head and looking at Edghar. "This is different."

"Of course, it is *different*," Edghar said with a look of annoyance. "What? Don't tell me you're going to say '*pass*' again?"

Varcade shook his head. "Nah, I'm doing this."

"Meeting those refugees opened your eyes, didn't it? It was not enough to hear it from me, you had to experience it yourself."

"Perhaps," Varcade admitted. "But it's more about the challenge for me."

"And the payment in God Dust is of no interest to you? I have a hard time believing that."

"Believe what you want," Varcade said. "I'm doing this because it excites me." Perhaps Edghar had been hoping for a more noble reason based on the look in his eyes. "What? You're disappointed by my answer? I'm a sellsword, what exactly did you expect?"

Edghar sucked in a deep breath then exhaled. "No, you are right. I shouldn't presume anything. I merely hoped that meeting the refugees affected you more–does not matter, forget it. The goal is all that matters in the end. And on that subject, we should go over some of the details."

Varcade groaned. "Do we have to?"

"Yes," Edghar said, then took a sip from his tea. "First you need to know, it's not going to be just the two of us. I'm putting together a crew."

"A crew? That's not how I do things. Hell, I don't even want to work with *you*. I do things solo."

"Not this time, you don't," Edghar said with a finality to his tone. "I am in charge of this operation. The sooner you accept that the less trouble we'll have down the road. You honestly expected me to put all my trust in you and you alone?"

"Hey, you came to me, man," Varcade said, surprising himself by how offended he felt. "Now you're telling me I'm not enough?"

"Thus far, you haven't given me a single reason to really trust you. Who knows, you might just turn tail and run whenever it suites you. I spoke with Patches and a few of the other sellswords last night. Do I need to tell you what they told me? About how fickle you are?"

"Fine, whatever," Varcade said, crossing his arms. "We'll do it your way then."

"That's right," Edghar said. "And do not forget it. Now, the reason we need a crew is because Clea is working with a band of Dusters."

"Clea?"

"The Bone Lord. That's her name."

"Okay. Go on. Band of Dusters."

"Once I learned she had hired them, I knew I had to leave Akrab quickly. And from what my sources told me; these are not your average God Dust-sniffing criminals. These are powerful people with frightening abilities."

"Powerful, eh?" Varcade said, feeling that tingle of excitement again. "I took down a Duster the other day. Frying Pan Pete. He wasn't that tough."

"I don't know who that is, but it doesn't matter. I promise you: these Dusters are on a different level. And that's why we need more people to help us."

"I guess we'll see about that," Varcade said, looking forward to the challenge. "So, who do you have in mind?"

"Luckily, Akrab's a big city with a lot of dangerous people. I have a list of individuals I kept track of during my years working for the Bone Lord. Potential threats then; potential allies now. One of them is a demon named Marduk. He's a revolutionary who has been causing trouble for years. I think we should start with finding him, but it will be challenging."

"Sure, whatever you say. And then what? What's your plan once we gather all these people together?"

"That *is* my plan. We need strong allies who can go up against everything the Bone Lord will be throwing at us. We'll figure out the rest one step at a time."

"Huh."

"What?"

"I just figured you being this former Spymaster an' all, that you'd have a more solid plan in place."

"It's not like I have done this before! My job was protecting the regime; not bring it down. I am doing the best I can, damn you."

"Geez, take it easy, relax. I was just asking. No reason to flip out."

"Fine. Forget it. Our immediate concern is putting together our crew. That's all you need to know. We will figure out the rest one step at a time. Who knows what might happen on the way."

"Sure, if you say so. Now can we go or are you gonna talk me to death before we even begin?" Varcade said.

After finishing up at the Nest, they had boarded the bumpy caravan that would take them all the way to Akrab.

Edghar cleared his throat. "Any reason this man is with us?"

Varcade and the Akrab refugee simply known as the Biter sat opposite of Edghar. The turbaned refugee stared at Edghar with a big closed-mouthed smile.

"Didn't I tell ya?" Varcade said. "He's coming with us."

"Hello," the Biter said, still staring at Edghar.

"Yes, hi," Edghar said before turning to Varcade. "No, no you did not. Why?"

Varcade exhaled. "What's with all the questions all the time? Ease up, man. Biter's cool. He kills people with his teeth. It's messed up."

"I rip the flesh from their bones," the Biter said matter-of-factly.

Edghar was speechless. He was used to being treated with respect and admiration.

"So, how you wanna to do this then?" Varcade said.

Edghar switched his focus to the task at hand and took out a list from his robe's inner pocket.

"As I already told you, working as the Spymaster for the Bone

Lord consisted of assessing threats to the city, and every name on this list caught my attention over the years—much like yourself. These are all dangerous people, but their skills and abilities are too good to overlook."

No reply.

Edghar looked up from his list and noticed Varcade sticking his head out from the caravan window. "Did you hear a word I just said?"

"Nay," Varcade said. "I thought I spotted a Cactilus. I've been trying to find one of the bastards for like a year."

Edghar took a deep breath. *Consider this practice. This idiot's going to drive you crazy, and you've only spent a day together. You either play along or you're going to end up strangling him—and we need him.* Agreeing with the voice of reason in his head, Edghar asked as politely as he could, "Ah, and what is this *Cactilus* you speak of?"

Varcade was still leaning out the window. "It's like a small cactus creature-dude with arms and legs. They're supposedly extremely fast and durable."

"I see. And what is your interest in this Cactilus creature?"

"I want one as a pet obviously; who wouldn't?"

Edghar rolled his eyes. "Not me."

"You're crazy, man," Varcade said. "Of course, you would."

"Fine. Let us agree to disagree. Can we get back to the question that *you* asked me?"

A moment of silence, then: "I didn't ask anything."

Edghar screamed internally.

"Kiddin'," Varcade's head returned inside with a large grin. "What's your plan? Go on."

Edghar sucked in a deep breath, attempting to regain his focus. "We need to find these people one by one and get them to join us, but I don't expect it to be a simple task."

"Jeez, do you overthink just about everything?" Varcade said, hands clasped behind his head. "Just pick one and we'll start there.

Don't make it such a big deal. You already mentioned that Marduk guy?"

Edghar frowned. "That's not how you do things. Especially with important matters like these. We need to think this through thoroughly and–"

With a lightning-fast motion, Varcade snapped the list from Edghar's hands. If that would've been a killing move, Edghar wouldn't have had a chance to react. The realization made him uncomfortable, but also hopeful for the mission.

"If you're having doubts about Marduk, let's go with this one first then," Varcade pointed on the list.

"Why that one?"

"How that isn't obvious is beyond me," Varcade said with a sigh. "It says *demon marksman* next to the name." The sellsword showed the list to the Biter. "Demon marksman, right?"

"I like," the Biter said. "You very clever man."

Varcade smiled. "You're not too bad yourself."

Edghar looked at the two strange men, thinking for a moment this was the beginning of a bizarre dream. When it finally dawned on him it was real life, he sighed. "Fine, let's do it your way then. We need to start somewhere, and the demon population are not exactly happy with the Bone Lord these days. That might be the incentive we need to get this person on our side."

"Why's that?"

"Complicated story. Or perhaps not *that* complicated, but we'll get into that later." Edghar asked for the paper back. "We know her name is Baaq and that she's a demon marksman from the First Contact War. She worked for a crime boss for some time before vanishing. But before she vanished, she was known to frequently visit a tavern called Three Sisters. It's located in the more demon-populated part of the city."

"Fine with me," Varcade said and yawned. "I'm gonna have a little nappy now. Wake me when we arrive."

THE CREW

In seconds Varcade was snoring, leaving Edghar alone with the Biter in an awkward silence.

Edghar kicked Varcade's leg with unnecessary force—but it felt good. "Wake up. We are here."

"Ouch," the sellsword complained, blinking his eyes open and rubbing his shin.

"Stop crying. We have work to do."

The Biter exited the caravan first, Edghar and Varcade coming out after. The three of them stretched their legs and arms after the long trip.

Edghar had instructed the driver to stop some distance away from the gates so their arrival wouldn't draw any attention from the city guards.

Edghar squinted from the light of the burning sun, holding up his arm for some shade. He'd only been away from Akrab for a couple of months, but in a sense, it felt like he was coming here for the first time. He'd been raised in the city-state, lived all his life there, but peering up at the high white walls at this particular moment made him feel like an intruder. For years he'd lived to protect Akrab, but now he was here to bring it down.

"I'm hungry," Varcade said, yawning. "Let's get something to eat."

"We can eat once we get to Three Sisters," Edghar said, pulling up his hood. He couldn't exactly be seen walking around on the streets. He was considered an enemy to the state after all, and the Bone Lord's soldiers were surely on lookout for him.

Edghar could see the Bone Lord's new security forces standing guard at the gates, inspecting anyone and everyone entering or leaving the city. They wore new armour and carried weapons the likes he had never seen. He still had some allies amongst the regular royal soldiers, but the members of the new security force were strangers to him.

"Is it weird to be back here, Biter?" Varcade said to the dark-skinned man in the turban. "You travelled all the way across the desert to get away from Akrab."

The Biter shook his head. "No problem. I only wanted to help the others across the desert. Being back is good."

"Alright, if you say so," Varcade smiled.

Edghar turned to the two of them but looked specifically at the rogue Educator. "Time to listen. I understand you are a reckless person, but that behaviour will not work from now on. We must not draw attention to us once we're inside those walls."

"Me? Reckless? Don't know what you're talking about. Let's go."

Edghar grabbed Varcade's arm and pulled him back. "Slow down, damn you. The city defence is on high alert. You think we can simply *walk* through those gates? Impossible. We'll have to go through the sewers and sneak our way into the city."

"Aw, man," Varcade groaned. "That sounds disgusting." He patted his stomach, "and I'm hungry . . ."

"Sewer not too bad," the Biter said. "Many rats. Delicious. We can feast."

Varcade gave the man a sideway glance. "Yeah, not sure about that. Think I'd rather wait."

"Well, this smells like *crap*," Varcade said, squeezing his nose.

"Who would have thought?" Edghar said dismissively, leading the way forward.

The sewers beneath the city were dark and disgusting as one would expect. Edghar had lit a torch using flint and steel once they had descended the ladder. Now they were up to their knees in dirty water as they slowly made their ways through the ancient tunnels beneath the city.

THE CREW

The Biter suddenly pounced on a rat and bit its head off.

Varcade leaned in close to Edghar. "Are all people from Akrab this weird?"

Edghar was unable to take his eyes off the Biter who squeezed the blood from the rat down his throat. "No, most certainly not. This man is something *special*. Quite fitting that *you* were the one to find him."

"Hey, what's that supposed to mean?" Varcade's voice made him sound like an idiot because he kept his nose clasped from the smell.

"Forget it," Edghar said. "I'm honestly surprised there are no patrols down here. The sewers have been a weak point for Akrab for years, and we've had countless smugglers and other criminals sneaking in this way. I would have thought, with the situation being what it is, that they would keep track of that."

"Whatever, man," Varcade said. "Just get me outta here as fast as possible."

"You need to know what's going on in Akrab if we're hoping to have any chance of getting to the Bone Lord herself. Listen to what I'm telling you, you bloody baby."

"I'm not a baby, you're a baby."

Edghar shook his head and drew in a deep breath. "I swear, I'm still not convinced you're not an imposter posing as a rogue Educator."

"Oh, that hurts my feelings. How can I go on with my life without your precious approval," Varcade said.

Edghar stopped in his tracks, holding up his hand. "Shut up," he whispered. "I heard something." He listened closer, and indeed, he wasn't mistaken. Something was sloshing around in the shallow sewer waters up ahead.

"What is it?" Varcade asked, his voice still distorted.

"It can be anything. Just be ready–"

Something tackled Edghar from behind, making him fly forward, landing flat on his stomach. Pushing himself back to his feet he turned and spotted his aggressor—or aggressors.

"What the hell are those?" Varcade said, finally forced to release his nose to unsheathe his swords from his back.

"Molks," Edghar replied.

The creatures made constant squeaking noises, jumping up and down in an agitated manner. They were amphibious and humanoid lesser demons, possessed with bulbous bodies and large mouths lined with rows of sharp fangs, and clawed hands and feet. They weren't exactly physically imposing, standing as tall as a regular human child, but there was quite a few of them.

"Some demons that came through the World Wound like these either couldn't assimilate themselves to human society or chose not to," Edghar said. "These lack the vocal cords to learn the common tongue, so they–"

"Fuck you, onion," one of them said, bouncing up and down.

"Huh. I was convinced they did not speak . . ."

"*Onion?*" Varcade said.

"You stink! Like onion!" one of the demons shouted, waving its hand in front of its face.

"Right," Edghar said. "Apparently, we humans smell like onions to most demons . . ."

Another one sniffed the air in the direction of the Biter. "You not onion."

Varcade looked at the Biter. "What the hell does that mean?"

The Biter shrugged.

Edghar took a step forward. "Listen, if you can understand me then there's no reason for us to fight each other. We are only passing through, that's all."

"You stink, and you ugly," another of the molks said. "We kill you."

Edghar sighed. "We don't have time for this." He drew up the sleeve of his robe to reveal the hand crossbow hidden beneath.

The molks' strategy of attack was apparently to curl their small bodies into balls and hurl themselves at their enemies. They came fast and strong.

Before Edghar could fire off a bolt, one of the molks slammed into his chest and knocked him over. With the demon on top of him, its jaw went for his throat. Edghar headbutted the creature, then grabbed the slippery skin of its neck with one hand and tossed it away like one would with an annoying toddler if one was an awful parent.

Two molks flew at Varcade but the only things they crashed into were his swords, which sliced through both like butter, spraying blue blood.

Another one snuck up behind Varcade without him noticing and threw itself up on him, clinging onto him like a backpack. Varcade dropped his swords and spun around in circles, trying to reach the damned thing, but it kept scuttling all over him. "Ouch, it bit me!" he said between clenched teeth, before finally getting hold of the demon's short leg. He slammed it to the ground face-first, knocking the creature out cold.

Edghar once again got to his feet, but more molks were already throwing themselves at him. One of them pulled his ear, and another scratched his face.

Varcade rushed to his aid and kicked the one latched to Edghar's ear like a ball, sending the demon crashing into the sewer wall. He punched the other one in the face, and its limp body slid off Edghar. "How many are there?" Varcade spun around, picking up his swords again.

"Disgusting onions hurt my children," came a gruff voice from the darkness behind them. "You will pay for that." From the shadows stepped a ... human? The man was dressed in tattered brown-yellow rags all over his body and dirty bandages around his face and arms. His mouth was full of rotten teeth, and he was severely cross-eyed. He had to angle his head to look at them. A rasping sound followed his slow advancement, as he held a large, spiked club dragging on the rock floor.

"Baba!" one of the molks ran to the newcomer. "Kill them!"

Edghar shook his head. "Wait, you're human?"

"What?" the man roared. "How dare you call me *that*?"

"Ehhh . . ." Varcade said, head tilted, both swords relaxing atop his shoulders.

"Because you are?" Edghar said.

"Baba one of us!" the molk next to the man screamed. "Molk, like us!"

"He is clearly a human," Varcade said pointing at the man, "You've gotta be kidding me!"

"I would rather be dead than be a disgusting onion!" The man-who-denied-being-a-man lifted his club menacingly. "I will hurt you for that." He picked up his pace and charged at Edghar, swinging his club like a madman—which he clearly was. Edghar had to duck and side-step to avoid having his face smashed-in, but the Molk-Man was relentless in his attack, and one of the jutting spikes scratched Edghar's cheek, drawing blood.

Edghar ducked under the club and shoved his shoulder hard into the man's chest, making him stagger back. With some distance between them created, he could use his hand crossbow again. He wiped the blood from his face with one hand, pointing the crossbow at Molk-Man with the other. "I will kill you if I must," he said. "Enough with this crap."

Molk-Man came at him again, but before Edghar fired a bolt, Varcade appeared from the side and smashed the hilt of his sword into the man's jaw. He toppled down face-first like a heavy bag.

The surviving molks ran to his limp body. "Baba!" they squeaked repeatedly.

Edghar looked at Varcade who sheathed his swords. "No need to kill him. The fight's over." He nodded at the small demons who were using their collective strength to lift the man-who-denied-being-a-man over their heads, disappearing down a sewer path.

"Did not expect someone like you to show mercy," Edghar said. "But I agree."

Varcade shrugged. "Whatever. Let's get the hell outta here now. I'm sick of these damn sewers. Hey, by the way, where's–"

The Biter who'd been missing during the whole fight jogged up to the two of them, holding one headless rat in each hand. "I hunted food for you. Here, please."

Edghar and Varcade shared a quick glance before reluctantly accepting the offering. When Biter didn't look, they tossed the rats over their shoulders.

CHAPTER EIGHT

Varcade was the last one up from the sewers and dropped the lid back in place with a loud clang. "For all that is sacred, can we go eat now?" the sellsword said, hands on his knees.

Edghar had his hood up again, peering around the corner from the alleyway. "Yes," he hissed. "We'll get you food, you damn child." He took another peek then added, "I was not sure we had climbed up the right place, but thankfully we did. We are in the demon ghettos of Akrab."

"But I give you rat? You don't eat it?" The Biter said, sounding offended.

"No, I *did not,* you bloody lunatic," Varcade said. "Because I'm human and I don't eat rats. I need real food."

"But rat very good!" the Biter said. "Delicious meat."

Varcade strode past the Biter, ignoring him, and tapped Edghar's shoulder. "Hey, are you not hearing me? I said I need to eat."

Edghar shrugged off the sellsword's hand. "Give me a moment—"

"No, you listen to me," Varcade said, grabbing Edghar and spinning him around, standing inches away from his face. "I like to think I'm an easy-going kinda person; but, and listen carefully, when I don't get to eat, I'm not responsible for my actions, 'kay? Take this—" Varcade shoved a couple of copper coins in Edghar's hand and closed it up, "–and run and get me some meat or whatever you can find." Edghar tried to say something, but Varcade silenced him, pressing a gloved finger on his lips. "No more talk. Go. Now."

Edghar slowly backed away from the unstable man and disappeared around the corner.

"I've no clue what I just ate, but damn, that was delicious!" Varcade said, licking the grease from his lips and exhaling with satisfaction.

"Okay," the Biter said, picking his teeth. "Not good as rat meat but okay."

"It's called Baaqba and is basically just chopped up mutton rolled up in bread, but the way they spice the meat and add their special sauce is really something, isn't it?" Edghar said, swallowing the last bite of his own food. He'd also been famished without realising it.

Many of the demon refugees made a living from serving their special cuisine. At first, it'd been frowned upon to touch demonic food, but their food had garnered a lot of attention and helped ease the bridge a bit between them and the humans in the city.

"Okay, let's go find this marksman now," Varcade said with a smile, tapping his belly - now a much less scary version from hungry Varcade.

"Aye," Edghar agreed. "I believe we can move around this part of the city without risking running into any soldiers. Due to the riots, they usually don't come here unless they can't avoid it. If I recall correctly, the Three Sisters tavern is not too far away from where we are."

The trio left the alley and found themselves on the busy streets running through the demon ghetto. While traversing the streets, it dawned on Edghar that he'd rarely visited this part of the city before. The buildings here had been hastily constructed to meet the demands of new houses for the incoming refugees as a result of the First Contact War. Some were constructed from hardened mud; others from stone, and they all shared the same trait: they were all rather ugly. Compared to the richer parts of Akrab that were known for their beauty, this whole area seemed to belong to another world.

Edghar suddenly noticed Varcade was staring at a demon passing them by. "Don't stare like that," Edghar hissed at Varcade. "What the hell is wrong with you?"

"Sorry," Varcade said in a hushed tone. "I told you I've never seen a demon before."

"Not good to stare," the Biter said. "It will get us in trouble."

All around were demons in all different shapes and forms. Where humans usually looked quite similar, apart from pigmentation, demons looked so vastly different from one another, you wouldn't even think they were the same race—and maybe they weren't. Not many studies had been done in that field.

Varcade's eyes widened. "That one has a trunk!" he whispered too loud. "I-I must pull it . . ."

"What?" Edghar said. "Absolutely not! Do not do that!"

"But . . ."

"I swear to the Lord of Flames, if you even attempt to–"

Edghar watched in horror as the sellsword reached for the demon's trunk. Edghar quickly reached out and grabbed Varcade's coat, yanking him back as hard as he could. "What did I just tell you?" Edghar hissed. The sellsword struggled to get free, but Edghar locked up his arms from behind and tackled him to the ground, blowing up a large cloud of dust around them.

The small, round, blue-skinned demon with the trunk looked down on them with its onyx eyes.

"Sorry about that," Edghar said between coughs from the dust in his mouth. "My friend is not well in the head."

The demon shrugged and walked past them.

"There is something seriously wrong with you!" Edghar said,

standing up and dusting himself off. "You'll bloody get us both killed if you do foolish things like that."

"'Kay, 'kay, I'm sorry," Varcade said, also dusting himself off. "I got a wee bit carried away, that's all."

"You are crazy," the Biter said and chuckled. "Very strange man."

"That's coming from *you?*" Varcade spat back.

Edghar rubbed the bridge of his nose. "What the hell have I gotten myself into," he muttered.

"I'll behave," the sellsword said with a big smile. "Promise."

Edghar sighed. "Fine. Let's go."

It didn't seem like Varcade, or the Biter picked up on it, but there was a palpable tension in the air. On the surface, nothing was out of the ordinary, but Edghar's role as a spymaster had trained him to pick up signals hidden to the average eye. The three of them had been observed and followed from the moment they surfaced from the sewers. There didn't appear to be an immediate threat, but it was clear their presence did not go unnoticed.

After about a ten-minute walk–during which Varcade actually kept it together–Edghar stopped. "This is it," he said, looking up at the sign above the door. "Three Sisters," he read aloud.

It shamed Edghar to admit, but he had rarely visited any of the demon-owned establishments before. Not that he had anything against it, it just never really happened.

But as they stepped inside, it became glaringly obvious that they were the only humans in there. Everyone turned and looked at them, and an awkward silence settled in the room.

"We're allowed to be in here, right?" Varcade whispered.

"Aye," Edgar said. "I do not believe it is common though. Especially these days with all the recent troubles."

"I have never been here before," the Biter said. "But I like it."

Standing there on the threshold, the first thing Edghar noticed was how different this tavern was compared to the human-run ones he frequented. The tables were slabs of polished stone, and the patrons sat cross-legged on cushions on the floors. The air was thick with smoke, but the smell was sweet and fruity–even pleasant. A quick glance around showed that most of the demon patrons were smoking some type of glass pipe–the reason for the smoky air.

"Come in, come in," a demon approaching them said. "Don't just stand there." She was tall and slender with a beautiful face, seemingly a cross between a human and a praying mantis.

"Hello," Edghar said with a smile. "We would like to come in for a bite and something to drink, if that's okay?"

"Of course it is," Mantis Girl said. "Why wouldn't it be? Follow me, please."

"Demons are so cool . . ." Varcade muttered behind Edghar as they were led deeper into the tavern. "Just being a human sucks, right, Biter?"

"Who say I am human?"

Edghar and Varcade shared a glance at each other.

"I make funny. Of course, I am human like you. Look at me. I talk and wear clothes."

"Riiight. I'm starting to have serious doubts about you," Varcade said. "Think I'm gonna keep a closer eye on you going forward."

"I think that's a good idea," Edghar said. "Something has been off about you right from the start."

"You two crazy," the Biter shrugged with a smile. "I am normal guy."

Mantis Girl led them to an empty spot in the corner. The three of them followed customs and sat down cross-legged on the pillows like the other guests. "We don't get many humans anymore. Before they would come from time to time, but lately, not so much. It's exciting having you in here today," she said. "My sister will be with you in a moment to take your order."

After a minute, a small humanoid demon came up to their table. She looked as if someone had taken a human girl and mixed her with a wasp.

"Hi, would you like to see the menu?"

"Yes, please," Varcade said with a grin. "I'm very hungry."

Wasp Girl giggled, like the notion of a hungry guest was somehow amusing.

"What do you recommend?" Edghar said, looking over the menu.

"Hmm," she said, curling her lower lip. "I'm not sure what humans like, now that I think about it. Would you like our special? It's very popular!"

"I'm sure that will be perfect," Edghar said. "Do you have some cider or–"

"I'd like a glass of milk topped with honey," Varcade said.

"I would like some tea, please," the Biter said.

More giggles. "Cider, milk, and tea. Got it. Coming right up."

A moment later, Wasp Girl returned with their drinks before leaving to attend other guests. Varcade downed his milk in one gulp. A second later he frowned.

"Something wrong?" the Biter said.

The sellsword smacked his lips. "It was salty. But also sweet. Can't decide if I liked it or not."

Edghar shrugged, sipping on his cider. Without being obvious about it, he looked around the room, trying to spot anything or anyone that might be of help in finding Baaq the marksman. He didn't know what she really looked like.

"We should try and find–"

"In due time," Varcade interrupted. "Let's eat first. And speaking of food . . ." he said, clapping his hands.

The doors to the kitchen swung open, and out came a chubby demon, carrying a large tray. This demon seemed to be a cross between a human and a beetle. Her face was round and long antennas sprouted from the top of her head. She appeared to be dressed in blue armour, but it might as well just have been her body.

"Not every day we get humans in here," Beetle Woman said with a gruff voice, lowering the tray on the table. She wiped some sweat from her flustered face. "Have you ever had mazz-mazz before?"

The trio shook their heads and studied the food before them. Things were pretty straightforward at first glance: a large piece of seared meat on top of a pile of red rice and cooked vegetables on the side. But one thing stood out and based on the glances they shared, none of them had any clue what it was. It looked almost like a jellyfish, but with a rubbery pink skin, and it had small, black eyes and thick lips.

"Eh, is that thing alive?" Varcade said, head tilted.

"'Course it is," Beetle Woman said. "Let me show you how to do this. It's simple. The course is named after this little creature," she said, picking up the mazz-mazz. "You simply hold it over the meat and give it a gentle squeeze, just like this." As Beetle Woman did this, the mazz-mazz secreted some type of clear liquid, dripping on the meat.

"Wait, what did you do?" Varcade asked. "What just came out of that thing?"

"The mazz-mazz."

Edghar threw up a little in his mouth, but quickly swallowed so no one would notice.

"What do you mean?" Varcade said. "I *need* to know what that was."

Beetle Woman shrugged. "We call it mazz-mazz, and it is unique to this creature. It lifts the flavour of the dish. Binds the spices together. You will like it."

"Yeah, not sure 'bout that," Varcade said, leaning back, his arms crossed. "Think I'll pass."

"You won't eat the food I've prepared for you? Is it not good enough for a human? Is that what you're saying?" Beetle Woman had a stern look on her face.

"Good stuff," the Biter said, shoving in a mouthful one after the other. "Very good. Even better than rat."

"Maybe we should at least try it?" Edghar said, watching the Biter go at it enthusiastically. "It would be rude not to."

"That guy eats *rats*," Varcade said.

"Well?" Beetle Woman said, staring at Edghar.

"Sure, I will try," Edghar said, unable to stop himself.

Beetle Woman crossed her own arms. "Fine. Then eat."

Edghar nodded, smiling awkwardly as he cut a piece of the meat, bringing it to his mouth.

"Stop." The demon chef said. "That piece had no mazz-mazz on it."

Edghar cleared his throat. "Oh, it didn't? My bad."

He forced himself to cut another piece, the liquid from the mazz-mazz covering it like a glaze. He put the piece in his mouth, trying to chew as fast as possible so he could just swallow. But as the piece of meat rolled around on his tongue, a wonderful sensation came over him. An explosion of taste all at once. He'd had good meat before–one of the benefits of being raised in the ziggurat was the quality of food–but he'd never, *ever* tasted anything this good.

Almost not believing it, he found himself reluctant to swallow. He wanted to savour the taste. "This i-is . . ." he stuttered, "amazing!"

The Beetle Woman snorted with pride. "Of course it is. And remember this: my mazz-mazz is the best in all Akrab. Nothing like it anywhere else."

Edghar was too busy taking another bite to acknowledge the words from the demon chef. All sense of etiquette went out at the window as he stuffed his mouth.

Varcade leaned closer, his eyes darting from the food–vanishing in an alarming rate–to Edghar to the Biter. "Is it really that good? But it's . . . weird."

"Then don't eat it," Edghar said, food flying from his mouth. "It's better if you don't."

"You would not like," the Biter said. "Order something else."

"To hell with it, I'll try a piece." The sellsword said. The same sensation that struck Edghar was now clearly written on Varcade's face. His smile stretched, close to reaching his ear lobes.

What followed was an intense display of gluttony. The three men did not utter a word as they shoved the food down their throat in a frenzy. When the meat, rice and vegetables were gone, they all reached for the mazz-mazz at the same time, struggling and arguing over who would get the last juices from the creature; but the Biter put an end to their bickering when he grabbed it and devoured it before their eyes.

Afterwards they sat there in a silence of three parts: the first part was one of shame, a shame at the animalistic behaviour that had overtaken them; the second part was one of lust, a greedy lust for more mazz-mazz; and the third and final part of the silence was one of spite; spite towards each other that the food had been shared between them.

"That . . . was something," Varcade said, wiping some sweat from his brow.

Edghar nodded, feeling dazed after the food. All he wanted was to go lay down somewhere.

The Biter had the hiccups and his eyes struggled to stay open.

"We should really find Baaq," Edghar said, forcing the words out. "That's why we came here."

"Sure, you go do it," Varcade said, rubbing his belly, a grimace of pain on his face. "I can't move."

"Right," Edghar said, forcing himself to stand.

He looked around discreetly, trying to spot anything that could give them a clue, but he doubted the marksman would be carrying a rifle around, so that was out the window.

Edghar saw a female demon at the far end of the room, leaning against the wall and drinking from a heavy ceramic jug. Her relaxed posture told him she was surely a frequent visitor here at Three Sisters. Perhaps she would know Baaq's whereabouts.

"What?" she said, wiping her mouth, barely looking up at Edghar when he approached her.

"I apologise for bothering you, but I'm looking for someone—"

"You got coin, human?"

Edghar frowned. "Aye. What of it?"

The demon got to her feet with a groan. "You wanna talk, the drinks are on you."

"I don't want to talk; I merely have a question—"

"One question, one drink," the demon said, looking around. "Where are you sitting?"

"Okay, fine," Edghar said, pointing to their table. "One drink."

Based only on looks, the demon was in rough shape, but as Edghar walked behind her, he also picked up that certain presence associated with a seasoned warrior. This woman had seen battle, he was sure of it. *Could this be Baaq?*

The demon sank down cross-legged at their table, not giving any attention to either Varcade or the Biter. "Where's the drinks? What's this piss?" she said, sniffing Edghar's cider. "You call that a drink?"

Edghar ignored her comment. "Forget about that. We are looking for someone. Her name is Baaq—"

"Yeah, yeah, I'm Baaq. What of it?"

Edghar suddenly noticed Varcade was staring wide-eyed at the demon's horns, and discreetly kicked his foot, breaking the sellsword's trance.

If the demon noticed, she didn't care. She whistled–rather rudely, in Edghar's opinion–at the Wasp Girl. "Hey, get us some al-kuhl over here. The finest you have. These onions are buying," she said.

"Al-kuhl?" Varcade said.

"Strong demon-made liquor. Too strong for humans," the Biter said.

"What the hell do you know about it?" Varcade said. "I can drink. Give me some of this *al-kuhl*. I'll show you."

"We are not here to drink, you fool," Edghar said. He turned his attention to the demon. "Your drink is on the way. So, you are Baaq? The marksman from the First Contact War?"

"I already told you yes," the demon snapped. "But here comes the drink. We'll talk after."

Edghar started to object, but Wasp Girl's arrival grabbed everyone's attention. She sat down a large ceramic jug and four clay cups. The moment Wasp Girl pulled out the cork, a sharp smell filled the air, immediately making Edghar's nose tickle and his eyes tear.

The drunken demon inhaled deeply. "Yes, now we're talkin'," she said, grabbing the jug and pouring up the drinks. "Let's drink."

The demon downed the contents of her cup in one swig and slammed it on the table. "Go on, your turn."

"I said we're not here to drink, dammit," Edghar said, pushing his cup away. "Listen, Baaq. I have something—"

"What is even in this?" Varcade interrupted, sniffing the drink and making a face.

"Who knows, but it's good for ya," Baaq said, pouring up another one.

"Maybe we should try it?" the Biter said.

Varcade nodded. "If we hadn't tried anything new, we'd never have eaten the mazz-mazz. What if this stuff is just as nice?"

"Good point," the Biter said. "I will try."

"Hello?" Edghar said, raising his voice. "Is anyone listening to what I'm saying?"

"Geez, just relax for one moment," Varcade said, pushing the cup in front of Edghar again. "We just found Baaq. Doesn't that deserve a celebratory drink?"

"*Fine*," Edghar hissed, grabbing the cup. "One drink. Just to make you all shut up about it."

"That's the spirit," the demon said. "Now drink up and let's have a good time."

About thirty minutes later . . .

"I looooove youuuuu, Cleaaaaa! How could you do this to me?" Edghar shouted, wobbling down the street. "It was me and you dammit. . . We made a promise to each other!"

"Come back, man," Varcade said, wobbling after him, trying to grab a hold of Edghar's robe. "Y-You're being too loud . . ."

"Lemme go," Edghar said, yanking his arm away with such force that he made himself spin around and topple over. "Ouch, what the hell," he groaned. "You punched me, Varcade."

"I didn't mean to!" Varcade said. "I swear, I'm sorry. Will you forgive me?"

"No," Edghar said, pushing himself up before falling over again. "You'll never hurt me 'gain . . ."

"I understand," Varcade said, bumping into a wall. "I don't deserve it . . ."

"Don't say that," the Biter said, slapping Varcade's face. "You are a good man!"

"Come on," Edghar said, finally back on his feet. "We need to kill the Bone Lord, man. Lessgo."

For some reason, Baaq, the drunken demon, picked up Varcade and carried him like a baby in her muscular arms.

Edghar stopped, scratching his head. "Hey, where are we by the way?"

Varcade shrugged. "I don't know, man, I don't live here."

"I am a liar," the Biter muttered to himself. "You do not know real me."

"I think I recognise that alleyway," Edghar said, ignoring the Biter. "Come on."

"Go after him," Varcade ordered Baaq who still carried him in her arms.

They reached the alleyway and Varcade noticed the sewer entrance. "Hey, I *know* what we can do," he said with a mischievous grin.

The Molk King froze as he suddenly heard noises. "Wait." He held out his arms, stopping the small molks with him from taking another step. Someone was climbing down the sewer ladder, giggling and laughing while doing so.

"Shhhhhh, man," one of them said. "They're gonna know we're coming."

"I am quiet! You're the one being loud!"

"Stop screaming, idiot!"

"What are we doing here?" a female voice said. "You onions are crazy."

The Molk King felt fear gripping his heart and the prickling of sweat on his brow. *It's those evil onions again . . . They're back to hurt us more . . .*

"What is it, baba?" One of the molks said.

"We must run, my children," the Molk King said. "They've come back for us. The bad men. Come, quickly. We must warn the others and get to safety."

Varcade blinked his eyes open. Everything was black. His head felt like a piece of lead, and it was a struggle just keeping his neck from straining. "Where the hell am I?"

Someone snored next to him.

Edghar.

"Wake up," Varcade said, shaking the man's shoulder. "Hey!"

"What, what's happening?" Edghar shot up, looking left and right. "Varcade?" After a moment he started sniffing the air. "What is that awful smell?"

Varcade forced himself to stand up, his legs barely able to keep him upright. "I think we're down in the sewers again?"

"Why the hell would we be–" Edghar stood and looked around, "–oh, seems you are right . . ."

Baaq and the Biter were asleep, spooning each other.

"What do you remember?" Varcade said, scratching his head.

They stood there a few minutes, trying to gather their memories. Everything was clear up until they'd . . . drank the al-kuhl at Three Sisters.

"What have we done?" Edghar muttered, face in his hands.

Varcade shook his head. "No clue. Why would we come down here again?"

Edghar exhaled. "I don't know and I don't care. We must get out of here and find a place to rest. I can't believe we did this."

"Well, it was your idea to drink that crap."

"What? You were the one who pushed me into it! You and the Biter!"

"Sure, blame me for everything," Varcade said.

"Okay, just forget it. Wake those two idiots and let us get out of here."

CHAPTER NINE

Vashi finally arrived in Akrab after a long journey.

He took in as much as he could of Akrab as he descended the ship's gangplank, his duffel bag casually thrown over his shoulder, and his wooden staff fastened on his back. Someone brushed into him hard as they walked by, showing no concern or offering an apology. But Vashi didn't mind. He had promised himself to stay true to who he was and wouldn't let himself be affected by the stressful lives of these foreigners. He would take one thing at a time, just as he did back in Karkan and the Educator Temple.

Vashi was far from being used to the climate of the scorching sun on this side of the world, but rather than letting himself be bothered by it, he simply took off his blue coat and held it under his arm. *Ah, that's better*, he smiled. *A simple solution to a simple problem.*

The majority of the buildings before him were built from white limestone, some square, others stood taller than the rest, and a few with golden domes gleaming in the sunlight. *Beautiful*, Vashi thought. *Strange, but beautiful.*

Vashi had only set foot in the harbour thus far, but he could already tell he was in a proper city-state, vastly different from the few scattered, secluded villages around the mountains back in Karkan. There was activity all around, different smells and sounds invading the mind at all times. *Where can one have a moment to think in a place like this?* Vashi wondered. *Doesn't matter. I won't be staying here for long. I'll put an end to my brother's foolery and return home.*

Vashi had been waiting years to hear anything about his brother's whereabouts, but once he heard what he was up to, a part of him wished it had remained a mystery.

His brother was accepting coin to hurt or even kill other people since he'd turned his back on the Educator Order, something not only absolutely forbidden by the Teachings, but also a despicable behaviour. *If I cannot make him see reason, I will have no other choice but to Release him.* The notion of it pained Vashi, but as soon as he acknowledged the emotion, he obliterated it before it could fester and weaken his resolve.

Being an Educator was much bigger than any personal relationships. They lived to serve *all* and sought to restore Balance to the world. The only way to do that was to have everyone accept and follow the Teachings; a set of rules on how people should behave in every scenario imaginable. But all attempts to establish an Educator presence in Harrah had failed thus far. These people strongly opposed the Teachings, something Vashi could not fathom. Following them made life easier and better for everyone. Why did they not want that?

Before the Masters had given Vashi his mission, they informed him about another Educator who had travelled to Akrab many years ago. No one had heard from her in ages, but Vashi still held hope she was alive and that she could assist him in finding his brother.

Vashi approached a bronze-skinned man with bulging, red-rimmed eyes. The man was seated cross-legged on the ground, holding a sign with something written on it—Vashi had practiced the foreign language spoken in the Harrah region, but hadn't mastered reading it. "Excuse me," he said, speaking slow and articulate just like he'd been instructed.

Remember to speak slow and drag the words out, his tutor back in the Temple had told him. *That way there will be no misunderstandings, yes?*

"I am looking for a person by the name of Xira. Would you be so kind and point me in the right direction?" Vashi said, brandishing an all-teeth smile .

"Why you talkin' like that? You a donkey?"

Donkey?

"My apologies, I am not sure what you mean." Vashi collected himself and tried again. "I am looking for a person by the name of–"

"I heard you the first time," the man said. "I asked why you spoke like *that*?"

"Your language is foreign to me," Vashi said with a big smile. "I am not from here."

"I can bloody see that with one look, boy. Why you stating the obvious?"

Vashi frowned. *But he asked me?* "I am sorry if I have offended you. I am only looking for–"

"Jeez. You are a donkey. Go away," the man said waving him away like a bad smell.

I don't think I would be wrong to assume that this man is being rude to me on purpose. Being rude to strangers is an offence stated in the Teachings. I must act. Vashi dropped his duffel bag and coat, then grabbed the man by his shirt and hoisted him onto his feet, slamming him into the facade of the building—all done in the blink of an eye. "The way you spoke to me is not kind, and I do not appreciate it."

"What the hell, let go of me," the man struggled feebly.

"I will, but only after you apologise and promise to think of this as a lesson for the future. Okay?"

"Get off, you crazy–"

Vashi gripped one of the man's fingers and snapped it in half. As a result, the man screamed, which was an expected response. "If your mind is not open to changing your hurtful ways, then pain must follow. This way you will learn the lesson. I shall repeat: apologise for your rude ways and promise not to do it to another person again. Ever."

"Okay, okay, I promise! Please let me go!"

Hmm. A conundrum. Is he only saying that so I let him go, or does he honestly mean it? I must be certain.

"Are you . . . sincere now, or only saying what you think I want to hear?"

The man sweated profusely, his already bulging eyes close to popping out from his head now. "Yes! I'm sorry I was rude, man! I won't do it again, I swear. I . . . just wasn't in the mood to answer questions and didn't think before I spoke!"

Vashi smiled. *Education complete.* He released the man, who slid down to the ground again. "You have passed the lesson, my friend. The next time, you will think before speaking, yes?"

The man nodded, clutching his bent finger. "Yeah, whatever you say, man, I promise."

Vashi held out a closed fist before the man.

The man looked confused and frightened.

"Bump it."

"Whaa?"

"To seal the agreement," Vashi said with a grin. "Bump it."

With a trembling arm, the man gently bumped his fist into Vashi's.

Vashi picked up his things: duffel bag over his shoulder, and robe under his arm. "Good day to you," he said with a nod and a smile.

The man did not reply.

Alright, let's go ask another person.

When no one was looking, Clea quickly snuck into Edghar's old living quarters. She gently pushed the door closed with a faint *click*. She turned around slowly, as if there was an inkling of a chance her former spymaster would be sitting at his desk as he used to, turning around to smile at her.

But he wasn't, and the room was empty and silent.

Clea sighed and walked up to the neatly—and untouched—made up bed and sat down on the edge. *What am I doing in here?* She thought, looking around the tiny room. *This is silly.*

As Akrab's spymaster, Edghar had been offered more lavish living arrangements, but that had never been in Edghar's interest. Instead, he had insisted on staying in the same room he'd always lived in; close to the others in the ziggurat that he considered family.

Clea glanced down at the bed she sat on, stroking the soft linen, recalling the times when she'd sneak in here as a youngling and spend the night–without her parents' knowledge. She and Edghar would stay up late after everyone else had gone to bed, having long conversations about anything and everything.

Sometimes Edghar would read one of the scary books his father had given him–after every trip his father had brought him a new book; that had been an arrangement and tradition between father and son. Clea had gotten scared on several occasions but never allowed it to show, and Edghar had jokingly said that one day he'd make her so scared she'd cry.

Clea smiled at the memory. *Back when things were simpler . . .*

Edghar was the former spymaster's son and had been raised in the palace just like herself. His mother had sadly died during the birth, leaving Edghar's father alone to raise the child. But old spymaster Pachinko hadn't been alone in Edghar's upbringing. He'd gotten plenty of help from the other royal staff with everything from feeding him, to changing diapers. The maids, the chefs, even the soldiers had all played a role in helping raise young Edghar. And they'd all done it happily. Edghar had rarely been any trouble and was an uncomplicated child.

Clea's own mother and father–the former Bone Lords–had been glad their only child had someone her own age to play with. But unlike Edghar, she'd always been more than a handful for everyone in the ziggurat. She had inherited her father's temper and was known to throw a fit if she didn't get her way. Edghar had always been able to ease her and not get bothered so easily. Clea hadn't considered it back then, but that was surely why her parents encouraged her to spend as much time as she wanted with the boy–hoping some of his demeanour would rub off on her.

But those days were long gone. Forced to inherit the throne after her parents' assassinations, she had to leave her childhood and become an adult overnight. Of course, she'd had help with her daily affairs, but she alone was the Bone Lord of Akrab, and the responsibility and the pressure had been–and still was–daunting. Edghar had taken over as spymaster after his father had passed from old age, and with him next to her, it had made things seem less intimidating.

Clea glanced at her right shoulder. Beneath the fabric of her dress was a stylised tattoo of the sun. It had been Edghar's idea, and he'd gotten the same tattoo himself–a secret pact between the two of them. He had said it would symbolise a new dawn, and that together they would tackle every challenge Akrab faced, one day at a time. *Just as the sun rises each dawn, we, too, will rise with her and work to create a better tomorrow. That is my promise to you.*

"That was easy for you to say," she hissed to herself, her nails biting down on the tattoo, ripping into the skin. "The crown was never on your head."

But each day the problems kept coming. No matter how many things they solved, new issues kept appearing. It'd been impossible to keep up. And as time went on, their relationship began to strain. Edghar's optimistic and serene attitude in the face of adversity had turned into something Clea had begun to despise. Instead of managing to calm her, he'd instead frustrated her more and more. She preferred direct action to get control of things, but Edghar had insisted there were better ways–more humane ways, as he explained it. He had warned her that if she continued down the path of ruling with an iron fist and using force to solve problems, the people of Akrab would eventually turn against her.

You were not wrong about that, Clea thought. *I'll give you that. But they will learn the consequences of turning against me.*

Clea took a deep breath and rose to her feet. It'd been a mistake coming here. Edghar was an enemy now, out there plotting against her; she could feel it in her gut. *The fool cares more for strangers he's never met than me.* And just like that, all her sentimental feelings were pushed away, and in their place came anger. *You betrayed me, Edghar. And you broke my heart. I'll never forgive you.*

CHAPTER TEN

Edghar sat on the side of his bed, face in his hands. *My head . . .* He groaned. *What the hell happened last night?*

Varcade was still asleep, snoring loudly, apparently not bothered the least by the glaring sun invading the room through the small circular window.

The alcoholic demon had been the first one to wake up and was rummaging around the room, making a ruckus as she fervently looked for something to drink. Edghar had tried to say something, but Baaq had shot him an I'll-murder-you-look, so he backed off.

"Would you stop staring at me?" Edghar hissed to the Biter who was seated in a chair in the corner. How long the man had been awake was unclear, and if he was feeling the effect of drinking the al-kuhl last night, it didn't show. The Biter smiled in response but didn't look away.

After finding themselves in the sewers the previous night–once again, for some unclear reason–they had thankfully found an inn where they'd spent the remaining hours of the night.

But Edghar had barely gotten any sleep. His mind was still in a painful haze from drinking that al-kuhl back at Three Sisters. Fragmented images from the previous evening kept flashing before his eyes. *Stupid, stupid . . . How could I have been so bloody reckless?*

Edghar couldn't believe he had embarrassed himself in such a pathetic way. That kind of behaviour was not like him at all. He gave each of the other people in the room a venomous look. *It's these fools I've chosen to surround myself with. They're bringing me down with them.*

Edghar blew out a deep breath. It was not fair blaming them for everything. He was a grown man who made his own decisions. But not only was Varcade a reckless buffoon, now they had also teamed up with yet another unstable person. Baaq clearly had a drinking problem. And the Biter . . . *What's his name even?* Realising he actually didn't know, made Edghar even more upset.

How am I supposed to save Akrab while having to rely on such people?

Baaq exhaled in relief as she finally found what she'd been looking for. Her ceramic jug had rolled under one of the beds. She picked it up and sucked the rice wine down her throat. "Oh, that's good," she said, wiping her mouth with her forearm. She sank down on the edge of Edghar's bed. "All is good in the world again," she said, giving Edghar a shoulder-bump. "You humans are way crazier than I expected. The things you did last night—"

"We do not need to bring that up," Edghar cut in.

Baaq half snorted, half chuckled. "Fine with me."

"Okay, listen to me, Baaq," Edghar said. "I never went through the things I wanted to—"

"Baaq? Ha, I'm not Baaq," the demon said, gulping down the wine then burped.

"*What?!*" Edghar said, his head snapping around so quick it almost broke his neck. "Please tell me you're not serious?"

The demon laughed. "Sorry, onion. I only said I was so you'd keep buying drinks."

The imposter was about to have another swig, but Edghar

slammed the ceramic jug from her hands, sending it crashing into a wall. Fake-Baaq dashed after it, watching wide-eyed as the translucent liquid poured out all over the carpet. "Why the hell did you do that?" she spun around with anger, but that quickly vanished as the demon came face-to-face with Edghar's hand crossbow staring her in the face.

"I have had it," Edghar said. "You understand? I don't want to, but I *will* put a bloody bolt through your eye if you don't give me information that leads to the real Baaq."

"Calm down–" the Biter said from the corner, half-rising from the chair.

"Shut up," Edghar said to the Biter, not releasing his stare on the demon. "Sit down and shut the hell up. This is not Baaq but a damn imposter. I am handling this."

The alcoholic demon raised her hands before her. "Okay, just take it easy. I'm sorry."

"I don't care if you are sorry."

"Fine," the demon said, her voice unsteady. "What do you want to know?"

"*Baaq*," Edghar hissed. "The real one."

"Right, Baaq. Yeah, I know her–I mean I know of her."

"Where can I find her? Think carefully. If you waste more of my time I will come back and find you."

The demon swallowed. "I believe she's a marsh farmer these days. East side along the river basin–"

"I know where it is. You're certain of this?"

"Eh," the imposter licked her lips. "That's the last I heard, I swear."

Edghar sighed and lowered his hand crossbow. "You better be right about this. Now get the hell out of here. Go."

The imposter demon scrambled for the door and left. Thankfully, last night's mishap had stopped Edghar from sharing anything about the plan to kill the Bone Lord. Letting her go wouldn't jeopardise their plans.

The Biter started saying something, but one look from Edghar made the man swallow his words.

Edghar felt depleted as he went to put on his clothes, and to make matters worse, a whiff of stinking sewage smacked him in the face as he picked up his robe.

"You, wake up," Edghar shouted at the sellsword as he slid on his dark-brown suede boots.

No response from Varcade. The sellsword was somehow still deeply asleep, laying on his stomach, one arm dangling down the bed.

Edghar stormed up to Varcade and smacked him in the back of the head. "Up!"

"What the hell?" the sellsword complained, startled from his slumber. "Would you *stop* hitting me when I'm asleep? I swear, I'll run my sword through your face next time."

"I tried calling your name, but it didn't work."

Varcade threw his legs over the side of the bed, looking like a person returning to life after years of being dead. "It's sure bright in here," he squinted. "And my mouth tastes weird. Yuck . . ."

"That's that awful crap we drank last night," Edghar said, adjusting the sash around his waist.

"Oh, that's right," Varcade chuckled. "Fun times."

Fun times? Edghar felt ready to snap. "Get dressed. Also, that demon turned out to not be Baaq. She was a bloody liar who only went along with it for the free drinks."

"Huh," Varcade said. "Bummer."

"Does not matter now. At least she knew the *real* Baaq's whereabouts. We need to leave right now."

"Well, aren't you a cranky bastard in the mornin'?" Varcade muttered. "Geez."

"Know why I am *cranky*, as you put it? Because you're not taking the job I hired you for seriously. You're dragging me down in your crap. I expected more from you."

"Hey," Varcade said, "I don't remember much, but I *do* remember you wanted to drink the al-kuhl, so don't put that on me. Hell, you even argued for it!"

"Nonsense," Edghar shook his head. "I did drink, yes, but it was far from my idea. You and that other idiot coerced me into it," Edghar said, giving the Biter a glaring look.

Varcade got up and pulled on his pants, bouncing on one leg. "You know what? I think you wanted to do it, even hoping something like what happened *would* happen."

"And why the hell would I want that?"

"Man, as uptight as you are, I could bet a thousand coins you were desperately looking for a way to relax and escape your troubles— even if only for a while. How 'bout you own that and move on. Stop blaming me."

"That's silly," Edghar said, trying to brush it off as nonsensical. "You don't know what you're talking about."

But was it silly?

The last couple of months hadn't exactly been the best of times. And if Edghar was being honest with himself, it was fair to say they had been the worst of his life.

Edghar's legs moved on their own accord, bringing him back to the bed where he sank down, rubbing his eyes with the palms of his hands. *Maybe he is right? When was the last time I even had a minute to myself? Just me and a good book?*

His books. Back in his quarters in the ziggurat. The books his father had given him after each trip as he returned to Akrab. *I miss them.* It was clear he wasn't only thinking of his books. He missed his father. He missed all the staff he considered family. And of course . . . Clea.

Edghar felt all his energy drained away in less than a heartbeat. The mental wall he'd built up crumbling away. *What am I even doing?*

"Hey, what are you doing?" Varcade said.

Edghar lay down in a fetal position. "I need to rest a bit."

"We just woke up, man."

"I don't care."

"Biter, will you help me out here?" Varcade said.

"I can bite his head off and make blood like a fountain."

Varcade rubbed his neck. "Yeah, not really what I meant."

The sellsword walked up to Edghar. "Hey, don't go all gloomy an' stuff. Come on. I'll be a good boy. We all will. Only serious business from now on."

"No, go away," Edghar said, throwing the cover over himself. "Leave me be."

"Can't do that. You dragged me into all of this, so I can't let you just give up. Come on. We'll grab something to eat. You'll feel better."

"Yes, I am also hungry," the Biter said, standing.

"*Fine*," Edghar said, throwing the cover to the side.

Varcade grinned at him. "That's better. Let's go."

The three of them went downstairs and gorged on bread, cheese, and a spicy soup to break their fast. Edghar's mood improved a bit from eating and Varcade tried not to annoy him. Even the Biter was on his best behaviour. Once they were done, it was time to leave and find the real Baaq.

Varcade opened the door to the inn and was startled by the dog standing right outside. "Oh, hello little fella," Varcade said with a big smile. He bent down to pet the animal.

"Don't touch me," the dog said.

Huh? So many questions popped up in Varcade's mind.

"That's him," the dog said, sniffing in Edghar's direction coming up behind Varcade. "I'm sure of it." The animal turned and looked at the sky, Varcade's eyes following.

An old and seemingly naked man sat on top of a small fluffy cloud hovering high in the air. The man's skin was like a shrivelled old plume, and he had no hair on his head. What he lacked up top was made up by having the longest and whitest beard Varcade had ever seen. The man on the cloud shouted some garbled words and pointed down at them with aggressive gestures.

What the hell is happening? Varcade thought.

"Did I just hear that dog talk?" Edghar said, brushing past Varcade before coming to a halt at the sight of the man on the cloud.

"I don't understand a word you're saying, Nimbus," the dog said to the naked man, "but this is the guy the Bone Lord's after. Now give me my Dust. My part's done."

The man on the cloud mumbled something and reached inside his beard, producing a pinkie-finger sized glass vial containing white powder. He dropped it and the dog caught it in his mouth. The dog padded up to the Biter, who stood closest. "Can you remove the cork?"

The Biter smiled and was about to accept the vial when Edghar snatched it from his hand. "Don't do that! It's God Dust, you idiot!"

"Hey, that's mine," the dog said. "Give it here."

Edghar pocketed the vial and pulled up the sleeve on his arm, aiming his crossbow at the dog. "You're the Dusters working for the Bone Lord."

"Yeah, technically, but I don't care about all that. I had one job and that was to find you. Now give me my Dust and I'll be on my way."

Varcade had unintentionally entered a staring-contest with the naked man on the cloud. The Duster called Nimbus said something unintelligible, but his tone was agitated, his eyes bloodshot.

"Oh yeah?" Varcade replied, pulling out his two swords. "Come down here and say that to my face."

Nimbus suddenly lifted a steel bucket. He reached inside and grabbed a . . . fish?

Yup, the crazy man on the cloud is definitely holding up a fish.

"Hey, Edghar, you really need to see this—"

The Duster did something and the fish suddenly started crackling and sparking with yellow energy. Nimbus took aim and hurled it down. Varcade moved out of the way and grabbed Edghar with him, which was a wise move, since the moment the fish landed it exploded, shooting up dirt all around the impact area.

"What the hell," Edghar said wide-eyed, his eyes going from the Duster on the cloud to the small crater on the ground.

"He throws fish that explodes," Varcade said. "Yeah, you heard that right."

"I *hate* these Duster bastards," Edghar hissed.

Another fish came falling and again Varcade and Edghar moved out of the way. The Biter didn't seem to care about what was happening and had engaged in a casual conversation with the talking dog.

Nimbus kept shouting incoherent things as his cloud manoeuvred left and right, and back and forth with impressive speed. The exploding fish kept coming down all around them, causing several explosions. Other people on the streets–humans and demons–screamed and ran away.

Edghar stopped whenever he saw an opening and fired one of his bolts up at the cloud. But so far none of them had hit the Duster himself. Varcade felt useless running around. He tried to think how he could reach the Duster.

"Okay," Varcade said over his shoulder, his movement never stopping, sheathing his swords. "You distract the bastard from down here and I'll try and get up to him somehow. I've got an idea."

"Do it," Edghar said, halting momentarily to fire off another bolt up at the cloud. "And hurry."

"You could help you know?" Varcade shouted at the Biter as he dashed past him and leapt up to grab the windowsill of the first floor of the square building.

"This dog talk like man," the Biter said. "Very strange, yes?"

"Yeah, I noticed that," Varcade said between clenched teeth, using his strength to hoist himself up the windowsill of the second floor.

Varcade finally reached the roof of the building and ran up to the ledge. Edghar still ran around below, throwing himself out of the way to avoid being hit by one of the exploding fish. The man was sweating bullets and breathing heavily, his movements turning more sluggish by the second. *Damn, he won't be able to keep up for much longer,* Varcade thought. *And how isn't the Duster running out of fish?! That stupid bucket is tiny!*

An explosion went off next to Edghar, the impact throwing the spymaster backwards violently. He was clearly dazed from it because he was taking way too long to scramble back to his feet. *Crap, he's not dazed, he's unconscious!* Varcade realised. The Duster on the cloud laughed like a perverted old man and prepared to hurl another fish to end Edghar's life.

Here it goes. One chance at this, Varcade thought. He backed away from the ledge to create some distance before he ran as fast as he could and leapt from the roof. Soaring through the air, Varcade slammed into the Duster with satisfying force, sending them both crashing to the streets below. Varcade's body could handle falling from such heights, but he was hoping the Duster's brittle old body wouldn't.

Varcade hugged the Duster in a tight embrace, grimacing from the fishy smell reeking from the old man. Varcade shifted and twisted his body so the Duster would bear the brunt of the impact as they collided with the ground.

They crashed to the ground and Varcade felt the Duster's bones crunch and break beneath him. Nimbus wheezed and mumbled something before his eyes rolled back in his head. The instant the Duster was gone, the cloud in the air vanished like it had never been. The only thing remaining was an empty bucket laying toppled over on the ground.

Varcade got up on shaky legs. It pained him to breathe. *Several ribs broken,* he groaned. It would heal in less than a day, but it would hurt like hell in the meantime.

Edghar rubbed his eyes, his vision blurry. He exhaled between clenched teeth as he forced himself to sit up. His body ached all over and his head felt heavy. "What happened? Where am I?" Edghar said, rubbing his neck.

"Welcome back."

Edghar realised he was back in their old room at the inn, laying in one of the beds. Varcade, the Biter and . . . The talking dog stood around him. "What is *he* doing here?"

"He's with us now," Varcade said with a factual tone, his arms crossed. "Me and Biter talked it over while you were unconscious. He's called Dog Man."

Dog Man winked at Edghar—actually *winked* at him.

Edghar sucked in a deep breath, rubbing the bridge of his nose. "Listen, the two of you do not decide who is added to the crew; I do. This dog is a bloody Duster working for the Bone Lord! He's the enemy."

Varcade waved him off. "That's in the past, man. Let it go."

"That's right," the dog said. "I was only hired to track you down. My part's done. Plus, I never liked those idiots anyway. These guys told me you're paying everyone in God Dust. I want in on that deal."

The Biter chuckled. "Listen to dog talk with voice of old man. Dog is not supposed to talk."

"I'm not a dog," Dog Man said matter-of-factly.

"Then what the *hell* are you?" Edghar said.

"I don't see how that concerns you," Dog Man said. "It's not like I'm standing here asking you for your life stories, am I?"

Varcade nodded. "Absolutely right. Stop being rude, Edghar."

Edghar ignored the sellsword. "Why should we take you along? What can you do for us?"

"I know stuff about the Bone Lord and what she's planning. You want me onboard."

Varcade nodded. "Definitely value in that. Also, he's a talking dog. What more needs to be said really?"

Edghar was too tired and beat up to argue. He didn't want to admit it, but if the canine had recently been close to Clea then he could perhaps even provide them with important details they wouldn't know otherwise. "Fine," he said with a sigh. "You're in." Edghar turned his direction to Varcade. "What happened to the other Duster? The naked man on the cloud."

Varcade stuck his tongue out and slid a finger across his throat. "Dead. Wasn't that tough to deal with if we're being honest. I expected more from these Dusters."

"That is easy for you to say," Edghar said. "He would've killed me if it was not for you. I couldn't even hit the bastard with my bolts."

"We didn't know a guy like *you* would be with our target," Dog Man said to Varcade. "You climbed a building and leapt off it to take him down, and you're standing here unscathed. If the Bone Lord knew, she would have sent one of the others instead."

"Looks like you made the right call finding me, eh?" Varcade said with a grin to Edghar.

Edghar still held some resentment towards the sellsword for the disastrous night before, but Varcade was not wrong. He had just proven he could actually go head-to-head against Clea's Dusters and come out on the winning side. Without him, Edghar stood no chance, and that was a fact.

"Aye, you did good," Edghar said. "Now let us get the hell out of here and find Baaq as quickly as we can. We can't keep wasting more time. I don't know how, but the Bone Lord somehow knows I'm back in Akrab, and that was not supposed to happen this early in my plan. This is a mess."

"You should know that when they don't hear back from me and Nimbus, they're gonna come after you even harder," Dog Man said.

"Let them," Varcade said. "We'll be ready."

CHAPTER ELEVEN

Edghar and the others made their way to the marshlands outside Akrab's high walls in haste. He knew exactly where they needed to go, which made things a lot quicker.

The four of them drifted down the river basins on a long and narrow canoe they'd rented to navigate the marshlands.

They passed small man-made islands created from reeds. The islands dotted the river and differed in sizes. Some carried one simple dwelling, while others were bigger and had room for several houses.

The scorching sun stood high in the sky, partnering with white, fluffy clouds to create a beautiful scene. The reflected rays from the sun glistened on the light-blue water as their canoe sent gentle ripples through the waters.

"So, these people live all their lives here?" Varcade said, standing in the front and using a setting pole to navigate the vessel. The sellsword was doing a good job, and Edghar was impressed. He would have done it himself, but he still needed to recover from the exploding fish that had almost blasted him into pulp—just thinking about it made his head spin.

"Aye," Edghar said. "They're known as marsh people. Some

breed and raise water buffalos, while others cultivate crops such as rice, barley, and wheat. I don't know what would have brought Baaq out here."

"It is nice and quiet," the Biter said, sitting in the middle next to Dog Man. "I like it here."

"Gotta say I do, too," Varcade said. "It's kinda relaxing, which is rare for me."

Edghar had asked people they passed if anyone knew Baaq's whereabouts. Luckily for them, many did. A demon moving out to the marshlands had not gone unnoticed. Some sneered at the mention of her name, followed by a derogatory curse word, while others spoke of her fondly.

The Dog Man kept sniffing, his nose running. Edghar had tried to ignore it, but the sound was getting on his nerves, and he was already feeling hostile towards the latest enforced member of the crew. "What is wrong with your nose?" Edghar said.

Dog Man shrugged. "Side-effect from using all that Dust. Messes up the nose."

"Big surprise," Varcade said. "Maybe you shouldn't snort the bones of the Old Ones? Ever think about that?"

The talking dog chuckled. "You're not wrong but it's way too late for me, boy."

"Boy? Just how old are you?" Varcade said over his shoulder.

"Much older than the three of you. That's all you need to know."

"Could you stop now?" the Biter said, his head tilted. "No more Dust?"

"That's not how it works. I'd die without it at this point."

"*Right*," Varcade said. "I bet that's what every Duster says."

"I'm not lying. That crap is addicting. I need it as much as I need water or air to survive."

"Are you serious?" Varcade said.

Dog Man nodded. "Aye. I did not know that the first time I used it. You don't need much of it before it changes your body forever."

Edghar was far from an expert on God Dust, but what Dog Man

said did make sense. The few Dusters he had come across over the years were almost always unstable and crazy individuals, snorting away their humanity one hit at a time. Surely, they would have stopped snorting the Dust when it began to change them if they could?

In Edghar's eyes, the Dust had always been like forbidden candy. Of course, a part of him wanted to try and see what magic abilities lay dormant in his blood, but he also knew there was no coming back from it. There was a reason why it was forbidden in all seven city-states. The God Dust locked in the vaults of the Bone Lords was simply there to act as an immensely powerful defence in the case Harrah was invaded. Only then would the God Dust be portioned out to the royal armies to give them the upper hand against the threat they faced. The World Authority feared the God Dust and would think long and carefully before they attempted to conquer the Harrah region like they had many other parts of the known world.

"Hey, Biter, take over for me a bit," Varcade said. "Let me rest."

"Of course, my friend," the Biter said and took the setting pole from the sellsword.

Varcade took the Biter's place next to Dog Man. He wiped off the beads of sweat running down his face.

"You know you could take off that coat of yours and it wouldn't be so hot," Edghar said, seeing the sellsword's discomfort.

Varcade shook his head. "Nah, it's my thing. I need to keep it on."

"Where did you even find such a strange attire?" Edghar said. "Never seen anything like it before."

"It's my old Educator coat that I have turned inside out. Pretty neat, eh?"

"So, it's a spite thing then? You want people to know you're a rogue Educator?"

"I don't care about other people. I want the Masters to know I'm out in the world sullying their precious Order. It makes me happy thinking about how upsetting it must be to them."

"Ah, that's why I recognised it," Dog Man said, looking Varcade up and down. "The Educator Order."

"You've seen an Educator before?" Varcade said, actual surprise in his voice.

"Aye."

"Huh," Varcade said. "Have you been in Karkan then?"

Dog Man nodded. "I've been to a lot of places, boy. I said I'm older than I look." The Duster scratched himself behind the ear. "So, you turned your back on them? I didn't think that was an option. Once you were in that was for life."

"It's not," Varcade said. "Escaped from them would be a more fitting way of saying it. I doubt I was the first, but if someone else has ever done it, I haven't heard about it. That would be a thing the Order would make sure to keep hidden."

Dog Man chuckled. "Well, good for ya. I always hated the bastards. Going around telling everyone how to live their lives and beating them up if they don't do as told; thinking they're better and more enlightened than everyone else because of those stupid Teachings. Give me a damn break."

Edghar was honestly surprised to see Varcade crack a genuine smile, but he understood why. The sellsword was not just a foreigner in Harrah; he was a unique individual. Meeting someone that understood his past was a rarity that Varcade clearly appreciated—especially someone who harboured the same feelings as he did towards the Educator Order.

"You think the Educators are still after you after all this time?" Edghar asked.

Varcade nodded. "Guaranteed. It takes years and years to train an Educator. In their eyes, we aren't people but property; an instrument used to restore Balance to a world that has lost its way. That's all we are."

"Messed up. You should get back at them some day," Dog Man said.

Varcade turned away and looked at the water. "Perhaps," he said.

No one said anything after that as they kept navigating through the river.

"I think this is house of demon, no?" the Biter suddenly said. "Red roof."

Edghar looked ahead and nodded. "Aye, seems right. Bring us up."

Their canoe came to a halt as it touched ground on the shore of the miniature island. The island had one arched reed house on it. The dwelling was not big and not small but seemed fitting for one person. Right outside the house were two poles with a line hanging between them. Several fish had been hung up to dry, flies buzzing all over them, the heat from the sun turning the skin crispy. Edghar had never understood how anyone would want to eat that.

There was no door to the house, and before they stood from the canoe, a demon stepped out, stopping in her tracks at the sudden appearance of strangers invading her island. She resembled a humanoid goat, but with bulging muscles and thick, short grey fur, wearing dark-green trousers and a brown top leaving her arms bare. She had large, backwards-curving horns with numerous ridges along them, and wore a brimmed straw hat.

"Who are you?" she said.

"Please tell me you are Baaq," Edghar said, standing up in the canoe.

She crossed her muscular arms. "I am. What do you want?"

Edghar felt relief wash over him, but he was not fully satisfied yet. "I'm sorry, but I need to be thorough. You are *the* Baaq; the veteran marksman from the First Contact War?"

"I already said yes, stranger. That is the second question I have answered while you still haven't answered mine. That needs to change, or we will have a problem on our hands."

Edghar nodded. "Of course. I will tell you everything if you are willing to talk?"

Baaq the marksman looked the others over, and Edghar instinctively felt embarrassed by the company he kept. "Fine. We can talk."

THE CREW

Baaq didn't have chairs for that many guests, so Varcade and the others had settled on the ground outside her house. The weather was still hot but not uncomfortable, and the demon had brought a jug of water and clay cups for everyone.

Several of the marsh people passed them on their canoes up and down the river, giving them "you're clearly not from here" looks. Varcade couldn't exactly blame them though. Their small crew would stick out as a sore thumb wherever they went from this point on; especially if the demon marksman was now added to the fold.

"Tell me why you are here," Baaq said. She sat with her legs crossed, hands resting on her thighs.

"I will get straight to the point," Edghar said. "We are going to remove the Bone Lord of Akrab. I am putting together a crew to do this, and I have been keeping an eye on you for years."

"I know, it's kinda creepy to be honest," Varcade said to Baaq. "He did it to me too. Kept following me around and stuff."

"You make it sounds much weirder when you say it like that!" Edghar snapped. He returned his attention to Baaq. "Ignore him. The reason I know who you are is because I was the former spymaster working for the regime. So, I kept track of anyone and everyone that could be a potential risk in the city. That is all. It was my job."

"And you want my help taking down the Bone Lord?" Baaq said. "Do I look like an assassin? I don't do things like that."

"I never claimed you were an assassin," Edghar said. "But according to everything I have heard about you, you're bloody good with a rifle. Humans and demons still speak of your deeds during the First Contact War to this day."

Baaq stared at the former spymaster for a moment before answering. "Is that supposed to make me feel proud? Or happy? That I have killed more men than I can remember? I never asked to be a soldier."

Edghar frowned. "But you were. When the demons came through the World Wound—"

"Don't call it that in front of me. *Wound*." Baaq said, her voice carrying an ice-cold anger. "What you refer to as a 'wound' was the portal my people went through to find freedom. We did not know what we would find on the other side. You humans attacked us the moment we set foot on your world, forcing us to go to war. I became a soldier so I could protect my people from dying at your hands. I did not *choose* it."

"I apologise," Edghar said. "I meant no offence. It's been a long time since the war happened and I will honestly say I don't know everything about it. What I do know, I have learned from the human side of the conflict. We rarely hear the demons' side of things."

Baaq closed her eyes for a second and breathed out before opening them again. "It's fine. Now, if that is all, please finish your drinks and go."

Edghar's mouth opened then closed, before opening again. "What about your people, Baaq? You must know what is happening in the city even though you don't live there. We're close to a civil war. Things have never been worse in Akrab and it all stems from the Bone Lord herself. She is out of control."

"Of course, I know," Baaq sighed. "But what can I do? What can you do?"

Edghar got his determination back the moment he noticed a crack in Baaq's armour. "I'm not saying removing the Bone Lord from power will solve *everything*, but it is a start. Her behaviour is not only harming the demons but *all* citizens of Akrab. I want to stop her. Now, before things reach a point we can never repair."

Baaq looked at Edghar with intense eyes, clearly contemplating his words. "You are serious about this?"

Edghar nodded. "I think we have a real chance. Especially if you are on our side. The Bone Lord has powerful Dusters working for her, so I need strong people on our side. Your expertise with a rifle could really come in handy."

Varcade shifted in his seat, feeling more and more uncomfortable as the conversation went on. He tried to turn off the part of his brain that drew parallels to him and the Educators. He, too, had moved away from his home and in turn turned his back on those other people still trapped by the Order, even if that had never been his intention. Baaq had, in a sense, done the same thing. Choosing to flee instead of fighting. The thought of young children being taken to the Educator Temples at this moment pained Varcade, and instead of doing something to stop the Order, he had left everything behind and ran to Harrah.

"What's crawling up your butt?" Dog Man whispered to Varcade, clearly noticing something was off. "Sit still."

"Nothing," Varcade said. "Shut up, leave me alone."

Baaq breathed in deeply, rubbing her temples. "I made some bad decisions after the war. I worked with a criminal known as Fat Pudding. I was his hired muscle you could say. Feeling bad about what I was doing, I started drinking heavily. The memories from the war and working for Fat Pudding became too much. I was losing my mind. So, I sold my rifle to him and left everything and moved out here. You coming here after all this time . . . Maybe we can change things. Maybe I can make up for the mistakes I have made in my life."

Edghar smiled. "We will get your rifle back, no worries. And yes, together I believe we can save this city."

Varcade couldn't take it anymore and stood up abruptly. "Okay, Baaq's in. Can we, like, wrap this up now?"

"Are you stupid?" Edghar said, staring at Varcade. "We are talking about serious stuff here."

"What more is there to say?" Varcade said. "Everything is terrible and we have a slim chance of really pulling this off. That's what you're gonna talk about now, isn't? How 'bout we focus on what's next instead?"

"We can't just rush things because you're bored. We need to think things through and adjust our plans—"

"No," Varcade interrupted. "You need to get your head straight.

The Bone Lord will have sent more Dusters after us now. Dog Man already told us this. Instead of reacting to everything she throws at us, we should instead do something that rattles *her*. Strike back and cause her to panic."

Edghar was taken aback as he contemplated what Varcade had just said. "That's actually not a bad idea. I am well familiar with Clea's temper. She will lash out and start making mistakes." The former spymaster nodded. "Damn it, Varcade, but you are right."

"Damn right I am."

"I have a suggestion."

Everyone looked at the dog.

Baaq was clearly surprised and started saying something, but Edghar met her eyes and shook his head, indicating to just let it go.

"Right before Nimbus and I left the ziggurat, that weird coin-guy said he was about to leave Akrab and have a meeting with the Bone Lord of Nuzz," Dog Man said. "If we hurry, we might be able to catch him out in the open. Feels like a no-brainer to me."

Varcade grinned at the look on Edghar's face. Varcade's impulse to recruit Dog Man had just given them a golden opportunity they desperately needed.

Edghar nodded. "Yes, that could work. We need to—"

Baaq cleared her throat. "Hey, remember what I said about my rifle? I don't have it anymore. If you want a marksman, I'm going to need to get it back from Fat Pudding."

"Why? Can't we just get you another rifle?"

"No. That's not how it works. I need *that* rifle."

Edghar sighed. "Alright, fine." He looked over at Varcade. "Can you handle Berenberg in the meantime? We'll meet up at Three Sisters once we're done."

"Who the hell is that?" Varcade said.

"The Treasurer–the coin guy!"

"Oh, yeah. Sure thing," Varcade shrugged. "I'll kill his ass, no worries."

"Don't say it so casually! You don't even know how the guy looks."

Varcade shrugged. "So what? I got Dog Man with me. You can track him for us, right?"

"Not a problem," Dog Man said. "I got his scent."

"I come with you and dog," the Biter said. "We have good time together."

"Yeah, that's probably best," Edghar said. "Then it's decided. Please don't get into trouble on the way. You need to hurry."

"I *know*, man. Stop talking to me like a child," Varcade said as he rose to his feet. "What will you do?"

"I guess me and Baaq need to get her rifle back . . ." Edghar said with a sigh.

CHAPTER TWELVE

Clea filled another cup of red wine and brought it to her lips. She sat in the magnificent gardens on one of the highest floors of the ziggurat, the sprawling city of Akrab spread out all around the royal building. The drinking along with the solitude of the garden was the only thing that helped her relax these days. The sound of birds chirping along with the fragrance from the various flowers was soothing. Clea closed her eyes and inhaled deep, feeling her tense body beginning to loosen.

The sky was a beautiful turquoise, not a cloud in sight. The parasol jutting up from the stone table shielded her from the blistering sun, and sitting there in the shadows, Clea felt herself as close to calm for the first time in what felt like forever.

"Pardon me, Your Excellency."

Fuck my life.

"Yes," she said, dragging out the word, trying hard to keep her composure. "What is it?"

The Keeper of the Royal Seal, Berenberg, stood rigid as a plank, his nose high in the air. "I'm close to being done with the preparations for my trip to meet with the Bone Lord of Nuzz. Everything seems to be in order and I should depart shortly if there aren't any unforeseen troubles." Berenberg cleared his throat loudly, making Clea shudder at the sound of phlegm being forced down his gullet. "The state treasure will get a much-needed boost after we receive the loan from the Bone Lord. The funding of the alchemy guild's weapon development has been a costly affair for us."

Clea rubbed her brow. "You still haven't said a single thing I didn't already know."

"My apologies, Your Highness. I simply wanted to ask if you've had a moment to look over the conditions for the loan? Without your approval–"

"Of course, I've looked them over! How many times do I need to tell you that?"

That was a complete lie.

"Give the bastard what he wants. We need that coin."

Berenberg gave a stale nod. "Very well, then. I should return in a few weeks' time, no longer than that."

How about you never return, you soul-sucking ghoul?

"Yes, yes, good. See you then," Clea said, motioning with the cup dismissively.

Berenberg turned on his heel and left.

The rim of the cup had barely touched her lips before both Khanon, the Army General, and Erikz, the Royal Guard Captain strolled up to her with urgency. Both men sank onto one knee, and said, "Your Highness," exactly at the same time.

Clea closed her eyes, feeling the veins in her neck pulsating. *"What now?"* she hissed.

"My apologies, Your Highness," Erikz said, "but we bring you urgent news. We just received word the Dusters we sent after Edghar failed. Witnesses confirm Edghar is indeed here in Akrab as you suspected, but he's not alone. It appears he's working with someone rather powerful. Together with this stranger, they took out the two Dusters. The . . . naked old man was found dead, and the . . . talking dog was nowhere to be found."

"Idiots! Who's that stranger you speak of?" Clea spat.

"We're still trying to figure that out," Khanon said. "But whoever he is, he seems to be a formidable foe. Those Dusters were the real deal."

Up until this point, Clea had hoped–no, wished–her thoughts that Edghar was plotting something weren't true; that he would never really do something to harm her. But now, with this information, that wishful thinking was obliterated. She gulped her remaining wine before immediately filling the cup again, her hands trembling. "Tarkus *promised* me working with the band of Dusters would solve our problems," Clea growled. "Those vultures are sucking our vault of God Dust dry and what do we have to show for it?"

Both the Royal Guard Captain and the Army General kept their silence.

"Bring Tarkus to me. Now."

Erikz bowed with his usual grace and left.

Khanon, ever the professional, stood like a statue, not bothered the slightest by the palpable silence. The general looked straight ahead, his mouth a thin line.

Clea took another sip, but the wine had lost its sweetness. It dawned on her that a small part of her was glad the two Dusters had failed. She wasn't really ready to hear a report that Edghar had been killed.

"Can we fix this without killing Edghar?" Before Clea could stop herself, the words had escaped her mouth. Her cheeks heated. She sat straighter, more befitting to a regal person of her position. "I mean, obviously I don't have a problem with it, but I'm just thinking we could use a man with Edghar's skills on our side, is all. It'd be a shame to waste someone like him, don't you think?"

Khanon offered her the briefest of smiles, but it was gone so quick, Clea couldn't be sure she'd seen it. "Edghar was wrong to openly oppose you. That wasn't his place. You are our Bone Lord, and we must do as you command. Edghar knew this, but still, he did what he did. A person taking that sort of liberty cannot be trusted,

I'm afraid. We need *order* or everything will crumble." The Army General sighed. "You *know* I care for the man. I have known both of you since the moment you came into the world. But what is done is done, My Lord. Edghar is now an enemy of the state, and he must be stopped."

Clea discreetly rubbed the tattoo on her shoulder—the one she shared with Edghar. She knew there was no going back. Edghar would always care more about what he thought was right. That was never going to change, and in his eyes, that meant removing her as Bone Lord of Akrab, regardless of how much it personally hurt him. She felt annoyed with herself for even breaching the subject and decided to change the topic quickly.

"What's taking them so long? Go and see–" Clea interrupted herself as Vizier Tarkus returned through the doorway at that moment. Erikz was next to him and behind them came the Duster who had introduced himself as the Baker.

Following the thin man were six identical . . . *Things? Creatures?* Clea's eyes widened at the sight, unable to determine what she was really looking at. They were humanoid with two legs, two arms and a head, but that's really where the similarities ended.

"Your Highness," Vizier Tarkus said with his usual smirk, rubbing lotion on his hands, arms, and legs, making a wet, squelching sound as he did so. It was so loud and disgusting to Clea, it was as if someone was smacking their lips and licking their mouth inches from her ears. "I can only apologise at the news that the Dusters we sent after Edghar failed in their task. I will admit I underestimated the man. But fear not, the Baker will not fail. I assure you of that."

The Baker stepped forward, the six creatures lining up behind him in a perfect formation. "My Lord, these beings are my own mercenary group collectively known as Dough Fest. I create them myself and they have never failed in executing a task given to them." He held another ball of dough in his hand, tossing it up and down. "If you want your former Spymaster eliminated, Dough Fest will get it done."

Clea was taken aback and seemed to have lost her tongue. She couldn't help but stare at the hairless creatures. They stood before her, butt-naked, their bodies made of some kind of sand-coloured clay —or dough she guessed was more accurate based on the name. Their eyes and mouth simply looked to be the imprint of a thumb pressed three times into their faces, and she couldn't imagine they filled any real purpose.

"Your Highness?" The Baker said.

"Yes, yes," Clea said. "Correct, whatever. What the hell are those things?"

The Duster took a step back. "Demonstration," he said and clapped his hands twice.

Immediately the six Dough Men sprinted into action, performing a variety of acrobatic tricks, ranging from forward rolls, backward rolls, handstands, cartwheels, backflips, and split jumps. Two of them boosted a third one who soared high above their heads before landing gracefully, while another one did a wall-run on the facade of the building.

"Weapons," The Baker said in a sharp tone, clapping his hands again.

The Dough Men hardened their soft arms and transformed them into an array of blade-like weapons.

Erikz and Khanon drew their own weapons and instantly formed a protective circle around Clea, their eyes tracking the Dough Men as they continued their arial tricks left and right.

"Enough," the Baker ordered with another double clap. The Dough Men once again formed a proper line behind the Duster. The man took out a tube from inside his coat. "Moisturise," he said and gave it to the Dough Man closest to him. The creature pressed out some skin cream before passing it to the next one. The Dough Men rubbed the lotion all over their bodies and face until they glistened in the midday sun. "Look how beautiful they are. Splendidly soft and doughy."

What the hell just happened? Clea thought with her mouth open.

"I believe that answers your question, Your Highness?" The Duster said with a satisfied smirk.

"What? Absolutely not!" Clea roared.

"No? Let's try this then. Exercise," The Baker said and clapped.

The Dough Men dropped to all four and began doing push-ups, then sit-ups. Clea wasn't certain, but it looked like one of them was imitating the act of thrusting in the missionary position during intercourse.

"Stop, stop it," Clea barked. "Enough!"

The Baker ordered the Dough Men back in line. "I assume *now* your question has been answered, Your Highness?"

Clea was about to explode. Thankfully the always watchful Erikz noticed his Lord's agony and stepped forward. "I believe Her Excellency has had enough demonstrations and would now like to know exactly what type of beings these are."

The Baker crossed his arms. "I already told you. I make them." He held up the dough ball in his hand. "Whatever I bake I can bring to life. But as I said, Dough Fest's track record speaks for itself. Better mercenaries you will not find. If I may borrow your sword."

Erikz looked at the Duster in confusion, but Clea rolled her eyes and nodded. The Royal Guard Captain reluctantly handed over his blade to the Baker. The Duster took the sword and chopped the Dough Man's head cleanly off in one slice, making it land on the ground with a sick thud. The decapitated creature bent and picked its head up and put it back on. "See?" the Duster said. "They are basically indestructible and will obey any order I give them."

The strangeness of the situation aside, it would be hard to argue that these creatures wouldn't complete their mission. "Fine," Clea said. "Send them."

The Duster returned Erikz's weapon and bowed before he left.

Clea rubbed her temples. She was getting a headache again. These days it seemed she couldn't go one day without having one. Feeling suddenly exhausted, she dismissed everyone with a wave of her hand. "Leave me. All of you."

Vashi had asked three other people where he could find the old Educator called Xira, but instead of getting answers, he'd been forced to educate all of them with pain, making them promise to forever change their ways.

I never imagined this city would be so tainted by horrible behaviour. A temple is clearly needed to help better these people. I need to speak with the Masters about that the moment I return home. The Teachings are desperately needed here.

But that was not why Vashi had travelled all the way to Akrab. He needed to find his brother and stop his destructive ways. Not only for himself, but also for the sake of the Educators. His brother's behaviour was tarnishing the Order's reputation, going against all the Teachings, and that was unacceptable.

Vashi would be lying to himself if he didn't confess that he was feeling slightly—just slightly—agitated that no one showed an interest in assisting him. All he needed was to find Xira and the rest would take care of itself. An idea formed. Maybe instead of simply walking around and asking these rude people questions of no interest to them, he could instead buy something from them, perhaps something edible, to win their favour. Surely, he would be allowed to ask a question or two afterwards and be met with respect and humility?

With that plan in mind, he looked around until he spotted a vendor selling something unfamiliar to him. He approached the old man with a smile, pointing at the orange strips displayed on the stand. "Hello to you. May I ask what it is you are selling, yes?"

"Sweets. They're called kulqum." The vendor was smiling at him, a seemingly rare occurrence in Akrab. "Would you like to try a sample, friend?"

"Yes, and thank you," Vashi said with a grin. The man handed him one of the strips. It was sticky to the touch; not hard, not soft but somewhere in between. Vashi bit down and had to work his jaw muscles quite a bit to get through it, but the taste was sweet and fruity, some type of citrus flavour. "This is good," he said as he chewed. He held up a finger. "I would like to purchase some of these . . . Kulqum from you."

"Of course," the vendor said. "It's two copper coins for five strips. Your pronunciation was rather good by the way. You're obviously not from around these parts."

"That is correct," Vashi said. "I have travelled all the way from Karkan."

Candy and copper exchanged hands.

The vendor's eyes widened. "Isn't that on the other side of the world?"

Vashi nodded. "It has taken me almost a year to get here. . ."

"To travel that far, you must have something important to attend to."

"Yes, I am here to find my brother. I'm certain he is in Akrab."

"Wow, you must really love your brother to make such a trip. I hope you find him."

"Love?" Vashi said. "I do not believe in that. That is not why I am here."

The vendor's friendly look changed to one of confusion. "Eh, okay. Anything else I can do for you?"

Vashi paused a moment. "Actually, yes. Would it be possible for me to ask you a question?"

"Of course."

Ah, faith in humanity restored, Vashi smiled.

"I am looking for a person by the name of Xira. Is that perhaps someone you have heard of?"

The male vendor frowned. "If it is who I think it is, then yes." His demeanour changed, the warmth in his voice vanishing; he even looked at Vashi differently, almost hostile. "That foreign freak lives in the demon ghetto part of Akrab. She used to go around and go *on and on* about some sacred teachings and would attack people if they acted in a way she did not approve. A real nutcase. But I don't think she does that anymore, thank the White Queen. People had enough of her."

Disappointment.

Talking about other people in rude and demeaning ways and trying to affect others into sharing those thoughts is wrong. Each person must form their own opinions based on their own experiences. An offence has been made, and a lesson must be taught.

Vashi sighed then punched the vendor right in the throat. The man toppled over, making gurgling noises as he struggled to breathe. Vashi leapt over the table using one hand and landed standing over the man on the ground. "Speaking ill of others is unacceptable. Say you are sorry this instant and promise to not do it again." The vendor wheezed, clutching at his throat. "You will say it and mean it sincerely or the Education must continue." More wheezing. "I am disappointed our encounter turned into this. We were having such a pleasant time together."

Vashi grabbed the man's foot and was just about to twist it when the vendor gathered enough air to speak up. "S-Stop, please . . ." the man said, looking up at Vashi with horror in his eyes.

"Say it," Vashi said, applying a bit of pressure to the man's foot.

"I-I'm sorry . . . I won't speak bad about anyone ever again, I promise. Please don't hurt me, I beg you . . ."

Vashi released the man's extremity and nodded. "I believe you." *Lesson complete.* Vashi held out his fist, and the man flinched at the motion, closing his eyes for an incoming blow. "The lesson is complete. No more violence required. Bump the fist," he said. The vendor carefully did as instructed. Vashi smiled, popping another piece of candy in his mouth. "I wish you a good day. Thank you and goodbye."

Vashi had to walk for hours before he finally reached the demon ghettos. The candy vendor had told him the old Educator Xira had last been seen in these parts of the city. By the time he arrived, the sky had darkened. The silvery moon illuminated Akrab with its soothing and mysterious light. The evening air had a bite to it, making Vashi put his blue coat back on. He much preferred this to the scorching sun.

Back in Karkan–the Land of Mountains–there was snow all year around. Even though Vashi and his younger brother had lived in one of the many remote villages in the valleys at the foot of the mountain range, the climate higher up in the mountains was on another level. It was close to those peaks where the Educator Temples were located. Vashi's brother had never taken a liking to the freezing weather, always complaining about the cold, but Vashi had grown accustomed to it over time. It was not an accident that the Order had chosen to establish their temples in such challenging conditions. The weather was a tool in their Educator training, honing the students' mental fortitude and toughness by pushing one's body to the extreme.

Vashi buttoned his coat and adjusted the round, high collar. The further he had walked from the city's core, the more Akrab changed. Here on the outskirts of the city, Vashi had gradually seen fewer and fewer humans, and more and more of the demon population.

When whispers of his brother's whereabouts first reached the Masters back in Karkan, they had been astonished to learn he had surfaced in Harrah of all places. That was on the other side of the known world. The Masters had ordered Vashi to go after him, and forced him to study the region and language before setting off on his long journey.

The Harrah region was mainly known for their God Dust and demon population. The demons had appeared out of thin air one day, stepping through a gateway known as the World Wound.

War between the two races had followed immediately. Once the war–called the First Contact War–had ended, it was decided by the Bone Lords that each city-state would welcome their share of demon refugees as part of the peace treaty. Some city-states held up their side of the arrangement, whilst others did not. The former Bone

Lords of Akrab had welcomed more demons into their city than all other city-states in the Harrah region combined. According to what Vashi had learned, things had been going well for Akrab for some time, but then the Bone Lords had been assassinated by a group of humans opposing the demon presence in their city.

Walking all the way here, Vashi hadn't encountered much trouble. There had been some chanting and yelling from a large group of humans, but he hadn't paid them much attention. But as he'd gotten closer to the demon district, the tension in the air became quite palpable.

Armed men and women–humans, by the looks of it–wearing armoured black and white robes were patrolling the streets. They wore cone caps that went down just above their noses, covering their faces, and some of them resembled human skulls. Their heavy weapons looked unlike anything Vashi had ever seen back in Karkan.

When the passing demons spotted the robed figures, they immediately turned their heels and went the other way. Clearly there was some type of conflict going on here, but that wasn't why Vashi was here. He needed to focus on his own mission.

The long journey was beginning to take its toll on Vashi. He was exhausted and was afraid to ask more strangers for help in case it would lead to further Educations. He decided he needed to find hospice for the night and get some rest. His search for Xira could resume in the morning, after some well-deserved sleep.

Vashi looked around and tried to make out the signs hanging above different doors but reading them was impossible. *I should have studied the language better,* he sighed.

Further down the street, two demons wobbled side to side, screaming and shouting. *Loud behaviour in public places is disturbing to other people and is not tolerated.* Vashi exhaled, rubbing the back of neck. He really was too tired for another education. Vashi was about to move closer and do his duty–

"A coin to spare?"

He turned and looked in the direction of the hollow voice.

Shrouded in the shadows of an alleyway stood a hulking figure, a hand with spindly fingers reaching out. The stranger was covered in rags, a drawn hood covering their face.

Vashi took out a copper coin and one of the candy strips he had purchased earlier. "Here you go, my friend," he said, placing them in the stranger's open palm.

"Thank you kindly," the voice said. "You are a good person. If only more people followed the Teachings..." The stranger muttered, returning to the shadows of the alleyway.

The Teachings? "Wait, please," Vashi said, following the stranger. "Xira?"

The stranger stopped. "No one has called me that in a long time... Who are you? Have you come to hurt me more?"

"No," Vashi said, holding up his hands. "I am Educator Vashi. From the Temples in Karkan. Master Habab told me about you. Are you indeed Xira? I cannot believe this. Truly the Saints guide me."

"I am, I am," she said. "Master Habab... I haven't seen him in... I cannot remember. Why are you here, Educator Vashi?"

Vashi hesitated. The subject of his brother brought him great discomfort. "I am here to find someone. A fellow Educator who has lost his ways. Master Habab believed you could help me in my search?"

"Perhaps I can." Xira shrugged. "Who knows. Follow me to my home and we will talk more."

CHAPTER THIRTEEN

Edghar and Baaq had left the marshlands and journeyed back to the inner city. The demon crime boss called Fat Pudding operated out of the demon ghettos and that was where Baaq was taking Edghar.

It was now early in the morning and the sun was slowly rising.

"Where are we going, exactly?" Edghar said, dropping a coin to a demon beggar. "We can't waste any time."

"We will not get there faster because you keep running your mouth," Baaq said. "We get there when we get there."

Easy for you to say, Edghar thought. He was annoyed at this whole ordeal if he was being honest with himself. Finding Baaq and recruiting her for the job was supposed to be the difficult part, not getting her rifle back.

"You never said why we can't just find you another rifle," Edghar said. "Does it have to be your old one?"

"Yes," Baaq said without sparing him a glance. "I am soul-bound to that weapon. It means only I can use it. *It* knows me and I *know* it. It's demon craft."

Edghar would be the first to admit the technology of the demons was a subject he wasn't familiar with. But he knew their unique weaponry had been what kept them in the fight during the First Contact War. But the Bone Dust-enhanced soldiers from the combined armies of the Bone Lords had been too much for the demons in the end.

"What does that mean?" Edghar said, realising this was an opportunity to educate himself. "*Soul-bound?*"

"It means I created that rifle using my own flesh and blood." Baaq pulled up her top to reveal a massive scar across her back. "It is part of me."

What the hell, Edghar thought with wide eyes. "Is that how every demon weapon is created?"

"No," Baaq said, pulling down her top again.

"But if only *you* can use it, why did this Fat Pudding buy it from you?"

"Powerful people like to collect rare things. Humans do this as well, do they not?"

Edghar nodded. "I see. Bragging rights."

"Sure, if that is what you call it. Now enough with the questions."

The two of them kept on for some time, now reaching areas of the city Edghar had never set foot in before. He'd always found the demon ghettos depressing but looking around now, he realised there were apparently even worse places. The state of degradation on the buildings and the tired-looks of demons they passed caused a knot to form in Edghar's gut.

Baaq suddenly stopped, holding out a muscular arm that caused Edghar to halt.

"Now, listen closely," the demon marksman said, facing him. "You might have been born in Akrab, but where we are going now isn't *Akrab* anymore. At least not the place you think of."

"What does that even mean?" Edghar said.

Baaq rubbed her brow with one of her large hands. "You need to stop with all these questions and just listen to what I am saying. These parts don't get many humans. So, stay behind me and pretend you're invisible or something. I will do the talking and we should be fine. You got coin, right?"

Edghar had had it with being treated like a child. "No, it is time you listen to me: I don't like surprises and I don't like being kept in the dark. Tell me where we are going and how we are doing this. Understand?" He met Baaq's eyes even though she towered over him.

Baaq took off her wide brimmed straw hat and ran a hand through her braids. "Fine. You are the one in charge. I can accept that."

"Good," Edghar said. "Out with it then."

"I already told you I made some bad decisions after the war, right? I was angry for how things turned out. All the pain and suffering crashed down on me. I started drinking and doing other bad things. I needed coin to get by, so I ended up working for Fat Pudding, doing whatever he told me to so I could eke out a living. I'm not proud of the things I did during that time. Finally, I had enough and realised I had to get out."

"And that's when you sold your rifle?"

Baaq nodded. "With the coin I made, I could buy what I needed to begin a new life out in the marshlands. But now you've brought me back here."

"Just remember you're back for a good reason. You were a hero for your people during the war. Now you can be a hero again and help create a better future for all demons in Akrab. That is worth fighting for, is it not?"

"Yes, it is. I would like that."

"Good," Edghar said with a smile. "Then let us go get your rifle back."

They continued until they arrived at one of the saddest places Edghar had ever seen. It was an old park, but it was completely run down. Trash and debris littered the place, and different symbols in the demon language–languages?–were painted everywhere. But the worst part was the group of demon kids playing there. Edghar's heart ached at the sight. The kids seemed to be in the middle of a game, all crouched on the ground in a circle.

Baaq walked up to one of the younglings with determined steps. "Fat Pudding. Where is he?"

"How the hell am I supposed to know that?" the demon boy replied, not even looking up at Baaq.

Baaq grabbed the boy by the neck and lifted him up, his short legs floundering in the air. "Hey, let me go you bastard!"

"Don't play with me, kid," Baaq growled in the boy's face. "Run and tell Fat Pudding that Baaq is here to see him." She put him on the ground and gently kicked the boy in the butt as he took off. Baaq turned her attention to the remaining youngsters. "The rest of you, get out of here." The kids cursed at Baaq but went their way.

Baaq sat down on an old and cracked stone bench. Edghar joined her.

The bad feeling in Edghar's gut was even stronger now. This wasn't a place for kids to be playing - demon or human. The realisation something like this even existed made Edghar disappointed in himself. He had been part of the ruling regime. He should have been aware. Even though his job was the state's security, he could still have done *something*, couldn't he? When had things reached this point?

"What is that look?" Baaq said, studying him.

Edghar sighed, shaking his head, not sure how to put his feelings into words. "Guess I am feeling bad about the state of things here. Of course, I knew things were bad in the outskirts, but I didn't know it had reached this point. Or maybe I had but chose to ignore it. I honestly don't know."

Baaq didn't immediately respond. Instead, they sat in silence for a minute before she spoke up. "I will not sit here and claim things were better in the Nine Realms. Far from it, otherwise we would not have fled in the first place. But this . . . existence here in your world . . . is something *new*. Something I could never have imagined."

Baaq leaned forward, her jaw resting on her knuckles. "It's true we demons all live in the same city as you humans; breathing the same air and all that, but at the same time we are not *really* here. We are not part of the *whole*. It feels like most humans want to forget we even exist. Our presence bothers you."

Edghar's immediate instinct wanted to argue that statement. He did not feel that way. Of course, there were humans who held nothing but hate in their hearts towards the demons. The group that had assassinated Clea's parents were of that sort–people who did not accept the demons in Akrab. But Edghar also knew many humans who loved the demons and saw them as equal citizens in the city. But instead of arguing with Baaq, he decided perhaps he should just listen.

Baaq continued talking without looking at Edghar, instead staring straight ahead, her mind somewhere else. "Do you understand what I mean? There is a big difference in *wanting* to have us here, and being *stuck* with us? My kind *knows* that; we are not dumb. And that constant feeling of being unwanted? After a while you can't ignore it any longer. You give in to it; even embrace it. It becomes both your sword and shield. The shield to protect you from the pain in your heart, and the sword to fight against it." Baaq sighed deeply. "I am not saying it is good. But it makes it easier to live. You hate us, so we hate you back. You want nothing to do with us, so we want nothing to do with you."

Edghar blow out a breath, rubbing his eyes. "I am not sure what to say, Baaq. I really don't."

"You don't have to say anything. I do not expect you to have the answers." Baaq turned and looked at him. "But I appreciate you listening. And I appreciate that you *care*. Otherwise, you would not do what you're doing."

"Of course," Edghar said. He wanted to say more, promise things would and could change, but how could he? The divide in not only Akrab but all of Harrah since the First Contact War would take years and years to fix—if it was even possible. But what he could do was start to make things better by removing Clea from power. Involving herself with the Alchemy Guild as well as having Dusters working for her... Her decisions were further fuelling this conflict and it needed to be stopped before it all reached a point of no return. Hearing Baaq's words had hit him deep, again reminding him why he was doing all of this.

"One-Shot Baaq!"

Fat Pudding was exactly what his name stated him to be: a fat, green pudding-looking creature with small wings that fluttered rapidly to keep the demon hovering in the air.

Next to him were two other demons, clearly Fat Pudding's cronies. One was a skinny demon who looked like a humanoid fly, two orange, bulbous eyes covering most of his face. Fly Guy carried two smaller demon-tech pistols.

The third demon–clearly female–had bright, pink skin and slanted yellow eyes. She looked at Edghar menacingly, her teeth shark-like.

"I see you have learned to speak the human tongue," Baaq said, rising from the bench.

"Better for business. Not only our kind that likes the good stuff," Fat Pudding laughed with his high-pitched voice. "Fat Pudding does not discriminate. Humans? Demons? I do not care as long as they pay."

The crime boss buzzed close to Edghar's face, his small eyes looking him up and down. "And who are you?" Fat Pudding looked over his shoulder at Baaq. "You running with onions these days, eh?"

"He's a friend," Baaq said. "Don't worry about it."

Fat Pudding hovered over Baaq. "I see. So, One-Shot, what brings you here? You want work? I always have a spot for you. My guy Ratzitt got himself killed a couple of weeks ago. I could use more muscle."

Baaq shook her head. "No, not why I am here."

Fat Pudding's demeanour immediately changed, he grimaced like he'd eaten something sour. "Then what do you want?" he hissed. "Do not waste my time."

The whole time that Baaq and Fat Pudding had been conversing,

Fly Guy had been staring at Edghar. He suddenly said, "I do not like your face. It is like shit."

Before Edghar could say something, Baaq overheard and cut in. "Shut it, Zipper."

"Or what?" Zipper said. "What will you do?"

"Both of you shut up," Fat Pudding said. "Get to the point."

"I need my rifle back," Baaq said.

Fat Pudding's beady, red eyes lit up. "Oooh, is that so? And what makes you think I still have it, old friend?"

Baaq crossed her arms. "Because the way your face lit up when I mentioned it. You can already smell the profit you are about to make."

Fat Pudding smiled. Edghar now noticed his small needle-like teeth, which turned his kinda cute grin into something out of a nightmare. "It so happens, I still have it. But it will cost you."

"What a surprise," Baaq muttered. "How much?"

"Well, actually," Fat Pudding said, "I have a proposal for you. You do this one thing for me, and I'll *give* you the rifle back."

Baaq sighed. "I don't have time to run your errands. Just tell me how much you want, and we will pay you here and now."

"Shame. This would have been a quick thing for someone like you. But if you want to pay instead, then that's your choice." Fat Pudding shrugged. "Five-thousand gold."

"Are you out of your mind?" Baaq growled. "You paid me five hundred for it!"

"The price has gone up. Market always changes!" Fat Pudding laughed.

"I don't have anywhere near that much," Edghar whispered in Baaq's ear.

Baaq exhaled through her nostrils. "This is how you treat your 'old friend?'"

"Business is business," Fat Pudding shrugged.

"What's that other thing then?" Baaq said.

Fat Pudding smirked. "I thought you said you were not interested running my errands?"

"Just cut the crap. What is it you need?"

"Not a big deal. No big deal at all. I am having some . . . trouble with another demon. He's called Fish-City. He is a thief. He waits for my men to do their business then attacks them and steals my coin. I need him dead. Dead and gone."

What the hell are we getting dragged into? Edghar thought.

"Where can I find him?" Baaq said between clenched teeth. "This Fish-City character."

"He owns this tavern called the Golden Coconut. Not hard to find."

"Why haven't you dealt with him yourself?" Baaq said.

"He is well protected," Fat Pudding said. "He has his own crew. But for the legendary One-Shot?" He scoffed, "It will be easy. No problem."

"It would be *easier* if you gave me my rifle first, don't you think?"

"Perhaps, but that is not how I do business. You bring me Fish-City's stinking corpse and I give you back your precious rifle."

Baaq turned to Edghar. "You said you were the one calling the shots. What do you say?"

Edghar blew out a deep breath, running his hand through his hair. "I don't see we have much choice. I can't have a marksman without a weapon."

Fat Pudding hovered up between them. "Looks like we have a deal, then? Good. Now go kill that fishy bastard."

"That's the place," Baaq said, nodding towards a two-story building with a sign that read the Golden Coconut. "Fish-City's place, according to Fat Pudding."

Edghar and Baaq were on the opposite side of the street, backs against the wall, discussing how to deal with the situation they'd been forced into by the demon crime boss Fat Pudding.

"I am not sure about this," Edghar said. "Killing someone just to get your rifle back. It's wrong."

Baaq shrugged. "It is your call. But remember, Fish-City is also a criminal. He's not innocent."

"Perhaps. How would we even go about it?"

"Either we wait until Fish-City steps out for some reason, or we charge inside and make it messy. The sooner you decide, the better."

Edghar tuned her out. His faith in the mission of saving Akrab had been nothing but ups and downs. One moment he felt confident then something happened that pulled the rug out from under him, making him fall face-down on the floor. Standing outside the Golden Coconut felt like a new low point. The whole thing was turning into a disaster. *Once I was the spymaster of the great city-state Akrab. Now I have turned into a street thug doing work for a demon crime boss.*

"Hey," Baaq said, bumping him with her shoulder. "Anyone there? I'm talking to you."

"Aye, I'm here."

"Then answer my question: How do you want to do this?"

Edghar took a deep breath and tried to regain his focus. They needed the rifle back. The whole point of gathering powerful allies for the crew was their capability of facing the Dusters working for Clea. Without the weapon, Baaq would be useless to him.

"We have already drawn more attention to us than I'm comfortable with. If we could keep this discreet, it would be best. This Fish-City, he doesn't know you, correct? He might have *heard* of you, but that is different."

Baaq shook her head. "No, I left the life on the streets a long time ago. Fish-City was not around back then. I would have remembered."

Edghar nodded, scratching his beard. "That's good. We can use that to our advantage. But the problem is *me*. I can't walk around these parts without attracting attention. Then again, you're not even armed, so that's another issue."

"Weapon or not, I can handle myself in a fight," Baaq said. "But it depends on how much muscle he has with him."

"We are in a tough situation, no matter how we look at it," Edghar said.

"If it'd been easy, Fat Pudding would have dealt with it himself. There's a reason—"

"Oy."

Edghar and Baaq both turned to face the armed group that had suddenly approached them.

Not now, Edghar thought.

The Bone Lord's new security force were clad in black and white robes, wearing funny coned hats. Steel masks in the shape of skulls covered their faces from the nose up, and they carried the newly created and experimental weaponry developed by the alchemist guild.

"This filth causin' trouble for you, sir?" one of them asked looking at Edghar.

Thank the Golden King, they don't seem to recognise me.

"No," Edghar said. "Everything is fine."

"You sure?" The soldier puffed out his chest, stretching his neck to make himself taller as he stared up at Baaq. "We'll gladly remove this filth from your presence. Just say the word."

"That's the second time you have called me *filth*," Baaq said, clenching her fist.

"Well, that's what you are, aren't you? Demon filth. Standin' here harassing this upstanding citizen." The soldier again looked at Edghar. "You really shouldn't be here, sir. It's not a safe place for good folks like yourself."

Edghar was having a really hard time biting his tongue. While it was true that Akrab had always been divided, treatment like this from soldiers was something new. *Are these the kind of people Clea would want in her service? What the hell is she thinking?*

"She's not harassing me. You are."

"Looks like we have ourselves one of 'em demon-lovers, eh?" One of the soldiers snorted, bumping his shoulder into his colleague. "Bloody disgusting if you ask me."

"I think you might be right about that," another one of them added. "A traitor, that's what he is. Running around with demon scum out in the open. 'Ave you no shame?"

The scene between them and the soldiers had now attracted the attention of several other demons. They stopped whatever they were doing to watch.

"Hey, hey, back the hell up you vermin," one of them said, motioning with his baton, but the onlookers didn't move a muscle. "I'm not warning you again."

"You better point that somewhere else," one demon said–somewhat resembling a humanoid rhinoceros–and took a step closer to the soldier. "Or I put it in your ass."

"Get the hell away from here you cone-head bastards," another demon–this one had a thin build with bulging large eyes like a chameleon. "This is our home. You have no reason to be here."

The situation was heating up. More and more demons appeared on the streets all around them, while others peered out from their windows to watch the scene unfold. Demon children ran around excited, calling for their friends to come and look at what was happening.

"Last warning," one of the soldiers said, taking a step forward. Two brass cylinders were strapped on his back, and from it was a tube attached to the strange weapon he held with both hands. "I'll gladly burn all you ugly-looking bastards to a crisp. Just try me."

Edghar had never seen a so-called flamespitter in action, but he was aware the alchemy guild had been experimenting with the concept for years. It appeared they had succeeded in creating the weapon, now that the Bone Lord was funding them.

From the corner of his eye, Edghar noticed the doors of the Golden Coconut open, and a new group of demons stepped out onto the streets. One of them had a certain poise the others lacked. His skin was a bluish-grey colour, and he wore an open red shirt, revealing thick muscles on his upper body. He stood taller than most men, and had a long, jagged nose that jutted out from his shovel-shaped face. Long, spiky, black hair ran down his back in a ponytail. He crossed his arms and observed the situation with a thoughtful look.

"That must be Fish-City," Edghar nodded in the demon's direction.

"He's got the look, all right," Baaq said after a quick glance, before returning her attention to the soldiers. "This situation is going to get out of control any moment now. There's no stopping it. But we can use it to our advantage."

"What do you have in mind?"

"Fish-City's crew are itching for a fight," Baaq said. "You can see that clearly in their eyes and posture. The moment this breaks out, they're going to join in and start cracking skulls. Trust me."

"Which leaves Fish-City on his own," Edghar added. "Got it."

The tension in the air was so thick you could cut it with a knife. Demons were pressing against Edghar and Baaq, the size of the crowd growing bigger and bigger. Neither the soldiers nor the demons seemed willing to back down. The Bone Lord's security force was greatly outnumbered, but their new weapons were clearly intimidating enough to make the agitated demons hesitant in making the first move.

"Ah, geez, I told you we shouldn't be patrolling this deep in these parts," one of the soldiers said, casting around nervous glances.

"Shut up, Fredrikk," another soldier snapped. "Just be ready."

Edghar didn't see who threw it, but someone hurled a stone and hit one of the soldiers in the back of the head. The soldier immediately spun in the direction of the throw and unleashed his flame-spitter into the masses.

Pandemonium.

Several of the demons on the receiving end of the terrible weapon were set aflame. They screamed and threw themselves on the ground, their arms and legs flailing as they tried putting the fires out, those around them desperately trying to help.

Edghar was horrified at the sight, and all notions about taking out Fish-City were forgotten. He needed to stop these fanatic bastards and their cursed weapons. A big part of him—perhaps he was naive—hadn't believed they would *use* the weapons, and certainly not like this. *This can turn into a massacre!*

Baaq apparently thought the same thing, because she didn't move towards Fish-City, but instead, grabbed the closest soldier by the neck and slammed the man's head into the nearest wall with a loud crack. The man's limp body sagged to the ground.

Thankfully, only two of the seven soldiers were equipped with flamespitters, and the first one who had opened fire was already tackled to the ground, surrounded by demons hitting and kicking him.

The other soldier backed up simultaneously as his weapon spewed out fire, making it hard for anyone to get a hold of him. The soldier was so focused on keeping the demons away, he didn't react in time as Edghar closed in on him. Edghar swiped his leg with a swift kick, making the soldier lose his balance and fall over. In moments he was swarmed by the masses.

The remaining soldiers were armed with batons that looked normal at first glance, but apparently also released flames—albeit smaller ones—upon impact. Whatever body part they struck, a flame erupted, so even though they didn't cause as much harm on a greater scale, the damage added up, and several demons were on fire as a result.

One soldier managed to get some space between himself and the demons and pulled a smaller instrument from his belt and pointed it straight up. A loud bang erupted as a flaming sphere shot up high in the air where it lingered for a few moments before descending again, leaving a long red trail behind it across the sky.

"That must've been a call for reinforcements," Baaq growled as she knocked out the soldier who'd sent the distress signal out with a powerful head-butt.

Edghar looked around. None of the soldiers were left standing, and by the looks of it, some of them had been killed in the chaos. But the same was said for a dozen demons who'd been burnt to death, their smouldering corpses littered on the ground all around them.

Edghar felt sick. *How can Clea support this? Damn her!*

"Come," Baaq said, grabbing Edghar's arm.

It took a moment for Edghar to gain his footing, but the logical voice in his head said that nothing would be gained from just standing around and feeling bad. This situation demanded action.

Regardless how things had gotten thus far, he wasn't stopping. The Bone Lord and her wicked regime had to go, and he wouldn't rest until it was done, or he was dead.

"Damn it," Baaq growled as they pushed themselves through the chaotic scene. "Fish-City slipped back inside. We need to go after him."

Edghar and Baaq slammed open the door into the bar, the two of them bursting inside. The Golden Coconut was empty—with all the patrons, and Fish-City's crew, still outside involved in the riot.

The interior of the establishment had one cavernous area in the middle of it, with a horse-shoe shaped bar counter against the farthest wall opposite the entrance. Along the sides of the room there were many smaller and open-vaulted sections adorned with small tables and couches.

Fish-City stepped out from the kitchen carrying two buckets. He stopped mid-stride as he laid eyes on Edghar and Baaq, making the water splash over the rims of the buckets.

"Who are you?"

Baaq strode up to the other demon. "Fat Pudding wants you dead."

Fish-City snorted and put down the buckets he'd been carrying. "Tell me something I don't know. Is that it? You're here to kill me?"

Edghar was surprised how calm the demon seemed to be at the notion the two of them had come to kill him.

Baaq was clearly also taken off-guard by Fish-City's easy-going demeanour, but she clenched her fists, nostrils flaring, trying to pump herself up. "Listen, I have no problem with you, but Fat Pudding has me at my throat. He has something of mine, and only way I get it back is either paying five-thousand gold or killing you."

"That's a lot of coin." Fish-City looked Baaq up and down. "You don't strike me as someone with that sort of capital. No offence, of course."

Baaq kicked one of the buckets and sent it flying. "I am not playing here."

"Neither am I. I'm assessing the situation," Fish-City said. "Fat Pudding wanting me dead is nothing new; but *you* two are," the demon said, glancing over at Edghar and acknowledging him. "If you really wanted me dead, you would have skipped all this talking and been done with it already. It's two against one and I'm unarmed. You *don't* want to kill me, but you feel your hand is forced because Fat Pudding has something of yours that you desperately need. You would rather pay the coin, but you lack the funds, alas, you *think* you must kill me."

Who is this man? Edghar thought.

"I don't see we have much of a choice," Baaq said.

Fish-City smiled. "There is *always* a choice. Few minutes ago, you came in here set on killing me the instant you laid eyes on me. But that's changed now. I'm not this person you made me up to be in your mind, am I? I'm real, and you're not Fat Pudding's usual thugs. You think before you act."

Baaq clenched her teeth. "Fine. You're right, I'll admit that, but I will still do what I have to do. This is bigger than you and Fat Pudding."

"Have you two asked yourselves why Fat Pudding wants me

dead?"

"He mentioned something about you stealing from him," Edghar said, recalling Fat Pudding hadn't gone into much more detail than that.

"If you'll give me a chance, I can explain," Fish-City said. "I have made it my mission to keep Fat Pudding from flooding our streets with God Dust."

"Wait, God Dust?" Edghar's eyes widened. "What do you mean?"

Fish-City walked over and relaxed with his back against the bar counter. "Somehow, God Dust has been making its way onto the streets. Not in all of Akrab, but the demon-populated sections. It has been going on for months; maybe even longer. And unlike you humans, we demons do not develop strange magical abilities when snorting the pulverised bones of dead gods. We experience a sense of relief, a blissful detachment from the physical world for a short time. But once that feeling passes, something about the Dust in our bodies turn us angry and uncontrollably aggressive. You could say it makes us see red."

Edghar couldn't believe what he was hearing. Was this the reason the demons had suddenly changed their behaviour? It must have been. Sure, the tensions and conflicts have always been there, but not like recently. The repeated demon attacks against human citizens had been the reason Clea started funding the alchemy guild to develop new weapons. The decision, however bad, had been a response to a growing problem facing the city.

Edghar was in disbelief, his head spinning. "How can this be possible? All the God Dust is securely locked up in the vaults at the ziggurat." He swallowed then exhaled. "This is no accident."

"Shit," Baaq said, rubbing her brow.

"Did it never strike you as odd why so many demons have been acting so differently lately?" Fish-City said. "Leaving their own areas and venturing closer to the inner-city only to cause trouble?"

"Of course it has," Edghar said between clenched teeth. "But I figured it was inevitable because of the great divide between our races. A growing tension that had to boil over sooner or later. I did not suspect something like this."

"I have no answers how the God Dust is reaching the streets, but I do know who is spreading it, and that's Fat Pudding. Me and my crew are doing what we can. We attack Fat Pudding's thugs whenever we can to stop them from selling the Dust. Whatever coin we get our hands on we give to those who need it the most." Fish-City sighed. "I can only do so much. Since we have no demon representative in the regime with any real power, I am doing what I can out here on the streets."

"Maybe *we* can do something about that," Baaq said under her breath.

"Perhaps you can, perhaps you can't," Fish-City said. "My focus is on what I can do. Ask anyone about me and who I am. You will learn I speak nothing but the truth."

Edghar let out a long breath, rubbing his neck. "Well, fuck."

"Pretty much," Baaq said.

Fish-City went around the counter and poured them both a drink. "I told you there is always a choice, and now a new one has presented itself to you. I have tried taking out Fat Pudding more than once to put a permanent stop to his operation, but he isn't easy to find. You apparently know him, which means there is some sort of trust between you. Perhaps you can get him out in the open."

Baaq said, "What do you have in mind?"

CHAPTER FOURTEEN

Varcade punched the man in the face, making it spray blood and teeth, while Dog Man had his jaws clenched around the same man's chin. The Biter had his arms raised, chanting something in an unknown tongue.

"Why are you doing this?" the man screamed as he fell over on his back, desperately trying to push off the dog.

"You said you wanted a fight, so that's what you got," Varcade said with crossed arms, standing over the man.

"I never said that!"

Varcade's eyes narrowed. "You didn't?"

"NO!"

"Are you sure?"

"Yes! My leg, please, get him off of me!"

"Fine, let go, Dog Man." The dog let go and sat down next to Varcade's legs like he hadn't been savagely biting someone a mere moment earlier. "You heard he wanted a fight, right?" Varcade said, scratching the back of his head.

"Nope, I just followed your lead," Dog Man replied with a bored look.

"Ah, a misunderstanding then." Varcade offered the man his hand to help him up. "My apologies."

The man accepted the help, but the look in his eyes made it clear it was out of fear and nothing else. Blood gushed from his mouth, and he tried wiping some of it off, but it just kept coming.

"I think we better get going, boss," Dog Man said. "Everyone is staring at us."

Varcade looked around the tavern, and indeed, their little skirmish had brought all eyes on them. The other patrons were horrified, and some were even crying.

The Biter crouched down and wiped some blood from the man's face with a finger then put it in his mouth, eyes locked with him as he did it.

Varcade grabbed the Biter's arm and pulled him up. "We need to go."

The trio rushed out the door, but before it closed Varcade heard, " . . . Are you all right, Jehry? What did they do to you?"

The three of them were back in the inner city and had stopped for a bite to eat at a fancy tavern in the richer part of Akrab when the fight had broken out.

"We should probably get a move on if we plan to catch that coin-guy before he leaves," Varcade said, shielding his eyes from the bright sun as he stepped outside.

"I *know*," Dog Man said. "You were the one who insisted on eating first and then started a fight for no reason."

"Sure, but the Biter was also hungry, right?"

The Biter nodded. "Yes. Very hungry."

"Anyway, I need a hit of Dust," Dog Man said, looking up at Varcade.

Varcade had been designated to carry the dog's God Dust for him. "Are you sure?"

"Yes, I'm *sure*," Dog Man said. "Give it here."

"Fine." Varcade uncorked the small glass vial and poured out the powder in his palm until Dog Man told him to stop. He held out his hand and Dog Man took a good sniff, snorting up the powder in one go.

"That's good, that's good," Dog Man said and exhaled.

"Dog using drug is stupid," the Biter said with a big grin.

"You can be stupid," Dog Man growled at the turbaned man. "Who are you even?"

The Biter shrugged. "I do not know how to answer this question."

"I don't even understand what the Dust does for you," Varcade said, looking down at the dog padding next to him. "You don't get any abilities or anything?"

"What you see before you is my ability."

Varcade scratched his head. "Being a talking dog?"

Dog Man nodded. "Aye. I was a regular human a long time ago. When using the Dust, I transformed into a dog for a limited time. But one day I didn't turn back. I've been stuck as a dog since."

"Huh," Varcade said. "And you're okay with that?"

Dog Man snorted. "I don't have much choice, do I, kid? It is what it is. I see it as my punishment for ever using the Dust to begin with. It's been so long now that I barely remember how it was being human."

Varcade shrugged. "Sounds about right, I guess." He stopped and looked around. "Where are we going?"

Dog Man, who naturally had an exasperated expression, gave him just that. "The south gate," the dog said. "I already told you that."

"Right," Varcade said, but didn't really remember Dog Man had told him that. "Well, we should hurry."

"We'll be there soon," Dog Man sighed. "Are you always this intense, kid?"

"I have been accused of that before, yes," Varcade said.

"He is very strange man," the Biter said matter-of-factly.

"*You* don't get to say that," Varcade said. "Anyone but you."

"You're both weird," Dog Man said.

People on the street gave the three of them strange looks as they passed, but Varcade didn't care; a part of him even welcomed the attention. After some time, they reached the outskirts and the south gate.

"Wait, stop," Dog Man said coming to a halt. "That's him."

"Who?" Varcade said without looking at the dog.

"The one we're after! The Treasurer!"

"Oh, that's right. Where?" Varcade said and looked where Dog Man was pointing with his paw.

A pale man accompanied by a group of four soldiers was next to an armoured caravan. They were loading it up for what must have been planned as a longer trip.

"That's the Bone Lord's coin-guy?"

Dog Man nodded. "Yup, I'm positive. He was in the throne room when we met with the Bone Lord herself. How you wanna do this?"

Varcade tapped his chin. "I need a horse or something. That way we can ride ahead and ambush them when no one's close. It'll just be us and the guards, and we'll make quick work of 'em. And it's all desert out beyond the gates, it'll be impossible for us to miss them coming."

"You better find a horse quickly then, because they're leaving."

A brilliant idea popped up in Varcade's head.

"Hey, how about I ride on your back?"

"Over my dead body."

"Come on? Why not?"

"Not a chance. It won't happen."

"Why are you ruining this for me?"

"You're not riding on my back."

If Varcade had more time he would have argued more, but time wasn't on his side. "Okay, but you can smell stuff, right? Can you pick up the trace of horses nearby?"

"Not a horse but . . ." Dog Man sniffed the air, "*Something* animal-like. No clue what, though. Come on, follow me."

"Amazing!" Varcade yelled, clapping his hands.

The large toad-like creature regarded Varcade with orange eyes and an air of indifference. Varcade gently patted it on the head, feeling the bluish, thick, rubberlike skin.

It made sense that Dog Man had picked up the scent of the toad because there were several of them tied up outside an isolated, run-down building. The air was thick with their funky smell that slightly reminded Varcade of peanuts. Ruckus could be heard from within the building, and from the sound of it, a large gathering was inside.

"What is this?" the Biter said, inspecting something that looked to be painted on the back of one of the beasts. "This is number?"

Dog Man padded up to look then nodded. "Looks like they're all numbered. And they're all saddled, meaning they're someone's mounts. But who rides beasts like these? Never seen that before."

"Whoever they are, I like it. This one's mine now." Varcade was still patting the beast before him. It was the largest of the bunch. "Hey, you. What's your name? Modzarellah, is that it?"

"Why the hell would *that* be its name?" Dog Man said. "You can't just randomly guess a thing like that."

"I just know these things. It's a perfect fit."

"I agree," the Biter said. "I also feel that is name of beast."

Dog Man gave both of them a sidelong glance. "Sure, whatever you say." And then under his breath, "I think I'm starting to miss Nimbus..."

Varcade moved around Modzarellah, studying the large beast. "Okay, Modzarellah, we're gonna go for a ride, 'kay? We'll be back here before you know it, so no cause to panic." The toad-creature croaked in response. Varcade leapt up and slid into the saddle, producing another croak from the beast.

"Come on, Dog Man, jump up in my lap. Biter, you get on behind me."

"Are you sure about this?" Dog Man said. "It belongs to whoever is inside. They're most likely not going to be happy about you stealing it."

"Right, like I care," Varcade said, making himself comfortable in the saddle and grabbing the reins. "Get on now."

The Biter helped Dog Man up then took his seat behind Varcade.

"Alright," Varcade said. "So far so good. Now the question is how to—"

Modzarellah leapt high and Varcade was barely able to keep from falling. The big beast landed several feet from the jump point–thankfully in the direction Varcade wanted to go–but immediately took off again, leaving a billow of dust in their wake.

Varcade laughed and Dog Man cursed as they went up and down and up and down. The Biter said nothing.

The sight of the leaping enormous toad caught the attention of several bystanders who all pointed at them, and Varcade waved with a grin as they passed by.

The plan to hide and ambush coin-guy's caravan was pretty much out the window, because it would be impossible to stay discreet when they soared through the air on the back of an enormous toad.

Modzarellah leapt over the city gates. From the air, Varcade could spot the dust trail of the caravan they were pursuing.

"You're a good girl, Modzarellah!" Varcade shouted. "Keep going!"

"I'm gonna throw up," Dog Man complained.

"Soon, we shall have blood," the Biter whispered.

"Get ready, guys," Varcade said, "we have our target in sight!"

Soldier Dhooli had a mind-numbing headache, and the rattle and jolting from the traveling caravan didn't exactly make things better. But what was by far worse, was the non-stop blabbering from the Keeper of the Royal Seal.

Dhooli and three other soldiers sat opposite Berenberg inside the caravan and were forced to listen to the treasurer go on and on about state incomes, taxes, and how the loan from the Bone Lord of Nuzz was absolutely critical.

But the only thing going through Dhooli's head was: *Shut up. Shut up, SHUT UP!*

". . . It's of vital importance that you read every word when dealing with a contract of this magnitude," Berenberg droned on, holding out the parchment for Dhooli to see. "Make no mistake, the Bone Lord of Nuzz has not agreed to the loan out of the goodness in his heart. He's well aware Akrab is in dire need of coin, and he's taking advantage of the situation. But he has us backed into a corner, so not much can be done about it."

Dhooli nodded, struggling to keep his eyes open. Him and the other soldiers in the ziggurat had drawn straws the evening before about which of them would have to accompany Berenberg on the trip. Obviously Dhooli had pulled one of the shorter straws.

". . . But that does not mean one mustn't be extremely thorough," Bergenberg continued, "You have to pay attention to the words between the lines." The treasurer pointed at a specific section of the contract. "For instance, just look at this–"

"What was that?" Markho, one of the other soldiers said and sat up, turning his head. "Did you hear that?"

Dhooli hadn't heard anything, but to be fair, he had been inches from falling asleep.

"Don't interrupt me, you scoundrel," Bergenberg said. "There wasn't any–"

"There it is again!" Markho said, and this time Dhooli had not only heard the sound but *felt* an accompanying vibration running through the caravan.

Dhooli pulled back the rectangular hatch on his side, and Markho did the same on his side. "I can't see anything but desert, desert and more desert," he said.

"Nothing here," Markho shook his head. "But you heard it, right?"

Dhooli nodded, but he still couldn't see anything.

(The problem was that none of them looked up, because if they had, they would've seen a massive toad about to land on top of them.)

The armoured caravan provided an excellent defence against the usual weapons of the marauders of the desert, but less so against a massive toad-beast descending from the skies.

The caravan buckled in on itself as Modzarellah came crashing down. Faint screams from within could be heard through the thick steel walls. The ropes tied to the two massive six-legged insects pulling the vehicle snapped, and the creatures took off, relishing their newfound freedom. The driver seated at the front of the caravan shot up high in the air and disappeared.

Modzarellah croaked and took off again, landing some distance away like nothing had happened.

Dog Man leapt from Varcade's lap down on the ground. "Never again, never again," he muttered, looking sick.

The Biter jumped off and stretched like he'd just woken from a nap.

Varcade got down and scratched the back of his head as he looked at the destruction before him. "Not exactly the plan, but the result is all that matters, right?" he said with a shrug. "Let's finish this."

"I need to catch my damn breath," Dog Man said, tongue sticking out, gasping for air. "If I don't throw up, that is."

"Fine." Varcade pulled his two swords from his back and made his way to the destroyed caravan. Without the two massive insects and a driver, it looked like a broken and discarded box left out in the scorching desert.

However, there were still grunts and other noises coming from within the wreckage. One soldier managed to crawl out through the half-opened and completely bent steel door. Unfortunately for her, she was greeted by Varcade's blade.

Another soldier made it out on the other side of the caravan. He stumbled and fell but got up again, dazed. Varcade appeared before him.

"Wanna live?" Varcade said, resting both blades on his shoulders.

"Yes," the soldier stuttered. "Please."

"Return to your Bone Lord and tell her what happened here. Got it? Tell her we're coming for her."

The soldier nodded frantically and limped away.

Varcade leapt onto the caved-in roof of the caravan and tried peeking inside. Two other soldiers were dead within, their bodies bent in unnatural ways that made Varcade wince. The pale man who had been their target was also clearly dead.

Varcade turned around and paced up to the others and Modzarellah. "Guess we're done here."

"Can we rest for a minute before—" Dog Man stopped and stared at the Biter, who was doing something to the soldiers. "What the hell is he *doing*?"

The Biter seemed to–no, he was *certainly* cutting off the ears from the corpses and putting them in his pockets. When and where he had picked up a large, serrated knife was a mystery.

Varcade shrugged. "No clue. I figure I should let him do his thing. It's the way we do things."

Dog Man rolled his eyes and sucked in a deep breath then sat down on his rump. "So, the Treasurer is dead then?"

"Extremely dead," Varcade said, sitting down cross-legged opposite the dog.

"The Bone Lord is going to have a fit once the news reaches her," Dog Man said. "I only met her the one time, but she didn't strike me as the most patient person."

"Good," Varcade said. "That's exactly what we need to buy us some time."

"For what?" Dog Man said.

"Edghar has other people he wants to recruit to the crew." Varcade shrugged. "Don't ask me who because I don't know. He's the one in charge of this whole thing."

Dog Man looked at him, searching Varcade's eyes. "Now that we have a moment, I've been meaning to ask you something. Why are you doing this, kid? What's in it for you?"

"What do you mean? I'm a sellsword. This is what I do."

"Sure, but there are easier jobs out there. And I have a hard time believing getting paid in God Dust is of much interest to you."

Varcade shifted in his seat. "What's with the interrogation? Why do you care?"

Dog Man shrugged. "Curious, I guess. Why aren't you back in Karkan using your skills against the Educators? Don't you want revenge or something for what they did to you?"

"Of course, I do," Varcade said. "But it's not as simple as that."

"Why?"

"It just isn't," Varcade growled. "You wouldn't understand."

"Fine, if you say so," Dog Man said. "Just know, your past always catches up to you. Take it from an old guy such as myself."

"Sure, whatever," Varcade said as he rose to his feet. "Thanks for forcing your *wisdom* down my throat. Maybe I'd be more open to it if it didn't come from a dog who's addicted to God Dust."

Dog Man snorted with a smile. If Varcade's words had hurt him, it didn't show. "Just thought you needed to hear it, kid." He got up on all fours. "Looks like break-time is over then? Can you please try and control that toad-monster this time around?"

"Modzarellah does what Modzarellah does. I control nothing," Varcade said over his shoulder, grabbing the toad's reins. "Come on Biter, time to go. You can snack on those ears on the way back."

"I do not eat human flesh," the Biter said, a piece of an ear sticking out from his mouth. "I am not monster."

"Whatever you say," Varcade said, not in the mood to argue. "Let's go."

Is it me? Do I attract these cannibal weirdos?

Vashi stood around feeling awkward as Xira rummaged through piles and piles of littered trash. She had taken him into an alleyway deep between the tall buildings in the ghetto. Apparently, this was her home.

Vashi had spent many hours with Xira and so far, she hadn't given him anything to help in his search for his younger brother. She went from saying incomprehensible things to trying to offer him something to eat. He was reaching a stage where it was extremely challenging to keep his composure. But having your emotions pushed to a degree where you lost control was forbidden by the Teachings.

"Just one moment," she said, picking up an old sock and inspecting it for a heartbeat before . . . *Did she put it in her mouth?*

"It is fine, really," Vashi said, scratching the back of his head. "I'm not hungry, I promise."

"Don't be silly," Xira scoffed. "You're a guest in my home, and not any guest at that. What would the Masters back in the Temple say if they'd heard you hadn't eaten a thing during your visit?" Between mouthfuls of old sock she said, "You want this? I don't need it."

Vashi leaned in for a closer look.

It was a dead cat. She just asked if he wanted a dead cat.

He forced a chuckle, taking a step back. "No thank you. Really, I don't need anything, Xira. Just some information. I have already been here longer than I'd planned. I need to go."

It was tragic to see a fellow Educator having sunk to this state, and his presence clearly made the woman nervous. If the Masters had known Xira's state they would not have told Vashi to seek out her help. Instead, they would have asked him to Release her . . .

"Ah, here we go," she said, picking up a cracked jar. She pushed her hand into it and when it came out, it was covered in a brown substance. She held her smudged hand close to his face, meeting his eyes with a smile. "Please, feel free. Eat this and we can talk after."

Vashi nodded, meeting her eyes with a strained smile of his own. "Oh, you're too kind. Thank you so much." He was really unclear on how to proceed, but this was obviously a losing battle. She wouldn't take no for an answer, and he couldn't be rude and decline. Vashi pushed Xira's wrist up, bringing her fouled hand to his lips, and gave the goo the tiniest of licks.

Huh, not too bad, he thought with amazement. "This is pretty good," he said, smacking his lips. "Has a nutty quality to it. What is it?"

"How would I know, silly man," Xira cackled.

"Ah." Vashi leaned his face away.

"That's it? You're already done?"

"Yes, I believe so. Thank you kindly."

I didn't just eat–

"So, why are you here, Educator Vashi? You mentioned your brother, yes?" Xira interrupted, as she sank down on a pile of trash. "Please, sit, sit. My home is your home."

Vashi looked around. None of the trash looked particularly welcoming, but he settled for a spot that didn't stink as much. "Yes. My brother." Varcade's betrayal of the Educators brought Vashi much shame. It wasn't something he liked to discuss. "He's here in Akrab, and I need to find him."

"No one should ever come here," Xira muttered. "These people are beyond enlightenment. No one can help them, not even the Educators and the Teachings."

"Careful, Xira, speaking like that is forbidden and you know it."

Xira didn't say anything, her attention instead focused on a small bug crawling on her tattered robe. "Oh, look at this one. A juicy boy, isn't he?" She snatched up the insect and popped it in her mouth. Vashi could hear how the bug's mangled carapace crackled as Xira chewed and chewed, a trickle of an orange liquid running down the corner of her lips. "Juicy indeed!" She laughed.

"Xira, please. I need whatever information you might have."

"Ask, ask," she said, waving her hand. "I'm listening, am I not?"

Vashi cleared his throat. "Have you heard anything lately that could be connected to my brother's whereabouts? A recent incident or anything? All I know is that he is working with a man called Edghar."

The sellswords in the Nest hadn't easily given up the information about his brother's whereabouts or who he was working with, and they had tried putting up a fight when Vashi had suddenly paid them a visit. But in the end, they stood no chance against an Educator, and he had left them in a heap of broken limbs.

"Hmm . . . Perhaps. Now that you mention it . . ." She shot up and started going through the trash pile closest to her. Her long arms dug and dug, and whatever was discarded was thrown back over her shoulder. "I'm sure it's here somewhere."

"What are you looking for?"

She muttered something he couldn't hear.

"What's that?" Vashi said.

"Here we go," she said, and turned to face him, holding a woven basket. "Egg-man is right here."

"Egg-man? I said Edghar." Vashi started saying as he peered down into the basket. "Xira, those are just cracked eggshells."

She nodded. "Egg-man died." The tone of her voice carried heartfelt sadness. "And he was the sweetest and most tender of lovers . . . I miss him dearly."

Vashi closed his eyes and took a deep breath, trying hard to keep his patience. *Saints give me strength.* "I'm sorry to hear that, truly, but that has nothing to do with what I asked. Please, Xira, try and think."

"I already told you," she said. "People have seen a silver-haired man here as of late. He was fighting a naked man on a cloud." Xira scratched her chin. "There might have been something about a talking dog too." She shrugged.

She did not just tell me all of that . . .

"Ah, I guess I must have forgotten," Vashi said with a smile, astonished he'd gotten through to her. The part about a talking dog and a naked man on a cloud made no sense, but Varcade's hair would certainly make him stick out as a foreigner. It wasn't much to go with but better than nothing. "Thank you—"

"I'm not going back to the Temple," Xira suddenly hissed. "You can't make me. I can see what you are thinking. All the guck moving around in your brain like slithering snakes. Don't think I don't see it."

Vashi sighed. He had anticipated this. "You are not wrong, Xira. You have fallen of the Path. You know this."

"Why should I care about the Path? These people do not want us here." Xira's demeanour drastically changed. She moved around skittishly, taking one step before stopping and going the other direction. Her voice seethed with anger, and she spat the words out. "They don't want to learn about the Teachings and restore the Balance. We should never have come here."

"We live to Educate," Vashi said. "What they want or don't want doesn't matter. It is our sacred duty to spread and uphold the Teachings."

Xira's back and forth pacing was now even more frantic, and she was muttering to herself. Vashi could only hear bits and pieces of what she was saying. "Don't understand. Beaten me. Called me names. Kicked me. Spit. Spat on me. Eyes. Hatred. Broken. Everyone. Can't change." She came to a sudden stop and shot out her hand, gripping Vashi's wrist. "Release me, Educator Vashi. Release me."

Vashi knew it would come to this. A part of him was imagining a scenario where he brought Xira back to the Temple with him, but deep inside, he already knew she was gone. And her presence in this state was only harming The Educators' cause. He couldn't allow that to continue. Vashi took one calm, deep breath, his hand reaching for the staff on his back. "I will."

It looked as if Xira's body almost gave out as she sunk down on her knees, one hand clutching the fabric of his trousers. "Thank the Saints . . . Thank you . . ." She was crying. "Tired . . . So tired . . ."

Saints give me strength to do what I must.

Vashi sucked in a deep breath and closed his eyes, attempting to enter a mental state completely devoid of all emotions that would hold him back from carrying out his duty. He gently removed Xira's hand from his leg and took a step back. "Close your eyes, Educator

Xira. You won't feel a thing." He gripped his staff firmly then delivered a lightning-fast strike that instantly broke Xira's neck. He grabbed her limp body before it fell and gently put her on the ground. "You have been Released, Educator Xira. May you find peace with the Saints in the Land Above."

CHAPTER FIFTEEN

"I wanna keep him," Varcade said.

"You can't," Dog Man replied.

"Why the hell not?"

"You *know* why."

"No, I don't."

"Because he's an enormous toad monster."

"And?"

"He already belongs to someone."

Varcade shrugged. "So what?"

Dog Man sighed, shaking his head. "You're really killing me here. Can you please–"

"What do you think, girl?" Varcade interrupted, gently patting Modzarellah's head. "Wanna come with us?" Modzarellah croaked in response. "That sounds like a yes to me," Varcade grinned.

"Seriously, people are staring at us . . . It's only a question of time before the Bone Lord's Dusters come looking for us, and we don't exactly blend in with the crowd. We need to get outta here and meet up with Edghar and Baaq."

Dog Man spoke the truth. Now that they were back in the city after killing the Bone Lord's Treasurer, their little party was indeed drawing a lot of attention from those who passed by.

"Fine, let's go, but Modzarellah's coming with us. It's been decided," Varcade said.

The Biter nodded. "I like toad. Powerful beast."

"What the actual fuck have I gotten myself into . . ." Dog Man muttered. "Do whatever you want. It's clearly pointless arguing with you."

"I always do," Varcade winked at the dog. "And ease up, It'll all work out. You gotta learn how to just go with the flow, doggie. You're too uptight, just like Edghar."

"Yeah, yeah, whatever, you lunatic . . ." Dog Man's eyes narrowed to slits suddenly, his nose sniffing the air. "Wait, something's coming."

Moments later the sound of marching boots stomping rhythmically could be heard, coming closer and closer. Everyone in the street stopped and listened, looking around nervously for the source. Suddenly, the army spilled out from around the corner of a large building; figures dressed in armour enforced white and black robes, wearing strange masks and coned hats, walking in a perfect square formation. They were heavily armed with odd-looking weaponry and shields.

"Who the hell are those guys?" Dog Man said to one of the bystanders who responded with a peculiar look at the talking dog before shrugging.

Finally, he said, "You been living under a rock? That's the Bone Lord's new security force. Her latest idea in how to deal with all the demon trouble we've been having lately. Must be another one of those riots down in the ghetto. A lot of those happening these days."

Varcade only half-listened to what the man was saying. His attention was on the strange individual at the front of the marching soldiers. *Is that a child leading them?*

The boy had pale, almost white skin–perhaps powdered?–and dark, short hair parted down the middle. Something about his facial features did not look right; it was more akin to someone wearing the wrong sized skin. *What the hell is that smug look?* Varcade thought, instinctively wanting to slap it off his face.

"Oh crap."

Varcade turned to Dog Man who was now also focused on the man-boy.

"That's Gloomy Glen. Another one of the Dusters employed by the Bone Lord. He's seriously bad news."

"Another one of her Dusters, eh?" Varcade said. "Good opportunity to take him out then and make the Bone Lord's life even more miserable."

"No, you don't get it," Dog Man said, looking up at Varcade. "You can't fight him. I'm serious."

"Why not?" the Biter said. "I bite him in throat, make blood spray. No problem."

"I said *no*, and that goes for both of you. You need to bloody listen to what I'm saying."

"Move," one of the oddly dressed soldiers growled at a civilian, shoving the man hard in the chest with his shield, making him fall on his ass. For a split second, it looked like the man in question wanted to argue, but he held his tongue and dusted himself off before slowly getting back up again.

Varcade took a step forward, arms crossed. "Hey, that wasn't very nice, was it?"

A few of the soldiers stopped, heads turning in Varcade's direction. "What the hell did you just say?" one of them said.

"Don't act like you didn't hear me," Varcade said, staring the soldier down. "I hate when people do that. You heard me loud and clear. What are you gonna do about it?"

Dog Man butted his head on Varcade's leg. "What the hell are you doing, you idiot?" he hissed. "*Shut up.*"

"Hush, doggie," Varcade said without looking at his companion, eyes still locked on the soldier.

"Oy, we've got ourselves a tough guy over here," the soldier shouted over his shoulder, before returning his attention to Varcade, a smirk on his lips.

"Don't listen to him, he's not all there in the head," Dog Man said. "We were just about to leave."

The soldier's eyes widened behind his skull mask as his head snapped down to the talking dog. "Filthy demon!" he spat, taking a step back and drawing his baton simultaneously. "Stay back!"

"I'm not a bloody demon," Dog Man protested. "Would you just stop and listen to what I'm saying?"

The rest of the soldiers had now noticed trouble was brewing, and a couple of them broke from their formation, jogging over to the soldier facing Varcade, Biter, and Dog Man.

"What's the matter, Darvid?" one of them said.

"That dog's a demon in disguise!"

"Huh?"

"It's true," the soldier by the name of Darvid said. "Speak again, you bastard. That's an order!"

Dog Man tilted his head, his tongue out, panting cutely.

"The fuck 'r you on, Darvid? We don't have time for this. We need to hurry our asses to the ghetto."

"I'm telling you the dog's a demon, dammit! It can speak!"

Dog Man barked a regular bark. Varcade couldn't help but laugh.

"What's the damn hold-up?" another soldier shouted to them.

"Darvid's claiming this dog over here is a demon in disguise or somethin'."

"I'm ordering you to speak again!" Darvid shouted, veins on his throat popping out. "Speak, dog! Speak!"

Dog Man sat down on his rump and offered his paw.

"Looks like a regular ol' dog to me," the other soldier said with a shrug.

"For fuck's sake." Another soldier stormed over, pushing anyone in the way aside violently. The moment he reached them he didn't hesitate and kicked Dog Man as hard as he could, sending the dog flying. "Fuck that stupid dog. Let's–"

The soldier's words caught in his throat. He coughed once, a spurt of blood trickling down his lips and jaw. He looked down with horror in his eyes at the red-slicked blade protruding from his gut.

"Shouldn't have done that," Varcade said, sliding his sword out with a wet sound.

"Bastard . . ." The soldier muttered as his legs gave out. He fell on his knees before toppling down, face-first, blowing up a cloud of dust.

The soldiers took a step away from Varcade, who had now unsheathed his second sword. "Dog Man, you okay?" he said over his shoulder.

"Fine . . ." Dog Man groaned. "Damn bastard kicked me . . ."

"Told y'all the dog was a demon . . ." Darvid said under his breath, which immediately drew an angry glare from the soldier closest to him.

It took a few moments for the soldiers to understand what had just happened, but when the realization hit, the atmosphere changed. In a second they drew their weapons and spread out in a circle around Varcade and the Biter, getting ready to engage.

"What 'r you all waiting for?" Varcade said, both swords resting on his shoulders. "Let's get it on then–"

"Well, what do we have here?" A gleeful and child-like voice said. The soldiers parted to allow the Duster called Gloomy Glen free passage. "A little unexpected trouble by the looks of it."

Varcade was weirded out by the creepy eyes and matching smile of the Duster. Gloomy Glen was about to say something when his eyes suddenly widened at the sight of Dog Man, who was trying to hide behind Varcade's legs.

"Dog Man! You're alive? We thought you were dead when Nimbus' body was found. Oh, how wrong we were; this is much, much worse." The grin on the Duster's face did not match the words he'd just said.

"Hey, man-boy," Varcade said, pointing one of his swords at Gloomy Glen, "You should be focusing on me, not him."

The Duster's smile vanished, replaced by a thin line and a bored look. "Why? You are *nothing*."

The instant the Duster said the last word, an immense feeling of melancholy slammed into every fibre of Varcade's being. He sagged down on all four, all his will to live gone. An aura of blue ethereal tendrils leaked out from Gloomy Glen and hooked themselves to Varcade's body.

What the hell is happening to me?

"I'm worthless . . . A coward . . ." Varcade heard himself say, unable to stop the words escaping his lips. "Pathetic. I don't deserve to live . . ."

From the corner of his eye, Varcade saw the Biter dashing at the Duster, but Gloomy Glen's head snapped in his direction before the turbaned man could reach him, shooting out more of the blue tendrils into the Biter. He immediately sagged to the ground in a foetal position.

"My life is lie . . ." the Biter muttered.

"So, what should we do with you, little traitor mutt?" Gloomy Glen said, strolling past Varcade and the Biter on the ground. "Kill you now or let Tarkus have a go with you?"

"Fuck him and fuck you," Dog Man said, staring up at the Duster with defiance. "I'm done with all of you."

Gloomy Glen laughed, a high-pitched, theatrical sound. "Of course you're *done*, you stupid idiot! Did you hear me offering you forgiveness? You will die, one way or another." The Duster turned to the large group of soldiers. "A few of you can stay. The rest can go deal with the troublemakers in the ghetto. This won't take long."

The majority of the soldiers did as ordered and left, leaving Gloomy Glen and a handful of the army behind.

Varcade tried to muster all the strength he could to move his body, but it was as if every part of him weighed a tonne. Sweat gushed from his face; his teeth clenched as he strained to move. *What is this cursed power he's using?* He managed to drag himself across the ground and weakly grabbed the Duster's leg with a trembling hand.

Startled, the Duster shot him a venomous look. "You dare *touch* me?" Gloomy Glen hissed and kicked Varcade in the face.

"What'r you gonna do about it?" Varcade stuttered, looking up at the Duster with a weak smile, tasting iron on his tongue.

"Huh, you're stronger than you look." Gloomy Glen squatted on his haunches. "Interesting. Perhaps it's worth a little look inside that mind of yours." the Duster closed his eyes and sucked in a deep breath, his long fingers stroking Varcade's scalp. "My, my, aren't you a pathetic one. All these suppressed feelings within you. Tasty goodness," Gloomy Glen said, clicking his tongue.

Varcade's body tensed, his eyes widening as a sensation unlike any other washed over him. He could somehow *feel* the Duster digging inside his mind. "S-Stop," Varcade said under his breath, forcing out the words, a rising panic building in his chest. "Please."

Gloomy Glen licked his lips, revealing an unnaturally long and green-coloured tongue. "Oh no, I haven't tasted anything as good as this in a very long time. Hmm, what do we have here? Who's this man you're trying to obscure in your thoughts? What are you hiding from dear Glen?"

Varcade was powerless against the Duster's abilities. He could do nothing to keep the man from rummaging through his most private thoughts like an open chest.

"Ah, it's your father, isn't it?" Gloomy Glen said.

"K-Kill you . . ." Varcade wheezed.

"Hah! You'll do nothing," the Duster mocked. "Let's see here, yes indeed, it is your father."

Varcade knew exactly what memory the Duster had gotten hold of. It didn't matter how much he tried to resist it, the scene sucked him deeper and deeper, drowning him in his own memory.

. . .

Varcade suddenly found himself back in that memory, observing his father and the stranger seated by the kitchen table. Young Varcade was hiding at the top of the stairs, his older brother Vashi next to him, both of them gripping the handrails. Present Varcade hovered behind the children like a spirit, Gloomy Glen next to him also in spirit-form. Varcade tried to grab the Duster, but his hands went through him like an apparition.

"Don't waste your time," Gloomy Glen said with a mocking grin. "You can't lay a finger on me. We're not really here. We're just observers."

"I'm going to kill you," Varcade said. "I don't know how yet, but I will."

"Yeah, yeah," Gloomy Glen waved him off dismissively. "You believe that if you will. Now shut your mouth. I want to see what the fuss is all about with this memory. Why did you so desperately try hiding it from me."

Varcade remembered this event like it had happened yesterday. Him and Vashi weren't supposed to hear the conversation, but something about the stranger in the pristine, white coat seated opposite his father had made Varcade's skin crawl. The stranger had looked at him and his brother like they were things, not children, before their father had ordered them upstairs.

"Is he one of the men from the Temple?" Child-Varcade said, looking at his brother. "One of the Masters?"

Vashi had nodded. "I think so."

"But Papa won't let him take us, right? Not like the other children?"

"I don't know," Vashi said. "Be quiet, I need to hear this."

Adult Varcade hovered behind the children, staring daggers at the Duster who was casually floating above the handrails, watching.

"Your boys are special, you're aware of this, yes?" *the man dressed in white had said, his fingers clasped together and resting on the kitchen table.* "Very special."

"Special?" *Varcade's father had said, scratching the back of his* head. "I don't know about that, but they are good boys most of the time . . ."

"The Saints have chosen them," the stranger said, leaning closer.

Varcade's father swallowed, his mouth the shape of an O. "For the Educators? The Order? I-I can't believe this," he stuttered, lowering his head like he suddenly wasn't worthy to look at the stranger directly.

"Yes," the stranger said. "It is a great honour to be chosen. Your boys will play a pivotal role in restoring Balance in the world."

"Are you sure?" Varcade's father said.

The man from the Educator Order nodded. "Of course. The Saints always know." He rose to his feet. "Time is of the essence. I am sure you understand. I will take them to the Temple where their Educator training can begin."

Varcade's father nodded. "I understand," he said, his voice cracking. After a moment he added, "My boys are going to be Educators, I can't believe it. Bless the Saints."

While Varcade's father beamed with pride and joy, Varcade felt sick to his stomach watching the memory unfold. He let out a primal roar from the deepest pit of his soul. He tried slamming his fist into the wall, but it went right through it. How could he have done it? Give away his children to a stranger just like that?

"I can't believe it," Vashi had said and put an arm around Varcade without looking at him.

"Doesn't he love us?" Child-Varcade had asked, fat tears rolling down his chubby cheeks. "Doesn't Papa love us anymore?"

Gloomy Glen suddenly laughed. "Such delicious misery!" The Duster licked his mouth and smacked his lips like he'd just been served the most succulent meal of his life. "More! Give me more!"

The bastard is somehow feeding on my memories, Varcade thought, a dark rage boiling inside of him. While his physical self in the real world was under the Duster's spell, this version of himself could at least think clearly. He wouldn't beat the Duster in physical combat; Gloomy Glen wouldn't let him. He would need to find another way, and just like that an idea popped up.

"Huh," Gloomy Glen said, noticing the door behind him creak open, a sliver of bright light escaping.

Yes, it's working, Varcade thought. Take the bait you freak. Take it.

"What do we have in there?" the Duster said, swirling around in the air.

"No," Varcade said. "Don't!"

The Duster shot him a disgusted look. "You can't tell me what to do. Don't try and keep things from me. It won't work."

"Please," Varcade said. "I beg of you."

Gloomy Glen grabbed the door handle and pulled it open. A bright light enveloped him.

Varcade blinked and then found himself exactly in the memory he had tried to conjure up: the worst one he had. One he hoped would be too much for the Duster to handle; one that terrified Varcade to his core still to this day.

Varcade watched the eight-year old version of himself strapped to a cold table in a dark room. His young self cried and strained against the shackles holding him in place, but his attempt to break free were futile. The Master Educators stood in a circle around the table and observed him. Their faces were cold, showing not a hint of sympathy or care for the youngling crying his heart out before them. Varcade could remember how he had felt at that moment: confused and beyond frightened. No one had told him why he was being treated this way or what they were planning to do to him.

The atmosphere in the dark room had changed the moment the Grand Master appeared. Unlike the Masters, he did not wear a white coat but a brown one, and his hood was up, obscuring his face.

"What the hell is this?" Gloomy Glen said, hovering next to him. "I don't like this."

"You don't?" Varcade said, crossing his arms. "Why not?"

"I just don't." The Duster turned and tried opening the door behind them, but it wouldn't budge. Gloomy Glen's eyes widened. "What? How are you doing this? Let me out!"

"Doing what?" Varcade said with a smirk.

"This shouldn't be possible!" the Duster spat. "I am the one in control!"

"Apparently not," Varcade said. "But hey, you wanted my most hidden memories, didn't you? This is the big one. So, relax and watch."

Gloomy Glen growled, pulling at the door handle with both his hands. His desperation almost looked comical as he struggled and failed to open the door.

The Grand Master approached young Varcade strapped to the table. He placed a cold hand on his arm. "Do not be scared, my child." The voice from within the darkness of the hood did not sound natural; it had an other-worldly quality to it, like it was coming from somewhere else entirely. "This is a great honour bestowed unto you. To be an Educator means that you are undertaking a sacred duty to restore the Balance and save this world."

"I wanna go home," young Varcade had said, barely able to utter the words through the clog in his throat. "Please, let me go."

"That's impossible, child. This is your home now."

"Please, I'm scared! I don't want to be here! Papa! Vashi! Help me!"

"Hush, hush, this is meant to happen. It is your destiny."

"No! I don't want to! Let me go! Let me go!"

The Grand Master covered Varcade's mouth with his hand, silencing the desperate pleading. Varcade trashed and kicked, doing everything he could to break the shackles, but it was to no avail. The Grand Master suddenly looked up and nodded once. "Yes, Holy Mother. I am ready."

"What is he going to do to you?" Gloomy Glen said with a tremble in his voice, pressing himself back against the door. "Tell me, damn you!"

Varcade did not reply. Watching the memory unfold made his rapidly beating heart hurt in his chest. All the emotions he had felt in that moment came washing over him again, making it hard to breathe. He had been scared before in his young life, but he had never experienced such terror as this.

The Grand Master had suddenly been engulfed in a bright light cast from an invisible source. The other Master Educators immediately fell to their knees, chanting things in a language Varcade didn't recognise.

The Grand Master convulsed, his body spasming, jerking up and down and back and forth in ways that filled Varcade with existential dread. The Grand Master then raised his arms and made guttural sounds as two additional arms grew out from his body on either side. The four new arms were unnaturally long and pale and did not look to belong to anything from this world.

Varcade howled as the deformed Grand Master approached him, his new arms dancing in the air, eager to get started with the cutting.

Pain followed. Pain that any living creature should never have to experience. Gloomy Glen screamed.

Suddenly Varcade was back in the real world, his eyes snapping open, the paralysis of his body gone. He was still weakened from the ordeal, but at least he was in control of himself again. Varcade saw Gloomy Glen on the ground a couple feet away from him. The Duster was on his back, his mouth open, frozen in what looked like a perpetual scream, eyes blank and still. Experiencing what the Grand Master Educator had done to Varcade had killed the Duster.

Slowly gathering his senses, Varcade got up on shaky legs that barely supported him. The Bone Lord's soldiers that had remained behind with the Duster were still in the midst of battle against Dog Man and the Biter. Not much time seemed to have past back in the real world.

This was bad. While his body healed faster than most, the mental torture Gloomy Glen had put him through had taken its toll on him. He instinctively reached for the swords on his back and realised he'd dropped them on the ground when the Duster had attacked.

Dog Man had his jaws clamped around one of the soldier's throats, his claws ripping into his chest. Animal and man toppled to the ground, Dog Man growling and sneering as the soldier spasmed in his death rattle.

Another soldier dashed up from behind, baton held high and ready to crack Dog Man in the head. But the Biter appeared in the nick of time, leaping up at the soldier's back, wrapping his long limbs around her. Unable to use her arms to fend him off, the Biter ferociously sank his teeth into the soldier's neck. She screamed and twisted around like she'd been set on fire, blood spurting in every direction like a fountain.

Varcade saw one soldier ahead getting up from the ground, shaking his head and groaning. He must have been knocked out at some point but was still breathing. Two brass barrels were strapped to his back and dangling from them was a long tube attached to some sort of apparatus unfamiliar to Varcade.

The soldier hefted the strange weapon in both hands and started moving towards Dog Man and Biter with a menacing look. But then the man suddenly stopped, his neck snapping over his shoulder at something behind him that demanded his attention.

Varcade felt the rumble beneath his feet before he spotted the same thing the soldier had seen. Coming at them at full-speed were Modzarellah's kin—the other toad beasts that had been tied outside where they had found her. But it wasn't just a large group of the toads. These had mounted demon riders. *Oh fuck*, Varcade thought, looking around and seeing Modzarellah standing off to the side with a bored look on her face. *Why didn't I just return her?*

The soldier spun and lifted his weapon against the demons, but before he could do anything, a large spinning three-bladed disc sliced through him, separating the man's upper and lower body. Varcade followed the flying weapon's arc as it returned to its owner, the mounted demon catching it one-handed from the air.

The good news was that only a couple of the Bone Lord's soldiers remained, and they were quickly mauled by the frightening onslaught of the demon riders, using a variety of weaponry Varcade had never seen before. The bad news was that Varcade, Dog Man and the Biter now stood alone against the demon horde.

Dog Man padded up to Varcade, breathing heavily, tongue out. The Biter–all bloodied up–appeared soon after, walking casually, like he was taking a morning stroll in the sun.

"I told you—" Dog Man began.

"I *know*, I *know*," Varcade muttered, quickly picking up his swords from the ground.

The demon leading the charge on toad-back raised a fist and made his fellow riders come to a halt before the three of them. The stocky and muscular demon stared right at Varcade with amber-coloured eyes. From the ferocious look on his face, it looked like Varcade had slept with his bride on their wedding night or something.

Dust hung in the air, and the chaotic sounds of battle were now replaced by a pressed silence dripping with tension that was occasionally broken by sporadic croaks from the toad beasts. Any civilian bystanders were already long gone.

The leader demon was bald with ash-coloured skin and had pointy ears, and he and all the riders wore matching simple trousers and vests with nothing underneath. The leader swung out of his saddle and landed on the ground with a loud thud, his boots crunching the dirt, his eyes locked on Varcade. "You steal my ride," he said with a growly low voice, a thick accent showing he hadn't fully mastered the human tongue. "Only Marduk ride Modza. Not onion."

Modza? Close enough, Varcade thought, forcing down the instinct to whisper "I told you so" to Dog Man in regards to guessing the stolen toad's name. "Wait, did you just say your name is Marduk?" Varcade said, slightly tilting his head.

He suddenly recalled that Edghar had mentioned that particular name when discussing who he wanted to recruit to their crew. A demon revolutionary who wanted to topple the Bone Lord's regime. *Huh, that's gotta be him.*

The demon grunted. "I am Marduk. Everyone know this."

"Okay, if you'll just listen to me for a minute," Varcade said, shifting where he stood. "I only borrowed your ride. Was going to return your toad, but then we kinda got into a fight with these guys."

Marduk reached inside his vest and took out a pair of menacing brass-knuckles. He slid them over his fists and cracked his neck. "I not care. I will smash your stupid face now."

Varcade was struggling just to keep himself standing. He was not winning a fight against this guy. "No chance we can talk about this–"

Marduk charged at him like a bull.

CHAPTER SIXTEEN

Edghar and Baaq were once again back in the run-down park where they had first met the crime boss Fat Pudding. The same group of demon younglings they had first encountered were also there, sitting around the park on broken debris acting as furniture.

"You really think this will work?" Edghar said in a hushed tone.

"Only one way to find out," Baaq said, adjusting Fish-City's body slung over her shoulder.

As Edghar and Baaq made it deeper into the park, one of the younglings stood and pointed. "Hey, that's Fish-City! They killed him!" The kids stopped whatever they had been doing and swarmed Edghar and Baaq, staring and pointing wide-eyed at Fish-City's corpse.

"Get Fat Pudding over here," Baaq ordered, before she dumped the body face-down on the ground. "Don't stand around, scram!"

The demon younglings did as ordered, running as fast as their short legs could carry them, leaving the desolate park silent and eerie. Edghar wiped sweat from his brow, his body tense with anticipation for what was about to go down.

"Here they come," Baaq said. "Be ready."

"One-Shot!" came Fat Pudding's high-pitched voice. The crime boss and the same two cronies he'd had with him previously emerged from around the corner. "Well, well, what do we have here?" the hovering demon said as they came up to the two of them. "So, you got the bastard, eh?" Fat Pudding's beady red eyes turning to slits with malice at the sight of Fish-City's body.

"Where is my rifle?" Baaq said, standing straight and tall, folding her muscular arms.

"All in due time," Fat Pudding clicked his tongue. "Zipper, make sure the bastard's really dead. Give him a good kick."

The demon that looked like a humanoid fly walked up to the corpse on the ground, but Baaq intervened, pressing her forearm into the thug's chest. "You want to play around with corpses, you do that on your own goddamn time. Enough of this, where's my rifle, Pudding?"

Fat Pudding laughed. "You have been off the streets for too long, One-Shot. You won't be getting crap until I'm satisfied you delivered on our deal and aren't playing any tricks on me."

"He's *dead*, isn't he?" Baaq growled, kicking Fish-City's limp body for emphasis. "What the hell more do you want?"

Edghar tensed. He discreetly put a hand on his wrist, ready to roll up his sleeve and fire his hand crossbow the moment it would come to that.

"You think I have lived this long due to luck?" Fat Pudding said, all previous playfulness in his tone completely gone. "I don't take chances. Move out of the way and let my guy do his thing."

"No," Baaq said, now forcefully shoving Zipper back, not letting the demon thug pass. "Show me my rifle or we're going to have a problem. I'm not joking."

"Oh yeah?" the pinked-skinned female demon thug said, taking a step forward. "You want to fight? Let's go, you goat-faced bitch."

Baaq growled and clenched her fist, drawing her arm back.

"Bah! Ease up, ease up!" Fat Pudding shouted. "Just show her the damned weapon, Doro. I don't have all day. Stand back, Zipper."

The demon called Doro kept her glare at Baaq for a few heartbeats but finally did as she was told. She reached for the case on her back and opened it, holding it out for them to see.

The weapon–if you could call it that–inside the case looked more like a bracelet. The almost organic-looking material had the colour of yellowed-bone, and there was no handle or trigger that Edghar could see. He couldn't imagine how this would be used as a rifle.

Baaq had an intense look in her eyes as she observed the weapon. She had briefly told him the rifle had been created using her own body; her tendons, flesh, and bone, and that it was Soul-Bound to her. But what that really meant, except no one else could use the weapon, remained a mystery.

Doro slammed the case shut, smirking.

"See? It's right there," Fat Pudding said. "Now move out of the way, Baaq."

Baaq grunted. "Sure. Do whatever you need to do." She lowered her arm and Zipper pushed past her, knocking his shoulder into her. The demon thug squatted down to turn Fish-City's body over, but then suddenly shot up to his feet like he'd been stung in the ass by a wasp.

"Surprise," came Fish-City's voice. He sat straight-backed like a man returning from the dead, aiming a double-barrelled demon-tech weapon at Zipper.

BAM!

The demon thug called Zipper was sent flying from the blast, crashing to the ground on his back, a massive gory hole in his torso.

Edghar winced, his hands instinctively protecting his ears. The loud noise rang in his ears, making him stagger back. "Holy shit . . ." Edghar said under his breath, simultaneously horrified and fascinated by the power of demon weaponry.

"Bastard!" Fat Pudding spat, flying high up in the air, his small wings straining to keep the pudgy demon afloat. "You're dead! Kill them!"

The pink-skinned demon, Doro, dashed back and reached behind her back, pulling out two small demon-tech weapons and started blasting, dropping the weapon case on the ground.

"Shit, shit, shit," Edghar said between clenched teeth as he leapt for cover behind a cracked old fountain. Bullets–or whatever it was demon-tech weapons fired–whizzed through the air. Going against his gut, Edghar carefully allowed himself a peek, trying to assess what the hell to do.

The air around several spots in the park suddenly rippled, revealing countless numbers of Fat Pudding's thugs. The thugs came from nowhere; like they had been there all along, but camouflaged by some demon magic. Whatever it was, it was *bad*. Edghar watched wide eyed as the catastrophe of the situation dawned on him.

"You think I came without a contingency plan, you stupid fuckers!" Fat Pudding screamed from above. "You'll all pay for this. No one crosses Fat Pudding and lives!"

"We will see about that," Fish-City growled, holding his weapon in both his hands, and firing shot after shot, killing one thug after another, not stepping back.

Fish-City's own crew had arrived many hours earlier and hidden themselves in the abandoned buildings adjacent to the park. They now entered the fray, fully armed and ready for action. The park turned into a war zone. Demons were dying like flies, the ground littered with bodies and blood, as the two demon crews showered each other in a storm of bullets and mayhem.

Edghar had lost sight of Baaq but finally spotted her taking cover underneath a stone bench a few feet away. The demon had her attention on the case holding her weapon, and she was half-sitting, like she was getting ready to go retrieve it. But making a run for it would be her death.

"Don't," Edghar shouted from the top of his lungs to get through the din of battle. "Stay down!"

"I need my rifle!" Baaq screamed back at him, her eyes darting between Edghar and the weapon case.

"Forget it! Just stay the hell down!"

"I can't!" Baaq said between clenched teeth. "Pudding's getting away!"

It was true, the demon crime boss was indeed making his escape. Edghar could barely see him so high in the air.

"I *need* to end this!" Baaq said.

Edghar sucked in a deep breath. "Fine, follow my lead," he shouted. He reached inside his robe and grabbed two bombs. Luckily, a quick glance showed one of them was an explosive one and not a smoke bomb. That could have been disastrous for what he had in mind. He replaced it with another smoke bomb and held them both up clearly for Baaq to see, and the demon nodded in agreement. Edghar took aim and hurled the two bombs so they landed close to the weapon case. A heartbeat or two after hitting the ground, smoke erupted out from them, filling the air in a matter of moments. "Go, go, go!"

Baaq shot to her feet and dashed into the smoke cloud, making her vanish from Edghar's vision. Edghar's eyes darted between the barely visible green outline in the sky that was Fat Pudding and the spot where Baaq had been engulfed by the smoke.

Come on, come on, Edghar thought, wiping sweat from his brow. *What's taking so long? Take the damn shot already!*

But the shot didn't come and Edghar's gut tightened in a knot. *Dammit,* he thought, and got up from his hiding place, making a dash after Baaq. A couple of Fat Pudding's thugs immediately spotted him, but Edghar was ready, unleashing two bolts from his hand crossbow. Both demons went down, but not before one of them had already fired their own weapon. The bullet glanced the side of Edghar's cheek, leaving a burning sensation and drawing blood, scarlet drops running down his robe. He ignored the pain and kept running until he was in the midst of the smoke cloud.

The sight that greeted him was far from optimal.

Baaq was down on all fours, the pink-skinned demon Doro latched onto her back, a tight chokehold around the marksman's neck. Baaq coughed and gurgled, desperately trying to get the other demon off her. Blood trickled down Baaq's face, colouring her grey fur into pink. The weapon case carrying the rifle was just out of arm's reach.

"Die, goat-face," Doro hissed between clenched teeth, readjusting her hands to further tighten the grip of her chokehold. Baaq's eyes started rolling back into her head, her mouth hanging open.

Edghar lifted his arm, trying to steady his aim. This was a game of inches. He could just as easily hit Baaq instead of Doro. He pulled the trigger but could instantly tell his aim was off. The bolt sank into the pink-skinned demon's shoulder. Doro growled and instinctively reached for the quarrel jutting from her, but in doing so she also released her chokehold.

Baaq sucked in a deep breath, the air rushing back into her lungs filling her with vigour and strength. She growled and reached up, grabbing Doro's hair.

Edghar had been so focused on Baaq, he was startled by the thug appearing right in front of him. Before he could act, the demon—who looked like an evil weasel/human hybrid—punched Edghar square in the face, making him stumble backwards and fall on his ass, his nose leaking blood. The demon loaded up for another punch, but Edgar shot out his legs and wrapped them around the demon's feet, making him trip to the side. Still sitting, Edghar scooched back, creating enough distance to fire off a bolt, hitting the demon right between the eyes. At least this time his aim had been right. Edghar blinked away the tears in his eyes from the blow to his nose, his vision clearing up.

Baaq and Doro were both on their feet, each hesitating to make the first move. But eventually, Baaq moved first and charged her opponent. Doro threw a wild hook, but the marksman ducked underneath and rammed her horns into Doro's gut with such force it sent her flying backwards. She landed some distance away, groaning and wheezing, surely several of her ribs broken. Doro wouldn't be getting up anytime soon.

"Baaq!" Edghar shouted, just barely able to make out a green blip high up in the sky. He ran to the weapon case and took out the weapon. "Here."

Baaq's chiselled shoulders rose up and down with each heavy breath, blood still oozing from the cuts in her dirtied face. "Give me that," she said.

The instant Baaq put the bracelet around her wrist, the material turned into thick, organic liquid. Countless yellow-white tendrils shot out from it, wrapping themselves around her hand and forearm, snaking their way up and stopping right beneath the elbow. Gone was her arm. Now it had been fully replaced by the long rectangular shape of the rifle.

Edghar watched wide-eyed at the completed transformation. He had so many questions, but he held his tongue. Now was not the time.

Baaq sank down on one knee, lifting her rifle-arm and taking aim.

Edghar squinted up, trying to locate the demon crime boss. "There! I think I see—"

Baaq's rifle erupted with such force the air around the pipe rippled the air, blowing up a cloud of dust in a large radius around them. The weapon boomed as it went off and Edghar could *feel* the vibration going through his own body from the released power.

"It's done," Baaq said, rising to her feet, resting her rifle-arm on her shoulder. Edghar watched, amazed, as the green blip that had been the crime boss Fat Pudding plummeted from the sky, crashing on a rooftop miles away. He couldn't believe the marksman had hit her target, and with only one try. One moment Fat Pudding had been celebrating his escape, but in a split second his life had ended.

"One-Shot, eh?" Edghar said with a smile, using his forearm to wipe off some blood from his battered nose.

Baaq grunted in response, but there was a hint of a smile on her lips.

Now that Edghar had a moment to gather his thoughts and surroundings, he realised the battle had ended. The smoke from his bombs had cleared up, revealing not a war zone, but a graveyard. Dead demons littered every surface, some still groaning as they died.

"There you are," Fish-City said, jogging over to them. "I've been looking for you." The demon bled heavily from his left shoulder, pressing his other hand against the wound to stop the crimson flow. "Seems Fat Pudding got away," Fish-City said, grimacing for a moment from the pain.

"No, he's dead," Baaq said.

Fish-City blinked, looking Baaq up and down like he was seeing her for the first time. His eyes went from her rifle-arm to her face and back again. "Wait a second," he muttered, unable to look away from Baaq's new arm. "Are you One-Shot? *The* One-Shot?"

Baaq nodded.

"You didn't tell me."

"You didn't ask," Baaq said.

Fish-City snorted. "Well, I'll be damned." The demon sucked his sharp teeth and looked around. "Nasty business, this, but at least it's over now. I lost some of my guys, but they lost even more." He held out his hand and shook both of theirs. "It might not feel like it right now, but you did a good thing today. I am in your debt."

CHAPTER SEVENTEEN

The demon called Marduk was on him before Varcade could react—surprisingly swift for his size. One hand shot out and grabbed Varcade by the throat, while the other one slammed into his face. After a serious pummelling that would have killed most people, Marduk finally released him. Varcade sagged to the ground like a deflated balloon.

"Pathetic," Marduk growled and spat then started walking away. "All onions weak."

Varcade groaned and began getting up. "I'll show you weak, you pointy-eared bastard..."

"Hah!" Marduk said, turning around. "You have more fight left? Come on. Get up. Show me."

While it was true that Varcade was in pain, it was more that his ego was bruised rather than his body. He refused to go down in a fight like this. He stood on shaky legs and grabbed his swords. "If it wasn't for that Duster freak I just fought, I'd easily kick your ass. You got lucky catching me at a bad time."

"Maybe you should just stay down," Dog Man whispered. "Not worth dying over this."

"He's on Edghar's list," Varcade hissed between clenched teeth only loud enough for Dog Man to hear. "Marduk. I remember the name."

Dog Man's eyes snapped to the demon and back to Varcade. "Really? That's good! Then talk to him. Maybe you can convince him to join us?"

"I will. *After* I beat him up."

"Are you stupid?" Dog Man growled. "You're not fit to fight. He'll kill you, and then he'll kill us."

Varcade nudged Dog Man with his leg. "Get out of the way."

"Biter, say something!" Dog Man pleaded.

The turbaned man shrugged. "Man must make own choices in life."

Dog Man sighed. "Great, you're gonna turn into a bloody philosopher all of a sudden? Idiot."

Marduk's companions were still mounted on their toads, and to his surprise, they actually cheered as Varcade rose to his feet, slapping the thick, rubbery hides of their beasts.

"My brothers and sisters want good fight," Marduk said, spreading his arms wide in open invitation. "Let us see how strong you are, silver-hair onion."

Varcade focused to steady his breathing and clear his mind. He could feel his body regaining its strength with each passing moment. If only he could buy himself more time, he would be in fighting shape again. "Hey," he said. "Want to make a bet?"

Marduk frowned. "Bet?"

"That's right," Varcade said. "You know what it means?"

"Yes, yes, I know this bullshit bet," Marduk said.

"Good. So, when I beat you, I get to keep Modzarellah."

"Modzarellah?" Marduk struggled to pronounce the name.

"Your toad. Modza or whatever you called her."

Marduk crossed his arms, glancing over at his mount that stood to the side. "And what I get after I crush you?"

Varcade hadn't thought about what he would offer. He looked around then shrugged. "Dog Man. You get Dog Man."

"*What?!*" Dog Man said with wide eyes. "No way in hell!" Before the canine could protest further, the Biter suddenly pounced on him, holding him in place. "Are you serious?! Let me go!"

"No," the Biter whispered close to Dog Man's ear. "Varcade is leader."

Marduk scratched his jaw then nodded. "Okay. I like this talking dog. You have deal. Now we fight."

The short respite had done its work; Varcade felt better again. He said, "Bring it on."

As Varcade expected, Marduk had one mode of attack, and that was to bullrush him headfirst. But what Varcade lacked in sheer brute force, he made up with swift movement and remarkable agility. Marduk came at him with arms outstretched like a wrestler, but before the stocky demon could get his meaty paws on him, Varcade leapt over him, making Marduk catch nothing but air.

"Need to be quicker than that," Varcade said with a sly smile that he turned up to eleven to further frustrate the demon who had spun around to face him.

Marduk roared and rushed him. This time Varcade did not leap over him, but instead, dashed to the side with the swiftness of a dancer. "This not fight!" Marduk growled as he came to a halt. "You bullshit coward."

Varcade shrugged. "We never set any rules, big boy. You think I'm just going to stand still and let you grab me? Think again."

Marduk's frustration was written all over his face, his amber eyes burning with rage. Realising he would have a hard time getting his hands on Varcade, the demon abandoned his half-crouched stance with bent knees and instead began bouncing lightly on his feet. He put up his fists and came towards him, swinging from side to side.

Brass-knuckles met blades in a shower of sparks as Marduk jabbed a series of strikes that Varcade deflected with his swords. The demon's punches came hard and fast, up and down, but they weren't fast enough. Seizing a small opening for a counterattack of his own, Varcade sliced a shallow cut across Marduk's forearm. The demon growled between clenched teeth at the sight of his own blood.

"You didn't like that, did you?" Varcade said, leaping backwards. "If this had been a contest of who drew first blood, I would be the winner."

Marduk did not entertain him with a reply. Instead, he kept coming towards him, but now, he lowered his arms, reversing to his previous battle stance. The demon walked him down, huffing and puffing, his coiled muscles ready to attack. Varcade was on the back foot, feeling the demon was getting closer and closer to him. Varcade realised too late that the demon was boxing him in; using their surroundings to limit Varcade's paths for escape.

Varcade felt his back bump into something, and before he could move out of the way, Marduk made his move and rushed him. Shooting like a spear, the demon wrapped his beefy arms around Varcade's midsection and drove him into the facade of the mudbrick house. The air exploded from his lungs as he crashed into the wall, both his swords flying from his hands. Using the wall to his advantage, Marduk yanked Varcade's legs out from under him, making him plop down on his ass. In a split-second, the demon had mounted him, his heavy weight crushing Varcade beneath his bulk.

Marduk tried to press Varcade down on his back with one hand, so he could use his other to smash his face-in. The only defence Varcade could offer was to limit the space between them and hug the demon with both his arms. But Varcade's arms were already straining, and it was only a question of time before Marduk would get the upper hand.

Marduk's companions' blood-thirsty cheering suddenly stopped and turned into loud mumbling. From the corner of his eye, Varcade could see the mounted demons fully turning their attention away from the brawl and onto something else entirely. Marduk must also have noticed because his body relaxed a bit.

"Marduk!" one of the other demons shouted. "Trouble! Big trouble!"

Marduk growled and hesitated for moment before pushing himself off Varcade. "We finish this later."

Varcade knew he had been moments away from being beaten to a pulp, so he held his tongue instead of offering up a cocky remark. He retrieved his swords and walked over to see what all the fuss was about. Instantly, a part of him wished he hadn't.

More of the Bone Lord's soldiers had arrived, but it was the *thing* in the center of them that caught everyone's attention. The monstrous machine looked like a massive vaguely humanoid iron-box walking on bent legs like that of a goat. Two slab-shoulders jutted from its upper frame and underneath each were long, powerful arms. One arm was equipped with a large talon-like claw, while the other one ended with a round hole like a mouth of a cannon. In the middle of its bulk there was a skull-like head with fiery red-yellow eyes, giving the whole construction a hunched and menacing posture.

The war machine came to a halt and raised its non-clawed arm and erupted in a continuous fluid stream of fire. The demon riders closest to the deadly construction were immediately set aflame. Varcade watched with horror how both demons and their mounts screamed and writhed in anguish.

Marduk shouted something in the demon tongue that made his mounted companions bounce away from the threat of the spewing fire. The demons were armed with three-bladed discs that they collectively hurled at the attackers. The discs travelled through the air and sliced through anyone not smart or fast enough to move out of the way, then travelled back to their wielders like deadly boomerangs. The royal soldiers dropped like flies, but any of the discs hitting the war machine did little against its armoured hull except getting stuck.

The deadly construct kept advancing towards them, but slowly, its movements cumbersome. The legs on the machine seemed to struggle under its own weight, and Varcade realised–and hoped–not much would be needed to take it off balance.

"The legs!" Varcade screamed at Marduk. "Go for the legs. I'll back you up."

Marduk's head snapped in Varcade's direction, locking eyes with him. He nodded once and ran into the fray with a mighty roar, Varcade following next to him. Dog Man and the Biter followed their lead and clashed with any soldiers standing in their way; both of them using their natural weapons of teeth and claws to shred through the Bone Lord's soldiers. Marduk's companions, who were now weaponless, whipped their toad mounts into a frenzy and charged the soldiers, crushing them underneath the bulk of the beasts.

Varcade was the first to reach the war machine and, standing up close, it dawned on him just how massive the thing really was, easily taller than three adult men standing on each other's shoulders. The construct hissed and spat as fumes and gas blew out from a series of openings all across the armour. To make matters worse, the two legs did not look as spindly and weak as he'd hoped from seeing it from afar. He sliced and diced at the legs with his swords but was only met by sparks as his blades failed to cut through the thick steel.

Marduk appeared next to him and slammed one brass-knuckled fist into one of the legs. The war machine immediately reacted to the impact, slightly losing its footing before regaining it again. Seeing the positive result, Marduk let out another roar from the pit of his stomach and unleashed a barrage of heavy strikes. Loud clanks echoed as his steel-enforced knuckles crashed into the metal.

Varcade, the Biter and Dog Man fought off the incoming assault of soldiers that never seemed to stop coming, in a small and tight circle around the war machine while Marduk kept up his attack. But the soldiers were armed with flame weapons of their own, and to say they were using them haphazardly was an understatement. The fires erupting from their weapons went everywhere, even hitting their fellow soldiers and setting them ablaze. The screams and thick black smoke along with the sickly smell of burnt flesh created a pandemonium unlike anything Varcade had ever experienced. It was as if they had been transported to their own little private pocket of fiery hell.

His eyes stung and kept watering and his lungs protested at all the fumes invading his system, making him cough non-stop as he wildly swung his swords cutting down one soldier after the other. It was close to impossible to make out what was actually happening but hearing the repeated clanking sound from Marduk's fists slamming into the war machine was somewhat reassuring amidst the total chaos. What wasn't reassuring was catching a brief glimpse of the Biter getting skewered in the back by the taloned arm of the war machine.

"No!" Varcade said, cutting down the soldier in front of him and dashing over to aid his friend.

The three claws burst from the Biter's chest and hoisted him off his feet, lifting him high in the air; white, odd-looking liquid gushing from the wounds. The Biter made no sound, but his body spasmed, arms and legs jerking uncontrollably, the white liquid pouring out of him and spraying in every direction.

Varcade sheathed his swords and leapt up high in the air, landing on the taloned arm of the war machine. He wasn't sure what he was planning to do, but he desperately needed to help the Biter somehow, if it wasn't already too late. He balanced on the war machine's long arm on the tip of his toes until he reached his dying friend. Varcade was just about to grab the Biter when the war machine gave off a metallic shriek and began tipping over. Varcade jumped off right as the massive construct crashed to the ground and caused an enormous cloud of dirt and dust to explode in all directions.

The Biter was flung loose, his limp body rolling away in the dirt. Varcade followed and sank onto his knees next to his companion. He turned him over gently and grimaced at the gruesome sight. The Biter's face showed no emotion at his impending doom and coughed once, more of the white liquid exploding from his mouth.

"Biter . . ." Varcade said under his breath, grabbing the man's hand. "What the hell, man. Don't die on me."

Biter looked up at him, his eyes blinking frantically, his body still spasming. "I am sorry. This body is ruined. I must go now. Forgive me."

"Don't be silly, there's nothing to forgive," Varcade said, sucking in a deep breath, slightly confused at the man's dying words.

"We will meet again, but first I must find a new shell. Walk away from me, my friend. I cannot control myself in my true form. I might attack even you."

Huh?

What happened next made Varcade panic and crab-crawl away from the Biter's body. A thick and red snake-like creature slithered out from the Biter's mouth and moved away from the corpse.

WHAT THE HELL?!

Varcade shot to his feet, feeling his skin crawling all over. What had just happened? He stood there a moment utterly dumbfounded and equally disgusted. Something nudged his leg and startled him, making Varcade jump back.

"Calm down!" Dog Man said. "It's just me!"

"Don't touch me," Varcade said under his breath. "Did you see that? Please tell me you saw that!"

"I saw, I saw," Dog Man said. "Poor Biter. He was weird but I kinda liked him."

"Not that part, did you see what came out of him?"

The canine gave Varcade a funny look. "What the hell is wrong with you, boy?" The canine muttered something else before padding over to the Biter's corpse. "Rest in peace. Hey, what's all this white goo? Is this blood?"

Varcade opened his mouth to explain what had just happened but then decided against it. It was too weird, and he had no idea how to explain it. "Forget it. Come on."

With the war machine down, the remaining demons had turned the tide of battle and made quick work of the last soldiers. Marduk stood on top of the felled construct and tore at the hinges on its back. Apparently, there was someone inside the machine controlling it. The bald demon yanked the steel door off and tossed it to the side then reached down and grabbed the driver who got a full serving of Marduk's wrath. Varcade almost felt sorry for the guy, but not really.

The aftermath of the fight was a gruesome sight. Smouldering corpses were littered everywhere, and fires still burned all around them. The ground was blackened, and nearby buildings destroyed. Varcade sank onto his hunches and took a deep breath, the exhaustion hitting him like a wall of bricks.

Marduk walked over to him and extended his hand. "Thank you. You did not have to help, but you did." Varcade clasped the demon's hand and stood up as Dog Man joined them. The demon looked down at the dog. "Are you his brother?"

"What? We don't look the slightest bit alike!" Dog Man barked.

Marduk shrugged. "Does not matter." He turned his attention to Varcade. "Forget about bet. You can keep talking dog."

"You know he *doesn't* own me, right?" Dog Man said. "Or maybe you don't . . ." He added under his breath.

"So, what now?" Varcade said, sheathing his swords on his back.

"Nothing. You live and I return to my mission." Marduk looked at the carnage all around them. "This only proof my fight is far from over."

"What is your mission?" Varcade said.

"Why should I answer you? What do you care?"

"Because I think we share the same goal."

Marduk laughed. Not a small chuckle, but a loud one, holding one hand on his stomach. Apparently, something about Varcade's statement had been extremely funny. "You are not bad fighter, but something wrong in your head, onion."

"And why's that?"

"My goal is death of all onions. I will take over this city."

"Oh," Varcade said, scratching the back of his head. "Okay, yeah, that's not my goal exactly. But we kinda still do have something in common."

Marduk crossed his arms. "What?"

"We're also looking to take over Akrab. And we're gonna start by killing the Bone Lord herself."

Marduk studied Varcade's face. "You speak truth, silver-hair?"

Varcade wasn't happy to admit they needed *anyone* for their task, but since arriving in Akrab it had been proven time and time again that Varcade alone was far from enough. "Yes," he said, his pride taking another critical hit. "We could work together."

Marduk ran a hand over his bald head. "Me working with onions? I don't know. It is wrong."

Varcade stepped forward. "Listen, we've got a guy who used to work for the Bone Lord. He knows a bunch of useful stuff that will help you achieve your goal. You have nothing to lose by teaming up with us. Plus, we have another demon in our crew. A marksman."

Marduk seemed to consider this for a moment that stretched out for what felt like eternity. He finally spoke up. "Maybe. What is your plan?"

CHAPTER EIGHTEEN

Clea slammed her hands down on the table, staring daggers at the people seated around her. "Well, say something damn you!"

The sudden news of Berenberg's death had shaken Clea to her core. All notion of keeping her composure as a dignified ruler was thrown out the window. An emergency council meeting had hastily been assembled, everyone in her most inner circle present. The group sat around the circular, wooden table, fresh fruit and a jug of wine before them.

"Why am I the only one speaking?" Clea said. "We still *need* that loan from Farouk. I will have to travel to Nuzz myself, then."

"I would strongly advise against that, Your Highness," Erikz, the Royal Guard Captain said. If the news of Berenberg's death had rattled him in any way, it was impossible to tell from his expressionless face. "It's too dangerous out there. And if word gets out that you've left Akrab, your citizens might see that as a sign of you abandoning them during the crisis at hand."

Khanon, the Army General cleared his throat. "Not only that, Your Excellency, but we now know for certain Edghar is somewhere in the city, plotting against you. The soldier who survived the attack against Berenberg was spared for the sole reason of delivering that message. You need to remain within the ziggurat at all times."

"Then what am I supposed to do? Sit here and wait for them to come and kill me?" Clea said. "How hard can it be to find and capture Edghar? We *know* he's right here in Akrab under our noses! And who is that damned man helping him?"

"I might be able to shed some light on the assassin's identity, My Lord," Vizier Tarkus said. But Clea was barely able to concentrate on the man's words, because in usual order he was rubbing that damn lotion on his bare arms, chest and neck, the sweet smell making her dizzy.

"Could you, for *once,* not do that right this moment," Clea sighed, rubbing her brow. "I can't stand that smell."

Vizier Tarkus had a smug look on his chubby face. "My deepest apologies, My Lord. But you know—"

"Yes, yes, your damn skin gets dry," Clea hissed, waving her hand dismissively. "Forget it, just tell me who Edghar's partner is."

The wet, squishy sound from the salve acted as a backup choir to the Vizier talking. "It seems the silver-haired assassin is a former warrior-monk of sorts who has turned his back on his order. He has made quite the reputation for himself working as a sellsword here in Harrah."

"They're known as Educators," Erikz said. "I came across them now and then back when I lived in Karkan. Religious types. And extremely dangerous. They are taken at a young age—"

"—I don't care about a history lesson," Clea snapped. She glared at the Vizier. "You promised employing the band of Dusters would take care of everything! But so far, they haven't accomplished anything. And what about those dough freaks?"

"Still no word from the Baker on that regard, but I have faith they will come through," Vizier Tarkus said.

"*Faith?*" Clea said between clenched teeth. "Like that has ever accomplished anything." She exhaled, her shoulders drooping. "Damn it all to hell."

THE CREW

Vizier Tarkus rose from his chair, the heavy beaded necklace around his fat neck clinking. His lotion-covered skin glistened in the sunlight coming through the window. "I may have an idea how to solve the matter with the Bone Lord of Nuzz. I believe we could convince him to travel to Akrab under the right circumstances."

"And what circumstances would those be?" Clea said. "We were sending Berenberg because Farouk wouldn't come here in the first place. What has changed?"

"Nothing has changed, My Lord," Tarkus said, his bare feet slapping on the stone floor as he walked around the small room. "The idea had merely not occurred to me at the time. You see, I have it on good authority that Farouk has a certain . . . *fondness* for the good things in life. In his case, that pertains especially to women and food. We have both exquisite food and women here in Akrab, wouldn't you say?"

"You seriously think those things would make the Bone Lord willingly come to a city on the brink of civil war?" The Army General said. "You can find food and women everywhere."

Vizier Tarkus again had that smug look on his face. "Dear Khanon, you are a military man. You live and breathe battle. What do you know of the urges of the rich and powerful?"

"Not much," Khanon said, "but I still doubt Farouk would risk his own life by coming here."

"Let Tarkus finish," Clea said. She was not fond of the way the Vizier was describing the Bone Lord's urges, but if history had taught her anything, it was that men would often make crucial decisions using other parts than their brains. That fact could be used to her advantage, and she would use any weapon available at her disposal. "Go on."

"Thank you, Your Excellency," the Vizier smiled. "I propose we arrange the greatest banquet Akrab has ever seen. In the ziggurat, of course. The cost for arranging it won't matter since the purpose of meeting the Bone Lord is to get him to sign off on the loan we need.

We will use the best chefs in the city and get the most beautiful women to attend. It will be an event for the ages."

Erikz and Khanon shared a glance between them, but it was the Royal Guard Captain who spoke first, unsurprisingly, since his primary job was Clea's safety. "A banquet? At this time? Please, My Lord, if I may, it's awfully risky inviting strangers to our doors when your life is under serious threat."

"Erikz speaks true," Khanon added. "We would basically be sending an invitation to the assassins as well."

"Perhaps they're right, Tarkus," Clea said. "It feels risky."

The Vizier came up behind her, the stench from his lotion invading Clea's senses. "Do you trust me, My Lord?"

"I do."

"Then believe me when I say this is the perfect solution to our current predicament. You will be perfectly safe."

Part of Clea didn't agree, but she suddenly lacked the energy or willpower to argue. And a steady sensation of pain pulsated right between her eyes, making it impossible to think. "Fine. We'll do as you advise," she said, closing her eyes and rubbing her temples.

"I urge you to reconsider, Your Highness," Erikz said. "This plan is terrible. The assassins—"

"Up the damned security then!" Clea exploded. "You *two* might not understand how to rule a city-state since you spend most of your time either playing with swords or planning military strategies, but I can't rule without capital." She drained the wine cup and rose to her feet. "We are doing this banquet. It will work, and that is final. Do you understand?"

Khanon and Erikz nodded.

Vizier Tarkus bowed and backed away.

"And one more thing," Clea said, glaring at the Royal Guard Captain and the Army General. "Perhaps the two of you should actually apprehend my assassins instead of just sitting here and worrying about them."

THE CREW

Vashi felt shaken after what had transpired with Xira. Rationally, the woman had asked for her Release, but the act of it still pained him. *It had to be done*, he told himself, seeking comfort in the fact she was at least no longer in pain. But he would not let his emotions linger on the matter anymore. He had done what was required, and in accordance with the Teachings.

Vashi had left the alley afterwards and once again found himself navigating the busy streets of the city. Now that he was certain Varcade had been seen in Akrab, it would be easier to simply ask people about a silver-haired stranger. *Someone must have seen him and could point me in the right direction.*

He noticed a group of demon younglings squatting in a circle, seemingly excited about something that Vashi couldn't see. Curious, he approached them and peered over their heads.

Some type of spider and a scorpion had been pitted against one and other in a deadly battle. The kids had long sticks they poked the insects with, both to keep them agitated and within the small confines they had created for them.

Cruel behaviour for the sake of entertainment is unacceptable. Vashi sighed. It seemed he couldn't go *anywhere* in Akrab without stumbling upon one offence or another according to the Teachings.

"This must stop," Vashi said and grabbed one of the children by his neck before tossing him to the side.

"Hey, what the—" another one started saying.

"Silence," Vashi interrupted, slapping the boy with an open palm right on the mouth.

The rest of the children broke their circle and shot up to their feet. But instead of running as Vashi had expected, they instead turned on him in force, peppering him with feeble kicks and punches as they cursed him out.

"Hey, hey!" came the voice of a burly older demon jogging up to them. He started slapping the kids on the back of their heads, yanking them off Vashi one by one. "Leave this man alone, you little savages. What is wrong with you?"

"He attacked us!" one of them said, her face in a grimace as the older demon held her by the ear. "We were just playing!"

"Yeah, we didn't do anything," another one chimed in, giving Vashi the stink eye. "Stupid onion came out of nowhere and started hitting us!"

The older demon's eyes narrowed as he turned towards Vashi. "This is true?"

"They are not entirely wrong," Vashi said, dusting off his coat. "But I did it because—"

"*What?* You admit to attacking our children?"

Vashi held his hands up. "If you will allow me to explain. The children were forcing insects to fight each other for their own cruel amusement. That is forbidden by the Teachings, so I made them stop. All sentient life must be respected and treated in an appropriate manner."

The older demon strode up to Vashi. "You don't tell our kids what games they're allowed to play," he snarled. "Who do you think you are? Coming here and telling us how to live our lives?"

"I am an Educator. It is my sacred duty to educate."

"Educator?" the demon grimaced. "What the hell is that? Never heard of it. You better take your ass away from here before we have a real problem on our hands." The younglings had lined up behind the older demon, giving Vashi mocking grins and making crude gestures.

Vashi nodded. "Certainly. But first, the children must promise to change their ways. No more cruel behaviour of this sort."

"Are you deaf or somethin'?" the older demon said, now inches away from Vashi's face.

"No, my hearing is perfect."

"You mocking me?"

"I am not. You asked me a question, so I replied."

The demon looked over his shoulder and barked something in his native demon tongue. In a matter of moments, more adult demons arrived. They gathered around Vashi, shouting incomprehensible things, and pointing at him.

"You shouldn't have messed with us," the demon said. "Especially not our kids."

Vashi frowned as he looked around at all the demons surrounding him. "This is a misunderstanding. The Teachings do not discriminate. *Everyone* must be educated, regardless of race and gender. Only when we come together the Balance can be achieved. Do you understand?"

The attempted thrown punch at Vashi's face indicated the answer to that was no. Vashi caught the demon's wrist before it stuck him and slammed an open palm into the attacker's chest, sending the demon flying in the air.

Vashi took two steps back, creating some distance between him and the now formed half-circle of demons facing him. "This is all unnecessary, I assure you. If the children would simply promise—" he ducked under a rock thrown at him, "—to not play more cruel games, I will be on my way."

More demons were now drawn into the street fight, and Vashi had to dodge a newcomer trying to hit him with a plank from behind. Vashi slid under the swing and planted a punch in the demon's liver, taking the air out of the attacker, who slumped to the ground wheezing in agony.

"Attacking an Educator is forbidden. If you refuse to back down, I have no choice but to educate you all." Vashi pulled the staff from his back, holding it out before him to keep the mob at bay. "This is my final warning."

The demons swarmed Vashi in mass.

The first line of attackers were struck by Vashi's staff in a wide sweeping arc. His weapon was made from iron wood, unique to Karkan, light to wield but strong as steel. Those on the receiving end had their faces cracked from the impact, toppling over in anguish. However, that did not stop the remaining demons. They leapt over their fallen brethren, murder in their eyes.

Vashi did his best to defend himself from the incoming buffet of violence which included punches, kicks, blunt weapons, and pointy things. He swiftly moved around them, dashing in and out, never standing still. He ducked and dodged the attackers and dished out some pain of his own whenever he saw an opening to counterattack.

The members of the Educators were trained to be one-man armies, and as the fight raged on, the demons fell one by one until only Vashi was left standing amidst a mountain of bodies. A chorus of groans sang a defeated melody all around him as he cracked his neck and returned the staff on his back.

"Education complete," Vashi said and looked around him. "Lesson: never attack an Educator. We live and work to make all *your* lives better. Next time, simply comply and violence will be avoided."

Vashi left the scene, making sure to not step on any of the fallen. He saw one of the demon younglings who'd been torturing the two insects standing to the side. The child's mouth was the shape of an O as Vashi approached him. He looked down at the boy and met his eyes with a smile. Then, he drilled a punch in the boy's flabby belly. The child wheezed and sank down onto his knees, hugging his body.

"Don't be cruel again, boy, okay? That goes for you and your other little friends." Vashi said, standing over him, holding out a closed fist. "Now bump it so we can get on with the rest of our day."

The child was struggling to breathe, but obliged Vashi's demand, offering a meekly fist-bump in return. "Good. Oh, one more thing: have you seen another silver-haired man who looks a little bit like me?"

CHAPTER NINETEEN

Varcade stood on Modzarellah's head with his arms crossed like a general making a grand entrance onto a battlefield. The toad mount still belonged to Marduk but he had given Varcade permission to ride it for the time being. The demon was more fascinated with Dog Man at the moment.

"Get off! What the fuck 'r you doing?" Dog Man said, running circles around Marduk who kept trying to get up on his back.

"You are animal. I ride." Marduk said.

"I'm not an animal, you bastard," Dog Man growled.

"Let Marduk ride you. Don't be such a bore," Varcade said.

"I'd rather get stabbed in the eye than let *anyone* ride me, so forget about it. Also, I'm too small, you idiots! It's not even physically possible!"

"I can ride any animal," Marduk said. "Rat, cat, dog. Size not matter to me. Come, I show you."

"Forget it!"

The strange group was making their way over to the demon owned tavern called Three Sisters where they would meet up with Edghar and Baaq. Them being the odd bunch out drew many stares from other people passing them by, but that couldn't be helped at this point, so Varcade had decided to just go with the flow and let whatever happen, happen.

Marduk eventually gave up his attempts to mount Dog Man and the three of them (along with Modzarellah) settled into a silence. The talking canine broke it when he looked up at Marduk and said, "Do you live near this part of the city? I wouldn't mind a short rest before we meet up with the others."

"I do not live here," Marduk grunted. "Only weak demons live here."

"What do mean by that?" Varcade said, having settled down cross-legged on Modzarellah's head instead of using the saddle.

"This is onion city. My kind deserves better. We should rule Akrab, not live with them or under them. Pathetic."

"Okay, but you still need a place to live?" Dog Man said.

"I am a warrior. I will have my home *after* the revolution. A home worthy for my people; built on top of human bones. Then, I will rest."

"Lucky me, now I'm around *two* hyper people . . ." Dog Man muttered under his breath.

Marduk spread his arms and looked around them, his face grimacing with disgust. "This is *not* worthy for my kind. The demons have forgotten we are the stronger race. But I have not, and I *will* remind them."

"Yeah, okay," Dog Man said, clearing his throat, looking sideways at Marduk. "Whatever you say, man. Just don't kill us when that time comes."

"I make no promises," Marduk said with a straight face.

"Hey, Varcade, can you maybe try to convince our new friend here casually mentioning he might kill us to maybe not do that?"

"That's gonna be a long time from now, isn't that right, Marduk?" Varcade said.

Marduk nodded. "Yes. Revolution will take time."

"See?" Varcade shrugged. "Don't worry about tomorrow, Doggie. No point in that. Just take life one day at a time and have fun with it."

"Yeah, that's not very reassuring . . ." Dog Man said, moving farther away from Marduk.

After a while Marduk suddenly came to a stop. His amber eyes narrowing and his back stiffening. "Scum," he growled.

They had left one gruesome scene of battle behind only to walk into a new one. But the dead bodies here were not like Marduk's companions, who fought for a cause; these looked like everyday demons. Their corpses were badly burnt, and the ground was blackened and bloody.

"Damn, so this is where the first soldiers we encountered were heading . . ." Dog Man said, shaking his head. "Imagine how much worse it would've been if we hadn't killed all those bastards. This is madness."

Demons were all over the street tending to those injured, while others removed corpses, and some putting out smaller fires that still raged. Those who cleaned up the aftermath did that in sombre silence, while those who'd lost loved ones either cried or watched with catatonic stares.

But that all changed with the presence of Marduk. Venomous glares mixed with loud mumbles spread amongst the demons as the warrior approached them and tried helping.

"We got this," a female demon said. "Do not need *your* help."

"I want to help," Marduk said. "Let me."

An elderly man who was tending to the burn wounds of a young child rose to his feet. "No," he said. "Leave us be. We don't want you here. We know who you are and what you do."

Marduk's mouth turned into a snarl. "Fight for our kind you mean? Yes, I do that, and I will continue until my last breath. You got problem with that?"

The older demon closed his eyes and exhaled. "You don't get it, do you? We have had *enough* with all the violence! We do not want another war; we want to live in peace. That is all we want. We do not want the poison your actions are spreading onto our younglings." The demon snorted. "You know some of them actually talk about you like you're some kind of hero. You are poisoning their minds."

"So?" Marduk growled. "I want to inspire them! They must learn we are strong. You want peace, old man? First, we must go to war." He looked the older demon up and down with a disgusted look. "What are you doing to help our kind? *Nothing*. You are old and weak. You stand here and let the onions come here and kill us. Our brothers and sisters slaughtered like animals." Marduk grabbed the demon by the neck like an unruly child. "I will not die on my knees," he said close to the man's ear. "You hear me?"

"Please, son," an older female said as she approached. "Leave us be. These people are mourning. Allow them time to grieve. This is not the time or place."

"Fine," Marduk said between clenched teeth, releasing his grip of the older man while simultaneously pushing him away. "I will go."

"Holy crap," Dog Man muttered and started walking. Him and Varcade had been sharing uncomfortable glances with each other during Marduk's outburst, both utterly clueless in what to do or say.

Varcade had, yet again, been reminded what was really at stake here in Akrab, and those feelings gathered up in his chest, creating a tight knot that almost made it hard to breathe. He hated it, and he had to fight hard to not give in to his instinct and just turn around and leave all of this behind.

Varcade exhaled with a satisfied and silly grin, both hands clasped across his bloated stomach. "That was *good*. I could easily eat mazz-mazz every day for the rest of my life. I mean that."

Sitting down at Three Sisters and eating a splendid meal had pushed aside the negative thoughts buzzing in Varcade's mind. Getting some food and drinks also had a positive effect on Marduk and Dog Man, and the tension had eased. They had been through a lot in a short period and some relaxation was clearly welcome.

Last time Varcade had been at Three Sisters he'd been with Edghar, but now he was in the company of a demon and a talking dog, making him the only human patron in the establishment. Growing up as an Educator had made him different from everyone else at an early age, and he found comfort in being around others who didn't fit any mould. Sure, some of the other demons at the other tables gave him funny looks but that didn't bother him the least.

The three of them had been given a table in the far corner of the spacious room. The air smelled richly of the varied and exotic spices used by the demon folks, and the dim lighting and shuttered windows created a cosy setting.

"I can't believe you actually ate that even after knowing what it is," Dog Man said, slurping water from a bowl on the floor.

"Mazz-mazz is a delicacy. Onion tongue not worthy," Marduk said.

"You say that but still you didn't eat?" Varcade said, glancing over at Marduk's full plate. "Look, you barely even touched your food. At least *I* appreciate your fine cuisine."

Marduk shrugged. "I am not hungry."

"Suit yourself," Varcade shrugged. "Give me like five or ten minutes, and I can finish yours too."

"No."

"Why no?"

"It is mine."

"But you're not eating it, are you?"

"Does not matter. You will not have it."

"That's just stupid."

"You are stupid."

"You can be stupid–"

"Can you both shut up," Dog Man said. "Look who just walked through the doors."

Varcade's face lit up. "Hey! Edghar and Baaq!"

Edghar's face was bloody–his nose looked broken–and his clothes were torn as well. Baaq didn't look to be in much better shape either, spots of her grey fur coloured pink from old blood. The air around them was heavy and grim as they came over to join them.

"We've been waiting for you," Varcade said, motioning them over with a wave. "Sit down. Meet Marduk."

"*Marduk.*" The way Baaq uttered the name was not said in a pleasant tone as she stopped dead in her tracks a few feet away from their table. Marduk cast a glance over his shoulder at the marksman and offered a dismissive snort. "What is he doing here?" Baaq said.

"Wait, Marduk?" Edghar said. "He's on my list."

Varcade grinned. "I know."

Edghar looked flabbergasted. "And that Duster dog is still with you I see?"

"I'm not an actual dog, you know," Dog Man said before proceeding to lick his butthole.

Edghar's look of confusion did not diminish. "If you say so . . ." He turned his attention to Baaq. "You know this man?"

"I know who and what he is," Baaq said.

"And what's *that*?" Marduk said.

"*Trouble*," Baaq sneered.

The stocky demon shot to his feet. "I can give you trouble–" Marduk stopped himself, confusion passing through his eyes. He walked to Baaq and Edghar, his eyes drawn to a strange-looking bracelet around Baaq's wrist. "That weapon . . . *Baaqarah*? Is it really you?"

Baaq said nothing.

Marduk offered his hand. "I am sorry for the way I speak. You are true hero for all demons. Stories about you inspired me–"

"Save it," Baaq said with a finality in her voice. "You're a mad man. We're nothing alike."

Marduk's eyes narrowed, clenching his fists. "I see. You also judge like that?"

"Damn right I do."

Edghar stepped in between them. "I'm not sure what this is about, but this isn't the time or place. Please."

"Edghar's right," Varcade said, food flying from his mouth as he spoke. "We're all friends here. Sit down and relax, get something to eat."

"I told you not to touch my food," Marduk said as he returned to the table.

Varcade shrugged. "Hey, you snooze, you lose."

Edghar placed a hand on Baaq's shoulder. "Come on. Let us sit down. We deserve some rest after everything we have gone through."

"No," Baaq said. "I won't share a table with him. I'll wait outside."

"Are you certain?"

"Yes." Baaq turned on her heels and walked out.

Edghar sighed and ran a hand through his dirty hair. The former spymaster sank down cross-legged on the floor cushion and ordered some food.

"Give me that," Marduk said, snatching back his almost-empty plate from Varcade.

"Hey, don't be mad at me because Baaq doesn't like you. That isn't my fault."

"Just shut up," Marduk said and turned his attention to Edghar. "You are the one who work for Bone Lord before?"

Edghar nodded. "And you're Marduk the Revolutionary."

"Some call me that. It is true you want to kill the Bone Lord?"

"It's not about killing her. I want to save Akrab. I will do whatever it takes."

Marduk grunted. "Good. I will help. When we are done maybe I kill you all."

Edghar almost choked on his food. "You *what?*"

"Ignore that," Varcade cut-in with a dismissive gesture. "He says stuff like that occasionally."

"Glad to see someone else react in a normal way about it at least," Dog Man muttered.

"Oh, I forgot to tell you," Varcade said, licking his fingers. "We took out that coin-person working for the Bone Lord."

"Really?" Edghar's face lit up. "Thank the Yellow King. I needed to hear that. How did you do it?"

Varcade smirked. "Did you notice that enormous toad beast right outside?"

"I did. What is it?"

"She's Marduk's mount. I call her Modzarellah."

"That not her name," Marduk said. "She is called Modza."

"That name sucks. Modzarellah is so much better."

"Fuck you and stupid name!" Marduk exploded and shot out of his seat.

"Hey! Hey! Calm down," Edghar said, putting out his arm before the stocky demon. "Sit down, please. Can we return to the topic? How did it happen?"

"I rode the big toad and crushed him into a pulp. It was pretty awesome. You should've seen it."

Edghar stroked his beard. "That's good. That's really good."

"Oh, and I also left one of the soldiers guarding him alive so he could spread the word," Varcade grinned. "Plus, I also killed one of the Bone Lord's hired Dusters and found Marduk, who was on your list. Not too bad, right?" After a brief pause he added, "So, what have you and Baaq been up to?"

Edghar swallowed then cleared his throat, scratching the back of his head. "Well . . . we got Baaq's rifle back."

Silence.

"That's all?" Dog Man said. "Are you serious?"

"Hey, it was easier said than done," Edghar protested. "We were caught in the middle of a riot and had to fight off a bunch of soldiers, and then we had to find this guy called Fish-City and make a deal with him, and then we were in this big battle with another demon gang led by a sleazy bastard known as Fat Pudding." Edghar licked his lips. "We were almost killed. It wasn't exactly easy. And why the hell am I even answering to *you*?"

"Whatever," Dog Man said, looking up at Varcade. "This guy wouldn't stand a chance without us, would he?"

"No, he wouldn't," Varcade said and looked at Edghar with an honest smile. "But that's why we are here."

Edghar exhaled. "You really came through, Varcade. I appreciate it. We might actually have a chance of succeeding."

"What's next then?" Varcade said.

"Let's see," Edghar said, moving aside some empty dishes before placing the list down on the table. "We got our marksman; now with Marduk in the fold we have the muscle. I have one more person in mind. His name is Zuba Ghul, but he's known as the Mad Puppeteer."

"What the hell does that even mean?" Varcade said.

"Who is this man?" Marduk said.

"From what I have heard, he uses corpses kind of like puppets and makes them explode."

"He's a Duster then?" Dog Man said.

"I think he's a Supreme," Edghar said. "The Ghul clan are rumoured to be behind countless assassinations stretching back almost a hundred years."

Marduk snorted. "Pathetic onions looking for ways to become stronger. Without bullshit God Dust we would have crushed your kind a long time ago. Stupid Dust will not help you in the end. Demons will always be stronger. You will see."

Edghar raised an eyebrow at Varcade.

"Hey, don't give me that look. You're the one who wanted him for our little crew. Just ignore it. So, how do we find this Puppeteer?"

"The Ghul clan have always carefully operated from the shadows and made it close to impossible to locate them," Edghar said, leaning forward, "But I do have a strong lead that my instincts tell me is right. It was brought to my attention that a certain gravedigger has been acting suspiciously, and that some corpses under his care has frequently gone 'missing' over the years."

"A gravedigger, eh?" Varcade said. "That would make sense. A person like that could move around burial grounds freely whenever they wanted without anyone really questioning them."

Edghar nodded. "Precisely. My instincts tell me this will be the way to the Ghuls. Let me talk with Baaq and then we'll leave."

Varcade yawned. "Perfect. I'll sneak in a nap then."

"Hey, Baaq, I brought you a plate," Edghar said as he stepped out the doors and laid eyes on the marksman. "Here. You need to eat."

Baaq sighed, but nonetheless accepted the plate and a fork. "Thank you."

"What happened in there?"

"Do you know who is in there with you?"

Edghar nodded. "I do."

Baaq gave him a look like she'd been expecting a different answer. "Then you should know it's because of demons like him that my kind will always be at odds with humans. Marduk is not looking for a way to co-exist; he dreams of a world where demons rule and mankind is either dead or enslaved."

"Let him dream all he wants," Edghar said. "That will never happen."

"You don't know that. More and more of my kind are siding with him; especially the younger ones who never experienced the war."

"How come he ended up like that then?" Edghar said. "I wouldn't be too surprised to hear my people played some part in it. Since meeting you, I've started to see the bigger picture, and it's not pretty."

"You are not wrong," Baaq said, putting her plate down. "Marduk was separated from his parents and placed in one of the demon camps when he was still a youngling. This was during the First Contact War, before there were even talks about finding a way for us to live side by side. You know about them, right?"

Edghar exhaled. "Unfortunately, I do. The camps didn't exist for long, but I have heard about the horrors that took place in them."

"Marduk is not wrong for harbouring hate in his heart, but his quest for vengeance could lead to another war. I don't want to see that happen. I agreed to help you because I want a better future for all of us."

"I know," Edghar said. "I am prepared to work with some dangerous people to accomplish what I've set out to do; people whose values I didn't share. Listen, everything we are doing is *wrong*, in a sense. I'm well aware about that, believe me. But the alternative is even worse. I can't just stand by and watch Akrab be destroyed; and trust me, that is what will happen. If we succeed in removing the Bone Lord from her seat of power, then we could maybe turn things around before it all goes to hell."

"I want to believe you."

"Then trust me. Even someone like Marduk could change his ways, but he needs a reason to dream of a less gruesome tomorrow. He needs hope."

Baaq gave him a long thoughtful look. "You really believe that, don't you?"

"Of course," Edghar said. "I wouldn't be doing all of this madness if I didn't."

"I'm not ready to believe in the cause as strongly as you, but the Bone Lord must be stopped. About that, I agree. I owe it to my people who are being slaughtered due to her actions."

"All we can do is try. Give Marduk a chance. Maybe you could talk to him and give him another way of thinking? One that does not end with the extermination of all humans?" Edghar smiled, trying to ease the conversation.

"Perhaps."

He nodded. "Good. Small victories, and all that. Let's go get the others. We need to find the last individual for our crew."

CHAPTER TWENTY

Edghar's suspicions about a shady gravedigger providing the Mad Puppeteer with corpses had proven true, and it hadn't been much of a challenge to break the creep and force him to lead them to the Ghul clan's mansion.

After cleaning up a bit, the crew boarded an armoured caravan–forcing the gravedigger to come with them–that took them far beyond Akrab's gates and into the heart of the vast desert surrounding the city. The ride had taken them hours. It hadn't been a sunny day to begin with, but now an army of dark clouds had seized the heavens with a menacing presence.

"Would you two stop pouting?" Edghar said, directing his annoyance at Varcade and Marduk. "There was no way we could bring that toad with us. Deal with it." The sellsword and the demon shared a glance between them and muttered something inaudible to each other. "What' that?"

"We just said that it's clear you have something against amphibians," Varcade said. "You hate them."

"What?" Edghar said aghast. "Absolutely not. The beast *physi-*

cally wouldn't fit in the caravan. I have *nothing*, I repeat, *nothing* against toads and frogs and whathaveyou. Don't just make up things like that."

The gravedigger cleared his throat, drawing everyone's attention to him. "Since we're here now, can I leave?" the young man pleaded. "Please, before they see me. I did everything you asked, didn't I?"

"You shut up," Marduk said, grabbing the gravedigger roughly by his neck and dragging him out of the vehicle. "This is where we find puppet man?"

"Not *puppet man*," Varcade said, climbing out after them. "Puppeteer."

"Same thing," Marduk said indifferently. "Puppets potato."

"What?"

"Human expression. When something is same," Marduk said matter-of-factly.

"That's not how you say it," Baaq said, rolling her eyes. "It's potayto, potahto."

Marduk turned and looked at the other demon for a brief moment then suddenly head-butted the gravedigger in the back of his head.

"Ow, why did you hit me for?"

"I get angry and I hurt you. That is rule now."

The gravedigger's eyes widened with panic. "What? That doesn't make any sense! I didn't say anything!"

Marduk hit him again.

"Varcade, can you please tell your friend to stop hurting the boy?" Edghar said over his shoulder as he was busy inspecting the large mansion before them.

Varcade shrugged. "I don't care if Marduk hurts him. He has an ugly haircut. He kinda deserves it, to be honest."

"What's wrong with my hair?" The gravedigger said.

"Looks like helmet, not hair," Marduk said, twisting the boy around to get a better look. "Helmet Head. That is your name now."

"Agreed," Varcade added.

"I don't like it . . ." Helmet Head muttered.

Edghar spun around. "Can we *please* focus on the task at hand?"

"Sure thing," Varcade said and walked up next to him, resting his knuckles on his waist. "Definitely has a 'corpsy' vibe to it, wouldn't you say?"

"If someone did weird things with corpses and magic, I'd definitely think of a creepy ol' place like this," Dog Man said, his head peering out between Varcade's legs.

"This is where I bring the corpses," Helmet Head said. "I promise. Can I please leave now? I really don't wanna meet *her*."

"Her?" Edghar said, looking back at the gravedigger.

"Zuba's mother. She's scary."

Varcade frowned. "Wait, the Puppeteer lives here with his mother?"

"Yes, yes. Now can I go?"

"Huh," Edghar said, ignoring Helmet Head's wish for freedom.

"Are we just going to stand around or actually find the man?" Baaq said, crossing her arms.

"Screw it," Varcade said and strolled up the short stairs leading to the magnificent double doors of the large mansion. Before he had a chance to knock, the doors swung open.

An older woman, perhaps in her fifties, stepped out and snapped the door shut behind her. She had long grey hair tied into two long braids that hung down her chest and wore a black raven-feathered cloak draped around her shoulders. "Who are you? What brings you here?" She spoke with authority, her milky lifeless eyes boring into Varcade's.

"Ehh, can Zuba come play?" Varcade said, awkwardly spreading his arms.

"There's no Zuba here!" the woman hissed. "Never heard the name. Now, leave or you'll regret it."

Varcade looked over his shoulder and noticed the rest of the crew had all moved several steps back away from him and the scary older woman. "Hey, what the hell? Don't leave me up here alone!"

The woman brushed past Varcade and down the steps, her eyes studying them one by one until her gaze landed on the gravedigger. "Jasper," she hissed. "You dare cross the Ghul clan and bring outsiders to my doorstep? Your vow means this little, eh?"

"No, please, I'm sorry, Lady Qanah! They forced me to tell them, I didn't have a choice!"

The older woman scoffed. "Silly boy, of course you had a choice. You simply made the wrong one. Now there will be consequences."

"Hey, what's happening out there?" a nasally voice whispered behind Varcade. He was still on the patio and noticed the door was slightly ajar, glimpsing someone on the other side of it. "Is Mother upset?"

"What? Yeah, I guess," Varcade shrugged. "You're Zuba then? Why are you hiding?"

Varcade heard the man lick his lips before replying. "Mother says I'm not supposed to leave the house without her permission."

"Eh, how old are you exactly?"

"Thirty-two."

"That's weird. You should–"

"Idiot!" Lady Qanah shouted as she noticed Varcade speaking with her son. "Go back inside!"

The door slammed shut instantly, leaving Varcade in a strange position as the elderly woman stormed up to him. "How *dare* you?"

"Look, lady, I didn't do nothin'. He opened the door and spoke to me. What's the big deal?"

"She'll kill him," Helmet Head said, tugging at Edghar's arm. "Don't underestimate her."

Edghar swore under his breath and walked to the bottom of the stairs. "Excuse me, Lady Qanah, is it? If you would just give me a moment to explain the situation, I'm sure you'll come to understand we got off on the wrong foot."

The elderly woman looked from Varcade to Edghar, her stern

expression regarding them with an air of clear disdain. After several heartbeats she finally said, "You better hope that's the case, since you already know too much about us at this point."

"This woman threatens us?" Marduk said, stepping forward. "I will rip out her tongue and kiss it gently."

Baaq rubbed her temples. "You can't just translate *our* demon sayings and expect them to work in the human language . . . What you just said makes no sense."

Marduk seemed to consider this for a heartbeat but then said, "I don't care. I will kill this woman now."

"You'll do no such thing, damn it," Baaq said, holding out her arm. "We're not here for a fight."

Marduk gave the other demon a look of disgust. "You are afraid of this old onion?"

"It's not about that, you bloody hothead. And this one's stronger than she looks."

"You are pathetic. Living together with onion-people make you weak. What happened to war hero I hear stories about all my life?" Marduk said. "Where she go?"

"She grew up and got wiser," Baaq said. "Now back off."

Marduk grunted but nonetheless seemed to accept the situation.

In the brief time since arriving outside the mansion, the weather had taken a turn for the worse with howling winds whipping their faces and a pitter patter of rain descending on the group. The clouds rumbled and flashes of lightning lit the dark sky.

"Bah, come on in then," Lady Qanah said, looking up with a disgruntled face at the nasty weather. "My old bones will freeze if we keep standing here." She motioned everyone inside. "I'll give you a chance to convince me why we shouldn't add each and every one of you to the Ghul collection."

"What the fuck does that mean?" Dog Man said, looking up at Helmet Head.

"You're about to find out . . ." The gravedigger said with despair written on his face.

THE CREW

The wooden floor creaked and groaned under their feet as the group entered the old house. Edghar wasn't alone in wrinkling his nose at the musty smell hanging heavily in the air. The mansion was massive with tall ceilings but somehow still felt cramped and cluttered. They passed rows and rows of bookshelves with dusty old tomes, and creepy and bizarre-looking statues depicting creatures and beings straight out of someone's twisted nightmares. Human skulls and skeletons replaced more mundane decorations such as plants and the thick drapes were black and embroidered with blood-red threads. Countless lit candles were put up everywhere imaginable, creating long shadows behind the crew as they went deeper into the bowels of the ancient house.

The group was led into the dining hall and seated on sturdy chairs with tall backs and large armrests. Massive, framed portraits of creepy-looking faces decorated the walls all around them. Lady Qanah took a seat at the head of the long table, studying each of the unwelcome guests–prisoners?–now inside her home.

Something about having those milky lifeless eyes focused on him made his skin crawl, and Edghar had to force himself to not look away. He needed to take command of the situation and show the matriarch he wasn't a pushover.

"Nice place you have here," Varcade said, drumming his fingers on the table as he looked around. "Not creepy at all. Who wouldn't want a bunch of stuffed humans lined up in the same room where they eat? Perfectly normal."

"Those are our ghoul servants, you fool," Lady Qanah said. "Behir, bring out some tea and sweets for our guests." She turned her attention back to Edghar. "We might still kill you, but until then you are still guests in our home and will be treated as such."

"As you wish, Mistress," the ghoul called Behir said with a formal voice as he casually stepped out from the line and left the room.

Varcade's eyes widened at the sight, his mouth open. "Okay, I take it back, that's cool! Can I buy one?"

"Shut up, Varcade," Edghar hissed between clenched teeth.

Lady Qanah snorted. "Of course, it is *cool* as you so eloquently put it; and no: they are not for sale, silly man."

Varcade swallowed, but his eyes still glittered with excitement as he kept staring at the animated corpses. Edghar cleared his throat, knowing he had to intervene quickly before the crazy sellsword would have a chance to derail the conversation with his usual stupidity.

"Lady Qanah," Edghar said, loud and clear. "We have come here seeking your help, or rather, your son's help, since I will admit I did not know of your existence until just now."

"Jasper failed to mention that, did he?" the woman said, her head snapping in the gravedigger's direction. Helmet Head shrank down in his chair, his eyes locked to the floor. "I'm surprised," she continued, "since he doesn't seem to have a problem blabbing his mouth these days."

"In Helmet–Jasper's defence," Edghar said, sitting straighter, "he didn't have much of a choice. I'm not proud of it, but we made it clear he either cooperated or we would cause him harm."

Lady Qanah chuckled. "Again, you bring up the term *choice*. The Ghul clan has been working with the Jespersons for close to a century. And not once before has anyone from that family betrayed our business relationship. Until now."

"Your name's Jasper Jesperson? Seriously?" Dog Man whispered to the gravedigger. "You never stood a chance in life, did you?"

"No . . ." Helmet Head said under his breath. "No, I didn't . . ."

"Tell them what happened to your father, boy, and his father before that?" The matriarch said. "Go on."

Helmet Head sighed. "They died protecting our arrangement and the vow."

"That's right," Lady Qanah said. "They had a choice, didn't they?

And they honoured our agreement. Unlike you. They would be ashamed of the spineless man you grew up to be."

Helmet Head clenched his fists, arms shaking then exploded up from his seat. "You know what? To hell with them! I never asked to be part of this sick arrangement to begin with! You think this is the life I wanted?" He hesitated, but then added, "Honestly, I'm kind of glad it came to this. Just kill me now or make me one of your freak puppets. I don't care anymore."

An intense silence spread across the room. No one had been prepared for the mild-mannered gravedigger to lash out like that. The silence was broken by the sudden sound of clapping, and Edghar wasn't the slightest bit surprised to find Varcade as its source. Everyone stared at the sellsword.

"What?" Varcade said. "If that doesn't deserve an applause, then I don't know what does. Good for you, Helmet Head. Fight the power!" He said, raising a fist in the gravedigger's direction. Helmet Head offered a weak and unsure smile in response.

"Tea and cookies," said the ghoul servant as he returned to the dining hall carrying a large silver tray, oblivious of the tension in the room.

"I stand corrected, it seems," Lady Qanah said, taking a sip from her tea. "You're not as spineless as I believed, Jasper. Now sit down again and have a cookie."

The gravedigger looked around for a moment like he was weighing his options, but what little fight he had in him escaped with a sigh and he sank down in his chair again.

"What is this bullshit *cookie*?" Marduk said, inspecting the treat close to his face.

"It's sweet. Just eat it," Baaq said to the other demon.

"No. Fuck you." Marduk clenched his fist and obliterated the cookie into countless crumbs seeping through his fingers.

Baaq sighed and rolled her eyes.

"As I was saying, we've come to acquire your services," Edghar said. "If that's not possible we're wasting our time."

Lady Qanah snapped off a piece from her cookie. "Don't think for a moment you're the one in charge here, foolish man."

Edghar pushed aside the irritation rising within him. "Fine. How do you want to do this, then?"

"Mother, can I have a cookie?"

Everyone turned to the new person who'd spoken.

Standing awkwardly just outside the entrance of the room–like a whipped dog fearing an invisible line they'd been told not to cross– was a lanky man wearing a turban, dressed in purple cloth wrapped around his body. He licked his thin lips awaiting a reply, his spindly hands twitching.

"Damn you, Zuba, you're not supposed to show yourself," Lady Qanah said, rubbing the bridge of her nose. "How many times have I told you this?"

"But I want a cookie and I'm bored. We never have guests."

Edghar couldn't help but grimace when he heard the man speak. *What an annoying voice...*

"Come have your damn cookie," Lady Qanah snapped.

The twisted smile that appeared on Zuba's face was disturbing, but even more disturbing were his leering, snake-like eyes. A reaction like that, to having been granted a cookie, was alarming.

"What are you all talking about?" Zuba said, pulling out an empty chair that scraped on the floor without a hint of grace. The man's whole demeanour had now changed after being invited to the table, instilling him with an air of superiority and obnoxious confidence. "Ah, Jasper's here."

"Hey, Zuba," Helmet Head muttered, nibbling at his sweet.

Zuba's eyes landed on Dog Man. "Excuse me, but what is a *dog* doing at our table, Mother?"

"I'm not a dog," Dog Man said.

The Puppeteer looked confused, but Lady Qanah interrupted any further inquiries about the talking canine. "These men have come here wishing to acquire your services, son. We were just about to go into the details."

Zuba grinned. "Well, do tell, do tell," he said, licking the crumbs from one of his fingers. "What can the great Zuba do for you?"

"Don't be obnoxious, Zuba," Lady Qanah said, rolling her eyes. "Shut up and let me handle this."

Zuba dropped his cookie and crossed his arms in protest. Edghar and Varcade shared a look, but said nothing.

"Now, tell us why you are here. Get on with it." Lady Qanah was clearly even more agitated now with the presence of her son at the table.

Before Edghar could reply, Varcade spoke. "We're gonna kill the Bone Lord of Akrab."

If the Ghul clan hadn't been notorious criminals themselves, Edghar would have worried about how easily they were sharing their plan.

"Oh, is that so?" Lady Qanah said, stapling her gnarly fingers together and leaning forward. "You believe the lot of you has what it takes to do it?"

"I do, and we won't fail," Edghar said. "But we could still need your help." He was momentarily distracted by the excitement on Zuba's face at the mention of Clea.

Lady Qanah turned her attention to Zuba. "Since you've already shown yourself, this is your chance to speak up. What do you say?"

The Puppeteer smiled as he got up from his chair and walked around the table until he positioned himself behind Edghar. Edghar suddenly felt the man beginning to rub his shoulders. "Hey, what the–"

"Shh, relax," Zuba whispered in Edghar's ear. "Let it happen."

Edghar jerked violently and shot up from his chair. "What the hell is wrong with you?"

Zuba held his hands up, laughing, the sound eerily similar to the rattle of a snake. "Calm down, we're just talking. Why so tense?"

Lady Qanah sighed. "Zuba, can you stop being a creep and just say what's on your mind?"

"Well, excuse me for trying to create a nice atmosphere," the

Puppeteer said. "Throw me in the dungeons and throw away the keys while you're at it."

As Zuba passed Marduk, the demon spoke up. "You touch me I will smash your face."

The Puppeteer stepped farther away from Marduk, shaking his head as he returned to his seat. "Such a feisty bunch . . ."

"You know what," Edghar said, "forget about this. It was a mistake coming here. We'll have to do on our own. Thanks for the–"

"Wait," Zuba said. "I'll do it. But I have one condition."

"And what's that?"

"I want the Bone Lord for my collection."

Edghar grimaced. "If that means turning her into one of your puppets, forget it."

Zuba crossed his arms, looking the other way. "Then I won't help you. Goodbye."

Edghar forced down the urge to punch the freak in the face, and instead said between clenched teeth, "You can have the Vizier. How about that?"

"Why does this bullshit matter?" Marduk said. "She will be dead. Give him woman."

"Defiling her like that . . . No. It will not happen."

"Why do you even care?" Varcade said. "Our goal is to kill her, you know?"

"I know," Edghar hissed, "but that doesn't mean I want to see her treated badly."

"Are you having second thoughts or what is this?" Varcade said, studying Edghar's eyes.

"No, dammit. I just don't want her turned into a freaking animated corpse. Is that so hard to understand?"

"Stupid onion head," Marduk added with a shrug.

"*Mother!* Tell him I want the Bone Lord!" Zuba said, running up and yanking at Lady Qanah's sleeve.

"I believe you've made that clear, son, but it seems he won't budge on that matter."

THE CREW

"But the Vizier sucks . . ." Zuba pouted. "He's *not* even really royalty."

"Why is it so important to you?" Varcade said.

The Mad Puppeteer dashed to the sellsword. "I want to create the most exquisite puppet collection the world has ever seen! Adding the Bone Lord of Akrab would be such a wonderful thing, wouldn't it?" Zuba attempted to look like a sad puppy but utterly failed because of his freakish snake-like features. "Convince your friend to say yes, please?"

Varcade grimaced. "Ehh, that's not up to me, and he's made it clear it won't happen. Just take the Vizier."

"It's not the same . . ." Zuba said under his breath, pouting as he sat in his chair. "Not the same at all . . ."

Edghar rubbed his temples. *I can't believe I'm even having this conversation . . .* "I've had enough of this. You won't get her, so either accept that and take someone else for your collection or we're done here. That is final."

"Okay I guess," Zuba said. "I'll take the stinky Vizier . . ."

"Then it is settled," Lady Qanah said. "We're onboard."

"*We?*" Edghar said.

"You think I'd let my son go on his own?" She shook her head. "I'm his protector."

"Protector?"

"We are of the Old Blood, and Zuba is the last living male of the Ghul clan, making his life sacred. It is my duty, both as a mother and a protector, to guard him and the future of our clan. Where he goes, I go."

"The future of your clan?" Varcade said, slightly tilting his head.

"An offspring," Zuba muttered, a look of disgust on his face. "Is there a more foul act in existence than that of mating with another human? All the human juices mixing . . . The thought of it alone makes me sick to my stomach."

"Your life literally revolves around corpses, but the idea of sex gives you the creeps?" Varcade said with a *really?* look.

"That's different!" Zuba snapped.

"Weirdo," Dog Man said, clearing his throat to masquerade his statement.

"Alright, whatever," Edghar said with a sigh. He turned his attention back to the crone. "If you need to come too, then so be it. I'm used to things like this at this point."

Varcade smirked and wiggled his eyebrows at him.

Lady Qanah nodded. "Very well. Tell me your plan. Preparation is key."

Dog Man suddenly started growling, his head snapping in the direction of the front door. His small paws slid on the floor and down the corridor as he rushed towards the door, barking furiously.

"That's new," Varcade said, then ran after and caught up to Dog Man. "Hey, what's your problem?" Dog Man kept barking, relentlessly scratching at the door. "Is someone out there?" Varcade carefully opened the door, leaning his head out, pushing his leg against Dog Man to keep him from rushing out.

"You better keep that *thing* away from me, or you'll be hearing from my employer."

Varcade's eyes widened at the sight before him. The man-sized creature hovered above the ground, its body the shape of a balloon wrapped in layer after layer of different coloured cloth. A shawl covered its face, leaving only a small slit which revealed a set of glowing white eyes. It reached for one of the rolled papers sticking up from its backpack, holding it out to Varcade.

"Well, what're you waiting for? Grab your paper and pay up. I ain't got all day."

"I have no idea what's happening right now," Varcade said, scratching the back of his head. He looked over his shoulder and said, "Hey, Lady Qanah, I guess someone's here to see you or somethin'? And will you shut up," he said to Dog Man who was still struggling to get past him. "For someone claiming *not* to be a dog, you sure as hell act like one!"

The creature at the doorstep sighed. "Not only do I have to make it all the way out here once a week—easily the worst route one can get stuck with, mind you—but now I have to deal with this crap as well."

Varcade couldn't help himself. "What the hell are you?"

The creature's white glowing eyes turned to bright red in a split-second. "Oh, that's funny. You're a jester, are you? Ha-ha. What an asshole."

Lady Qanah appeared in the doorway, elbowing her way past Varcade and kicking Dog Man at the same time, making him scamper away. "That's just perfect. You made the jinn upset," she sighed.

"I'm confused, man," Varcade said.

"The shit I have to put up with," the jinn muttered.

"He's a news jinn, you fool," Lady Qanah snapped at Varcade, before turning her attention to the hovering being. "Please forgive this man, he was most likely dropped as a baby." She accepted the rolled newspaper and paid the jinn. "There's a little extra there for the troubles we have caused you. Your boss doesn't need to hear about this, right? I need to keep getting my news delivered."

"Oh, lucky me, an extra two coppers. Look at me, Ma, I'm rich, we made it!" the jinn said with a snort-chuckle.

Lady Qanah rolled her eyes. "Fine. Here." She added a couple of coins. "I trust it is settled then?"

"Yeah, whatever," the jinn said, before vanishing in a puff of smoke that left a spicy scent behind.

Lady Qanah slammed the door shut, giving Varcade an angry glare. "How is it even possible you don't know what a news jinn is? How do people get their news where you're from?"

Varcade shrugged. "Lady, I don't know. I don't pay attention to boring stuff like that."

"You're an utter buffoon, that's what you are," she said and rolled out the paper. Her head moved up and down and side-to-side as she glanced over the articles. "Oh, would you look at this," Lady Qanah said with a smile.

They returned to the dining room and Lady Qanah splayed out

the paper on the table. "A royal banquet," she said. "In three days' time. Now, isn't that an interesting coincidence."

"Not a coincidence," Edghar said. "Doing this at the banquet has been the plan all along."

"It has?" Baaq said. "This is the first I hear of it."

"Yeah, you've never mentioned that before," Varcade said.

"That's because you have the attention span of a fly," Edghar said.

But in fact, the banquet had not been the plan along—this was the first time Edghar was hearing of it as well. But there was no reason for them to know that. His mind was his greatest weapon, and a plan was already shaping up in his head.

"It's certainly a splendid opportunity," Lady Qanah said. "But I can already tell you countless things that makes the plan extremely—"

"Did I say I was finished?" Edghar interrupted, staring at Lady Qanah.

Lady Qanah smiled. "You did not. Please continue."

Edghar stood and leaned forward, hands resting on the table. His mind was racing. This was it. Everyone on his list had been gathered and it was finally time to set things in motion. The room was silent, expect for the raging storm outside. Howling, fierce winds barraged the building, making the old mansion creak and groan in protest.

"Okay, so this banquet is happening in three days' time. Assembling this crew took longer than I expected, but we still have time to get things in order. The Bone Lord and her people *obviously* know we might attack on this specific occasion and will have ramped up their security. That's fine, because we're going to have a couple of surprises in store they won't be anticipating.

You see, by making it so obvious we're going to attack the banquet, all their security measures will be centred around it. That will leave the rest of Akrab in a compromised state, wouldn't you agree?"

"Much talk," Marduk said. "Shut up and tell us plan."

"Fine," Edghar said, pushing down his annoyance. "Since you

asked, Marduk, let's start with you. You're itching for some bloodshed, aren't you? A chance to get back for how the demons are treated?"

Marduk nodded. "I will drink the blood of our enemies and dance the night away."

Baaq took a sip of her tea and set the cup down. "That's not what you're meaning to say . . . What you want to say is . . ." The marksman sighed. "Whatever, forget it."

"It doesn't matter," Edghar said. "Marduk, on the day of the banquet, I want you to gather your followers and rile up the demon slaves working the fields outside the city walls."

Marduk spat on the floor, drawing a horrified gasp from Zuba. "Those demons are weaklings! They have no will to fight back. They are not warriors."

Edghar nodded. "I'm aware, but you're not going to give them a choice. You will *force* them to fight because you're going to kill the task masters first. When the soldiers discover their bodies, they will attack the slaves, and then it's a matter of survival. Fight or die."

Marduk's smile was wicked. *"Force them,"* he repeated. "I like this."

"Once news reaches the banquet of an on-going uprising in the fields outside the city, they will have no choice but to send some of their forces to deal with it. I wouldn't be surprised if the Army General himself will lead the charge, so keep that in mind, Marduk. Do not underestimate him."

"I will crush him, do not worry," Marduk said, his amber-eyes flashing at the prospect of fighting a worthy opponent.

"Are you serious?" Baaq said, staring at Edghar. "Do you know how many of those slaves might die during your staged uprising?"

"We're talking about ending a regime," Edghar said, looking at each of them. "Did you expect it to happen peacefully? Blood will be shed and innocent people will die. Once we're done, we will have created the foundation for a better tomorrow."

"I guess, but I still don't like it," Baaq said.

Edghar ignored that comment and continued. "That takes us to you, Baaq. You're going to convince Fish-City to rile up the demons in the city and take to the streets. Before you say anything, I'm not telling you to start killing innocent people. The goal is to create yet *another* distraction; chaos is what we're after. I want the biggest riot Akrab has ever seen. Once things are in motion, I want you to position yourself with that rifle of yours and start taking out the incoming soldiers and whoever is leading them. The faster you do it, the less chance innocent people are harmed."

Baaq gave Edghar an icy glare but nonetheless nodded in agreement.

Lady Qanah chuckled. "Clever. This will force another response from the Bone Lord, dividing her forces even further."

"Indeed," Edghar said. "I count on this also drawing out the Bone Lord's Dusters away from the ziggurat, meaning it won't be as well protected. The one thing that I haven't figured out is how to gain entry to the banquet itself."

Lady Qanah scoffed. "That part is simple. I can get us in."

"You can?"

"There are countless powerful people in the city who owe the Ghul clan. There is a certain noble who recently hired us to assassinate his father so he could take his place in the parliament. I will force him to take us as his retainers for the evening. Either that, or his dirty secret comes out."

"Excellent. That takes me to you, Zuba. I need you to get us into the vault carrying all the God Dust. Your explosions should do it."

"Child's play," Zuba said, nonchalantly inspecting his long fingernails.

"Varcade, once the explosions go off, that will be your cue to go wild. Got it? Everyone will be distracted by the sudden commotion."

The sellsword nodded. "Sounds good."

"Remember, the Royal Guard Captain won't leave the Bone Lord's side; that, I can promise. You must go through him to get to

Clea. And Erikz is a master swordsman, so keep that in mind when going against him."

"I'll deal with him," Varcade said and let out a long yawn. "Don't worry."

Lady Qanah rose from her seat. "It's getting late. There's no point in traveling to Akrab during this storm and in the middle of the night. I don't like it, but it would probably be for the best if you all spend the night here."

Zuba's eyes lit up with unhinged excitement. "Sleepover!"

CHAPTER TWENTY-ONE

"What do you think? Do you like it? Isn't it great?"

Varcade shared a discreet look with Helmet Head.

When it had been decided that the crew would spend the night in the Ghul mansion, Zuba immediately singled out Varcade and Helmet Head to share his room. Varcade hadn't been excited about sharing quarters with the creepy puppeteer, and when he'd started to protest , Zuba had gotten the look of someone who'd just lost their puppy. To avoid having the fickle puppeteer possibly throwing a tantrum, Varcade yielded and went along with it.

Zuba had then taken them to his bedroom on the uppermost floor of the mansion and was now showing off his things. The room had the basic furniture one would expect: a rather large bed and a desk, but what one wouldn't expect was the extreme amount of *human* taxidermy. Preserved corpses lined the walls in a variety of positions that really made them look alive. Some stood with their arms behind their backs with their chins tilted up in stoic poses, whilst others had been positioned more dynamically like they were running or throwing a punch.

"It's definitely weird," Varcade said with a wrinkled nose, a slight odour of oil and rotting flesh creeping into his nostrils.

"Sure, sure," Zuba said, nodding eagerly, "but in a great way, right?"

"I'm not sure that *weird* and *great* belong in the same sentence, but you do you. I can see you've put a lot of effort into this."

"I have! I want the largest collection in all the world."

Varcade was willing to bet this was probably the *only* collection of human taxidermy in the world.

Helmet Head had a defeated aura around him and barely said anything, following them with stooping shoulders and dragging his feet.

"Right," Varcade said, rubbing his neck, "but what's the point of all this? Are these the corpses you use when carrying out an assassination or what?"

Zuba frowned in response like he'd been slightly offended. "Absolutely not. These don't ever leave the house. They're for display only. Also: that's not how my powers work. To create exploding corpses, I need freshly dead people. They still retain some of that good lifeforce that I can manipulate."

"Lifeforce?"

Zuba seemed to contemplate Varcade's question for a moment before replying. "Mother says I'm not supposed to really talk about my abilities and all that ... But I can trust you, right?"

Varcade shrugged. "Sure, whatever. I was just curious, but you don't have to—"

"No, no, I'll tell you. That's what friends do, isn't it? Tell each other secrets?" Zuba said, moving unnecessary close to Varcade's face.

"I guess ... Maybe?" Varcade said, moving his head away.

A leering grin appeared on the puppeteer's lips. "Okay, so when someone dies unexpectedly, their corpse retains some of their *being* or lifeforce for a short time. It's like this extremely intense feeling of anger and confusion that their life has suddenly ended. Instead of letting those feelings just dissipate, I grab them and use them as a fuel to bring them back. But that lifeforce is seething and can't be contained for too long before it outright makes them physically explode. So, once I animate a corpse, I have a short window when I need to direct them towards whatever it is I want blown to pieces. And that's pretty much it. Neat, huh?"

"Riiight... That's really messed up, man."

"Ha ha, you're such a joker," Zuba laughed and awkwardly punched Varcade's shoulder.

"What about your ghoul servants?"

"Those don't explode. They just do whatever I tell them to do. Come on, you have to look at this one, it's one of my favourites," Zuba said, motioning Varcade and Helmet Head to follow.

The puppeteer stopped in front of one of the corpses. It was a large and muscular man wearing skin hide boots and a loin cloth to cover his private parts. His arms were held out on either side, two massive axes gripped in his hands. But what really stood out was the face.

Varcade blinked. "Is that a beak?"

The Puppeteer nodded. "It's a duck-man."

So many questions...

"I can see that," Varcade said, "but... Is it *real*?"

Zuba chuckled in his typical rattlesnake-like laugh. "Of course not! There's no such thing as a 'duck-man'. Hah, my best friend is so silly, isn't he?" Zuba said shaking his head and looking out before him like he was addressing an invisible audience.

Best friend?

"He's my own creation," Zuba continued. "I surgically added the beak. And I did a pretty fine job."

"Why?" Helmet Head said, speaking up for the first time since entering the puppeteer's bedroom.

The puppeteer shrugged. "I thought it would be interesting. Don't you like it, Jasper?"

"I guess... I just don't see the point."

Zuba scoffed, crossing his lanky arms. "Well, that's because you aren't an artist like me. You wouldn't understand the creative process."

Helmet Head didn't argue and went over to one of the large windows instead. He looked out like a fairy-tale princess trapped in a tower who longed for their freedom. Rain peppered the glass and the wind shrieked and howled as if it was a crazy person demanding to be let inside.

"Hey, it's getting late," Varcade said. "We should probably try and get some sleep."

"Already?" Zuba said with clear disappointment. "I thought we were going to stay up and hang out? I have more things–"

Helmet Head suddenly gave out a yelp and staggered back.

"What's wrong?" Varcade said.

"I-I saw something outside the window."

"You sure? What was it?" Varcade said as he moved closer to the window.

Lightning flashed and lit the penetrating darkness for a second, revealing a humanoid shape plastered against the glass. Varcade's eyes widened, and he immediately stepped back and reached for the swords strapped to his back.

"You'd think we could've gotten our own rooms in a house this big," Dog Man said.

"You would think a *dog* would sleep on the floor and *not* in the bed," Edghar said, lying on his back and pulling the comforter up to his chin.

"How many times have I told you I'm not a dog?"

Edghar sighed. "If you're not a dog, then you are just a guy, meaning we're two men sharing a bed."

"So? I don't care 'bout that," Dog Man said, resting his face on his paws. "You really are uptight just like Varcade says. You need to loosen up."

Edghar wanted to argue the point but decided it wasn't worth it.

The room was claustrophobically small and cluttered with old things. It was more like a storage area where a bed had been jammed inside even though there was no real space for it. The ceiling was angled in a way that one would bump their head if sitting without care, and there was practically no room between the bed frame and the walls. The only way to get on and off was by either crawling or scooching down to the end.

The storm assaulted the old mansion, and the lone window in the room wasn't properly insulated. Now and then a gust of wind would suddenly reach inside like long, creepy fingers gently caressing one's face.

Edghar shifted from his back to his side, then onto his back again, finding it unable to relax and get comfortable. "Doesn't the bed feel damp? It feels damp; almost wet."

"Maybe, I don't care. What's bothering me is that mouldy smell. It's bloody everywhere. Have these people ever heard of cleaning?"

Edghar blew out a long breath. "We're not going to get any sleep tonight, are we?"

"Probably not . . . Wait." Dog Man suddenly stood up on all four, sniffing the air intensely. "Hey, do you smell that? It smells like . . . *Yeast?*"

"Yeast? What, do you think Lady Qanah decided to bake bread in the middle of the night?"

"How the hell should I know. But I'm telling you I'm picking up a strong odour of yeast. It's everywhere."

Edghar shook his head dismissively. "Fine, but I don't really—"
CRASH.

The sudden sound of glass breaking sent a jolt through Edghar's heart. Dog Man shot him a look with wide eyes. "What was that?"

"Not sure," Edghar swallowed, then added, "But we better check it out."

Even though Edghar had said the words, neither him nor Dog

Man tried to move. Hearing sudden and unexpected noises was the last thing one wanted when being in an old mansion out in the middle of nowhere during a thunderstorm.

"Well, what are you waiting for?" Dog Man said.

"I'm not waiting for anything," Edghar said defensively. "You are the dog; shouldn't you go first?"

"Alright, fine. Just because you're scared."

"I'm not *scared*. It simply makes more sense if you take the lead."

"Whatever," the talking canine said and leapt off the bed.

Baaq waited for Marduk to step inside the room then shut the door. The muscular, stocky demon grunted as he looked around.

"Shrivelled onion lady gives *us* most shitty room. Big surprise."

"I doubt any of the other rooms are any better," Baaq said as she walked past Marduk. She put the oil lantern on the floor and sat on the edge of the bed. "Don't make a big deal out of it. I'm already annoyed I'm forced to share the same space as you."

Marduk ignored her comment.

The room they'd been given for the night was more like an attic. It had no windows and no furniture except for the one lone bed. Stacks of books and other throwaway items were coated in dust and undisturbed cobwebs hung around like no one had stepped a foot inside there for a long time. *Maybe we really did get the worst room?* Baaq pondered.

Marduk crossed his arms and stared at her.

"What is it now?" She said, rubbing her eyes with the heels of her hands. "Or you know what: whatever it is you can just keep it to yourself. I don't care."

"What happened to you? How you become so weak? Bow down to onions like pet. This worst room in house and you *know* this."

Here we go again . . . Whenever Marduk had the opportunity, he would pester her about how disappointed he was that his childhood hero didn't live up to the fantasy he had in his head. "Maybe it is, but I really don't care. I'm not going over this again. It's late and I want to sleep. So shut up."

Marduk snarled, clenching his meaty fists. "Watch your mouth," he said. "*No one* talks to me like that."

Baaq's immediate instinct was to say, 'what will you do about it?', but she knew that would lead into a proper brawl, and even though her honour wouldn't allow her to back down, she was far from sure she could take Marduk on in a fist fight. Instead, a slight sigh escaped her lips, and she rolled her eyes. "Fine, I'm sorry. Will you go to sleep now? You can even take the bed."

Marduk unclenched his fists, his face turning sour like he'd been insulted. "No, you are older. Bed is for you."

"I really don't care. I can sleep on the floor."

"No," Marduk said. "It is final."

The tautness of the other demon's muscles finally seemed to relax a bit as Marduk sat cross-legged on the floor. Baaq took off her brimmed straw hat and lay on the bed, her hands clasped behind her head. The room was silent except for the creaking from the walls as the storm outside kept smashing its invisible fists on the facade of the old mansion.

Baaq couldn't help but discreetly observe Marduk from the corner of her eyes. Sitting on the floor with a natural expression with no one to fight or argue with, he looked almost lost; like he didn't know what to do under quiet ordinary everyday moments. Everything in his life revolved around fighting the injustice done to their demon brethren. That was the fire that fuelled his whole being and he had turned himself into the ultimate warrior for that sole purpose. He had sacrificed anything and everything that resembled a normal life.

Seeing him from that perspective made it a bit easier for Baaq to begin to understand him; even though she wouldn't abide by his murderous methods. But at the same time, Baaq herself had now agreed to stage a city riot for the greater good of Akrab, which begged the question: how different was she really, when compared to him?

Baaq cleared her throat. "Hey, listen. Don't think I don't understand you; because I do."

Marduk looked up at her with a faint smirk. "Heh. Sure. If you say so."

"I mean it," she said. "I can still understand you even if I don't agree with your methods. But in the end, we both want the same thing, don't we?"

"What you talking about? You not warrior anymore. You live in river and catch fish. Silver-head onion tell me this. I don't even know why you come."

"I'm here, aren't I?" Baaq said and sat up, heat in her voice.

Marduk shrugged.

Baaq exhaled. "Listen, I don't know if we'll be able to pull this off, but if we succeed, Edghar really believes we will be able to change Akrab for the better. Maybe I'm a fool, but I want to believe that."

"You believe word of onion?" Marduk grunted. "I think you are fool then."

"Then why are *you* here? Why are you doing this?"

Marduk contemplated the question for a moment before answering. "Together we have better chance of killing Bone Lord. When she is gone, real revolution can begin. All onions will pay for what they have done."

"No, damn it," Baaq snapped. "I won't let you and your followers lead us into another war. That's not the way forward. Can you get that into that thick skull of yours? There is a future when we live side by side as equals. There must be . . . If not, this will all be for nothing."

"Why live side by side? We are *stronger*; we should rule, not them. We can build new empire."

Baaq blew out a long breath. "It's impossible to talk to you. You're so hellbent on bringing about a bloody revolution you won't even *consider* another option."

"Because your option bullshit. It not real; only in your head. Onions do not want us on same level; they want us *under* them."

"We don't know if it's real or not if we don't even try. But I *want* to believe it can be true. I've been through enough wars. This is it for me. Either this works or . . . I don't know."

Marduk rose with a grunt. "You are fool, like I said. Weak fool. I find other room to sleep."

"Fine with me," Baaq said, shaking her head and cursing herself for even trying with the radical demon. "Go and find—"

The moment Marduk opened the door, *something* long and pale wrapped itself around his face and violently yanked him out of the room.

Baaq shot to her feet and pressed the white bracelet around her wrist, activating the needle-like teeth to bite into her flesh and draw blood. The organic accessory transformed into a liquid that spread up and down her arm until it solidified into its rifle-form.

She ran after Marduk ready for a fight but was instead met by nothing but an eerie silence in the dark corridor stretching out before her. "What the . . ." She said under her breath.

With careful and slow steps, Baaq moved down the corridor, the floor now and then groaning under her boots. The candles in the sconces reacted to the wind finding its way inside through various nooks and crannies, making the soft light cast dancing shadows around her. The silence was so prominent it turned into an invisible force pressing on Baaq from every direction.

She suddenly noticed the vague shape of something up ahead. The shape did not move and Baaq raised her rifle-arm straight out, ready to blast whatever it was into oblivion. But as she came closer, she sucked in a deep breath and allowed herself to relax, lowering her weapon.

"Why the hell are you just standing there, Marduk?" she said. "What—"

The words caught in her mouth as it dawned on her she was not speaking to Marduk at all, but rather a hastily put together clay or dough sculpture of him that never would have tricked her if not aided by darkness. Baaq spun around, her weapon raised and her heart beating loudly in her ears. But before she could react, something descended from the ceiling and knocked her out.

Moving through the old mansion was like trying to navigate a maze. But at least Dog Man's heightened senses of smell prevented them from walking in circles. Without the canine, Edghar would have been lost.

"You picking up anything?" Edghar said, moving slowly and on guard. He'd thrown on his clothes and armed himself with his hand bow before leaving their bedroom.

"Just more of that weird yeasty smell," Dog Man said. "It's getting even stronger; like it's everywhere. Not sure how to explain it."

Edghar sniffed the air. If he focused, he could somewhat pick up on the scent Dog Man was describing. "Well, whatever it is, it didn't come from the kitchen, we covered that."

"Wait," Dog Man said and came to a stop. "You hear that?"

If the talking canine was trying to make Edghar feel bad about having less developed senses of smelling and hearing he was succeeding. "*No*," Edghar snapped. "Just assume that I never do and just tell me straight away."

Dog Man shot him an annoyed look over his shoulder. "I don't think I like you very much."

"I don't need you to like me," Edghar said. "Out with it."

"I'm not sure, but I heard something. It came from upstairs."

The two of them kept moving until they reached the staircases leading to the upper floor of the mansion. Edghar had barely taken his first step up when a loud voice spoke from behind them.

"What the hell are you two fools doing, sneaking around in the middle of the night?"

Edghar and Dog Man both spun around in a panic like they'd

been two children caught stealing sweets they'd been told not to touch. Lady Qanah stared at them with her milky-white eyes, her wrinkled mouth taut with displeasure.

"So, you're the ones stomping around and causing a ruckus that's interrupting my sleep?" The crone marched up to them and poked a bony finger in Edghar's chest. "Is that how you repay me for my hospitality?" Edghar had found the old matriarch quite intimidating when they'd been in a well-lit room earlier in the evening but facing her in the darkness was the nightmare-version of the woman. "Well?" Lady Qanah hissed, poking him again, even harder this time, making Edghar take an involuntary step back.

"No, it's not us," he blurted out. "We also heard something. And Dog Man is picking up a weird smell. We're following the scent."

"I smell yeast," Dog Man said, but with a slight hesitation in his voice, like saying it out loud to the old woman somehow now made it sound silly.

"*Yeast*? What the hell is that supposed to mean?"

"We're not sure," Edghar said. "That's why we're looking into it."

"Idiots," Lady Qanah spat. "Come on then. If you're wrong about this, one of you will pay."

The old matriarch brushed past them and ascended the stairs with a spring in her steps that could have rivalled someone in their twenties.

"What does she mean by that?" Dog Man said, looking up at Edghar. "Pay?"

"How the hell should I know?"

"Fine, but you can take the lead with the old crone. I'd rather keep my distance from the Ghul family members."

Edghar and Dog Man caught up to Lady Qanah who had already reached the second floor. Edghar wasn't sure if his mind was playing tricks on him, but not for the first time, it felt as if the layout of the mansion made no sense; like there were too many corridors and doors in all the wrong places. Thankfully, the old matriarch took charge, so

Edghar simply followed. But the woman moved in a brisk pace, and he almost had to jog to keep up.

"You haven't said anything in a while," Edghar said to Dog Man. "No more smells or sounds?"

No answer.

"Hey, I'm talking to—" Edghar said and glanced over his shoulder.

An icy chill ran up his spine at the discovery that Dog Man was nowhere to be found. Edghar came to a sudden halt. "Dog Man? Hello?"

Lady Qanah stopped and turned around. "What it is now?"

"Dog Man! He's gone," Edghar said. "He was right there and now he isn't."

"Don't be silly. I'm sure he's somewhere around here—"

But before either of them could investigate the canine's sudden disappearance, loud and sudden noises from down the corridor reached them, and this time there was no mistaking the sound of battle.

CHAPTER TWENTY-TWO

Varcade watched the window explode inwards as a strange being crashed through. The creature rolled on the floor in a summersault before jumping up to its feet to face them.

"What the hell are you supposed to be?" Varcade said.

The hairless creature stood before him without a shred of clothing and looked to be made entirely from dough, and three dents in its face formed the minimalistic features of eyes and a mouth. The Dough Man said nothing as it held up its chubby arms that suddenly hardened and transformed into pointy things akin to sword blades. The bladed arms took on a darker, golden-brown colour and the previous soft texture was replaced by a crusty layer like a well-baked loaf of bread.

Helmet Head gave off another yelp as two more Dough Men came flying in through other windows. Mimicking the first one, they, too, weaponised their arms. One of them turned its hands into large axe-heads whilst the other one decided a spiked mace was their weapon of choice.

"Get behind me," Varcade said over his shoulder to Zuba and Helmet Head. "I'll deal with these . . . doughy bastards."

The one with blade-arms rushed him, hacking, and slashing at him with a ferocity and speed Varcade had not expected based on how the creature looked. Varcade went on the defence and deflected each strike until he got the opening he needed. With one swift motion, Varcade's sword sliced the Dough Man's head clean off its shoulders and sent it flying across the room.

Varcade was about to turn his attention to the next attacker when he noticed the headless body didn't topple over like he'd expected; but instead remained standing with a dumbfounded look even though there was no face to express that particular feeling. In the next moment, the Dough Man turned and ran after the ball of dough that had been its head moments ago. The creature bent to pick it up and plopped it back on.

Are you serious? They can do that?

The Dough Man with axe-hands acted on Varcade's momentary distraction and charged. This one moved slower and swung at him with heavy and powerful blows meant to kill with one hit. Varcade ducked and evaded the blows until he countered with an attack of his own, crossing both his swords right through the Dough Man's midsection. His blades sliced through the creature like . . . well, dough, cutting it clean in half. But the sense of victory was short-lived. The upper and lower body parts on the floor started moving by their own accord, reaching for each other like long lost lovers. Varcade's eyes widened as the Dough Man put itself together and rose on slightly wobbly legs.

"Behind you!" Helmet Head shouted.

Varcade spun around and barely got his sword up in time to parry the incoming spiked mace aiming for his head. Using its other unweaponised hand, the third Dough Man slipped in a sneaky punch and hit Varcade straight in the face. The doughy–but hardened– punch was delivered with impressive power, and it sent Varcade stumbling back, briefly making him lose his footing.

"Cheap shot, eh?" Varcade said with a challenging smile, wiping off blood from his lip with the back of his hand. He adjusted his stance and said, "Try that again. I dare you."

It was unclear if the Dough Man actually understood him since none of them had uttered a word, but no words were really needed: their intent was quite clear. The Dough Man rushed him again, its spiked mace held high. Varcade dashed forward and used his superior speed to deliver an array of attacks that turned him into a bladed blurred tornado. In a matter of seconds, the Dough Man had been sliced and diced into pieces and scattered in every direction. It was clear to Varcade that cutting them up wasn't enough to kill them, but he counted on it taking longer to reassemble itself with its body parts strewn all over.

The Dough Man–the one who'd been headless but wasn't any longer–had turned its attention to Varcade's companions. Zuba had positioned himself behind Helmet Head and gripped the young boy's shoulders, trying to either use him as a shield or push him out in front of him.

"S-Stop it," Helmet Head pleaded through gritted teeth, fighting to break free from the puppeteer's grip.

"I am too important to die," Zuba screamed. "You're expandable!"

Zuba was apparently stronger–a small feat when it came to the two involved in the physical struggle–and succeeded in shoving the younger man. Helmet Head fell onto his hands and knees and avoided the slicing motion delivered by the Dough Man by sheer luck. The Dough Man paid the boy no further attention as it moved past him, its "eyes" fixed on the puppeteer instead.

Zuba offered the worst defence imaginable. He closed his eyes and feebly held up his hands like that would somehow shield him. The Dough Man stepped forward and raised its bladed arm.

"Stay away from my son!"

Lady Qanah and Edghar stumbled into the room. Three long needle-like objects flew from Lady Qanah's outstretched fingers and sunk deep into the Dough Man's face and chest with a *thud, thud,*

thud. But if that had any effect on the creature it didn't show. The Dough Man slowly turned its head back to Zuba to finish what it had started.

The old crone did not hesitate and dashed forward with her back hunched, her arms hanging low and her long sleeves fluttering in the air. Lady Qanah leapt forward with her leg straight out, delivering a hard kick that made the Dough Man stumble several steps to the side.

Varcade seized the opportunity granted by Lady Qanah's efforts and went for the attack. The Dough Man didn't turn in time before Varcade's blades had cut the creature into chunky pieces. He repeated this with the last standing Dough Man, making quick work of the creature in a similar fashion. But there was no real victory in sight. More Dough Men were already entering the fray. They came in through the windows and a few even came through the doorway like they'd already been inside the mansion.

Helmet Head had been halfway out one window and onto the balcony trying to make his escape from the madness before he suddenly returned inside with panic in his eyes. "There's a man on the balcony! He's creating *them!*" he said.

"One of Clea's Dusters," Edghar said, who had moved into the room and now stood next to Varcade. The spymaster unloaded a couple of bolts into a Dough Man charging them, but it didn't stop the creature from advancing.

Varcade met the incoming Dough Man head-on and sliced its head off in one clean swing. He shot Edghar a look over his shoulder. "Can you handle the Duster? Me and the old crone can deal with these bastards momentarily, but it looks like they'll just keep coming if you don't kill the source."

Edghar clicked a new bolt in place and nodded.

Edghar zig and zagged between the countless Dough Men who had swarmed the room until he reached the window. Climbing onto the balcony was like entering a different world where penetrating darkness ruled, and he was immediately barraged by harsh winds and biting rain that whipped and clawed at his face.

The square-shaped steel balcony ran all the way around the facade of the old mansion and had waist-high railings to prevent any unfortunate incidents. Edghar hadn't been outside for more than a couple moments but was already completely soaked. He brushed away his wet hair plastered to his brow and held up his hand bow. The nasty storm assaulting him made it hard to see, and he blinked frantically to clear his vision. The only light source to combat the darkness was what dimly spilled through the windows.

Edghar had strategically climbed out the one window that would allow him to approach behind the man Helmet Head had spotted. He hoped this would take the Duster off guard. Edghar winced and moved slowly, and the balcony rattled from time to time, making him grip the railing to steady himself.

Edghar reached the corner and pressed himself against the facade to peek around it. The Duster had his back turned to him exactly like Edghar had hoped. He raised his hand bow and took aim. Hopefully, one well-aimed bolt would be enough to kill the Duster. But before he could make his shot, something gripped his neck and slammed him into the wall face-first. His already broken nose cracked against the facade, and the force made him bounce against the wall which made him fall back on his butt. Edghar blinked away tears and rain, shaking his head. A loud noise rang in his ears and it felt like he was floating.

The Dough Man who stepped forward was vastly different from the other ones Edghar had thus far encountered. The creature was tall with broad shoulders and unproportionally short legs. Its skin was dark brown and the pits that were its eyes glowed yellow, cutting through the darkness.

Edghar used his feet to inch away from his attacker and fired two quick bolts that thudded into the chest of the creature. The Dough Man ignored the bolts jutting from its body and stomped toward him. It shot one hand out around Edghar's throat and hoisted him up high in the air. Edghar clenched his teeth, trying with all his might to break the grip, yanking, and tearing with both his hands, but the creature's strength was on another level.

"Wait, my doughy child."

The Duster's voice was thick and slow; like there was too much air and saliva in his mouth. He walked towards Edghar and the Dough Man with relaxed steps, his long black coat fluttering behind him. His dark-blonde hair was slicked back with a prominent receding hairline and his angular face was cleanly shaven. Meaty lips underneath a large nose smiled at Edghar's agony.

Edghar finally managed to squeeze in a couple of his fingers inside the Dough Man's grip which allowed him to suck in a much needed breath. He could see the Duster was kneading two dough balls, one in each hand. A violet substance seeped out from the skin of his palms and mixed into the dough. He tossed both dough balls over his shoulders without even looking, but Edghar could see how the balls transformed into new Dough Men mid-air.

The Duster finally stopped right before him and looked up at Edghar with eyes that carried no emotion.

"You are that traitor, aren't you? Edghar, was it? Tarkus wanted me to send you a message before killing you if I had the chance. He wanted you to know that he's been aware of what you've planning and that he *wants* your silver-haired friend to succeed in the assassination. So, me and my doughy children will spare his life. But you have served your purpose."

"Tarkus?" Edghar croaked.

The Duster smiled. "You really did not know, did you? The bald man is a Duster. He has been using his abilities to play you and the Bone Lord against each other like puppets."

"W-Why . . . the hell . . . would you tell me this?" Edghar struggled to get the words past his mangled throat.

"The Vizier has quite the ego, hasn't he? Not unusual for people in power. He will be glad when I report the look you had on your face when I told you." The Duster looked up at the Dough Man. "Now you can kill him, my great big fat one."

Apparently, the Dough Man had been holding back. The grip on Edghar's throat tightened, forcing him to make undignified guttural sounds as his windpipe was being crushed. A sense of dread washed over him. This was how it felt to die. But he couldn't go like this; especially now that he'd learned Tarkus was behind everything.

I can't die here . . . Do something! Anything!

Edghar reached inside his robe with a trembling arm. His weak fingers clawed at the buckle holding the sphere-shaped bomb in place. The damn thing was stuck. If the Dough Man noticed what he was doing it didn't seem to care.

Got it!

Edghar gripped the explosive and yanked it out. He pressed the button then shoved the sphere right into the creature's chest with as much power as he could muster. His hand holding the bomb sunk deep into the dough and he quickly pulled his arm out.

BOOM!

Edghar was violently thrown to the side from the blast. He crashed onto the balcony lying flat on his back, doughy chunks splattered all over him. He groaned and sat up, rubbing the back of his head, which, he realised, was bleeding. What most likely saved him from blowing himself to pieces was that the Dough Man had been keeping him at arm's length from itself, as well as the denseness of its dough body.

The Duster had not been so lucky.

A sense of accomplishment and relief washed over Edghar as he spotted the dead Duster. He had been caught in the blast. Half of his head and torso blown off.

Unfortunately, the massive Dough Man was still on its feet and turned to look at Edghar.

No . . . Please no.

The creature had a massive hole in its chest and its body looked to be deteriorating at a rapid rate now that the Duster was dead. The soft doughiness was turning liquid, slowly melting away. But even if the creature was dying, it wasn't happening fast enough.

The Dough Man stomped towards him and transformed one of its arms into the biggest blade Edghar had ever seen. He swallowed and forced himself back up. An eerie calm settled into his body. He had no more tricks up his sleeve and there was nowhere to run. This was it.

I will die on my feet, Edghar thought and straightened his back.

Varcade dashed across the room, cutting through Dough Man after Dough Man but it wasn't enough. The doughy bastards just kept coming. Lady Qanah fought impressively, using her hand-to-hand combat skills to fight the creatures invading her home.

Where the hell is Edghar? Varcade thought as he leapt and sliced the head off of one of the creatures. *He should've taken care of that Duster by now?*

He wanted to run outside and help but the old crone wouldn't be able to keep up on her own. Helmet Head had hidden, and the idiot Zuba just ran around the room screaming with his long arms flailing above his head. One of the Dough Men had been chasing the puppeteer non-stop, apparently extremely eager to kill specifically him for unknown reasons.

"My collection!" Zuba shouted. "It's getting ruined!"

The puppeteer's corpse collection had indeed taken quite the hit in the melee. Much of the taxidermy had been destroyed by a variety of sharp blades and other pointy things. The stuffed corpses lay scattered all around the room, making it look like a massacre had taken place.

One of the Dough Men came at Varcade hard. The creature chopped at him ferociously with its blade-arms, forcing Varcade to parry while being on the retreat. He bumped into something that turned out to be Lady Qanah's back. The old woman was being pressed from her side too.

"This isn't working," Varcade said between clenched teeth, allowing himself a glance over his shoulder while deflecting the blades cutting at him.

"*I know,*" Lady Qanah hissed.

From the corner of his eye, Varcade saw the old woman deliver an open-palmed strike into her foe and sent the Dough Man flying. He returned his attention to his attacker and decided enough was enough. Varcade spun around with lightning speed, appearing behind the Dough Man and sliced the creature in half.

"AAAARRRRGHHHH!"

Varcade immediately recognised the voice.

Marduk roared as he stumbled into the room. The stocky demon had what looked like a doughy substance all over him, and he was tearing it away from his face. His eyes were full of murder. A Dough Man made the mistake of getting in Marduk's way which resulted in the demon slamming his fist right through the creature's face. He grabbed hold of another one in close proximity and tore its arms off before proceeding to beat the armless Dough Man with its own severed limbs.

Varcade grinned. "Glad to have you back, big man!" He turned and gave Lady Qanah a look. "You two need to handle this. I'll take care of the Duster."

"Go," the matriarch said as she kicked a Dough Man away from her.

Varcade made his way across the room in a matter of seconds and leapt out the already opened window. His feet clanked on the steel balcony for a split-second before he took off. The rain peppering him was a nuisance, but at least his heightened senses allowed him to see in the dark.

He turned a corner and what he witnessed made him halt for a brief moment. The man who must have been the Duster lay dead before him, his corpse a grotesque mess. Edghar was pressed up against the railing of the balcony and in front of him was a massive Dough Man. The creature's arm had the shape of a giant blade. Edghar turned his body as the blade came chopping down. It sliced the spymaster's left arm cleanly off at the shoulder. Edghar screamed as blood sprayed from the open wound. The Dough Man followed up with a backhanded fist across Edghar's face that sent the man flying over the railing.

Varcade was stunned. Had Edghar just been killed?

The Dough Man slowly turned around. Varcade tried to prepare himself for a fight, and think about Edghar later, but something was clearly wrong with the creature. Its body was dissolving. The dying Dough Man stomped towards him, its weight making the whole balcony rattle and shake like it would come crashing down. But with each stride, the creature deteriorated more and more, and before it even reached him, the Dough Man melted into a puddle carried away by the rain.

CHAPTER TWENTY-THREE

"Look, he's waking up."

Edghar opened his eyes, his vision blurred. He could make out the shapes of the faces looming around him. The room was dark with only a handful lit candles offering light. "W-What happened?" he rasped. He was laying on a slab of rock that'd been turned into a table, its surface cold against his bare skin. He had a booming migraine, and his head was heavily bandaged. "Where am I? And why am I only wearing pants?"

"We're in my laboratory," came Zuba the puppeteer's nasal voice. "In the mansion's basement."

Edghar tried to sit up, but someone—Varcade—placed a hand on his chest and gently kept him down. "Easy there, man," the sellsword said. "You shouldn't get up."

Edghar licked his dry lips, trying to make sense of the situation. His mind was scrambled, and he couldn't string his thoughts or memories together. "What happened? I'm dizzy . . ."

"That's the anaesthesia," came Zuba's voice. "I had to put you under for the surgery."

"What surgery?" Edghar said, feeling a trickle of panic. "What did you do to me?"

Varcade scratched the back of his head, swallowing. "Eh, don't you remember anything? Anything at all?"

Edghar frowned. "I..."

A rapid series of images flashed in his mind: bizarre dough creatures. Fighting. A giant blade passing before his eyes; unable to react in time. And then falling... into darkness.

My arm ... Edghar felt sweat trickling down his brow, his eyes avoiding looking at the left side of his body.

"Oh, for the love of the Red King, stop dragging it out," Lady Qanah said, pushing past the others until she stood next to Edghar. "You lost your arm in the battle. But my dear boy saved your life. He acted quickly and for that you should be thankful. He even gave you a new arm."

"It's not too bad, actually," Varcade said, looking over Lady Qanah's shoulder at Edghar.

Edghar closed his eyes. The moment the sellsword uttered the words, a sickening horror grabbed hold of him. He took a deep breath and forced his gaze upon that which he'd been avoiding.

"Oh, look at that. A baby arm." Edghar made the statement devoid of emotion. "You attached a baby arm to my body. That's neat."

"He's losing it," Dog Man whispered to Helmet Head. "Oh man."

"What? Losing it? Nah, I'm fine. I'm good," Edghar said, the words flooding from his mouth in a high pitched and squeaky tone. "Why shouldn't I be good? I lost my arm and almost died, right? So, to save me, this man here, Zuba, attached a baby's arm to my body. There was no other choice, right? I was surely bleeding profusely, and decisions had to be made on the spot, am I right?"

He sat up, smiling. Why he was smiling, he didn't know. He studied his new arm, nodding. "Oh look. It even has that extra fat when you're really young. That pudgy quality that folks find so cute." An involuntary sound pushed itself out of his mouth. It had been meant to be a chuckle but came out as something else entirely. "Too bad the skin-tone is much lighter than the rest of my body, but who cares, right?"

"Hey, Edghar, you'll be fine, I'm sure—" Varcade began.

"Fine? Of course, I'll be fine, you silly man. It's just an arm, right? A baby arm let's not forget that. Less than half the length of a grown man's arm. Completely useless, for all purposes, but who cares, right? Oh look, I can't even really move it. It just flops around when I try." He pushed his shoulder up and down, the baby arm flapping against his body. "Isn't that sound funny? Flop, flop, flop."

"Why you put little baby arm on him?" Marduk asked. Everyone turned to the demon standing farther back in the room. "You have big cold box here with adult arms," he said, holding up two perfectly looking arms that had belonged to grown people at some point.

"Shut up, man," Dog Man hissed. "*Shut the fuck up.*"

Edghar laughed hysterically. "Now isn't that a great question!" He was still a bit dizzy but jumped down from the table, the soles of his feet slapping on the cold floor. Everyone took a step back away from him. "Hey, don't be scared, I'm good. Who cares? Adult arm, baby arm, what does it matter in the end?"

"You don't seem fine," Baaq the Marksman said. "Rather the opposite."

"What? You couldn't be more wrong," Edghar said, shaking his head. "Just let me—"

He leapt on Zuba, making the man topple over on his back. Edghar sat on top of him, slapping Zuba's face with his new arm. "Baby arm, baby arm," he repeated with each slap. "You like that, you sick bastard?"

Baaq grabbed Edghar roughly from behind and dragged him off the puppeteer. "Calm down," she barked, wrapping her arms around Edghar to keep him still.

Varcade dragged Zuba to his feet. "Can't you fix this?"

Zuba dusted himself off, glaring at Edghar with slitted pupils. "No."

"Why not?"

"He could die from an infection if I operate on him again. Plus, he's ungrateful and rude."

Varcade sighed. "Yikes."

"What're you talking about, Varcade? I'm not even upset," Edghar said, unsuccessfully trying to wrestle himself free from Baaq's grip. "Here, just let me talk with Zuba for a moment. I won't hurt him."

"Maybe I can fix it once he's healed from this surgery," Zuba hissed, still glaring at Edghar. "But it's gonna be weeks before that happens. This will have to do for now."

Lady Qanah strolled up to Edghar. "That's the first and only time you lay your hands on my son, understand? You should kiss his feet for what he's done for you."

Edghar's reply came out as a murmur since Baaq covered his mouth.

"Back off, lady," Varcade said to the old crone. "That's not helping."

Lady Qanah scoffed and went over to her son. "You did good, my boy."

"Can I leave now?" Helmet Head suddenly said, making everyone look at him. "Please?"

"No," everyone said in unison.

Helmet Head's shoulders slumped with an accompanied sigh.

"Once this guy calms down, we need to get back to the city," Baaq said, still covering Edghar's mouth, holding him in place. "We're clearly not safe staying here."

"Yes. Time to kill Bone Lord. I am tired of this bullshit," Marduk growled.

The marksman nodded. "Yeah, we don't have much choice. We need to get everything ready for the banquet or we'll miss our window to take her out."

"So, how do we do this?" Dog Man said.

Varcade noticed everyone was staring at him. "Why're y'all looking at me for? Edghar's the one in charge of this whole thing."

"I wouldn't count on this guy for anything right now," Baaq said, still stopping Edghar from leaping on Zuba.

"Shit." Varcade said.

Varcade exhaled, rubbing the bridge of his nose. "Edghar, can you please say something, man? We *need* you with us."

The group was back upstairs, standing around the large dining room table. The spymaster was there as well, but he wasn't really *there*. With a blank stare, he sat in an old wheelchair that had once belonged to Zuba's father, his face sagging like it was in the process of melting.

After Edghar had calmed down from his primal urge to harm Zuba, he'd entered some kind of catatonic state to the degree where he couldn't or *wouldn't* even stand up on his own. Now and then he would mutter "baby arm" to himself but that was pretty much it.

"Edghar is in shock," Baaq said, crossing her arms. "I saw similar things happen with soldiers back during the war. We need to give him some time to wrap his head around what happened to him. He's not gonna respond to us pestering him, so we need to proceed without him."

"You need to make a decision," Dog Man said, looking at Varcade. "Like it or not, this plan revolves around you being the one to kill the Bone Lord. We're just the support."

Varcade didn't respond.

"You're being dramatic for no reason," Lady Qanah said, pressing her index finger on the splayed-out newspaper on the dining table. "We *know* what the plan is. Edghar laid it all out before his mental collapse, did he not?"

Varcade nodded. "Fine, you're right. The royal banquet. When is it?"

"In two days," Lady Qanah said. "In honour of the Bone Lord of Nuzz, who is coming to Akrab. As I already mentioned, I can get you, me, and Zuba in there."

"But how?" Dog Man said. "You can't just *walk* in there."

"I'm well aware of that, *mutt*," the old crone hissed. "The banquet will be filled with nobles, and not too long ago, one of these nobles paid for the services of the Ghul clan to assassinate a rival of his, the man's own father more specifically. If it wasn't for us, that man would never have reached his position. We'll simply pay him a visit and force him to bring us with him to the banquet as his guests."

"Huh," Varcade said nodding. "Blackmail. That's actually not bad."

"Thank you for stating the obvious," Lady Qanah snorted.

The gravedigger–now caretaker–returned from the kitchen and sat down next to Edghar, and gently shoved a spoon of mushroom stew between the man's lips.

Marduk suddenly roared and shot up, making his chair topple over. "All you do is *talk, talk, talk!* All time bullshit. I can do better on my own."

Varcade shot the demon a lazy look and crossed his arms. "Yeah, and how's that? Exactly what have you accomplished before we met?"

The demon clenched his teeth, his amber coloured eyes promising death and destruction. "You remember what happened last time you fight me? This time I smash you dead."

"Stop talking and get on with it then," Varcade said, grabbing the pommels of his swords. "I'm sick of your attitude."

Baaq rose, slamming both hands on the table. "You both need to shut up! We don't have time for this."

"Mommy!" Zuba startled, reaching for Lady Qanah who gave her son a look of disgust and pushed him off her.

After a moment of intense silence, Varcade finally exhaled. "Fine, fine," he said, holding up his hands. "Baaq's right. We need *each other* for this plan to work. Edgar's current state is a big setback, but we can still pull this off. This isn't the time to fight amongst ourselves."

Marduk snorted but nonetheless sat down again in peace.

"Are you fools done with your outbursts?" Lady Qanah said. "Good, because we don't have much time. We travel back to Akrab together and split up once we reach the city."

Varcade stroked his jaw. "It's important the riots outside and inside the city don't start until *after* the banquet has begun. You got that?"

Baaq and Marduk shared a glance with each other and nodded.

"Lady Qanah," Varcade said. "What about Dog Man? Can we bring him to the banquet?"

"I don't think that's a good idea," she said. "It'll draw unnecessary attention."

"That's okay, boss," Dog Man said, looking at Varcade. "I'll go with Baaq."

"Don't think that's a good idea either," Baaq said. "You're not going to be much help to me up on the rooftops. Better if you help Marduk take out the task masters and get the slave uprising going."

Dog Man nodded. "I guess, but I'm not sure Marduk wants me with–"

"You can come, dog child. We create chaos together."

"*Dog child?* That's—"

"It's settled then," Varcade cut-in before Dog Man had a chance to object his new moniker. "I guess we're doing this. Let's go—"

"Umm . . . hello?"

"God, what is it, Helmet Head?" Varcade sighed with closed eyes, rubbing the bridge of his nose.

"How long am I supposed to stay here?" Helmet Head stuttered, averting his eyes from Varcade's. "I've done everything you asked of me, haven't I?"

"Don't be selfish, boy," Dog Man said. "Someone must care for

Edghar until he recovers. It wouldn't be right leaving the poor man in this state, would it?"

"You can stay here and tend to Edghar," Lady Qanah said with a dismissive hand gesture. "Our ghoul servants will be at your disposal and the pantry is full of food. Make yourself at home."

"Oh, okay, I guess . . ." Helmet Head said.

"Baby arm," Edghar chuckled.

"Yeah, baby arm . . ." Helmet Head sighed, feeding the spymaster another mouthful of stew.

CHAPTER TWENTY-FOUR

They gathered outside the Ghul mansion as one of the undead servants went around the building to bring Lady Qanah's personal armoured caravan.

"Exciting, isn't it?" Zuba said, putting his lanky arm around Varcade's shoulders. "It's been a while since I've had the opportunity to perform my art and add to the collection."

Varcade shifted uncomfortably. "Have you ever heard of personal space? Why are you touching me?"

"Ignore the boy," Lady Qanah said. "He doesn't get out much."

"Ah, here comes Zababa," Zuba said with a smirk–not the least offended by either Varcade's or his mother's comments.

"Eh... What's *that*?" Varcade said, head tilted in study.

"That, my friend, is one of my proudest creations," the puppeteer said, spreading his gangly arms introductory. "A very special kind of ghoul; one of a kind, actually."

The massive ghoul called Zababa gripped the two long iron shafts jutting out from the armoured black painted caravan, seemingly holding it all up by way of brutish strength. The ghoul's skin was blue grey with veins bulging out everywhere on his body and he wore ragged purple trousers. His head was shaped like a potato; uneven and bumpy.

"Why's he smiling like that," Dog Man said, shuffling back a bit as Zababa came closer. "It's creepin' me out."

Zuba shrugged. "He's just a happy kind of guy. Always a big ol' smile on his lips and ready to serve."

Varcade seriously doubted that was the whole truth.

"What did you do to this poor thing?" Baaq said with a frown, looking the muscular ghoul up and down.

"A little bit of that, an' a little bit of this," Zuba said. "I doubt you'd be able to comprehend the inner workings of my craft."

"Master." The ghoul said, his sophisticated accent a stark contrast to his monstrous appearance.

"Zababa." Zuba replied.

"Are we done with all the chitchat?" Lady Qanah said, rubbing her arms beneath her raven-feathered cloak. "Get onboard so we can leave. It's freezing."

The crew climbed onboard the caravan and slid the heavy door shut. Once inside, they sat on the two benches opposite one and another. "The ghoul's gonna drag this big thing all the way back to the city?" Dog Man said.

"Indeed," Lady Qanah said. "Zababa does not get tired."

"That guy not stronger than me," Marduk said out of nowhere, looking out through the slits in the door, trying to catch a glimpse of Zababa's back. "I can smash him."

No one bothered to reply.

The caravan moved in a steady pace for an hour or two, shaking gently with each heavy thump from the ghoul's stomping feet. No one said much. They knew it was time for action from the moment they arrived back in Akrab, and the tension was creeping up on each of them.

Varcade still harboured annoyance he'd been forced to take the reins on the whole thing, but in the end, he had one job, and that was to kill the Bone Lord. That part he was comfortable with. Lady Qanah carried the burden of actually getting them into the banquet, and Baaq and Marduk each had their hands full with their respective riots.

The journey back to the city took a while, and Varcade was moments from falling asleep when the caravan came to a sudden halt. He sighed, rubbing his eyes. "Why'd we stop?"

"Don't know," Lady Qanah said. "Go look."

"Fine," Varcade said and slid the heavy door to the side and stepped out. "Zababa is it? Why did you stop?"

The massive ghoul turned his lumpy head as Varcade approached him. Zababa's smile was as big as ever, looking to be forced in position by invisible needles and strings, while his blood-shot eyes conveyed an eternal panic. The contrast was so freaky Varcade avoided looking directly at him.

"There seems to be a rowdy group of individuals obstructing our path, sir," Zababa said, pointing one sausage-like finger.

Varcade scanned the horizon and spotted the group. "Yup, you're right. Marauders probably." He turned to Zababa "Keep going but stop a safe distance away before we reach them. No need risking them attacking the caravan. I'll take care of it."

"As you wish, fucker," the ghoul said with his gentle voice.

Varcade turned his head with a frown. "Sorry, what was that?"

"Pardon?" Zababa said.

"Did you just call me *fucker*?"

The ghoul shook his head. "Certainly not, sir. I would never utter profanities directed at one of the master's companions."

"But I clearly heard you say it though?"

"Impossible, sir."

Whatever, Varcade thought, shaking his head as he climbed back on the caravan.

"What's going on?" Baaq said. "Trouble?"

"Marauders."

Baaq got up and inspected the hatch on the roof of the caravan then used some force to get it open. "I'll cover you." She pressed the bracelet around her wrist and seconds later her arm had transformed into a rifle. The marksman noticed Varcade staring at her with his jaw open. "Are you going to do that *every time?*"

Varcade nodded foolishly.

A short while later the caravan came to a full stop, once again.

"I trust you will handle this?" Lady Qanah said. "I need not remind you we are pressed on time."

"Yeah, yeah," Varcade said. "You all just sit nice and tight, and I'll be right back. This shouldn't take long."

He climbed out of the caravan and marched past Zababa, stopping a short distance away from the group of marauders obstructing their path. There were three men and two women, all wearing mixed pieces of leather and plate armour and armed with a variety of nasty weapons meant to inflict much bodily pain.

One of the women with unruly brown hair and a pig-like nose stepped forward, a confident smile on her lips. "Oi, oi, traveller," she said, but it could as easily have been oink, oink instead. "You think you're tough o' what in that fancy red coat of yours? And who's that big ugly bastard dragging the caravan? Never seen one like 'im before."

"That would be Zababa the ghoul," Varcade said, "But you don't need to worry about him."

"Oh, but we're supposed to worry about a silvery-haired bastard as yourself, eh?" One of the men said. His whisker of a moustache and wide-set eyes made him look like an ugly catfish. "Who are you? One of 'em foreigners from across the seas, yeah?"

Varcade ran a hand through his hair. "Yup." He let his eyes wander over the group of marauders. "Soo . . . I'm guessing there's a so-called toll to pay before we can pass? Or is this more of a "we're gonna rob and kill you situation"? Just so I am clear on what I'm dealing with."

"Bingo, motherfucker," Pig Nose said.

Varcade frowned. "That doesn't answer my question—"

"It'll cost ya fifty silver coins if you know what's best for you," Catfish said. "Cough it up."

"That's quite steep, wouldn't you say?" Varcade said, cracking his neck.

"Enough with the bloody talk," one of the other marauders cried out.

Varcade could swear the woman who'd spoken looked like a rat. And he wasn't just giving the marauders animal-like attributes for fun, because the remaining two men actually looked like horses with their long faces and big teeth. "I'm sorry, but I gotta ask: do you call yourselves something?" Varcade said. "Like, do you have a name for your little group of marauders?"

"As a matter of fact, we do!" Pig Nose said, puffing up her chest. "If you get to live another day—which you won't—you can spread the word that the Beast Gang controls this slice of the desert."

Varcade nodded. *Yup, there it is.*

"Well, hand over the coin," Catfish said.

Varcade reached behind his back, gripping the two sword handles. "You really don't know how this'll end?"

Rat Face stuck two fingers in her mouth and wolf whistled. "Do you?" she said with a smirk.

Varcade looked left and right but couldn't see anything he needed to worry about. If there was more of them, he would've already spotted them - not exactly much to hide behind in the middle of the desert. "Pretty sure I do," he said and drew his swords. "Let's do this then, you thieving—"

The sand around them exploded in several places all at once. Revealing themselves from their cover, four red-skinned humanoid creatures shot in the air, descending into a half-moon formation behind him. They reminded Varcade of reptiles in appearance, yellow slitted eyes and black sharp talons on their hands and feet.

"Ah, I did not see this coming," Varcade said, turning around and positioning himself with the marauders to his right and the newcomers to his left. "What are these things?"

"We got demons on our side, you bastard," Pig Nose said.

"Huh, that is a new one. A band of marauders partnering with demonkin. So, who approached who in a scenario like this? What type of arrangement do you have in place—"

"Kill him!" Catfish screamed, spit flying from his fat lips. "Do it now!"

A loud noise erupted and a second later a bullet from Baaq's rifle slammed into Catfish with such force it sent the man flying. Everyone except Varcade took a step back, fear written on their faces as they desperately turned their heads left and right. Catfish was on his back a few feet away with a steaming hole the size of a man's fist in his forehead.

The booming sound came again, and this time one of the Horse Men literally flipped around in the air from the impact. He landed awkwardly in a heap of limbs face-down.

"What the fuck's happenin'?" Pig Nose shouted, spinning around in a circle.

"You messed with the wrong group of people, that's what," Varcade said and dashed forward, slashing one of his blades through Pig Nose's armour like it wasn't there.

One of the demons threw itself at him with talons extended, but Varcade swiftly stepped out of reach. The demon landed on its stomach with a loud thud, blowing up a cloud of dust into its own face. It had a dumb look on its face as Varcade drove his sword through its neck.

Rat Face and the other Horse Man both came at him at once from opposite sides, thrusting their spears with bad intentions. Varcade felt both spears cut through his skin as they drove into each side of his stomach. Both marauders stopped, hands gripping their spears tightly, their eyes gleeful with perceived victory.

"Oh no, you got me," Varcade groaned, gripping both wrists of the marauders. "Or did you?"

He forced both spears deeper into his body until they went straight through, then kept pushing them, making the two marauders stab each other. "Hey, would ya look at us? Hanging out shish-kebob style. Isn't this something?" Varcade said.

Rat Face and Horse Man both looked utterly confused as their knees gave out and they sagged to the ground, leaving Varcade standing upright with two spears jutting out from his body.

"Why you not tell me we have fight!" Marduk roared as he came charging. "This not okay."

Marduk spread his thick arms and bull rushed the two enemy demons, bringing them both to the ground, then rained down nasty elbows which turned their faces into pulp.

The last marauder-demon stood frozen between its dead allies. Marduk got up and grabbed it by its throat and gave it a couple of open-handed slaps across the face. The demon held up its hands in surrender. Marduk released his grip, and the marauder-demon ran in what appeared to be a random direction. Why it didn't burrow down back into the earth was a mystery.

Varcade pulled out the spears from his body and dropped the bloody weapons in the sand. The wounds hurt but would heal up in a short time. He strode up to Marduk and slapped his shoulder in a friendly thank-you gesture.

Making their way back to the caravan, Varcade noticed Baaq looking down at Zababa from the roof hatch, seemingly having a heated argument with their driver. The moment she spotted the two of them returning, she spread her arms and said, "The ghoul just called me a 'whore goat!'"

"I did no such thing," Zababa said.

"He would never say something crude like that," Zuba said, head sticking out from the open caravan door. "Don't be silly and make things up."

"Just ignore it," Varcade said to Baaq, giving the massive ghoul a sideway glance. "Something's definitely wrong with that guy."

THE CREW

"We're here," came Lady Qanah's voice as she nudged Varcade awake. "Time to go."

Varcade rubbed his eyes with his knuckles and yawned. "Great."

The others were already outside as Varcade stepped out from the caravan and joined them. Thankfully there had not been any issues passing through the city gates. Either the Ghul name carried some serious clout, or the guards had been too scared to argue with Lady Qanah.

"Thank you, Zababa," Lady Qanah said to the giant ghoul. "Take the caravan and return to the mansion."

"As you wish, Mistress."

"I guess this is it," Varcade said, scratching the back of his head as Zababa and the caravan took off.

Baaq nodded. "Once we get the plan rolling, there's no turning back. We're about to send this city into utter chaos. Are we sure this's the way to go?"

"We have a plan that we will execute," Lady Qanah said. "The time for discussion is over."

"Yes, no more bullshit talking," Marduk agreed.

There was an uncomfortable silence and Varcade sensed everyone waiting for him to say something. He cleared his throat. "So, everyone's clear on what to do then?" All of them nodded in response. "Okay, that's good. Anything else we need to—"

Lady Qanah scoffed loudly. "Hearing you talk is torture. Listen, the banquet is tonight. We have just enough time to get everything in order. Remember that both riots need to start *after* the banquet is well underway. We need the news to reach the dear Bone Lord at the worst timing possible. We want her to panic, and her forces divided."

"How we know when is right time?" Marduk said.

"You'll know when the Bone Lord of Nuzz arrives in the city," Lady Qanah said, eyeing Marduk and Baaq. "Everyone on the streets will be making a fuss about it. It will be impossible to miss."

"We got it," Baaq said. "Anything else? If not, I need to find Fish-

City. We don't have much time and it's going to take a lot to convince him to go along with our plan."

"I know what I must do," Marduk said. "You come with me, dog-child."

"How about you *don't* call me that?" Dog Man said. "Is that too much to ask?"

"Yes."

Dog Man cursed under his breath. "Fine." He turned and looked up at Varcade. "I need my stuff."

"Ah, right." Varcade forgot he'd been carrying the talking canine's God Dust. He took the vial and handed it to Marduk. "Give him a sniff now and then."

Marduk took the vial then suddenly crushed it in his fist.

"What the hell are you doing?" Dog Man barked, running over to the spilled white dust in the sand. He desperately tried to use his paw to remove the tiny glass fragments but quickly realised it was impossible. "Why did you do that, you bastard? I won't survive without it!"

Marduk shrugged. "If you die, you die. Now we go." The stocky demon gripped Dog Man's neck and lifted him up. "We must gather my followers to help attack the Taskmasters."

"Help me, boss-man," Dog Man pleaded, staring at Varcade with panic in his eyes.

"Sorry," Varcade said with an awkward smile. "I'm sure you'll be fine! Good luck!"

Baaq shook her head and exhaled before walking away. Marduk and Dog Man went in the opposite direction.

With all of them gone, Varcade was left alone with the two members of the Ghul clan.

"*Finally,*" Zuba said and wrapped his arm around Varcade' shoulder. "Thought they'd never leave. Now it's just us like it's meant to be."

"What the hell does that mean?" Varcade said and slid out.

"You know, just *us.*"

"No, I don't *know.*"

"Be quiet, son, and stop bothering the man," Lady Qanah snapped.

The puppeteer crossed his arms and gave Lady Qanah a defiant look, but he didn't argue

"Well, stop standing around the both of you," the matriarch said. "We need to pay nobleman Sharif a visit. Come on."

Why did I have to be the one who ended up alone with these two. .
.

CHAPTER TWENTY-FIVE

Nobleman Sharif woke with a smug smirk. An easy thing to do when every day began in the beautiful Shariba estate in the esteemed nobles district in Akrab. *That's right, it's my house. It belongs to me and no one else.*

Not too long ago, the master bedroom had been his father's, but that was in the past since Sharif had had the old goat assassinated. Now he was the head of the Shariba noble family, and everything had played out perfectly exactly like he'd planned it.

He wiggled and stretched against the soft, fine linen covering his bed. The texture felt cool against his skin despite the blistering heat outside. The sun cast his room in a soothing yellowish light, making the space bright and inviting for a new day.

Sharif sat up slowly, scratching the stubble on his cheek. *No, no, that won't do at all.* He would need a clean shave. The Bone Lord's great banquet was in the evening, and he needed to look his best. This would be the first grand occasion since he'd been selected as a senior member of the parliamentary council—a position previously held by his father.

On paper, the Bone Lord held ultimate power in Akrab, but she could not manage all affairs of the great city-state or even defend it would a military conflict arise. She needed the support of the noble class. While the Bone Lord mainly focused on the big picture issues facing Akrab, the nobles had their hands in everything from water supplies to the wheat fields and farms outside the city's walls.

Now that Sharif was head of the family, he had the right to maintain a standing army of slave soldiers. The soldiers primarily served their noble masters, but in a state-wide emergency the Bone Lord could freely call upon these armies to supplement her own troops.

But Sharif was getting ahead of himself. *One thing at a time.* The virtue of patience and strategic planning had been key to having his father assassinated so Sharif could take his place.

"Muneer! Adnan!" Sharif bellowed. "Attend me."

In a perfect world, his servants would magically know the precise moment their master woke and immediately stand ready beside his bed to see to his needs. This shouting business felt improper and below a man of his stature. *I'll have to do something about that.*

Sharif cocked his head, staring at the door and waiting for it to open. Already ten heartbeats had passed and still no sign of his servants. *How dare the lousy dogs make me wait?*

This was not the way Sharif wanted this special day to start. There could be no valid reason why the servants weren't already in his room attending him. He cursed under his breath and stood. *My father was always too gentle with these lazy scoundrels. Seems I'll have to take out the whip so they learn how things will be from now on.*

There was no point in getting dressed since he still needed to bathe and shave. In an undignified manner, Sharif left the room in nothing but his underpants, his bare feet slapping on the stone stairs. He started cursing and shouting before he even reached the spacious room on the lower floor, but the moment he stepped off the stairs, his stream of profanities died in his throat.

Lady Qanah and her son Zuba of the Ghul clan sat on *his* cushions around *his* table, eating *his* fruit and bread. Another strange man–a foreigner based on his ghastly silver hair–lay on the floor, hands clasped behind his head. Sharif's two house servants, Muneer and Adnan, stood next to them like they were waiting to serve them. The moment the two noticed him they looked down in shame.

"What the hell is going on?" Sharif said between clenched teeth. "What are *you* doing here?"

"We figured we would break fast before waking you," Lady Qanah said, not even giving Sharif the courtesy of looking at him when she spoke. "You like to sleep in, Sharif? Life of a senior nobleman treating you well, it seems."

"Hello," Zuba said, waving a spindly hand at Sharif. "Good to see you again."

Sharif couldn't believe his eyes or grasp what was happening. He was part of the parliament! This was unacceptable on every level. "How *dare* you come into *my* house—"

A flying bread bun smacked him right in the face. Sharif was stunned; his eyes blinking, unable to fathom *that* had just happened.

The foreigner smirked at him, bouncing another piece of bread up and down in his hand.

"Don't be childish, Varcade," Lady Qanah said half-heartedly, unable or unwilling to hide a ghost of a smile on her lips.

The man called Varcade shrugged and took a bite from the bread like it was an apple.

"Come sit," Lady Qanah said. "Have something to eat. We need to talk."

Sharif moved to the low-set table, his posture one of defeat. It didn't matter if you were the greatest warrior or the highest of kings, having something thrown in your face mid-sentence was a sure way to take the wind out of any man. He sat cross-legged on the cushion next to the people who had invaded his estate.

He knew how dangerous the Ghul clan was first-hand, and the foreigner had two swords laid out next to him. Now that his initial anger had subsided, Sharif was forced to admit the severity of the situation at hand. His life could very well be in danger, and anger gave away to fear.

"What do you want from me?" Sharif said, his voice that of a different man than the one who'd stormed down the stairs cursing and shouting like a buffoon. "I already paid you, Lady Qanah. Our business is concluded."

The old woman nodded as she took a sip of her tea. "That is in the past. You are correct. But we have new things to attend to. The Bone Lord's grand banquet."

"What about it?" Sharif said, feeling queasy.

"We're gonna be your guests tonight," the foreigner said with his mouth full of bread. "You're bringing us with you."

Sharif's fear was tackled to the side by an immediate instinct of self-preservation. "Are you insane? I can't do that!"

"You *can* and you *will*, dear Sharif," Lady Qanah said, her milk-white eyes staring into his soul. "This is not a request."

"You don't want the other nobles to learn you paid us to assassinate your father, do you?" Zuba said, a sinister smile on his lips. "Politics is a nasty business, sure, but that's crossing a line, even in your dirty world."

Sharif licked his lips, his mouth feeling as dry as the sand and dust outside his home. He didn't regret killing his father; he was weak and close to senile, not fit to be head of the Shariba family any longer. The old man would dose off and drool during parliamentary council meetings for god's sake! He was turning their family into a laughingstock and ruining Sharif's own chances to succeed him. No, he did not regret sending his father to the grave. The only thing he regretted was getting involved with the Ghul clan.

"You're blackmailing me? I paid you a hefty sum of coins and did everything according to our agreement . . ."

"That's correct," Lady Qanah said. "Hence why you have no choice in the matter. You are bringing us with you as your personal retainers for the evening's festivities. You will do everything we ask and will do so with a smile on your face. Understand?"

Sharif rubbed his temples and let out a long sigh. "Can I at least ask why? I don't understand why you'd want to attend the banquet.

Surely there must be more exciting things to do for . . . folks as yourselves."

"We're just gonna kill the Bone Lord and perhaps a few others," Varcade said. "It's not exactly set in stone."

Sharif stared at the foreigner, blinking frantically, and shaking his head. "I'm sorry, could you repeat that?"

"You heard the man," Lady Qanah said. "The Bone Lord of Akrab dies tonight and you're going to be our key to making it happen. Is that clear enough for you, dear?"

"Ah, I see."

Sharif fainted.

A large area around the Western gate of Akrab had been cleared of the general public to allow the Bone Lord of Nuzz and his retainers to enter the city safely.

Clea and her inner circle stood rigidly on a newly built dais as the stream of guests made their way into her city in a long line that stretched farther than she could see. She hid her hands behind her back to conceal the fact they were trembling.

So much was at stake. Clea was well aware how disastrous the timing for this banquet was, but without an iron-clad alliance with the Bone Lord of Nuzz, her role as ruler of Akrab wouldn't last long; that was simply a fact.

The unrest plaguing the city was close to the tipping point. She knew she had a short window to regain control or she'd have a full-blown revolution on her hands. If that happened, it would be the nail in the coffin; the Seven would turn on her without mercy, deeming her unfit to rule and someone else would take her place. The other Bone Lords couldn't allow a weak city-state on Harrah; the combined might of the Seven was all that prevented an invasion from the World Authority, and right now Akrab was the one chink in their united armour.

I can't think about that right now, Clea thought, taking a subtle deep breath. *I need to make sure the big bastard's visit goes without a hitch; there's no room for mistakes here.*

A tall woman separated herself from the long line of people and marched up to the edge of the dais. She wore the typical robes worn by court Viziers, with the exception hers was white and embroidered with violet and gold. The Vizier of Nuzz bowed low before allowing herself to look up and meet Clea's eyes. The woman had straight black hair ending just below the jawline and wore elegant yet excessive kohl mascara; her upper eyelids painted black, and the lower ones painted violet.

"Your Highness," the woman said. "I am Shana, the Royal Court Vizier serving the great city-state of Nuzz. It is my honour and privilege to introduce His Excellency, Bone Lord Farouk."

Amidst the sea of people now through the gates, Clea saw a custom-built palanquin carried high by eight servants (a typical palanquin was carried by two or four at the most). Even from this distance, Clea could see the flood of sweat streaming down the faces of the servants as they struggled to hold the massive thing aloft.

Marching along and surrounding the vehicle in a perfect square formation were Bone Lord Farouk's notorious elite cadre of all female bodyguards known as the Ghosts of Nuzz. They wore loosely fitted white uniforms with plated cuirass and large pauldrons painted black. Expressionless silver metal masks covered their faces and identities.

People moved aside to allow the palanquin to manoeuvre up to the dais where it stopped. The open sides of the vehicle revealed a giant of a man laying comfortably on his side on top of a sea of pillows. The Bone Lord was clad in white and golden silk draped around his gargantuan frame. His eyes had the size of raisins when compared to how big his bald head was, but somehow Farouk still had an intimidating presence.

"Your Highness," Clea said. "It is my great honour to welcome you to the great city-state of Akrab. I hope your travels–"

"Such pleasantries are below us, dear Clea," Farouk said loudly, waving a fat hand decorated with ridiculously sized jewellery on each sausage-like finger. "We are practically family, are we not?" The man's voice had a rasp tone and his speech mumbled together at times since he tended to breathe in and out between words.

Clea forced a smile.

"I loved your father like a brother, may the Golden King rest his soul. I don't want him looking down on his only child and seeing how the great city-state he built with his own blood and sweat is being ruined." Farouk clicked his tongue. "How could you let this happen, child?"

Child? I will stab you in your fat neck— Clea bit her tongue, the jolt of pain pushing her dark thoughts away. Farouk had never been particularly close with either of her parents. That he'd come to help now as some kind of duty was nothing but a blatant lie. But of course, she could say nothing about it and had to play along.

"Even though it hurts my pride, I can do nothing but carry the shame and extend a hand in hopes of getting things back in order. I know my father would have wanted me to ask for your help, dear Farouk."

Farouk motioned for Clea to move closer out of anyone else's earshot. "You've never been a good actress; I'd even say you're terrible," the Bone Lord said, his voice now carrying a menacing tone. "It's better to simply nod than put on a poor performance and embarrass us both. We both know exactly what made me come. Let me handle the theatrics for all the sheep."

Clea was boiling on the inside. Once again, it was clear she'd never been cut out for the world of politics. She carried her heart on her sleeve and her temper was always a looming presence ready to tear down the charade and reveal the ugly truth. Why did she desperately cling to her seat of power when it was such a miserable existence? Was it simply the burden of carrying her parents' legacy? Bound by duty? The introspection swarming her mind could not have come at a worse time. *Focus, damn you,* the voice inside her head spat at her.

She met Farouk's eyes and said nothing but offered a nod.

Farouk smirked in response. "That's better, dear. Now wrap this thing up so we can get to the banquet. Farouk hungers."

Nobleman Sharif blinked his eyes open. His vision was blurry, and it took a moment to gather his wits about him. He was back in his bed upstairs, laying on his side. Someone was shouting down the hall outside his room. Not someone . . . that foreigner . . . Valkad or whatever his stupid name was.

"I see you're awake," a voice whispered, inches away from his ear.

Sharif flew up from the bed like he'd been stung by a hornet. He backed up until he collided with the wall. "Why are you in *my* bed?!"

Zuba lay on his side, head propped up on his elbow. "I wanted to see how you were doing is all. Is that so wrong of me?" he said, one of his fingers gently tracing the soft linen where Sharif's body had been moments ago.

The snake-like features on the man's face and his leering eyes were something out a nightmare. Why was that vile man in his bed?

"What did you do to me?" Sharif stuttered, swallowing a big lump of saliva.

"Me? I did nothing much."

"Much? What do you mean by that? *Much?*"

"Oh, you know, just some cuddles. That's all really. To help soothe you from your earlier episode downstairs."

"Did you . . . *Finger* me?" Sharif wasn't sure why he'd just accused the man of *that* specifically, but somehow Zuba fitted the type of a person who would do such an abhorrent act to an unconscious person. The boy was obviously deranged.

"I did no such thing. I mean, I could if you want but—"

"No! Never you nasty freak!"

Sharif looked around the room in panic. He ran up to the sole glass-less window and peered down. Would he survive the fall? Most likely but not without breaking something. It would be worth it though. Anything to escape the madness of this day.

"Look at you," Zuba said with a chuckle. "All panicky. Relax. You're not going anywhere."

Sharif was grabbed from behind and pulled back in as he was halfway out the window.

"Take your hands off of me!"

"Mother," Zuba called out, his arms tightly wrapped around Sharif's waist. "Some assistance, please. Sharif is being very naughty."

A moment or two later, Lady Qanah marched inside the room, visibly distressed by the look on her face. "Yes, you *will*," she hissed over her shoulder. "Stop arguing!"

"I'm *not* wearing this! You can't force me, you old hag," the foreigner said, following Lady Qanah inside the room. The man was dressed in a long, turquoise gown with a tall cone-hat on his head.

Why is that man wearing my late mother's evening gown and my parliament hat? Sharif was utterly confused by the sight and momentarily forgot about his attempt to escape.

"Well pick something else then, you stupid man-child! What don't you understand about blending in?"

"How is *this* blending in?" the silver-haired man said.

"Please, for the love of all that is sacred, take off my late mother's gown . . . " Sharif sighed, covering his face in his hands. This was all too much. *What have I done to deserve this?*

"I told you it was a dress," Varcade said, crossing his arms. "Just admit you were wrong."

Lady Qanah waved him off dismissively. "Doesn't look like a dress to me." The old matriarch turned her attention to Zuba. "What are you shouting about in here? Don't I have enough on my plate dealing with one lunatic?"

"I'm sorry, Mother," Zuba said. "But our dear nobleman tried to make an escape out the window. But I stopped him. Yes, I did."

"Good." She approached Sharif and grabbed him hard by the cheeks. Her grip was surprisingly strong for an old woman. "Go sit on the bed and don't move a muscle. You hear me?"

"Your son molested me while I was blacked out," Sharif said, his lips smushed together.

Lady Qanah released her grip, her head snapping in Zuba's direction. "Tell me he's lying, Zuba . . . Say it isn't so or I will—"

"I swear I didn't," Zuba said, holding his hands up. "I promise."

Lady Qanah sighed, rubbing the bridge of her nose. "See, he did no such thing. Why would you even make up something like that? You sick, and perverted man."

Sharif's eyes bulged as he caught Zuba winking at the foreigner and the foreigner grimacing in response. Sharif tried to say something, but the old matriarch slapped him hard right across the face.

"I don't want another peep from you. You will speak when asked to speak, otherwise you will keep your mouth shut. I am *this*"–she showed the barely visible space between her thumb and index finger–"close. You understand? *This close.*" She turned to Varcade. "You don't want to wear that? Fine. Pick something else. You can forget about wearing your silly red coat and you need to hide that awful hair of yours. I don't care how you do it, just do it. That goes for you too," she said to Zuba. "Find a suitable disguise. Now. We're only hours away."

CHAPTER TWENTY-SIX

Jasper sat next to the bed in the master bedroom of the Ghul mansion. Steam rose past his face from the mug in his cupped hands. He tried taking a sip from the sweet tea, but it was still too hot.

One of his captors, the man called Edghar, had been asleep for hours, and Jasper had contemplated leaving more than once. *Why am I even still here?* That was the big question plaguing him. Perhaps he simply felt sorry for the man. Having your arm chopped off and then replaced with a baby's arm was a cruel fate for anyone. Also, Edghar had been the one in the group who had been nicest towards him, all things considered. It wouldn't be compassionate to have the man wake up all alone in a deserted mansion full of ghoul servants. Jasper had been raised better than that.

Helmet Head. Does my hair really look that bad? He tried running his fingers through his thick hair. He put his tea to the side and got up to inspect himself in the tall mirror fastened to the wall. After receiving his new moniker, Jasper couldn't un-see it. It truly was shaped like a helmet he was forced to admit with a sigh. *Is this why girls have never liked me?*

"Are you enjoying your stay, sir?"

One of the ghoul servants stood at the doorway, peeking inside with his upper body but his feet remaining in place like they'd been fastened to the floor. He was a thin built man wearing a black jacket and matching pants. A pencil moustache adorned the grey and saggy skin of his face, and only a few wisps of hair sat atop the bald head.

"I'm okay," Jasper said with a smile. "Thank you."

The ghoul butler stepped inside the room; arms clasped behind his back. "Are you certain, sir? Anything we can do for you? Anything at all?"

"Nope, I'm good. But thanks."

In truth, Jasper was feeling a bit peckish, but he'd rather avoid the ghoul servants as much as possible. Their demeanour made his skin crawl.

"Very well, sir. You just let me know if any need arises. We live to serve. Well, we don't live in that sense, but I'm sure you are aware of the saying."

Jasper smiled at the ghoul, but the butler didn't leave. After a moment of awkward silence he said, "Still don't need anything," accompanied by a nervous chuckle.

"What about my *needs*?" the ghoul said slowly, his smile fading, his blank eyes fixed on him.

In a heartbeat, Jasper went from uncomfortable to terrified. "What do you mean?" he said, trying to keep his voice natural.

The ghoul came closer. "I have needs as well. I feel it right here," he said, a white-gloved hand pressed against his stomach. "There is an emptiness inside me. A hollow pit. It hungers."

"I-I'm not sure—"

"Do you know what it's like? To have a primal *need* natural to all living creatures that cannot be sated?"

Jasper backed away from the ghoul, bumping his legs against the small table next to the bed. "No, I can't say I can . . ." A bead of sweat dripped from the tip of his nose down on his upper lip. "Have you . . . I don't know . . . Talked with Zuba about it? Maybe he can help?"

The ghoul butler's mouth had now turned into a snarl as he kept coming closer. His fingers twitched in the air, extended before him like someone overly excited to dig into a succulent meal.

"Boy . . ."

Jasper startled from the sound but felt instant relief as well. "Edghar? I need your help–"

The ghoul's eyes darted to Edghar for a brief second before turning back to Jasper. His face changed back to his usual demeanour as quickly as putting on a mask. "Are you enjoying your stay, sir?"

Jasper blew out a long breath and nodded. "All good. Don't need anything at all. Please go away and stay away. Thank you very much."

"As you wish, sir."

The ghoul butler turned around and left.

What the hell was that?! Jasper wiped away a rivulet of sweat that had formed on his brow.

Edghar grimaced as he forced himself to sit up in bed. "Water . . ." Jasper could see some blood had seeped through the white bandages wrapped around the man's head.

Jasper had already brought a jug with him for when the man woke up. He poured him a mug and handed it over.

"I thank thee," Edghar said after downing the liquid in three loud gulps.

Thee?

"You feeling better? If you do, I think it would be a good idea to get out of here."

"The Golden King willing, I shall live yet another day." The man glanced at his new arm then looked away with disgust. "However, I do require my clothes."

"They were torn to shreds in the battle," Jasper said. "But I found this shirt and some pants. I think they'll fit."

Edghar got up on shaky legs and got himself dressed. The white tunic was too tight, but the dark blue trousers were a good fit. He sat on the edge of the bed. "And my cape?"

Jasper frowned. "Cape? You weren't wearing one?"

THE CREW

"I SHALL HAVE MY CAPE, DAMN YOU."

Jasper shot up from his seat, completely unprepared for the explosive outburst. "Okay, gimme a second. Just calm down." He was positive the man had never worn a cape as long as they'd been together. He needed to think fast. He strode up to the black curtain covering the window and ripped it down. *Will this do?*

Apparently, it did, because Edghar accepted it without complaint. "A hand, boy. I . . . I am not the man I once was."

Jasper fastened the curtain-now-cape around the man's neck with a simple knot.

"Yes, that shall do I believe." Edghar looked around the room. "And my eyepatch? Where is it?"

"Eh, you don't—"

"EYEPATCH, BOY!"

What is even happening right now? Jasper didn't know what to do, so he ripped off a piece of his own trousers and handed it over.

"Yes, yes, that is good," Edghar said. "Help me put it on."

Jasper once again did as he was told. Anything to contain the rage boiling inside the man.

Edghar stood, his chin raised in the air, staring longingly at *nothing*. "Ready the mount, boy. We must ride."

Why has he suddenly changed the way he talks? How bad was that hit to his head?

"Where are we going? I'm not sure you're well enough—"

Edghar groaned loudly, rubbing his temple with his one functioning hand. "The city . . . I have a strong feeling there is *something* I need to remember. Something of vital importance. I cannot recall at this moment, but time is of the essence. Of that, I am positive."

Jasper cleared his throat. "Okay, but we don't have a mount—"

Edghar's eye widened and he stiffened. He suddenly grabbed Jasper by his collar. "Don't you understand, boy? We have been deceived! Played for fools! My dear Clea is not the foul woman I was tricked to believe; nay, it has been the machinations of her Vizier all this time!"

"I-I really don't know what you're talking—"

Edghar's grip tightened, and he brought his face even closer to Jasper's. "We must stop the planned assassination!"

"But we still don't have—"

"MOUNT! NOW!"

"Okay, okay! I'll see what I can find!"

I should have escaped when I had the chance . . .

Edghar looked the gangly creature up and down. "What is this foul beast?"

Luckily for Jasper, he had found a stable behind the mansion. And within the building stood a lonely and strange being.

Jasper scratched the back of his head. "It *was* a camel, I think? But it's dead now. Or was. Now it's *undead*. I'm not sure."

"Will it carry us like the wind?"

"Wait, what do you mean *us*?"

"You shall come with me to rescue my loved one. Are you not my squire?"

"Eh, no?" *And you're not a knight, as far as I know.*

Edghar unwrapped the bandages around his head and tossed them aside. "Do you wish to be? My squire, that is."

"Honestly, I'm not even exactly sure what it means."

"You would continue to serve my needs, as you have done excellently thus far, I must say. Once we regain control of the ziggurat you will have a sleeping quarter close to my own. And when time allows it, I shall teach you the art of combat and turn you into a formidable warrior like myself."

"Are you serious? I would *live* in the ziggurat? No more grave digging?"

"Correct."

"And that includes food and everything?"

"Correct again."

Jasper beamed on the inside. *Finally, the Yellow King blesses me!*

"Okay, I'll do it!"

"Excellent. Now saddle this beast so we can be on our way. We must make haste."

Vashi had lost track of how long he'd been aimlessly wandering around the city. His legs ached and he hadn't eaten in ages. Before his search could continue, he decided he needed some rest and sustenance. The sound from a nearby building caught his attention. There seemed to be a lot of people both inside and outside.

A young woman was leaning up against the wall and eating the leg of a chicken.

"Excuse me," Vashi said and approached the stranger. "If I may ask, did you purchase that piece of meat from in there?"

The woman nodded then tore off a chunky piece from the bone. The chicken had a crispy skin and left a trail of grease at the corner of her mouth. "You've never been to Yuba? Best chicken in Akrab. You need to try it."

The savoury smell reached Vashi's nostrils, and his mouth started to water. "Really? Then I will do exactly that. Thank you," he said with a smile.

As Vashi stepped through the door to Yuba, his mind was bombarded with different impressions activating all his senses. The sensation was so strong it almost felt like a physical blow. The bar was packed with people, carrying a mixture of strong scents that hung in the air, stinging Vashi's nose with each inhale. Everyone was talking loudly, and the floor creaked and squeaked from the amassed weight as people scrambled around the cramped space.

A four-man band in the corner smashed a variety of instruments together in a savage attempt to create music. The resulting tune sounded like a desperate and primal plea for help.

"Move, fuck-face," someone growled, elbowing past Vashi, making him stumble a step.

Calling someone derogatory names is not accepted and must be–

Someone else bumped into Vashi, making him lose his train of thoughts. The person hadn't even bothered to excuse themselves.

Rude behaviour with no regards to the feelings of others is forbidden and–

"What's your poison?" A red-haired woman shouted, appearing inches away from his face.

Vashi took a step back. *Shouting is rarely accepted if not during dire circumstances. I deem this instance does not qualify and must be punished–*

"Hello? I don't have all day," the woman said, glaring at him. "You need to order something."

Vashi was thirsty and hungry, but his own needs did not take precedent over the Teachings. The woman's shouting could not go by unpunished.

Vashi drew back his arm to begin the education, but another person bumped hard into his back, making Vashi lose his balance and crash into the woman who, in turn, fell on her butt. The tray in her hand crashed to the floor, glasses shattering, their liquid contents showering them both. For some obscure reason Vashi couldn't fathom, the patrons in the room started cheering, clapping their hands, and stomping their feet.

"Get off me, you idiot," the woman hissed, scrambling to her feet.

Three offences in a matter of seconds, Vashi thought, feeling a slight pressure in his chest as he got up. *Offences must be ranked in other of severity before correct education is applied.* He swallowed, having a hard time focusing. He closed his eyes and took a deep breath then exhaled. *Guide me, Saints, my body and mind betray me.* The Saints heard his pleas, and a sudden calm washed over him. *Gather yourself.* Once again master of his domain, Vashi swiftly moved between the crowd until he spotted a table underneath the stairway. Two people sat at the table, but one of the stools was unoccupied.

"Hello," Vashi said and nodded at the two figures before planting his rear on the empty stool. *Yes, this is better. Here I can assess the situation at hand before I decide how to–*

"Hey, what're you doin'? You can't sit here." The man who'd spoken had his hood on—*peculiar since we're indoors*, Vashi thought—his face hidden in shadow. "This table's taken."

"But no one is using this seat?" Vashi said.

"So what? We have this table. Get outta here."

Vashi frowned. "You still have the table. I'm only using this empty seat."

The other figure also wore a hood, but it stuck out in odd angles like the person was wearing another piece of headgear underneath. "Are you trying to be funny?" The voice was female but also hollow.

"There is no attempt at humour from me," Vashi said. "A seat was empty and available, so I sat down. Is that not the intended purpose for its construction?"

The first man spoke again. "Okay, I don't know what your deal is, but we don't want company. Get it?"

Vashi couldn't understand what was happening. He said, "But we are in a public facility built with the intention to attract guests. You can't expect to be alone when you are outside with others. Your logic is flawed."

"Is this guy for real?" the man said, looking at his female companion. "I can't tell if he's yanking my tail on purpose or not."

"I'm not sure, but it's not worth it. Come on."

The two hooded strangers got up and left.

A servant–not the red-haired woman–passed by Vashi and took his order. He ordered chicken clubs and a yoghurt drink. The food arrived shortly later, and he dug in. The crispy chicken skin crackled between Vashi's teeth, and the meat was juicy, not at all dry. It had been seasoned with lemon, black pepper and other herbs he did not know the name of. Between bites, he drank the salty yoghurt drink that tasted good but also strange to his palette.

"Bloody hell," an older man exhaled as he plopped down at the table next to Vashi. "I'm exhausted. How're you?" The stranger turned his head and reached to clap Vashi's shoulder.

Vashi pulled his arm away. *Physically touching a stranger without their consent is forbidden.* "You should not touch others without their consent."

"What?" the man had a hollow face with dark rings under his eyes. The few wisps of hair fighting a losing battle were slicked back. "I meant nothing by it, just a friendly greeting. I don't want any trouble."

"Fine," Vashi said, "but please keep it in mind for the future."

The man gave him a questioning look then shrugged. "Sure, if you say so." He drank from his large clay cup then burped loudly.

Vashi grimaced at the crude behaviour but returned his attention to the last chicken club and devoured it. He could have eaten more, but he felt satisfied for now. He did not have time to linger around longer than necessary.

After some time when nothing else had been said, the man suddenly scoffed, shaking his head. "Can you believe it?"

"Believe what?" Vashi said.

"The big banquet. What else?"

"I am not sure what you are referring to? I have not heard anything about a banquet."

The man looked at Vashi. His breath reeked, making Vashi tilt his head away. "How's that possible? Wait, you're not from these parts, are ya? Guess it makes sense then."

Vashi was confused. "But what is it you want to say about this banquet?"

"What I want to say?" the man said, suddenly raising his voice. "I have loads to say! It's a bloody joke it is. The whole city's going to shit and the rich and mighty decide to have a feast."

"Rich and mighty? Will the Bone Lord be there?"

The man laughed. "Of course! She's the damn one throwing the whole thing together. It's taking place in the ziggurat."

Vashi could feel it in his bones: the banquet would be where Varcade would try and assassinate the Bone Lord. He knew it hadn't happened yet, otherwise he would have heard something, foreigner or not. He still had the chance to stop his brother from forever tainting the Order's reputation and standing.

"I must go there."

"Hah! I'm sure they'll just let you in. Better yet: I'll even come with you!"

Vashi stood up. "No thank you. I will go alone. I do not enjoy your company."

The man frowned. "What the hell? You don't say that to someone's face like that."

"But it's the truth," Vashi said, throwing on his coat. "The Teachings tell us to be honest."

"I don't know what 'teachings' you mean, but words can hurt, you know?"

"That isn't my problem. Goodbye."

Vashi made his way through the rowdy crowd and stepped outside. He sucked in a deep breath of fresh air. Finally, he had a clear next step. It was about time he faced his fool of a brother.

CHAPTER TWENTY-SEVEN

Young Haroon leapt down from the carriage, his small feet blowing up a cloud of dust as he landed.

"Don't do that," his father–Lord Wakil–said, smacking Haroon in the back of the head. "We do not have time to change clothes before the Bone Lord's banquet, you understand? I have urgent business to attend, then we're leaving."

"Sorry," Haroon said, rubbing the sore spot on his head.

"That's fine. Now go look at the slaves or what have you, while I speak with the Overseers–ah, here they come, right on time. Go on now," Lord Wakil said, pushing Haroon aside.

This was Haroon's first time visiting the wheat fields beyond Akrab's walls. He couldn't count how many slaves there were but there sure were a lot of them. He hadn't even fully grasped what being a slave meant. Were the servants at his house also considered slaves? He shrugged and walked over to get a closer look.

The slaves were bare chested and had dirty loin cloths wrapped around their waists. Some were humans like Haroon himself, bronze-skinned with varying degrees of dark hair and eyes, and some were demons, coming in many different shapes and sizes. They worked the fields with bowed heads and crouched backs. No one was talking. They just worked and worked.

What an awfully boring life, Haroon thought. Why would anyone want to do this? He'd only been outside the shade of the carriage for a couple of minutes and the heat was already bothering him. *They're just out here all day every day?* Haroon shook his head.

His father had told him some people weren't meant for anything else in this world. Their brains were too small to grasp more demanding types of work. "The slaves are thankful when they are told what to do," his father had said during a rare occasion when he'd taken the time to sit down and talk with Haroon. "The stressful lives of nobles and freemen would be too much for such simple folks to handle. They aren't equipped for it. Work, eat and sleep is the foundation these people need for a happy life. Anything beyond that, and you get a whole mess of problems on your hands. Too much thinking isn't good for them. There is a certain order to things, you see, and that order is what makes Akrab one of the greatest city-states in all of Harrah."

Haroon guessed his father's explanation made sense, but it sure seemed boring. There were other men who marched up and down on the fields. They wore colourful cloth wrapped around their heads and down their backs, and sandals, unlike the slaves who were barefoot. Haroon recalled his father had called them taskmasters. Now and then one of the taskmasters would strike one of the slaves with a three-headed leather whip. The slave on the receiving end would simply grunt between clenched teeth and continue working.

Why are they being hit if the slaves want to be here? Haroon scratched his head. That part didn't make sense. His father was prone to striking him and his siblings when they misbehaved or the worst offence being talking back to either of their parents. None of the slaves were doing anything wrong, so why were they being hit? Perhaps he'd ask his father about that later, on the ride back into the city.

"Get over here," his father called out. "Just a couple more things to finish up in the house then we'll be on our way."

Haroon walked over to his father who stood next to three other men. Two slaves held up parasols to shade the group against the blistering sun.

"These are the Overseers," his father said. "Say hello."

"Hello," Haroon said.

The three men smiled at him. These men wore nicer clothes, like himself and his father, which meant they were important.

Together the group strolled over to a large square building constructed from mudbrick. The house was placed on a slightly raised hilltop that overlooked the fields below.

Once inside, they sat on cushions on the floor. The slaves brought jugs of water with slices of orange, and some bread and cheese. In a matter of minutes Haroon was already bored out of his mind. His father and the overseers talked about things that weren't the least bit exciting. Adult stuff that he barely understood.

"Father, can I *please* play outside? I won't go anywhere, I promise."

Lord Wakil looked at the overseers. "It's perfectly safe, My Lord," one of them said. "The dogs know better than to ever step one foot outside the crops in this direction."

"Very well. Stay *right* outside then, you hear me?"

"Hello, little boy."

The child sat on his hunches, drawing something in the sand with a stick. He looked over his shoulder, his eyes widening at the sight of Marduk and Dog Man coming towards him.

"You don't have to sound so creepy," Dog Man said, glaring up at him. "Geez."

The boy dropped his stick and stood up to face them. "Did the doggie just speak?"

"I sure did, kid."

"Wow!" the child's eyes lit up. He ran to them and squatted to pet the talking canine.

"My name's Dog Man. Who are you?"

"I'm Haroon," the boy said with a big smile, still petting the dog. "My father is Lord Wakil. He's having a meeting with the Overseers."

"A *Lord*, huh?" Marduk said. "He must be important man."

The boy nodded. "I guess."

"Okay, kid, that's enough," Dog Man said, squirming away from the child's eager hands burrowing into his short fur. "I think it's time for you to leave now."

Marduk crouched down, arms resting across one knee. "Yes, boy. You go now."

The boy frowned. "Leave? I'm waiting for my father."

Marduk leaned a bit closer, his growly voice barely a whisper. "Your father not coming back."

"I don't understand. We're going back to the city and to the Bone Lord's banquet tonight."

"Sorry, kid, that's not happening," Dog Man said.

It took longer than expected–perhaps the onion child was dumb– but he finally seemed to pick up on a sense of danger. "I don't think I should be talking to you anymore." The boy tried to walk past them, but Marduk gripped his arm and held him in place.

"Listen, kid," Dog Man said, "do as I tell you and everything will be fine. March right over to the carriage that brought you out here, okay? The driver's still waiting. Go to him and tell him *exactly* what just happened here."

The little onion's eyes teared up. "W-what about my father?" Fat tears rolled down his chubby cheeks.

"That between us," Marduk said. "Adult things. Tell driver father not coming back."

"Okay . . ." the boy said, snivelling. "I'll go now."

Marduk stood up and crossed his arms. "Good, boy."

The child walked away, throwing them a look over his shoulder now and then. Marduk waited for the little onion to descend the small hill, so he was out of eyeshot.

"I guess you'll handle the next bit?" Dog Man said.

Marduk nodded and slid his brass knuckles on, one for each hand. He pushed the reed mat covering the door aside and marched inside the house.

Four men sat on the floor. The nobleman Lord Wakil stood out with his fine linen clothing and the other three were the overseers. Out of the four, only the overseers would fight back. Three versus one: Marduk smiled.

Before any of the men could react, Marduk rushed inside and slammed his fist into the back of the head of the closest overseer. The man's neck broke, killing him instantly. The two other overseers scrambled to their feet, spilling out the cups in front of them and pulled up the cudgels tied to their waists.

The overseers weren't equipped to hide the fear in their eyes. They had no idea how to deal with this; they'd grown lazy over the years. *These scum have been beating up other onions and demons who has never fought back; it's a whole different thing when you're facing someone who won't back down.*

Marduk charged one of them and delivered a right hook that cracked the overseer's jaw with a loud *pop*. The force from the blow sent the man crashing into the wall behind him. Marduk followed up with another fist that buckled the man's face into itself.

The last overseer made the foolish decision to try and grapple with Marduk from behind; like his puny onion strength would be his match. Marduk broke free from the grip and slammed his elbow into the overseer's throat. The man fell over, gasping for air that would never come again, his body spasming on the floor.

"Please," the nobleman said, holding up his hands. His panicked eyes darted across the dead overseers in the room. "I have coin; anything you want you can have. I can make you a rich man!"

THE CREW

Marduk took off his brass knuckles. He wanted his own bones to be the tools that ended this man's life. He grabbed a handful of the nobleman's hair and yanked him closer to his face. "Coin will not save you."

He made quick work of the nobleman and rose to his feet, blood dripping from his knuckles. Lord Wakil's body lay limp on the floor, his head sagging to the side at an unnatural angle. This was a statement that couldn't be misunderstood. Once the soldiers found his corpse it would be clear: *We are coming for all of you.*

While Marduk had dealt with the overseers and Lord Wakil, his demon followers had ambushed the taskmasters in the fields. They had arrived mounted on their toads and slaughtered the taskmasters one by one. Marduk strolled through the crops and stopped to look at one of the dead taskmasters laying before his feet. Next to the dead man stood Ghonza, one of Marduk's most trusted followers. Ghonza had green-grey skin with an oblong face and thin moustache that hung down to his chest.

"You did good, Ghonza," Marduk said and squeezed his friend's shoulder before taking a seat on the taskmaster's corpse to rest his legs.

"It is pleasure killing these bastards," Ghonza said.

"Here come the slaves," Dog Man said, sitting next to Marduk. "And they don't look particularly happy about being liberated."

Word of the attack on the taskmasters had spread across the fields like wildfire. All the slaves had stopped working and were now coming closer to see for themselves. Many of them huddled together, whispering, fear and panic plainly written on their dirty faces.

An older, white-haired human slave approached Marduk, trepidation in his steps. The man's skin was leathery and dark, shaped by countless years of tolling the fields in the harsh climate on Harrah.

"What have you done?" the old slave stuttered, sinking onto his knees next to the taskmaster's corpse like the bastard had been a loved one.

"Get up, you fucking weakling," Ghonza said, grabbing the old man by the neck and throwing him to the side.

"You've doomed us all," the old man said, rocking back and forth on the ground.

Marduk clenched his teeth at the miserable sight. He wanted to hurt the slave; punish him for being so weak. But Marduk also knew, deep down, the old man had been shaped into the pitiful wreck before him. It wasn't all his fault. Perhaps he'd been born into the life of slavery and never known anything else.

Marduk rose with a groan and wiped sweat from his brow. He stepped over the pool of blood that had formed around the corpse's head. "Your owner, Lord Wakil, is dead. I smashed in his face," Marduk proclaimed, speaking loud and clear for every slave to hear. "Overseers also dead. Taskmasters dead, you already know."

Some slaves reacted with utter defeat like the older slave had; many others threw themselves on the ground in tantrums. Several turned hostile and yelled and cursed at Marduk. A few stood in silence and watched.

"This moment you all free. But now you must make big choice," Marduk said. "Soon they will hear about this back in city. I make sure of this. Bone Lord soldiers will come. Sand under your feet will drink blood today. You must decide whose blood that will be."

Those slaves that had already reacted with panic and defeat had a new intensity of primal fear at the notion of having to fight the royal army. They sank onto their knees, weeping and hitting their own faces in anguish. The older slaves had little fight in them, but the young faces Marduk observed among the masses told a different story; they stared back at him with blazing determination.

These younglings, humans and demons, men and women, still carried hope in their hearts. Hope for change. But hope would get them nowhere. Anyone could hope. It wouldn't bring about change. Change happened when people fought for it and took it; showing those in control you have had enough. No, Marduk did not want these young slaves' hope; he wanted the fires within them and it would only take one spark to light the flames of fury.

"You are free to make own choice. You can run and maybe find safe place somewhere. But where is that place? Other city-states will not welcome slaves who killed their masters." Marduk added a chuckle to bring home the point. "Also, desert much dangerous for travel. Marauders maybe kill you; or foul fiends hungry for your sweet flesh." Marduk shook his head. "I think not good idea." Marduk could see those slaves whose immediate instincts had been to flee begin to second-guess themselves.

"So, what can you do? It is easy. You *fight*. This is chance to fight back against those who want to keep you shackled. You must say, enough now; and you say this with language everyone understand: violence. Action, not bullshit talking."

"But we don't know how to fight!" a young human woman said. "We won't stand a chance against the Royal Army."

"She's right; we'll be slaughtered," a young demon said. "They have real weapons and the best armour; what do we have? Simple farming tools."

Marduk nodded in understanding. "You are not wrong, but you forget big thing; the thing *they* always want you to forget: together we are many, and they always few. This is, and will always be, big hole in their fancy armour. We not *ask* for change, we *take*, together."

"Your words seem to be working," Dog Man said, looking up at Marduk.

Marduk scoffed but allowed his lips to form the hint of a satisfied smile. What had been faint whispering now developed into a full on discussion among the slaves. Some nodded their heads at each other, while others argued. Whatever happened next was up to the people. He had helped light the fuse because that is what they needed, but in the end, only working together would mean something. Even though this rebellion had been orchestrated for a bigger purpose, now that

Marduk stood there, he made up his mind: he would fight with the slaves until the end.

Fish-City strolled back and forth; the demon's hands clasped behind his back; a frown on his face as he contemplated Baaq's request.

"I know it's a lot to take in," Baaq said. She was seated at a table at the Golden Coconut–the bar owned by Fish City. "And I felt exactly the same as you when Edghar first proposed the idea."

Fish-City stopped in his tracks. He turned and looked at Baaq. "Then why did you decide to go along with it? Staging a city-wide demon riot? How is that going to help our standing in society?"

"The riot in itself won't, but what we'll accomplish will. We're talking about creating a new Akrab. The Bone Lord must be removed from her seat of power. Otherwise, we'll have more than occasional riots, we'll have a civil war on our hands. It might sound mad, but this is a way to prevent that from happening."

Fish-City exhaled, tapping his fingers against his knuckles. "I don't know, Baaq. I really don't."

"I'm sorry to put you in this position, but there's really no time left to discuss this. The banquet could start at any time. We need to act now." Baaq stood up and grabbed Fish-City by the shoulders. "Listen, we do this together and make sure the riot is controlled and doesn't get out of hand. You have to trust me."

"Fine, Baaq," Fish-City said, looking up and meeting her eyes. "I'm far from convinced, but I do trust you. If you think this is what needs to be done, then so be it."

After agreeing to go along with Baaq's plan–if done on his terms–Fish-City had immediately sent a scout to the Royal District to observe when the banquet got underway. Once it did, the scout would return and let them know. Then he'd called in three demons whom he referred to as his captains - young demons who'd been with him for years and who helped run his whole operation and briefed them of the plan. The captains now stood before Baaq and Fish-City, ready to hear their orders.

"Listen, I'm going to rely on you three once this gets going," Fish-City said. "This will be a *controlled* riot; that means keeping our people in check. You see someone getting too excited and deviating from our goal, you put a stop to it. I won't allow any senseless destruction of property or pillaging. This city is *our* home. I will not see it burned to the ground."

"We understand, Boss. We won't let you down." The captain who'd spoken had cream-white skin and black eyes.

"Good," Fish-City said. "That also means not hurting innocent citizens. Our fight is against the Bone Lord's soldiers, especially her new security forces. Those, you are free to give hell. They've chosen their side."

"Are you sure about this?" Another of the captains said. The demon woman had silvery, scaled skin that gleamed beautifully. Her head was shaved except for one long braid that ran down her shoulder, and she had tattoos below and above her eyes–symbols that were unfamiliar to Baaq.

"I'd be lying if I said yes, but it's decided now," Fish-City said. "I trust Baaq and I believe in what she's doing. I'm not saying it isn't risky or that it might not fail, but it's worth a try."

"I'll be with you all every step on the way," Baaq said. "I'll follow the march from the rooftops and have your backs covered. The ziggurat is our end destination."

"I'm ready," the third captain said. She had an arrow-shaped head and large red eyes. Her skin was a golden-brown and her four arms were thin as twigs and ended with three menacing claws.

A minute later, the door to the Golden Coconut swung open and a demon kid rushed inside. "Mr. Fish-City," he said.

"Speak," Fish-City said.

"The banquet is underway. I watched all the guests arriving like you asked then ran straight back here."

Fish-City nodded. "You did good."

The demon child beamed with pride.

Baaq rose to her feet. "Alright, that's our cue. Let's get this started."

CHAPTER TWENTY-EIGHT

The banquet was now in full swing. Clea was seated in her throne on the dais, holding a bejewelled goblet filled to the brim with wine. Bone Lord Farouk was on the floor, eating and drinking with the appetite of ten men. Most of the Ghosts of Nuzz cadre were seated on a table of their own in the corner, but two of the silver-masked warriors always kept themselves in close proximity to their master, following like shadows.

Most invited guests were in the central court down the hall from the throne room. Some were nobles, others were freemen–the most revered craftsmen and artisans of the bunch, along with the more famous merchants as well as higher ranking military personnel.

Only the senior nobles part of the parliamentary council was allowed in the throne room itself; them and Bone Lord Farouk's retainers.

Clea emptied her goblet in a manner that would have been more fitting in a lowly tavern than for a woman of her stature, but she did not care. She took no pleasure from the festivities; this was a forced event at an exceptionally catastrophic time, and that fact sucked out all enjoyment from the occasion. Thankfully, the nobles carousing the room were too busy drinking and eating to keep a close eye on her, which suited her perfectly.

All she wanted was for the evening to end. Tomorrow she would properly discuss the future of Akrab with Bone Lord Farouk; the first major step in bringing about change for the city-state she ruled. In the meantime, she had to patiently sit in her throne and observe the debauchery tainting the halls of the ziggurat.

"Would you relax," she snapped at Erikz the Royal Guard Captain standing next to her. "Your tension is ruining my wine; and right now, it's all I have."

Erikz shifted his feet, making a poor attempt to relax his stoic posture. Like always, he donned his golden plated armour, and the clinking and clanking from it annoyed Clea to no end.

"I apologise, Your Highness, but I must stand vigilant and be prepared. I will not lower my guard if it means risking your life. You would not postpone this banquet as I suggested, which is your right, of course, but that means I must be ready for anything. The assassins are still out there."

Neither Clea or Tarkus had heard anything from the Duster called the Baker and his Dough Men for days, and not reporting back equalled failure in Clea's mind.

She rolled her eyes. "*Fine*. Would you at least tell that awful band to play some other music? It's absolutely appalling, and I can't stand it."

Khanon, the Army General arrived before her right in time to hear her complaint. "I believe our dear Vizier specifically requested that band, Your Excellency." The old veteran smiled with his eyes.

"Of course, he did . . ." Clea sighed. "If I am to get through this awful evening, I need my goblet refilled and that ghastly music changed. I don't believe that's too much to ask, is it?"

Khanon motioned for one of the servants carrying the wine jugs to come forward, while Erikz attended the band.

Bone Lord Farouk strolled up to the throne, his cheeks rosy from all the drinking he'd indulged in. "Are you going to just sit here for

THE CREW

the rest of the evening?" he said. "I don't know if you have noticed, my dear, but there's a banquet taking place."

"It gives me great pleasure seeing you enjoy yourself, dear Farouk," Clea said, "But I assure you, I'm fine right where I am."

Bone Lord Farouk's head snapped in the direction of the hastily assembled stage where the band was playing. "Why did they change the music? I was enjoying that song." He shrugged, turning his attention to her again. "No matter."

As Erikz returned to resume his position next to Clea, Bone Lord Farouk looked him up and down. "Are you going to bring me a chair, or am I supposed to simply stand here, Golden Boy?"

Erikz looked at Clea and she nodded a sympathetic nod.

"Certainly, My Lord," Erikz said and left, shortly returning with a chair.

Bone Lord Farouk sank his massive frame into the seat, still eyeing Erikz. "You're not from here, are you, boy? Where are you from?"

"I am not," Erikz said. "I was born in Rizale."

"*Rizale*," Farouk spat—literally. He turned to Clea. "How did this man snake himself into your service, Clea?" He snorted like a bull ready to charge. "A man from the conquered lands of the World Authority working for *you*? Are the other Bone Lords aware of this? I can't imagine they are."

"If I may, My Lord, I in no way associate myself with, nor serve the World Authority. I came to Harrah willingly to leave that life behind," Erikz said.

"So you're a deserter on top of it!" Farouk's head again snapped to Clea. "This is beyond acceptable. Even for you."

If Clea didn't handle this properly all hell could break loose. If there was a pivotal moment where she needed to control her temper, this would be it. "Erikz has proven his loyalty to me time and time again, Farouk. He was captured on our shores and was taken to be a slave gladiator. He fought splendidly and won his freedom like anyone else and was then handpicked by Khanon himself to serve me."

"Is this true, Khanon? You—"

"Are you questioning *my* word, Farouk?" Clea said, staring him in the eyes. "Don't forget who I am or where you are. I will not be so blatantly disrespected within my own halls."

Before Farouk could respond, Khanon cut in. "Indeed, Your Highness. If I may say, seeing Erikz perform in the pit reminded me of myself in my younger years. Say what you will about the vile World Authority, but whatever Erikz received in training overseas was excellent. I consider it an honour to fight beside him."

Erikz nodded with a smile at the word of admiration coming from the older veteran.

"I believe this subject is closed, Farouk," Clea said. "I will hear no more of it."

It was clear that Farouk wanted to argue further, but he decided against it. He instead funnelled his anger toward something completely different–unfortunately a trait Clea herself was prone to–and barked at the poor servant who happened to be standing nearby. "How long must I wait before being offered another bite to eat? Farouk hungers, damn you!" The startled servant ran like his life depended on it.

The atmosphere still remained tense, and Clea worried she wouldn't have what it took to make it through the evening without a disaster. She had never liked Bone Lord Farouk, but it was now safe to say she *despised* the man. *Why does he have to sit here? Go on, you bastard! Go eat and drink yourself to a stupor. Get out of my sight.*

As if the Yellow King himself decided to grant her a blessing, the Bone Lord suddenly rose to his feet with a groan. "I believe there are still some people I should greet."

Clea nodded. The moment he turned his back, she released a big sigh of relief.

"I'm sorry, Your Excellency," Erikz said. "I did not wish for my past to cause strain between yourself and Bone Lord Farouk. Should I—"

"It's fine," she said, waving her hand dismissively. She could see Erikz was uncomfortable by the whole thing, and he had never been anything but good to her. "Don't spend another moment thinking about it."

Erikz was mid-bow when he suddenly spun around, his gauntleted hand reaching for his sword. "It's fine, Erikz," Khanon said, motioning for the Royal Guard Captain to stand down. "It's one of our men."

It took a moment or two for Clea to get a sense of what had even happened, but then she saw a soldier had entered the throne room. *Did Erikz hear the soldier's armour and react that fast? Was that it?* The soldier was breathing heavily, like he'd been running. "Permission to approach," he said between laboured breaths.

Khanon nodded. "What's the matter, son? Out with it."

"Lord Wakil has been killed by the slaves working his crop. They even killed the Overseers and all the Taskmasters on the sight. We have a full-scale revolt on our hands."

"How did you hear this?" Clea said. "Tell me."

The soldier licked his lips, blinking from the sweat in his eyes. "His young son. The child was with his father right before the attack. He was spared so he could return here and tell us what transpired."

Damn you, Edghar, Clea thought, biting down on her teeth. This was not the first time a similar tactic had been used to send her a message. "It's Edghar's doing," she said. "I *know* it."

"I concur, Your Highness," Khanon said. "This was planned. The timing is too suspect to suggest anything else."

"My, my, what seems to be the matter?" Vizier Tarkus said as he shuffled up the short stairs to the dais. The Vizier had dressed up for the banquet, wearing light-green and dark-violet cloth wrapped around his pudgy body. "Such a tense atmosphere on this delightful evening. What could—"

"Slave revolt in the Southern wheat fields," Khanon said. "They killed a senior nobleman along with the Overseers and Taskmasters. We've got a disaster on our hands."

The Vizier clicked his tongue, shaking his head. "Such scoundrels. How dare they?" Tarkus took out the small jar filled with cream from within his make-shift robe. A moment later he rubbed his hands together, producing a wet and squishy sound as his dry skin absorbed the lotion. "Well, what are you waiting for, Khanon? Gather your soldiers and squash the revolt immediately. We can't risk it spilling into the city itself, can we?"

The Army General looked at Clea. "My Lady, I don't feel comfortable leaving your side; especially now."

"What choice is there?" She said. "If Farouk even sniffs a hint of potential danger he will leave instantly, and damn it all, but I *need* him."

"Don't worry, dear Khanon," Tarkus said, putting a hand on the veteran's shoulder guard. "I will send one of the Dusters with you. Together, you will crush those slaves in no time and that will be the end of it. I'm certain you'll be back here before you know it."

"Your Excellency," Erikz said. "This is an obvious plan executed to divide our soldiers. We can't play along. It's *exactly* what they want."

"Erikz," the Vizier said. "You are the Bone Lord's bodyguard and nothing more. Matters involving the security of the city itself is handled by the three of us—not yourself." Tarkus turned his attention to Clea and looked her deep in the eyes. "Your Highness, you know what needs to be done. A slave revolt demands action."

Clea knitted her brow as she struggled to string her thoughts together. The sweet smell from the Vizier's lotion was nauseating; the scent even more pungent than usual. She felt light-headed and cursed herself for the amount of wine she'd had. Of course, Erikz's assessment made sense, but her hand was forced. *A slave revolt, of all things!* Clea couldn't imagine anything worse to demonstrate how weak her rule was. "Go, Khanon," she said. "Take the Duster with you and end it *quickly*, you hear me?"

"Very well, My Lord," the Army General said with a bow. "Tarkus, tell your Duster to meet me outside straight away. I shall rally the troops."

The Vizier nodded. "Certainly, dear General."

Less than five minutes after the Army General had left, another soldier entered the throne room. Clea could tell the soldier wanted to run but forced himself to approach in a calm manner to not distress the surrounding guests.

"What now?" Clea said between clenched teeth.

The soldier cleared his throat and averted his eyes. "I just received word, so the details are scarce, but it appears a massive crowd of demons are marching through the city. If the report is correct, they're numbering in the thousands. So far things have been peaceful but we're not sure what their goal is."

Clea closed her eyes and rubbed her temples. She felt dizzy, almost faint. This was too much. "I—"

"No cause for alarm, Your Highness," Tarkus said. "This is the exact reason why we established the new security forces. I'll order them to mobilise immediately to deal with the filth and have one of the Dusters to support them."

"This is madness," Erikz said, eyes darting between Clea and the Vizier. "Divide our forces even further?" The Royal Guard Captain sank down on one knee before Clea. "My Lord, please, I implore you, we need to call an end to this banquet and move you to safety. We're playing right into Edghar's hands! You know this is his doing."

"There is no place safer than within the walls of the ziggurat," Tarkus hissed. "We do not run and hide at the first sign of trouble. We will face them, and we will crush them."

"Are you serious?" Erikz said, looking over his shoulder at the Vizier. "This is more than *trouble*. We're talking about a slave rebellion and a potential city riot happening at the same time." Erikz slowly rose to his feet, his eyes narrowing at the sight of the Vizier like he was seeing him for the first time. "What are you up to, Tarkus? What's really going on here?"

"Your Highness," Tarkus said, placing his slightly sticky hand on Clea's wrist. "Will you allow this man to speak to me in a such a way?"

"Stop it, Erikz. You will hold your tongue," Clea said. It was strange; like her lips had moved on their own. A part of her not only shared the Royal Guard Captain's worries, but she also even *agreed* with them. But something in the core of her being felt off, like it was impossible to string together her thoughts or articulate her worries into words. Her mind was covered in a thick haze.

"As you wish, Your Highness," Erikz said, forcing the words out.

"Tarkus," Clea said, gathering herself to the best of her abilities. "I need you to usher everyone away from here and contain all guests in the court room. We can't risk any of them overhearing what we're talking about and spreading rumours. Also, stick to Farouk and keep him occupied. You need to make *damn* sure not a single word of any of this reaches him."

"Certainly, Your Excellency," the Vizier said with a smile that went from ear to ear. "I thank the Lord of Flames we have such strong leadership at a critical time as—"

"Just go!" Clea hissed, rubbing the bridge of her nose, and closing her eyes. "Erikz, tell the guards to stop letting more people inside or freely go out. We need to isolate the banquet and minimise the chance any of this reaches our guests."

The Royal Guard Captain nodded.

Clea tried to steady her breathing and remain calm, but the tense and worried look on Erikz's face right before he left did not make it easy.

It took Vashi hours of walking until he finally reached the building that was Akrab's heart. He had seen it from afar since his arrival but standing before it now demanded his full appreciation. The great ziggurat not only towered above the rest of the buildings in the sun-baked city-state, but it also stood out like a rare and colourful flower in a sea of sand. In the centre, an immense staircase ran from the base to the summit reaching for a silvery moon that hovered in a clear, starlit sky. The people of Akrab were savages in desperate need for the Teachings, but their workmanship was exquisite and could not be denied; even rivalling the Educator Temples back in Karkan.

Vashi strolled to the two soldiers standing guard at the base of the great staircase. "Hello, I would like to go inside, please and thank you," he said with a big smile.

The two guards shared a look between them before the male one spoke up. "Oh yeah? You want to attend the banquet? Well, of course. Please, go right in."

"Wonderful," Vashi said and took but a single step forward before the female guard gripped the hilt of her sabre.

"Are you stupid? He was being *sarcastic*," she said, her blade half-drawn. "Step back. You're not setting foot inside the ziggurat."

Sarcasm, Vashi recollected. *A hidden way to mock or show hostility in a–*

"Well, what do we have here," someone giggled, coming down the stairs. "Let me see."

Vashi's thoughts were interrupted by a woman at least twice his age. She was a stocky lady wearing a colourful silken gown along with a lavishly decorated golden circlet. She looked him up and down with wolfish eyes, wetting her lips with the tip of her tongue. She tried getting between the guards who attempted to stop her.

"Please, madame," one of the soldiers said. "We have been given strict orders to not let *anyone* in or out. I must ask that you remain—"

"Oh shush," she said, tapping the soldier on his nose as she passed him by before returning her attention to Vashi. "Well, aren't you quite the exotic man. What are you doing out here all alone?"

Vashi wasn't sure how to respond. "I—"

"Why don't you come inside as my guest? I imagine the two of us could have a wonderful time together."

"Please, madam, I told you—"

"Do you *know* who you're speaking to?" the woman spun around, jabbing a finger in the female soldier's face. "I am Nazila Aman. Does the Aman Trading Company sound familiar perhaps? It *should* since we operate in all the seven city-states of Harrah!"

"Of course," the soldier stuttered, "but we've been given—"

"*I. Don't. Care.*" she hissed. "Now be silent before you make me real upset, you hear? One word from me and you'll be thrown in the Pit."

The soldier sighed and lowered her gaze.

Nazila turned her attention back to Vashi, the tone of her voice again gentle and alluring. "Now where were we, sweet one? You coming inside with me?"

If there was one glaring thing lacking from the Educator Teachings, it was how to handle yourself in a situation adhering to the more . . . biological nature of being human. The celibacy part was simple and clear enough to understand. Vashi had no issues with that. But there–

"Oh, stop just standing there," Nazila said, clearly losing her patience. "Come on, I won't take no for an answer." She grabbed his wrist and pulled him to her, their faces inches apart.

The woman had a deep and sweet fragrance, and her hot breath on his skin made Vashi's body tingle in places that were *definitely* frowned upon in the Teachings. "I really should not—"

"Hush, hush," Nazila smiled wickedly. Still holding his wrist, the woman dragged him along past the soldiers who meekly attempted to protest mostly for show.

However uncomfortable Vashi was, he couldn't deny the perfect timing for the woman to have appeared. *Are the Saints perhaps aiding me?* He would find Varcade at the banquet, of that, he was sure, and this was his *last* chance of stopping him. A rogue Educator assassinating a ruler of a foreign nation would be something the Order could never recover from.

After ascending the never-ending staircase, the two of them finally stepped into the ziggurat and into an antechamber where servants stood lined up to serve them welcoming drinks. The woman grabbed a goblet for herself and handed one to Vashi. "Is this spirits? I don't—"

"You don't have to drink if you don't want to, sweet one," the woman said. "Just hold on to it for appearances at least. You already stick out as it is." She studied him again, making it clear she *liked* what she saw. "Say, what's your name, dear? Tell me a bit about yourself."

Vashi realised he hadn't properly introduced himself. "I am very sorry, that is rude of me. My name is Vashi and I'm an Educator."

"Educator? What's that? A religious thing or something?"

Vashi nodded. "Yes, our mission in life is to spread and enforce the Teachings of Balance. But truthfully, I travelled to Akrab to locate my missing brother. I am certain he will be here tonight, among the guests."

Nazila smiled. "A religious man, how intriguing. Now I understand why you're so uptight. But let's see if we can't get you to *loosen* up a bit tonight, eh? I'm not one to shy away from a good challenge, after all," she winked.

Vashi flushed, feeling excited and uncomfortable simultaneously. He wasn't used to having his feelings being conflicted in such a stark way. This was the exact reason Educators took a vow of celibacy; to not have their minds tainted and muddled by thoughts and feelings born from the urges of the flesh and heart. Those thoughts did not fit the Balance; they were too chaotic and incomprehensible. "Please, I must find my brother. It is very important."

Nazila waved her hand dismissively. "Yeah, yeah, don't worry your cute head about that. If he's here I'll help you find him, okay? Come on."

Instead of grabbing his wrist, she took Vashi's hand, their fingers interlacing. The touch of her skin made his body tingle again. Nazila led him into the central courtroom: a vast square space with rows of marble columns lining each side. The room was packed with people, but the atmosphere wasn't as rowdy and invasive as the tavern Yuba had been.

"Quite something, isn't it?" Nazila said, sneakily putting her arm around his waist. When Vashi tried to manoeuvre himself free, the woman held him in place even tighter–and the worst part was that Vashi liked that. A lot.

Saints forgive me. I am lost...

A tall man with dark hair wobbled up to Vashi and Nazila, the drink in his hand spilling left and right. "Now who's this, eh, Nazila?" The man slurred his words, his eyes barely open. "Found yourself a new pet, have you?"

"What if I have? You *jealous*, Lord Lutfi?"

"What if I say I was, eh?"

Nazila smiled a cheeky smile.

Vashi was confused by the ongoing exchange between them.

"What's this louse have that I don't, huh? You should be with *me*. You know we've had some good times together; you can't deny it."

Nazila turned to Vashi. "I'm not sure. I like his strange hair." She ran her fingers through it, making Vashi shiver with forbidden pleasure. "He's different, it's exciting. Something *new*."

"What about *that* damn hair? He looks like a bloody fool to me. Why does it stick right up like that?"

"I am not sure, it has always—" Vashi said.

"You're old news, my dear," Nazila shrugged. "What we had is in the past. It's over."

Lord Lutfi hesitated a moment then leaned in close to Vashi, his wretched breath stinging Vashi's nostrils. "You should leave if you know what's good for you. I'm a nobleman. You do not want me as your *enemy*."

"Very well," Vashi said, head leaning back, feeling a sense of relief that he could be on his way and resume his task. "I will go and find my brother." He turned to thank Nazila for helping him inside when he was suddenly pushed from behind. Vashi stumbled forward a step but managed to keep himself upright.

"I told you to go, didn't I? Lord Lutfi doesn't ask something twice."

Vashi turned and faced the nobleman. Lord Lutfi threw his goblet over his shoulder and put his hands up in a–poorly looking– fighting stance.

"You're making a fool of yourself," Nazila said, rolling her eyes at Lord Lutfi. "Stop this pitiful behaviour. Ignore him, Vashi."

Ignore him? Impossible. Intentionally pushing someone in an attempt to instigate combat is forbidden. Education of wrongful behaviour must be enforced. There was no way around it, even though the timing couldn't be worse. But he couldn't call himself an Educator and represent the Order if he simply walked away from such a blatant offence.

"Come on, fight me, you lousy freak," Lutfi shouted, specks of spit hitting Vashi's face.

"I am standing right here, am I not?" Vashi said.

That statement seemed to be the tipping point for the man. He rushed Vashi and threw a sloppy punch.

Vashi's hand shot out with the speed of a lunging snake, gripping the man's wrist mid-air, while his other hand–open palmed–struck Lutfi's chin from a downward angle, making the man's head snap back like a clam snapping shut.

Lutfi fell backwards flat on his back, making a wheezing sound.

Vashi walked up to the man and looked down. "A civilian attacking another person in an environment that is not a battlefield is not allowed." He pressed his boot on Lutfi's mouth and rubbed it around. "You will never do this again, understand?"

"What's wrong with you," Nazila shouted, trying to pull Vashi away from the nobleman.

Vashi tore his arm free, his head snapping at the woman. "Do not involve yourself or interrupt Educator Teachings. That is forbidden."

Nazila stepped back, her eyes wide with horror. "What? You're insane . . ." She shouted for the guards.

This is not good, Vashi thought, shaking his head, his foot still pressing down on Lord Lutfi's mouth, *but the Education must be completed.* "Make this easy on yourself and promise you will never do something like this again." The nobleman blinked frantically, his head bopping up and down. "Good. Bump it." Vashi put his fist out.

"Step away from the man right this instant."

"Do it now!"

Vashi looked around the room as more and more soldiers surrounded him, their weapons drawn. The other guests had all backed away from the scene, but they watched with excitement in their eyes.

Hmm . . . this is really not good. He still had to find his brother; nothing was more important. That meant he couldn't let himself be captured and removed from the banquet. *What must be done must be done.*

He stepped away from Lord Lutfi and positioned himself in the centre of the circle. He threw his robe back, pulled out his staff and entered a battle stance suited for fighting multiple opponents.

"I am sorry, but I must do this," he said with a solemn nod. "I must complete my mission. Nothing can stand in my way."

The soldiers charged.

"We have arrived," Lady Qanah said, looking out the side of the carriage as it came to a stop outside the ancient ziggurat. "Seems like the banquet has already started."

"Please, I beg you to reconsider this," nobleman Sharif pleaded. "There must be another way—"

"Shut up, we're doing this," Varcade said. "Get your butt moving."

Varcade, Lady Qanah, Zuba and nobleman Sharif all got out of the carriage one by one. Surrendering to Lady Qanah's demands of wearing a disguise, Varcade had put on a dark, pleated cloak over his coat that covered him from his neck to his feet; as well as a funny-looking hat with colourful feathers to hide his silvery hair. Zuba's weird bandage-outfit that he usually wore was covered up by wearing a lime-green one-piece tied at the waist. *He should've worn something to cover his creepy face too,* Varcade thought.

"What an ugly place," Varcade said as he walked over and looked up at the massive ziggurat. "Whoever built this should be ashamed of themselves."

"Shut up," Lady Qanah said. "Don't speak if not absolutely necessary."

Before Varcade could argue, the puppeteer put his hand on his shoulder. "You better do as Mother says," Zuba whispered.

"I'll do that if you stop *touching* me," Varcade said and shrugged Zuba's hand off.

A large crowd of common people had gathered outside the ziggurat to catch a glimpse of the festivities and all the important people attending the banquet.

Varcade and the rest of the group made their way through the masses until they arrived at the bottom of the giant staircase where two soldiers—one female and one male—stood guard.

"Go on," Varcade whispered harshly to nobleman Sharif who had frozen still with a dumb look on his face. "You better play your part convincingly or remember what happens."

Nobleman Sharif nodded, using a silken handkerchief to wipe away the stress-induced sweat peppering his brow. "Fine, fine." He patted himself down, getting rid of any wrinkles sustained during the carriage ride over and walked up to the guards.

"Lord Sharif and . . ." He glanced over his shoulder, clearing his throat. "Party of four."

The female soldier swayed to the side so she could get a closer look at the group. "Four? Each guest is allowed a maximum of *two* additional guests, and that includes personal retainers."

"Ah," Sharif said, again patting his brow with the handkerchief. "Someone must have failed to inform me of this. Unfortunately, the members of my party were personally invited by myself as my guests and have travelled all the way from Karthalah to attend the banquet. Surely an exception can be made for such special circumstances?"

The soldier shook her head. "I'm sorry, My Lord, but even if we could, we are not allowing more guests inside. Strict orders from the Royal Guard Captain himself. I'm afraid you arrived too late."

"Oh well, that's unfortunate," he said with a shrug–not even *attempting* to hide the relief and chipper in his voice. He turned around and marched back to Varcade ten times lighter on his feet than he'd been walking up to the guards.

"Sorry, but it looks like none of us are going inside. Nothing I can do about it; my hands are tied."

Varcade put on a big smile for appearances sake as he leaned in close to the nobleman. "How can I say this . . . Forget about revealing to the other nobles that you had your father killed; if you don't get us inside, I'll just *kill you*. How do you like that, *My Lord*?"

Sharif swallowed, his hands hanging in the air awkwardly. "Ah. Well then. Perhaps I admitted defeat a little too easily. Why don't I go give it another try then?"

"I think you should do that," Varcade winked. "Go on."

Sharif was just on his way back to the guards when a new guard came running down the long staircase, stopping midway. "Attack! We're under attack!" After delivering the panicked statement, he spun on his heels and rushed back up the stairs again. The two soldiers at the bottom shared a confused look between them for a split-second before they ran after their colleague.

Varcade frowned. "An attack? What?"

"Forget about that," Lady Qanah said, already running up the stairs. "This is our chance to get in, you idiot. Move it!"

"Right!" Varcade said and followed, Zuba behind him. "Guess we never needed you after all," Varcade shouted over his shoulder at the nobleman.

Sharif was left standing alone in the dirt, his mouth an O.

"What the hell is happening out there?" Clea bellowed, half-rising from her throne.

Erikz had just rushed back into the throne room after investigating the commotion coming from the central court. It wasn't like him to not immediately respond to her, but he was scrambling to push the two massive doors shut.

"Damn you, Erikz, answer me!" Clea felt sick to her stomach. *Something* was seriously wrong.

"We're under attack, Your Highness," Erikz said with a glance over his shoulder, clenching his teeth and straining himself to finally getting the doors closed. He pulled his sword and ran up to Clea. "We need to leave *right now*. Please follow me, My Lord."

Countless emotions swarmed Clea's mind. She felt utterly lost, not sure what to do. "An attack? *Who's* attacking us? Is it Edghar?"

"I don't know," Erikz said, speaking so fast he forgot to address her properly. "I don't think so. But it's bad. Our guards are getting destroyed out there."

"But Farouk," Clea stuttered. "He was in that room! He can't be harmed under my own roof!"

Erikz shook his head. "Nothing I can do about that right now. I won't leave your side and we can't stay here. Please, I implore you to allow me to bring you to safety."

"I can't believe this is happening," Clea said, her voice trembling. "Where's Tarkus?"

Erikz held out his gauntleted hand and she grabbed it. "I don't have any answers. All I know is we need to create as much distance as we can from the enemy. There's no way out of here except from the front so we're stuck in the building. The inner throne room is our best chance; either that or the residential suite–" The Royal Guard Captain pulled at the door in the far corner of the room, but it wouldn't open. He tried again more violently to no avail.

"It's locked?" Clea said, eyes going wide. "It's never locked."

"No worries," Erikz said, not doing the best job of making her believe him. "We'll try the other side."

But that door turned out to be locked as well. "Fucking hell," Erikz said under his breath.

"We're trapped . . ." Clea said, turning to look at the double doors behind them; the only thing separating them from the ongoing assault in the next room. "Erikz, what do we do?"

"I . . . don't know."

Hearing the tone in Erikz's voice made Clea even more scared than the attack itself.

Varcade heard the commotion coming from the court room the moment they set foot inside the empty antechamber. "What the hell is happening here?"

"No clue," Lady Qanah said, "But this changes everything. If the guards are already distracted, you should be able to get to the Bone Lord without much opposition. Be thankful."

"What about us then?" Zuba complained. "I was going to show Varcade what I can do—"

"Be quiet," Lady Qanah said. "There's no time for your foolery."

A group of nobles came running from the court room, their heads snapping over their shoulders, eyes wide with panic.

"A mad man!"

"He's killing all the soldiers!"

"A Duster has come to assassinate the Bone Lord!"

The guests rushed past them and out through the doors, paying no attention whatsoever to Varcade or the Ghuls.

"Well, screw it then," Varcade said and tore off his silly disguise. "No point for that anymore."

Zuba did the same, following Varcade's lead like a younger sibling imitating a cool older brother.

"If you deal with the Bone Lord, me and Zuba can focus on finding the God Dust vault. Change of plans or not, we will not leave here empty-handed."

THE CREW

"Fine, you do that," Varcade said, trying to gather himself at the unexpected events unfolding before their eyes. "You two should be able to move around more freely if the guards are occupied with this mysterious attacker. Go and get as much God Dust as you can."

"I'll kill someone and use their corpse to explode the door to the vault," Zuba said, licking his lips. "I'm sorry you won't be able to see it yourself, but I'll tell you all about it later when—"

Lady Qanah pulled her son's arm and dragged him along before he could finish his sentence. The three of them entered the central court room trying to look as casual as possible, even though it failed completely since most other guests were running past them, *away* from the threat they were walking towards. Varcade shared a quick look of determination with the Ghuls before they each split up and went their separate way.

The raging battle was mostly confined to the left side of the spacious room, so Varcade simply stuck to the right, brushing against the wall as much as possible. From every open doorway more guards came flooding in; too many for Varcade to count. He tried to catch a glimpse of who the mysterious attacker was, but they moved so fast they weren't more than a blueish blur. The *thing* darted from one guard to the next, striking with such force it sent soldiers flying in all directions.

Varcade couldn't put his finger on it, but *something* in the air felt almost familiar to him; like a presence he knew. He wanted to get a closer look, but the sight of the two doors slamming shut ahead of him squashed his curiosity.

Varcade kept moving towards the throne room, swiftly darting left and right to avoid clashing with the panicked guests running past him like their hair was on fire. A massive man–somehow frighteningly obese while still looking muscular–was being rushed out by a group of silver-masked soldiers.

From the corner of his eye, Varcade could still see the guards being demolished by the attacker, and no one was keeping track of his own movements. He arrived in front of the closed double doors and pried them open with a loud creak.

The throne room was empty except for a lavishly dressed woman and a man in golden plated armour. As Varcade stepped inside, the golden-armoured man immediately spun around while simultaneously shoving the woman behind him. The two of them matched Edghar's description perfectly: This was indeed the Bone Lord in all her glory and the Royal Guard Captain. Varcade reached behind his back and liberated the two swords from their sheaths.

"Don't take another step," the guard captain said, aiming his longsword at Varcade. "You'll be dead before I allow you to harm a single hair on the Bone Lord's head."

The Bone Lord had not stopped staring at Varcade from the first moment he appeared before them. She looked scared and stressed, true, but there was something else gleaming in her eyes; a feral determination that clearly stated she would not die without putting up a fight. "You're him. The silver-haired man who killed Berenberg."

"Who?"

"Berenberg! My Treasurer!"

"Oh, the coin-man!" Varcade nodded, "Yeah, I killed him. That's actually quite the story—"

"*Edghar* sent you, isn't that right?" the Bone Lord said, venom in her voice at the mention of her former spymaster. "You're his assassin."

"That's right; or at least, that's how it all started," Varcade said, cracking his neck. "But what began as a job has turned into something else now, and I'm actually looking forward to this. Your reign of terror must come to an end."

"Keep your tongue in your mouth, scum," the Royal Guard Captain said. "'Reign of terror', how *dare* you?"

"Scum? How rude. I'm not in here calling you names, am I? I'd think we could at least keep this somewhat civil."

"*Why?*" The Bone Lord shouted, pushing past her bodyguard to his startled dismay. "*Why* is Edghar doing this?"

Varcade frowned. "Are you seriously asking that question? Ehhh . . . How about because you're completely mad? I mean, have you been outside lately? The whole city's coming apart, if you hadn't noticed." He shrugged. "Sorry, lady, but you need to *go*. And since you don't seem willing to do it on your own . . ."

"Don't waste your air on this villain, Your Highness—"

"Quiet, Erikz," the Bone Lord said, staring daggers at Varcade. "Do you have the slightest clue what is really going on here? What it *takes* to rule a—"

"Listen, Your Highness or whatever," Varcade said, "I'm not in the mood for a bunch of jibber jabber. What say me and golden-guy get to the fighting part since we all know that's inevitable."

The Bone Lord took a deep breath, the rage on her face close to comical. "Erikz, I order you to *destroy* this man. I want his head."

The Royal Guard Captain nodded and stepped forward. "It will be my honour, Your Excellency."

Here we go.

CHAPTER TWENTY-NINE

The slaves who had decided to stay and fight were lined up behind Marduk. The slaves were armed with simple farming tools such as hoes, rakes, and flint-bladed sickles, while Marduk's followers–mounted on the massive toad beasts–had their three-bladed throwing discs along with an array of spears and blades for the melee.

A palpable silence hung in the air, only interrupted now and then by the nervous clearing of throats or anxiety-ridden shuffling of feet. The one constant sound came from the great river; sloshing and splashing as it flowed through the channel between the banks. The scorching heat of the midday sun had been replaced by chilly winds now that the sky had darkened. Marduk had ordered torches to be lit and placed all around them to aid their vision for the forthcoming battle.

"What the hell am I doing here . . ." Dog Man muttered. "I'm too old and weak for a battle of this magnitude. I just wanted some Dust . . ."

"Shut up and fight," Marduk said. "No Dust for you."

"Easy for you to say; you live for this crap."

Before Marduk saw them, he *felt* them: the thunderous hooves of the royal mounted cavalry. He took a step forward, separating himself from the hundreds of slaves lined up behind him. Marduk knew that fear would cripple the slaves' hearts and make them lose what resolve–however small–they'd built up once the battle began in earnest. The time for talking was over, and now he needed to be the fearless leader they needed and *show* them that even though the odds were stacked against them, he would not falter.

"Here they come . . ." Marduk heard one of the slaves say. "It's really happening. Bless us, Lord of Flames."

"Get ready!" Ghonza shouted, mounted on his red-skinned giant toad next to Marduk. At the demon's words, the rest of Marduk's followers all raised their three-bladed discs and pulled their arms back. "Wait for it! Wait for it! NOW!"

The moment the Royal Army descended upon them they were bombarded by the three-bladed discs hurled by the demons. Razor-sharp steel sliced through armour and flesh, taking the incoming soldiers by complete surprise. Many fell to the first volley; even more fell with the second one.

Marduk slid on his brass-knuckles and bounced lightly on his heels. There was no point in running a long distance to reach his targets; let them come to him instead; let them enter his personal realm of rage and death.

Now.

Marduk charged for the mounted soldier closest to the front. The rider had a look of surprise seeing the demon running towards him instead of fleeing. The soldier swiped down with his curved blade, but Marduk sank onto his knees, sliding forward in the sand and making the man miss, smashing the horse's hind leg which snapped it like a twig. The mount buckled and crashed violently to the side, spraying up sand and sending the soldier flying.

Marduk rushed to his feet as the other mounted soldiers rode past. *Now it's up to you,* he thought, glancing back over his shoulder as the battle commenced. *Fight or die.*

The two armies collided in a violent frenzy that created a

cacophony of maddening sounds. But the time for Marduk to observe was over, he was himself in the midst of it, and the slightest distraction could spell the difference between life and death.

"*You.*" A deep voice bellowed.

Marduk spun around.

A large man dressed in a gleaming silver armour leapt down from his black steed. His deep-red cape fluttered in the wind behind him as he marched straight at Marduk. He was an older dark-skinned man with a neatly trimmed white beard. The man drew two rectangular-shaped blades, locking eyes with Marduk. "To think Edghar would sink so low to ally himself with the notorious *Marduk*. The man has truly lost his mind and abandoned all honour in his bones."

Marduk cracked a challenging grin, wiping off his bloodied brass-knuckles on his trousers. "You are Army General Khanon. Edghar tell me you will come." Marduk studied him and scoffed. "You not so strong. I will smash you."

"You're welcome to try," Khanon said. "I'll put an end to you and this revolt before more unnecessary blood is spilled. This ends with your death."

"Come, big man, I will destroy you."

The Army General held his swords out far to the sides and started spinning them, turning the blades into circled blurs. He moved around Marduk, changing his distance constantly, ebbing and flowing in and out, never standing still, each of his strikes coming sudden and as quick as the lash of a whip.

Marduk had an instant to react to block the incoming strikes with his brass-knuckles. The room for error was non-existent; an inch to the left or right and Marduk would lose a hand. His weapon of choice was not best suited for defence.

The onion-bastard is trying to make me tired so I make a mistake, Marduk thought, never allowing himself to lose concentration. *I need to disrupt his tactic.*

Waiting for the precise moment when Khanon attacked, Marduk

blocked and kicked up a heap of sand in the man's face. "You like?" Marduk barked between clenched teeth.

Khanon stumbled back, blinking frantically to get the sand out of his eyes. He continued swinging his swords, but recklessly, a forced course of action to keep Marduk at bay while he struggled to regain his sight.

But Marduk wasn't waiting for that and charged the Army General with the force of a frenzied desert beast. He needed to close the distance and would accept a cut or two to get his hands on the man. Khanon tried backing up to remain in optimal distance for his lashing blade strikes, but Marduk broke through and dove for the man's waist in a bear hug that tackled Khanon to the ground.

Creating some leverage from his dominant position, Marduk punched Khanon twice, one splitting his eyebrow and drawing blood, while the other smashed the man's nose. But the Army General was physically stronger than Marduk expected and was able to push him off using brute strength.

Khanon scrambled back to his feet and started spinning his swords again. The sand in his eyes didn't seem to bother him anymore–or at least, not as much. Marduk cursed under his breath. He was bleeding from his shoulder and felt a sharp sting of pain running up his back. He had been cut open when closing the distance and tackling the man. They locked eyes, the tension rising with each heartbeat at who would make the first next move.

"Marduk, watch out!"

Marduk heeded the warning and allowed himself a glance over his shoulder.

A massive figure stomped toward him. The warrior was covered in heavy armour from top to bottom and swung the largest hammer Marduk had ever seen. It slammed into the royal soldiers and slaves alike and sent them soaring through the air like they weighed nothing.

"Those are our men!" Khanon bellowed at the figure. "What the hell are you doing?"

The giant arrived before Marduk and the Army General, holding the long shaft of its hammer in a two-handed grip. The warrior wore a round faced helmet depicting a smiling cherubic child.

Why does it sound like an infant crying? Marduk frowned. The crying echoed, seemingly coming from *within* the armour.

"What the hell are you doing, Bonky-Bonk?" the Army General barked.

"You all must die," came a soft female voice from inside the helmet. The voice sounded ethereal; otherworldly, each vowel dragged out when spoken.

"What bullshit this?" Marduk sneered as he backed away from the giant warrior.

Khanon's nostrils flared, his teeth clenched. "We've been betrayed," he said under his breath, more to himself than to Marduk. "Soldiers! The Duster's not our ally!" he shouted from the top of his lungs. "She's an enemy!"

The massive warrior called Bonky-Bonk leapt forward–a move Marduk was not expecting from someone that size–the hammer raised high above her head. Marduk rolled out of harm's way as the massive weapon smashed the spot he'd been standing, making a tower of sand erupt like a volcano. Bonky-Bonk moved fast and charged Khanon, gripping her hammer like a battering ram. The Army General was quick on his feet, leaping backwards to dodge the incoming blows.

What am I supposed to do here? Marduk thought, shuffling to his feet. Should he fight *with* Khanon against this new and sudden threat? *Damn it.* Could he even take on this Duster on his own?

"Listen!" Marduk roared, hoping the slave fighters and his followers would hear him. "Metal giant is Duster! Kill her!"

Word about a Duster amongst them spread quickly, and Marduk could see slaves and soldiers switching their attention to the monster. Khanon tried to get in an attack whenever he saw an opening, but his blades did nothing against the armour of Bonky-Bonk, barely leaving a scratch. If the Army General's swords weren't enough, then what the hell was Marduk supposed to do with his brass-knuckles against that *thing*.

"Why are you doing this?" Khanon hissed, still relying on his speed to avoid being hit by the hammer that would surely pulverise the bones with one blow.

"You have fulfilled your part and are not needed any more," Bonky-Bonk said. The smooth female voice was such a conflicting contrast to the armour and gruesome helmet. The disturbing infant cry from within the Duster's armour was also getting louder and louder, echoing out across the battlefield.

One of the soldiers armed with a crossbow released a quarrel that found its mark in Bonky-Bonk's back. The bolt pierced the Duster's armour, causing thin tendrils of violet smoke to seep out. That caught the attention of the Duster. She turned around, ignoring Khanon, and charged for the crossbowman, a trail of the violet smoke following her.

The soldier was mid-way to loading up another bolt when she noticed the Duster coming at her. She dropped the weapon and her quiver, fleeing for her life.

Marduk cursed the coward and ran as fast as his legs could carry him to snatch up the crossbow. He had little experience with using onion-weaponry, and his brass-knuckles made it damn impossible to operate the stupid device.

"Here, let me!"

Marduk looked at the new soldier who'd ran up to him. She nodded once, determination in her eyes. "Hurry," he said, handing over the weapon to her.

With the efficiency only achieved after countless hours of practice, the soldier had the crossbow loaded with a new bolt in a matter of seconds. The ground shook as the Duster came running. The soldier's hands trembled but she sucked in a deep breath and steadied her aim. The crossbow fired off the bolt with a loud twang. Marduk's head followed the trajectory and grunted with approval as the bolt slammed into the eye of the Duster's helmet.

More of the violet smoke billowed out, causing the Duster to halt mid-stride.

Marduk didn't know *what* the violet smoke was, but it seemed to cause distress or even pain to the Duster, and that was all he needed to know. "Can you again?" he said to the female soldier. "I will distract bastard." She didn't need to be told twice and prepared another bolt.

Demons in the thousands had taken to the streets of Akrab and begun their march towards the ziggurat. Baaq observed the masses from the flat rooftops of the square buildings, sprinting across and jumping from one to the next. She had been astonished how quickly word had spread and just how many demons had turned up outside the Golden Coconut to join the hastily put-together march. Fish-City's word indeed carried some weight in the demon community.

The crowd moved at a steady pace and so far, hadn't encountered any of the Bone Lord's security forces; something Baaq found increasingly odd. *Word about this must have spread around the city by now? Where are the security forces? They've been called in for much less than this in the past.* The whole point of this was to force the Bone Lord to divide her military power. If they didn't show, this was all for nothing.

"I'm gonna run ahead and see what is happening," Baaq shouted down to the three captains Fish-City had briefly introduced to her. "Something about this isn't *right*."

Baaq was mid-leap between two buildings when she caught sight of a black pillar of smoke rising in the distance. She frowned, not sure what to make of it. She picked up her pace and got her answer a minute later when she saw the raging fires. *What the hell?*

The Bone Lord's security forces had indeed been called into action, but clearly, they had no intention to clash with the marching demons; instead, the soldiers had turned their alchemy powered fire weapons on *anyone* and *anything* in their way. Baaq's eyes widened with horror as the soldiers unleashed their fires on the human citizens, burning and killing with the aim of wreaking as much havoc and destruction they could.

If the demons would be blamed for this senseless massacre, any chance of a peaceful co-existence between the races would be doomed. Baaq didn't know how or why, but they had been tricked. Someone was playing a game of their own, and whoever that was, they were several steps ahead of them.

Baaq spun around and dashed back across the rooftops as fast as her legs could carry her, jumping between the buildings until she reached the marching demons. She raised her rifle-arm and fired a shot to draw attention to her. "The security forces are slaughtering humans and burning everything in their sight. We need to stop them."

"What? Why would they do that?" One of the captains said.

"To blame it on us," Baaq said. "We need to go right now."

Word spread quickly among the demon masses and what had previously been a steady march now turned into a running mob pumped up for a fight.

Baaq took off once again, her heart beating in her ears. She reached a building that would be optimal for her skills with the rifle. She dropped down flat on her stomach right on the ledge and steadied her aim.

In her sights were a cluster of soldiers who had spread out in the Golden Plaza. Ancient statues had been smashed and torn down; vendor tents set ablaze, and citizens trying to flee were chased down and killed. Among the soldiers were large bi-pedal constructs that spewed fire with one arm and skewered their victims with massive steel talons with the other.

Baaq took a deep breath, trying to clear her mind to focus on the task at hand, but it was challenging. Anger unlike anything she'd experienced in a long time burned inside. Not only at the massacre playing out, but also blaming herself. She had *known* in her heart how bad things were getting in Akrab, and instead of doing something, anything, about it, she had turned her back and hidden herself away. *I'm not hiding anymore.*

She pushed her thoughts aside and willed her rifle to fire. Her first target was a soldier standing over a fallen man and bashing him with a fire baton. The energy-bullet slammed into the soldier's head and killed him instantly. The badly injured citizen looked around surprised before dragging himself up and limped away.

The other soldiers saw their colleague drop dead and turned left and right, trying to locate where the shot had come from. Baaq fired off four rapid shots in succession and took out four more soldiers. "That's right," she said under her breath. "How do you like—"

"Get in my sack?" a voice suddenly said right behind Baaq.

She immediately rolled from her stomach to her back and fired a shot in the direction of the voice. The bullet slammed into the stranger and knocked him off his feet. But a moment later he started moving again and slowly got back up like waking from a nap.

The man was tall and lanky, wearing a long, tattered coat and a wide-brimmed hat. Thin, white wisps of hair ran down to his lips, obscuring his face, but she could clearly see the purple glow in his eyes. A large and dirty old sack was slung over his shoulder. He looked down at his chest where the bullet had entered, his eyes following the violet smoke pouring out. "Why do you wish to hurt me?"

"*Who* are you?" Baaq said, shuffling up to her feet, aiming the rifle at the stranger. *And how the hell are you still alive? I got you in the heart!*

The stranger tilted his head like he was contemplating the question. "I do not remember anymore," he said with a hoarse voice. "Now I am Hangman-Daddy. Please get into my sack?"

Baaq cursed to herself. The man's glowing eyes marked him as a Duster; she should have anticipated this.

Hangman-Daddy lunged at her and grabbed her arm. His touch

was cold as death itself. Baaq instinctively head-butted the Duster which made him release his grip and stagger back.

Using the created distance, Baaq got off two shots that hit him in the head. Hangman-Daddy fell over on his back, but almost immediately began to rise again, more violet smoke leaking from the bullet wounds. "You must get into my sack," the Duster said with a sigh, his voice tired like a parent pleading with their child. "Please."

Hangman-Daddy stumbled forward awkwardly and made another attempt to grab a hold of her. "Don't touch me, you freak," Baaq said and slammed her rifle-arm in the man's face.

Hangman-Daddy stepped back, his free hand touching his face. "Why are you hitting me?"

Baaq frowned. "*Why*? Because you're trying to kidnap me or stuff me in your sack, you sick bastard."

"Kidnap you? Hmm . . ." The Duster said, stroking his chin. "Yes, I guess you are right. But please, get into my sack now?"

"*No!*" Baaq said between clenched teeth and fired a series of energy-bullets into the Duster. She grimaced as a jolt of pain ran through her rifle-arm. Her weapon did not use external ammunition and instead channelled Baaq's own life force to produce the energy needed to fire it. Her body paid a small toll for each bullet, causing her harm, but using it without care was not only dangerous but possibly lethal. Her frustration had gotten the best of her, and now she would pay the price.

Hangman-Daddy was already back on his feet, violet smoke leaking from several holes in his tattered coat. Baaq was in pain and her mental command to fire another round failed; her body's need for self-preservation kicking in. The Duster backhanded her, and the impact sent her crashing down face-first. Hangman-Daddy leapt on her back, his long legs wrapping around her waist to hold her in place. Before she knew it, the sack was being pulled over her head.

Baaq expected the inside of the sack to be pitch-black, but instead, she found herself amidst a sea of stars in a pitch-black void; her head floating as if it had been removed and shot up in space.

What the actual fuck? She gasped, squirming as much as possible to stop the rest of the sack from swallowing her.

Mid-struggle, Baaq faintly heard a whispering voice echoing across the vast darkness all around. The sound made her ears hurt; like whatever was being said wasn't meant for an insignificant mortal like her to comprehend. Panic gripped her from two directions now; physically she still fought Hangman-Daddy, but mentally she went through a primal fear unlike anything she'd ever experienced, facing this *force* hidden among the stars.

"Get me out, get me out," Baaq screamed. Her sound was muffled from the sack over her head, but her voice *inside* the sack was crystal clear. The whispering was growing stronger and stronger; and whatever the source of it was, it was also coming *closer*. Baaq didn't know how she knew, but she was certain she would instantly die–or something worse–if the hungry presence among the stars reached her.

In a moment born from desperate need for survival, Baaq's mind cleared enough to make her swing her head back repeatedly. She felt herself slamming into something–most likely Hangman-Daddy's jaw–which made the wrapped legs around her body loosen their tight grip. Using as much strength as she could possibly muster, she exploded free, her body twisting and turning in any shape or form to get the Duster off her. Hangman-Daddy's weight vanished and Baaq shot to her feet and ripped the dirty sack off her head.

The Duster was down on his back, looking like a bull-rider violently thrown off from the beast he had tried to conquer. She was now that liberated beast and leapt at the man before he had a chance to get up. Baaq transformed her rifle back into its bracelet-form so she could use both arms to physically beat up the disgusting Duster.

She chocked Hangman-Daddy with one hand and kept him in place, while her other one rained down punches in his face. "*Get in your sack?*" Baaq screamed, spit flying. Perhaps the physical violence wouldn't kill the Duster, but she could *feel* his body growing weaker, going more and more limp from each hit. Overtaken by rage and feeling defiled, Baaq shot up to her feet and ran to snatch up the sack.

Hangman-Daddy was already sitting up again, but Baaq threw herself on top of him, using all her weight to push him down. *"You get in the fucking sack!"* She said, forcing the sack over the Duster's head.

That this wasn't any ordinary sack was obvious by now, but she was still surprised to see how the fabric itself seemed to adjust its size depending on the victim. Baaq kept pulling the sack down; first covering the Duster's head then his torso and arms. Hangman-Daddy's legs kicked violently, his body squirming desperately to free himself. Baaq had no way of knowing if he was experiencing the same thing she had, but whatever was happening inside the sack seemed to work, because the Duster screamed for his life, his legs kicking for dear life.

Baaq wrapped her arms around the sack and squeezed as hard as she could, keeping the sack in place. What had been deliberate physical attempts from Hangman-Daddy to free himself now turned into uncontrollable spasms. "That's right, how do *you* like it?" she hissed.

Less than a minute later, the Duster's body finally went limp. Baaq released her grip and crab-crawled away from the corpse. The insane fight had come to an end and Baaq's mind was racing. *What the fuck just happened?*

She felt dirty and violated; her heart trying to beat itself out of her chest. But there was no time to digest the harrowing experience. From the corner of her eyes, she could see that the battle raging in the plaza had reached new levels now that the demons had arrived, and the soldiers had called in reinforcements. But not only that, the human citizens had banded together with the demons, fighting side by side against the Bone Lord's soldiers. Baaq forced herself up and transformed her arm into the rifle again.

CHAPTER THIRTY

Varcade was faster than his opponent, but the Royal Guard Captain demonstrated a type of precision with his blade Varcade had never encountered before. The two men circled each other now, allowing for a short respite from their intense back-and-forth battle.

"You're good; actually, more than *good*," Varcade said, eyes locked with his opponent, his body tensed and ready to react in the blink of an eye.

"I know," the Royal Guard Captain said, attempting a feint to make Varcade flinch.

Varcade had to push himself to his limits to keep up with the man. The tiniest of mistakes could end the fight. He tried a feint of his own but drew no reaction from Erikz. *This isn't working*, Varcade thought. *Gonna have to try something else.*

Varcade attempted a sloppy attack that deliberately left his stomach exposed, but the Royal Guard Captain instead sliced the bend of his arm, cutting a large gash. Varcade tried to not grimace from the pain. Sure, the wound would heal but that would take time, and for the moment one of his arms was now useless. In a strategic battle like this, that was a disaster.

"I know what you are," Erikz said, flicking his sword in the air and making the freshly drawn blood fly. "Your tricks won't work against me."

"Is that so?" Varcade said. His wounded arm dangled to his side; his fingers barely able to grasp the blade which dragged on the floor. "And what would that be?"

The Royal Guard Captain circled Varcade, never standing still. "You're an Educator. I know of your abilities. They won't help you against me."

Oh, this is bad for real, Varcade thought, a feeling of panic starting to build.

Erikz suddenly exploded in a series of stabs and swings and Varcade did his best to block most of them using only the one functioning arm. His opponent was telling the truth: he purposely wasn't aiming for any of his vital organs, instead attacking sections of Varcade's body that would render him useless in a fight. Varcade successfully blocked the whirlwind of attacks but just barely. He wasn't sure he would be able to pull it off again.

Varcade felt like a fool. For years he'd been relying on the powers forced upon him as an Educator, and thus mostly ignored to hone his skills as a swordsman. His opponent was the exact opposite: a man with no abilities or tricks up his sleeves who had dedicated his sole existence to mastering the art of combat one day at a time like a true professional. It was becoming glaringly obvious that Varcade's laziness had now reached the stage where it would bite him in the ass.

Doesn't matter now, Varcade thought. Using his enhanced speed, Varcade unleashed a savage barrage of attacks focused more on output than precision.

Erikz's movements were so light; his feet moved across the floor more akin to that of a dancer than an armoured knight, and he not only blocked all of Varcade's attacks, he turned it into a performance.

After a brief stand-off, Varcade saw the change in Erikz's movement but couldn't react in time. The Royal Guard Captain shifted his defensive stance to an offensive one mid-block; dancing past Varcade and slicing the fold between his left leg with a clean cut. Immediately Varcade's knee buckled and now he only had one leg to support himself with.

Erikz moved in behind him and would deliver the final swing that would separate Varcade's head from his neck. Using his heightened senses, Varcade felt the Royal Guard Captain's breath on his neck. Varcade reacted with pure instinct and plunged his sword in an upward angle into his own chest, driving it hilt-deep. The long blade came out through Varcade's back and tasted new flesh, producing a guttural sound from the Royal Guard Captain.

The Bone Lord screamed, the shrill sound echoing in the cavernous room.

Varcade slowly pulled the sword from his chest and turned around. Erikz was frozen in place, blood gushing from his throat. His sword fell to the floor with a *clank*. His eyes blinked rapidly at the scarlet running down his gleaming armour. He tried saying something but instead coughed, blood trickling from the corner of his mouth.

Varcade hobbled away a couple of steps before his working leg gave out. Blood poured from the wound in his chest, and he felt faint. The Bone Lord reached Erikz a moment after he crashed to the floor. The woman sank to her knees, placing the Royal Guard Captain's head in her lap. Varcade did not feel proud having used such a dirty tactic to best his formidable opponent, but if he hadn't, he would be the one dying instead.

"No, no, no," the Bone Lord cried, rocking back and forth. "Erikz, please!"

"You had me worried there for a moment."

Varcade looked up at the man who had entered the throne room soundlessly. He was bald, and his body had a gravy-like quality beneath layers of colourful cloth wrapped around him. His face reminded Varcade of a fat boy beaming with happiness at the anticipation of devouring a succulent meal and then having a mountain of cakes as desert.

"Who the hell are you?" Varcade said, chipping for air. He had never felt a pain like this before and a part of him feared he'd overestimated his regenerative abilities.

"Ah, that's right, we've never actually met before," the man said with a honey smoothed voice. "I'm Tarkus, the Vizier of Akrab. I have been eager to finally meet you."

"Why are you talking to him like a friend?!" The Bone Lord screamed, tears running down her cheeks. "He *murdered* Erikz!"

The bald man slowly turned towards the woman. The big smile on his lips faded into a thin line and his small eyes turned cold. Any semblance of the happy boy was gone like a mask had been removed, revealing the sinister presence hidden beneath. "Shut your mouth."

The Bone Lord's eyes widened with disbelief. It was as if she'd walked in on her parents during sex; something her mind wasn't equipped to comprehend. "W-What?"

"You heard me. Shut your fucking mouth."

What the hell is going on here? Varcade shifted slightly, making his body scream in protest. But at least the blood had stopped gushing from his chest, which hopefully meant he wasn't actively dying.

Clea gently lifted Erikz's head from her lap and got up on unsteady feet. The woman appeared to have been rattled to her core; her face carrying a look of pure terror and despair. "What's the meaning of this, Tarkus? What has gotten into you?"

"'What has gotten into you, what has gotten into you?'" Tarkus imitated, his words dripping with venom. "Do you even comprehend how *long* I have been waiting for this moment? All this time I've been forced to listen to your whiny voice. Poor little Clea who was gifted a country to rule; oh, such a burden!"

The Bone Lord was too stunned to speak. She stood completely still, staring at the Vizier in the same way one would watch a horrible accident too intriguing to look away from even though one should.

"You still don't get it, do you?" Tarkus spat. He reached inside his robe and yanked out a small jar. "The cream, you stupid bitch. There's God Dust in the cream. Your thoughts haven't been your own for years! I've had your brittle mind in the palm of my hands all this time." The hateful words flooding from the Vizier's mouth assaulted the Bone Lord like a barrage of invisible punches. Each sentence caused a physical reaction: she winced, closing her eyes, her lips quivering. "And your dear Edghar . . ." Tarkus laughed. "His steadfast presence was the last wall I had to tear down to fully control you. With him out of the way, there was nothing stopping me."

The mention of Edghar seemed to be the final nail in the coffin. Clea staggered and had to put her hands against the wall to steady herself. Her face went blank, her tears dried up. This was, in some ways, worse than a physical death; this was the annihilation of a person's soul.

"I needed you to be killed at the hands of an assassin so no one would suspect I had anything to do with it. With you dead, I could naturally step forward as the saviour of Akrab and prove my worth as the rightful man to become the new Bone Lord. The other Bone Lords would not be able to deny me!" Vizier Tarkus smiled at the human husk that was the Bone Lord.

"You," the Vizier said, turning his attention to Varcade. "It is time to finish what you came here for. Get up and kill her."

Varcade could barely understand what had just taken place here. But what he did know, was that he felt a surging hatred towards the vile man speaking to him. "Not a chance," he said. "That's off the table."

"No?" The Vizier shrugged. "Oh well, there's enough meat on the bone to support the narrative that the Bone Lord was assassinated. People all over Akrab has seen you with their own eyes. If she dies by your hands or mine are only minor details at this point."

"Don't touch her," Varcade said. Again, he tried to get up, but he psychically couldn't. He cursed his body for not obeying him. The best he could do was try to drag himself towards them, but he wouldn't get there in time. Especially since the woman made no attempt to move or flee as Tarkus strolled toward her. It was like she welcomed the death he would deliver. The Bone Lord closed her eyes as the Vizier's chubby hands shot out and wrapped around her throat.

The Duster called Bonky-Bonk now had four bolts jutting out from her armour. One in the eye of the helmet, two in the lower back and one in the chest. Violet smoke billowed from each hole, and the Duster's frantic and wild movements clearly stated their tactic was working.

Marduk and Khanon both danced around the iron giant and the frenzied swings from her hammer. Whenever Marduk got an opening he slammed the Duster with his brass-knuckle covered fists. Their impact did not do much, but the force was enough to make Bonky-Bonk stagger and momentarily loose her footing. The Army General kept hacking away with his two swords, not causing any real damage but still enough to draw attention to him.

But mortally damaging the Duster wasn't their specific purpose; their tactic was to keep Bonky-Bonk distracted while the soldiers peppered her with bolts from their crossbows.

Unfortunately, their aim wasn't the best, and the damned weapons took forever to reload. Either that, or the soldiers were simply bad at handling them.

Marduk noticed how Khanon's movements were beginning to slow. He still managed to dodge the incoming blows from the hammer, but he was clearly struggling to keep up. "You tired, old man?" Marduk said.

"Focus on yourself," Khanon said between clenched teeth.

The split-second Marduk had taken to mock the Army General proved costly.

Bonky-Bonk spun around and slammed a gauntleted fist into his face. Marduk was sent flying from the power of the blow. He landed on his back; the air knocked out of him. The serene view of the starlit sky was interrupted by a massive shape appearing out of nowhere.

The Duster had leapt straight up in the air and was now crashing down towards him.

Marduk roared in defiance as death descended on him, but something grabbed his foot and pulled him away right before the Duster's impact would have crushed his bones to powder.

"Up, you fool," Khanon said, dragging Marduk to his feet.

In a somewhat comical display, the Duster landed on her rump in a billow of dust where Marduk had been just a moment before.

"Why you save me?" Marduk said.

"Because I can't win this fight alone," Khanon said. "Not against a Duster. Come on."

Bonky-Bonk shot up again and immediately charged at them with her hammer held out before her like a battering ram. The sound of the infant crying had now reached super angry baby levels.

The twang of another bolt loosed rang out and slammed into the thigh of the Duster. More violet smoke leaked out, but the Duster did not slow down; if anything, she seemed to be getting more hysterical and unpredictable in her attacks.

"How we stop this *thing*?" Marduk shouted as he leapt back from the hammer. "What must we do?"

Khanon was about to say something when one of the slaves crept up behind him and slammed a large rock in the back of his head. The Army General sank down on one knee. As he turned to look over his shoulder at his attacker, the rock once again slammed into his face with a wet crunch. The man who had moments ago saved Marduk from death was now face down in a pool of his own blood. Maybe dead.

"I did it!" the slave said. A thin and young man. "Look, Marduk! I felled their leader!" The slave's celebration was cut short as Bonky-Bonk's hammer crushed his head like a watermelon.

The Duster stopped for a moment, staring straight at Marduk.

Marduk stared back, clenching his fists.

He could hear the words of "retreat" coming from the Royal

Soldiers as notice of the Army General's death spread around the battlefield.

"If I die, I die," Marduk said before unleashing a guttural roar and charged the Duster head-on.

Bonky-Bonk met his charge with her own.

Marduk had no plan except to avoid being hit by the massive hammer. He waited for the absolute last moment before ducking beneath the wild swing and slamming his weight into her like a flying spear. The Duster lifted off her feet from the force and crashed to the ground onto her back. Marduk swiftly mounted himself on top and unleashed a barrage of strikes and elbows. Blood sprayed from the torn skin opening on his knuckles, but Marduk was beyond caring at this point.

Using all the might he could muster, Marduk ripped off the gorget from the Duster's neck then grabbed the helmet. *My fists will taste your foul flesh even if it's the last thing I do*, he thought as he wrenched and pulled violently. But as the helmet finally came off, there was no face there to greet him. Instead, a thick cloud of violet smoke billowed out.

The Duster's body spasmed and rattled, arms and legs flailing as the smoke poured from the hollow armour and rose in the dark sky. Marduk followed the smoke with a dumbfounded look as the violet smoke coalesced into the giant shape of a human woman cradling a babe in her arms. The infant screamed from the top of its lungs and the woman's face was distorted into something straight out of a nightmare. Their presence did not last long as a gust of wind passed by, making the woman and child dissipate into nothing.

Marduk pushed himself off the Duster's hollow armour. With the Royal Army in retreat, and the Duster defeated, the battle was finally over. Marduk looked around and saw bodies littered everywhere. The sand had indeed quenched its thirst this night. He returned to the Army General and flung his corpse over his shoulder. "You not bad onion," he said mostly to himself. "I bring you back to your people."

"I'm *never* ever going *anywhere* with you again."

Marduk could not help but crack a smile as Dog Man appeared next to him. The canine's white fur had turned pink, and he walked with a limp. "I forget you here. You survive. That is good."

"Fuck you, man. Seriously."

Marduk laughed a hearty laugh. The two of them began the journey back to the city.

Clea had been ready to die when Tarkus seized her throat in his hands. But as he started choking her in earnest, applying his full force to prevent her from drawing a single breath, a primal need for self-preservation had flared up within her very core.

She would not give this treacherous snake the satisfaction of ending her life and get away with everything. She *refused* to let him win. Tarkus did not expect any resistance, so when Clea suddenly reached up and pressed her thumbs in the man's eyes, his celebratory wicked smile turned into anguish. He unleashed a harrowing scream as Clea burrowed her fingers as deep into his soft eyeballs as she could.

Tarkus released his grip and staggered away from her, trails of blood trickling down out the corners of his eyes. Clea was overtaken by mad fury and ran after him, slashing his face with her fingernails. Tarkus screeched in anger and punched her right on the nose, felling her to the floor. Clea's eyes teared up and her head spun. She tried her best to defend herself from the barrage of kicks raining down on her from Tarkus, but she could barely hold up her battered arms anymore.

"I was going to make it quick, but now I'll wait until you *beg* me to kill you," Tarkus spat, his eyes black with malice. "You hear? Beg!"

I'll never beg you for anything, you spineless worm, Clea thought, trying to keep her composure, refusing to surrender. As long as she drew breath she wouldn't go down without a fight, and him underestimating her was her greatest weapon.

As Tarkus bent down to grab her hair, Clea seized the opportunity and kicked up her knee with all the strength she could muster, cracking the fat man's jaw with thunderous force. Tarkus was stunned from the blow and wobbled back, momentarily dazed.

Clea scrambled to her feet fast as she could and lunged at him with the ferocity of a desert fiend. She scratched and punched and perhaps even bit him–she wasn't entirely sure–, causing the man as much harm as she physically could dish out.

Unfortunately, it proved to not be enough. Tarkus backhanded her and followed up with a powerful punch to her gut. Clea's legs gave out and she slumped to the floor on her knees, wheezing. *I tried*, she thought, gasping for air. *At least I tried . . .*

Tarkus' hands wrapped themselves around her throat and this time she had no more fight to give. Her vision was slowly fading to black when the massive stained-glass window of the throne room suddenly exploded with a deafening shatter. Tarkus released his grip and Clea screamed as a shower of glass rained down all around them. Sweet breath once again entering her lungs, she blinked with utter confusion at the impossible sight before her.

The camel–if that's what it was–came through the window and skidded on the floor, its hoofs sliding and slipping, making the poor animal's gangly legs bend in comical and sad angles as it struggled to regain its balance. The rider holding on to dear life wore an eyepatch, his blue cape fluttering behind him. Long dirty-black hair ran down his face and his beard was rugged and unkempt, but there was no mistaking it: Clea knew who it was the moment she laid eyes on him.

"E-Edghar?" she said, barely a whisper, unable to close her mouth.

The clickety-clack of the camel's hoofs finally came to a stop as the animal stilled. Something moved behind Edghar in the saddle, but it was obstructed from view by the heavy blue cape her former spymaster was wearing. A rather young boy popped his head out from under the fabric, gasping for air and untangling himself. He leaped off the animal and landed on shaky legs. Clea couldn't help but acknowledge the boy's hairdo might very well be the worst one she'd ever seen.

"What the hell, man?! What the actual hell?" the boy shouted, his hands on his knees, staring up at Edghar still seated in the saddle. "You did *not* tell me you were planning to do that! You're insane!"

But Edghar paid the boy no attention. His one eye darted between Clea and Tarkus. Before Tarkus could make any move, Edghar raised his hand bow and fired a quick bolt in the man's chest. Her former Vizier staggered back with wide eyes and crashed to the floor.

The boy dashed over to the silver-haired foreigner and crouched next to him. "Hey, Edghar, it's Varcade. He's alive."

"Quite the entrance, Helmet-Head," Varcade said with a weak smile. "Impressive."

"Clea . . . Thank the White Queen," Edghar said. "You have no idea how relieved I am to see you're still alive. I'm . . . I don't know where to begin . . ."

Clea wanted to feel nothing but hatred for the man, but her heart refused to cooperate and open the gates to where her darkest thoughts resided. What she really wanted, more than anything else, was to throw herself into the familiar comfort of his arms.

But she couldn't do that.

Edghar unmounted and took a couple of cautious steps towards her, but she raised her hand which made him halt immediately. "Don't come closer," Clea said, trying her best to keep her voice from breaking. Uttering those words went completely against what she really wanted.

Edghar opened his mouth to say something before snapping it shut. Again, he tried saying something, raising his arm to begin explaining before it feebly fell to his side. He shook his head and took a deep breath. "You're hurt."

"I'll live."

"Tarkus. It was him all along."

"I know," Clea said. "He told me everything right before he tried to strangle me to death."

Edghar clenched his fist, not saying anything for a moment or two. "We've both been fooled, Clea. For a long time. I had no idea Tarkus was a Duster. I should've known but I didn't. My job was to defend you against any potential threat, and it turns out the biggest one was right under my nose this whole time. I not only failed you, but all of Akrab. The city I was sworn to protect. But—"

"What happened to your arm?" Clea blurted. She hadn't noticed it until just now, and she found herself unable to look away from it. It was much too small for his body and looked deformed.

Edghar stiffened and quickly draped his cape to cover it up. "That's . . . I'd rather not talk about it."

"It's a baby arm."

Clea and Edghar both turned to look at the boy with the atrocious hairdo crouched next to Varcade.

"His arm got chopped off in a fight so a guy we know fixed him up."

"*Baby arm?*" Clea said with a grimace. "What does that even mean?"

"I said I don't wanna talk about it!" Edghar said. "Shut up, Jasper."

Clea took a couple of steps closer to Edghar. With a trembling hand she reached for his face. "You lost an eye too," she said softly, her fingertips touching his cheek.

"No, he didn't."

"What?" Clea said.

"He did not lose an eye," the boy said. "It's fake."

"You must've hurt your head pretty bad from that fall, eh?" Varcade chuckled.

"I–" Edghar stuttered.

Clea lifted the patch and indeed saw Edghar's eye, and it was perfectly healthy. Edghar snatched the eyepatch off and threw it to the side. "Forget that. I was hit in the head and wasn't myself for a while. It's a long story."

"Told you," the boy muttered.

Clea couldn't help but smile. She grabbed Edghar's face with both hands and looked deep in his eyes. "I've never seen you like this. Where's the stoic and all too serious Edghar Ligaro I've always known?"

Edghar shrugged, also allowing himself to smile now. "As I said, a lot has happened. I doubt we'll ever see that version of me again. I mean, look at me." He pulled his cape aside to fully reveal his new arm. "What the hell is *that*?"

Clea tilted her head to have a better look. "That's . . . seriously disturbing."

Edghar laughed awkwardly, rubbing the back of his head. "I'll fix it somehow. Don't worry."

Clea's smile faded, and she turned around, suddenly unable to look at him. She wished this could be nothing but a loving reunion, but that would be too simple. As Edghar had said, so much had happened.

"Clea?" Edghar said, placing his regular hand on her shoulder.

"You plotted to have me killed. You sent assassins after me." Saying it out loud felt strange. Like she was making it up. But she wasn't. It had really happened. The man she'd always loved on some level had planned and orchestrated to end her life.

"Clea, look at me." Edghar gently made her turn to face him. "I thought I was doing the *right* thing. Words can't express how much this whole ordeal has pained me. I know how sick it sounds, but I saw no other way. You *did* order your men to kill me, you know? I did not make that up. You broke my heart that day. How should I have known Tarkus was manipulating you?"

Clea sighed. That part was true. And the worst thing about it was that she wasn't even entirely sure Tarkus could be blamed for *all* of it. She had been angry, furious even, on that day. Perhaps her own bad traits had been the key Tarkus needed to affect her to begin with. It was time she owned up to her mistakes and stopped blaming everyone else. "You're not wrong about that. I know. I failed this city long before this—"

"Hello, excuse me."

Everyone in the throne room turned their attention to the stranger. The man wore a blue coat and his silvery hair pointed straight up in the air, defying all physical laws.

"I'm looking for my brother," the stranger said. "His name is Varcade."

CHAPTER THIRTY-ONE

Varcade slowly pushed himself up on his elbows, struggling to comprehend the sight before him. "It can't be . . . Vashi?"

But it was. There was no doubt about it. His brother that he hadn't seen in years had now suddenly appeared right here in Akrab. Vashi faced the collective group, blood and dust caked his face, his blue coat torn and ripped.

"You're the mysterious attacker?" Varcade said. "What the hell is going on?"

"Swearing is forbidden, little brother. You know this," Vashi said.

"Really?" Varcade said. "You've come all this way across half the world to start lecturing me?"

Vashi did not answer. Instead, his focus had shifted to Edghar. "You're the man behind this, aren't you? The one who paid him to come here and assassinate the Bone Lord."

Edghar was about to reply when Varcade cut in. "Don't answer him! Anything you say can be used against you. Better to just shut up, trust me." Varcade finally felt good enough to force himself to stand on wobbly legs. "You have nothing to do with this, Vashi."

"Of course, I do. You represent the Educator Order. I can't allow you to sully our reputation and cause irreparable harm by your foolish actions. I thank the Saints I was able to stop you in time. I have been looking everywhere."

"Everywhere?" Varcade said. "Wait, how long have you been in Akrab?"

Vashi tilted his head, contemplating the question. "A couple of days. Maybe a week."

"A week? How haven't you been able to find me before now? It's not like we've been keeping a low profile."

"I had to enforce the Teachings almost everywhere I went. This city is a bad place."

"The Teachings?" Edghar said, speaking up even though Varcade had explicitly asked him not to.

"Don't bother, it's basically just a way to justify beating people up if they don't behave a certain way."

"That's not true," Vashi said. "I educate them in accordance with the Teachings. I make the world better and help restore the Balance."

Varcade scoffed. "Yeah right."

"You'll be quiet now, little brother. You have caused enough problems for the Order as it is. Come on, let's go."

"Are you stupid?" Varcade said. "I'm not going with you."

"You will come. You have no choice."

"I don't know the story between the two of you, but if Varcade doesn't want to go, then maybe you should respect that."

No, Edghar you idiot . . .

Vashi's head snapped towards Edghar. "Interfering in Educator affairs is forbidden. You must be–"

"I'm *not* an Educator anymore," Varcade said, demanding his brother's attention. "How can you still not understand that after all this time?"

"Because one does not abandon the Order. The only way to leave is to be . . ." Vashi hesitated, the first sign that his brother had a shred of humanity left in him.

"*Released*," Varcade said. "That's what you were about to say, wasn't it? Are you really going to kill me, Vashi?"

"Hey," Edghar said, taking a step towards Vashi, "If he doesn't want to go then you can't—"

With lightning speed, Vashi slammed an open palm into Edghar's chest and sent him crashing into a wall several feet away. The Bone Lord screamed and ran after her former spymaster. Varcade limped forward to grab his brother, but Vashi's hand shot out like a cobra and gripped Varcade's wrist. "Enough of this. We go now."

Varcade tried yanking his arm free, but his brother held him in place. "Are you really going to force me to fight you?" he said between clenched teeth.

"That will be your choice, but you will not win. You know this."

"Stop this!" the Bone Lord shouted from across the room. Edghar leaned up against her, his arm around her neck. "Enough. I don't know who you are, but I *demand* you to stop."

"You hold no authority over me," Vashi said, meeting Clea's stare. "And you don't have the right to interfere with Educator affairs. I will Educate you if I must."

"Wait, you came all the way here to stop *me* from assassinating her and now *you* are threatening to beat her up?" Varcade said. "Don't you see how messed up that is?"

"The Teachings states that no one except another Educator are allowed to—"

"Uh, guys," Helmet Head said with a tremble in his voice.

"Not now!" Varcade roared. "Can't you see we're having a crucial discussion?"

"Y-You should listen to the boy . . ."

Everyone's heads snapped in the direction of Tarkus' breath-less voice which somehow still sounded menacing. The fat man clutched his heaving chest where a bolt jutted out, blood trickling down his stomach and dripping to the floor. The jar of lotion that had contained his God Dust lay hollowed out at his feet, and Varcade could see the white cream smeared all around his mouth.

"What have you done?" The Bone Lord stuttered, eyes darting from the empty jar to Tarkus' face. "You ate all the Dust? You'll be *Taken!*"

"I'll not be defeated," Tarkus hissed. "Not now; not ever. You'll all die with me."

Tarkus' face suddenly contorted with pain. The flesh around his chest, arms and legs turned taut as the muscles underneath bulged out; the God Dust spreading throughout his body. But what had initially been a change in his physical appearance by way of gaining muscle mass now quickly turned Tarkus into something barely resembling a man at all. It was as if his bone structure was morphing rapidly, becoming something that would no longer be contained by the prison of human flesh. His facial features were distorted into something monstrous; the lips receding from his mouth creating a perpetual sick grin. The last semblance of humanity in his eyes were replaced by obsidian pits, violet smoke leaking out.

Edghar had not waited for Tarkus to fully transform before he had grabbed the Bone Lord and dragged her towards the dead-looking camel still idly standing around. He'd called for Helmet Head who'd ran up to him. After a quick–and heated–exchange, Clea and Helmet Head mounted the animal and took off.

Tarkus' head turned towards them making their escape, but Edghar fired off three bolts with his hand bow that drew his attention. The bolts bounced off Tarkus as if they'd slammed into a wall of rock, but the distraction had been enough for the Bone Lord and Helmet Head to flee through the double doors of the throne room. Edghar ran to Varcade and Vashi. Together, the three of them now faced the monster Tarkus had become.

Tarkus stepped towards them before he suddenly let out a harrowing scream that echoed out across the throne room. The thick snaky veins running up his arms and legs bulged out even more than before, pumping with blood and looking close to bursting. Tarkus' body spasmed, accompanied by guttural sounds escaping his lips. His body was spasming so fast, only the vague shape of a man was visible.

"This was *not* what I signed up for," Varcade said. "Holy shit."

"Can someone please tell me what is happening?" Vashi said. "I don't understand."

Edghar had a disturbingly calm look on his face. "Doesn't matter, we'll all be dead soon."

The heavens exploded with a sound a thousand times louder than regular lightning. A heartbeat or three after the sound, the whole roof of the ziggurat came crashing down in a deafening explosion. Through the new opening in the roof came a massive bolt of violet lightning that struck Tarkus right where he stood. But instead of obliterating the man, the energy went *into* him. The instant it did, a massive force exploded outwards from Tarkus, trashing anything and everything hit by the immense blast. Varcade, Vashi and Edghar were all sent flying like pebbles caught in a hurricane.

Varcade blacked out for a moment before coming around amidst a pile of rubble. He shook his head, coughing, trying to clear out the cobwebs and stop his head from ringing. The whole ziggurat was coming down slowly but surely, the floors and walls vibrating. The amount of dust in the air making it close to impossible to see.

"Varcade!" someone shouted amidst the ruins and grime. "Can you hear me?"

"Over here, Edghar," Varcade said, slowly sitting up. A moment later, he could see the contour of a man coming closer towards him through the wall of dust.

"Good, you're alive," Edghar said, covering his mouth with his one functional hand.

"Tarkus," Varcade coughed as he got up to his feet. "He's a Taken now? It really happened, didn't it? We need to find the whole crew if we're even gonna stand a chance."

"First things first," Edghar said. "We need to get the hell out of here. Whole place's coming down any moment."

Varcade groaned. A rib or two were broken. "Need to find Vashi first."

"No need, I am here."

Vashi made his entrance out of the smoke like a performer taking the stage. "I heard your voices and followed the sound."

"Let's go," Varcade said. "Come on."

The three of them moved towards the exit, rock and dust from the roof still falling all around them. Edghar took the lead since he knew the ziggurat inside out even in this ruined state.

"There's someone up ahead," Edghar said. "I hear voices."

"As long as it's not Tarkus, we still have a chance of making it out alive," Varcade said.

They finally reached the corridor leading out from the building, and to Varcade's surprise and joy, the voices had belonged to Zuba the Mad Puppeteer and his mother Lady Qanah.

Lady Qanah was trying to drag Zuba with her, but her son was refusing to go, instead trying to return deeper inside the ziggurat.

"He's my friend!" Zuba said. "I won't leave without him!"

"He's *not* your friend, you stupid boy! He doesn't even like you! No one likes you!" Lady Qanah said, grabbing her son with both hands and pulling him away.

"You're wrong! I'm sure he's still in there looking for us. He wouldn't leave us behind—"

Varcade cleared his throat. "Eh, so this is a bit awkward..."

Lady Qanah released her son. "Told you," she muttered.

Zuba crossed his lanky arms, his snake-like eyes starring daggers at the three of them. "Did you even *try* to find us? Did you?"

"We did!" Varcade said. "I swear!"

Vashi's head snapped to look at his brother. "That is a complete lie. Meaning the statement you just said does not contain a single grain of truth. Lying is forbidden by the Teachings. We did not attempt to look for anyone before trying to locate the exit. You must be reprimanded—"

"NOT. NOW." Varcade screamed in his brother's face. "Will you give it a rest for once?!"

Zuba scoffed, looking away. "So that's how it is then."

Edghar closed his eyes, rubbing the bridge of his nose. "Two minutes back with you all and I already have a headache . . . And this isn't even the whole—"

The doors to the ziggurat slammed open with a bang as Marduk awkwardly riding Dog Man came into view. The dog swayed side to side, unable to keep his balance under the hefty size of the demon.

"Get off me!" Dog Man said the moment he noticed Varcade and the others. "Get the hell off!"

"I can't believe you let him ride you," Varcade said as Dog Man and Marduk caught up to them. "I don't think I can ever look at you the same way again."

"He played the *emergency* card!" Dog Man said with a panicked voice. "We saw the bolt in the sky and the roof exploding! Time was of the essence, and we had to . . . We had to move quickly . . . Life and death . . . I thought we had to save you . . ."

Marduk patted Dog Man's head. "That was fun. You are good boy."

"I feel dirty . . ." Dog Man said, looking down at the floor.

"Before anyone asks, this is my brother Vashi," Varcade said. "That's all the explanation you'll get for now so shut up about it. Let's get outta here before the whole place—"

The tremors and rumbles going through the palace before had been nothing compared to those that came now. No one had to say anything. The crew bolted for the double door as rocks the size of grown men came crashing all around them. The floor cracked, opening long fissures threatening to swallow them.

They ran as fast as their feet could carry them. Inches from the doors, Varcade slipped for a moment and crashed into Edghar's back which made him fall into Lady Qanah. One by one they all fell on top of each other, spilling out through the doors and down the massive staircase in a heap of rolling limbs.

The ziggurat imploded from within. Boulders and bricks flying in every direction as *something* gargantuan rose from within the ruins, shaking its arms and legs as if the building had been a tight skin it was now shedding. Rising on its feet accompanied by a sickening roar stood an Elder God in the flesh.

"We're so fucking dead . . ." Dog Man muttered.

CHAPTER THIRTY-TWO

Varcade and the rest of the crew all scrambled to their feet and ran as fast as their legs could carry them. Behind them, the Elder God's reign of destruction began. The titan swung its arms, obliterating the surrounding buildings like they were made from sand. Its feet crushed any poor bastard who had the misfortune of literally being in the worst place at the worst time possible.

The crew made their way down a long street and created enough distance between them and the Taken to have a brief moment and catch their breath.

"We've gotta do something," Edghar said, chipping for air. "The Taken's going to destroy the whole city. Everything we've been fighting for will have been for nothing. It can't end like this."

"What would you have us do, silly man?" Lady Qanah said. "That's an Elder God back from the stars. It is over." She grabbed Zuba's hand. "Come on, son. We're leaving. This is not what we agreed to."

Zuba pulled his hand away. "If Varcade's staying then I'm staying."

"Guess you're staying then, because I'm not going anywhere," Varcade said.

"You're not?" Edghar said, looking at Varcade wide-eyed. "I mean, good, it's just, I thought I was going to have to convince you to stay and help."

"Is it a surprise that you won't have to?"

"Hell yeah it is."

Vashi put a hand on Varcade shoulder. "It should not be. He is an Educator, and we live to serve and protect the people. It is our duty."

"I am *not* an Educator, and that's not why I'm doing it," Varcade said. "I just refuse to let that fat bastard Tarkus get away with this. So, with that said, if you're all onboard, I say let's go take down an Elder God."

Marduk clenched his fists, a wild grin on his lips. "I am ready."

Dog Man sighed. "I'm going to die today, aren't I?"

Varcade cracked a smile. "Not if I can help it, doggie."

"Enough with this nonsense!" Lady Qanah said. "Zuba, I *refuse* to let you entertain this foolery. We are leaving and that is that."

"Shut up, *mom!*" Zuba said, staring his mother in the face. "Stop telling me what to do! If you want to go, then just go! I'm staying."

The old crone was taken back by her son's outburst. "Stupid child . . ." Lady Qanah muttered. "This will be the death of the Ghul clan. But if you refuse to go then I must stay as well." She turned to Varcade. "Well, how exactly do you propose we do this?"

Varcade laughed. "No bloody clue. We'll wing it or somethin'." When no one opposed that, Varcade looked at Edghar. "No objection? Really?"

Edghar shrugged. "Believe it or not, but I trust you. So, if you say we wing it then we wing it."

"I like this new you," Varcade said, punching Edghar in the shoulder. "Let's go."

Varcade took the lead as they made their way back down the street where the Taken was behaving like a child throwing a tantrum. The Elder God was still tearing down buildings and stomping his feet to crush anything catching his attention. While the crew ran towards the Elder God, countless other panicked citizens of Akrab ran as far away from it as possible.

"Zuba, there are a lot of corpses in the streets," Varcade said mid-run. "We're going to need you to do your thing and reanimate as many as you can. This is your chance to perform your masterpiece. We need you." The Mad Puppeteer beamed with joy. It would have been an inspiring sight if the man didn't look so gleefully twisted when smiling. With a nod, Zuba stopped running and began performing his dark arts, Lady Qanah staying with her son to protect him from harm's way.

Varcade turned his head to Marduk. "This is your chance to go head-to-head with an Elder God and let it taste those fists of yours. You're always looking for a bigger challenge and it doesn't get any bigger than this. Go get it, big man." Marduk laughed and took off. Seeing the fearless demon rushing head on to face a Taken was a sight to behold.

"Vashi—"

The Educator put his hand on Varcade's shoulder. "I know what I need to do. We will speak again once this is all over."

Varcade nodded. "Be careful. Also, we want to save this city, not destroy it. Remember that."

Vashi dashed to the side and leapt up to climb the closest building. He would need to position himself perfectly for what he was about to do. They could see him jumping across the rooftops for a few moments before he vanished out of sight.

Three rapid, loud *booms* suddenly sounded. A second later, the Taken screeched as three energy-bullets struck it.

"Looks like Baaq is now joining the fight," Edghar said, looking up to the taller buildings and trying to spot her. "I'd recognise the sound of her rifle anywhere."

"Perfect timing," Varcade grinned. "Let her blast that bastard to pieces."

Varcade called them to a halt some safe distance away from the Elder God. He was now alone with Edghar and Dog Man.

"What exactly are we supposed to do?" Dog Man said, looking up at Varcade.

"Nothing."

"*Nothing?*" Edghar said. "Are we just to stand here while they fight for their lives?"

Varcade crossed his arms. "I trust our friends will pull this off. You'll see."

Edghar smiled. "Looks like I'm not the only one who's showing a new side. They're *friends* now, eh?"

"Yeah, yeah, you've both learned crap about yourselves through all this. We get it, now shut up about it," Dog Man said. "I approve of this plan. I approve very much."

"Hey, there's Vashi. Up there." Edghar said, pointing. "What's he doing?"

The Educator had positioned himself on the ledge of a tall building in extremely close vicinity to where the Elder God was running amok. Vashi raised his staff to the sky and screamed, "Tears of One Thousand Saints!"

A beam of lightning shot from Vashi's staff. The Educator held it upright with trembling arms, straining to keep it straight, the energy a constant flow. The sky which was already dark turned even darker, and the clouds came together to become one with each other. The heavens rumbled and a slow and steady pitter-patter of fat droplets descended from the heavens above.

"You're probably not going to like this," Varcade said to Edghar. "We need to take cover quickly."

"What do you mean?" The former spymaster said with a worried look, as Varcade led the three of them inside the ruins of a newly destroyed building.

"You'll see."

Baaq had no clue what was going on.

One moment things had seemed simple and clear: provide ranged support for her fellow demons taking the fight to the Bone Lord's security forces. That was before a strange man had appeared next to her on the rooftop and tried stuffing her inside a sack that turned out to be anything but a regular sack.

Shortly after dealing with the Duster, before even getting the chance to properly catch her breath, she sees and hears the sky explode, followed by a bolt of lightning striking the ziggurat.

That seemed like ages ago, because now a giant had exploded out of the ruins of the building and was destroying everything and anything in sight. She had spotted Varcade and the others first running away from the giant, before then turning back and running towards it.

So Baaq naturally shifted her focus from shooting the Bone Lord's soldiers on the streets, to directing her bullets to the humongous being with evil written all over it.

She lay on her stomach on the edge of the rooftop, firing bullet after bullet, all of them obviously hitting the target. "Don't know how much this is really doing," she said under her breath. "But it's all I got."

The giant did show pain when her bullets tore through its skin, giving off a deafening screech that was music to Baaq's ears. However, it clearly wouldn't be enough to fell the monster. But if she could provide any distraction at all, she would do it. Akrab was still her home, and she would rather die defending it than flee.

The giant was now clearly getting annoyed by her bullets, spinning around to see where they were coming from. Baaq's heart froze in her chest as the monster stopped and looked straight in her direction. It reached down and grabbed a massive chunk of stone that had once been a large part of a building.

"Oh shit."

She scrambled to her feet and ran. She didn't need to turn around to sense what was coming. Reaching the other side of the rooftop, she threw herself off just as the building she'd been on was decimated.

Vashi gritted his teeth, his body crackling with ethereal blue lightning. *I call for your help, Saints in the Land Above,* he thought, watching in awe as a portion of the sky above the Elder God split open. *Let your precious tears help cleanse away this stain from our mortal realm.*

Vashi's staff acted as a beacon to signal the Saints he was in the presence of ultimate evil. Feeling the pain in an Educator's heart, the deities would begin to collectively weep from their halls in the Land Above where they resided in the afterlife.

"Tears of One Thousand Saints!" He cried out for a second time.

One could not be faulted if for one moment thinking what fell from the heavens was a heavy downpour of rain; but as the droplets descended closer and closer to the ground, each one lit up with a white glow. Impossible to mistake it for usual rain, the Tears of the Saints looked more like countless shooting stars.

At first, the Elder God didn't take notice of what was happening, swinging its arms and legs to continue its senseless destruction, but as the first drop landed on its skin, the Taken definitely took notice. The man who'd once been the mortal called Tarkus looked at the sky for a moment before being bombarded by the Tears of the Saints.

The Elder God screeched as the tears sizzled its skin, tearing through flesh and bone like a hot knife through butter. *It's working,* Vashi thought in amazement, still giving it his all to keep his staff steady. He guided the Saints where to direct their attack, doing the best he could to avoid collateral damage. In the past, on rare occasions, Educators had used Tears of One Thousand Saints to annihilate complete cities when determined they were beyond redemption.

Unfortunately, Vashi couldn't completely control it, and some tears missed the Elder God, destroying anyone or anything they touched. But thankfully, Vashi was doing more than a decent job of mostly directing the tears to hit the intended target.

The damage on the Elder God's body was gruesome. The melted skin was sloughing from its body, landing in smoking heaps on the streets beneath it. The Taken screamed and trashed, clearly looking for the source of its pain.

"Not good," Vashi muttered as the Taken finally spotted him on the ledge of the high building. "Not good at all." His natural instincts screamed for him to run, but Vashi did not move.

Self-preservation does not take precedence over my duties. I must stand my ground for as long as psychically possible. That is my calling and–

Vashi couldn't complete his thought as seeing the hammer-fist coming down on top of him was a rather distracting view.

Marduk was still hurt from his fight with the Duster called Bonky-Bonk, but the challenge of fighting an Elder God lit a fire in his belly that pushed aside all concerns about his physical well-being.

He ran towards the Taken as fast as his legs could carry him. The Elder God towered over the tallest buildings in the city, and Marduk only really saw two massive legs before him. He had no clue how to actually fight an Elder God but getting his hands on his target was usually the first step.

Strange rain had briefly fallen from the skies, showering the Elder God. It had ripped its skin to melted shreds. Whatever that had been, it had thankfully stopped now that Marduk was finally close. The stench from the steaming heaps of skin on the ground was disgusting. He passed one skin pile and saw a man trapped underneath it; his arm outstretched.

"Please help me," the man said with both a panicked and disgusted face. "I-I got it in my mouth..."

Marduk gave him a quick glance and said no.

The ground shook and trembled as the Taken moved around, its feet dreadnoughts of destruction that pulverised anything they came in contact with. Marduk waited for an opening and leapt up on a pile of rubble, then in the same motion threw himself as high up as he could and grabbed onto the Elder God's leg, right below the kneecap. He dug his claw-like fingers as deep in the flesh as he could, struggling to get a firm hold.

It dawned on Marduk how insignificant he was to the raging Elder God. If the Taken had even noticed him–which Marduk doubted–it showed no sign of it. At the same time, Marduk was clinging on to dear life, slipping and sliding, close to losing his grip over and over. Whatever that magical rain had been, it had caused extensive damage to the body of the Elder God; and in turn, that made Marduk's climbing almost impossible. Flesh and gore squished between his fingers as he readjusted his grip repeatedly. It was like a tender piece of meat that falls off the bone at the slightest touch.

This will not work, Marduk realised. *There is no way for me to get high enough.*

His short-sighted goal had been to climb up to the throat of the Elder God and cause as much damage as he could before eventually falling off. But at this rate, he'd soon be thrown off without having achieved anything. He'd only reached the upper thigh thus far, and almost been thrown off several times.

Marduk tilted his head and realised the Elder God's groin was within reach. *That always works*, he thought with a savage grin.

Clea couldn't believe what was happening. She sat mounted behind the boy with the ugly hair on the undead camel, the animal racing down narrow streets, taking them away from the destruction caused by a giant monster.

"We've gone far enough," Clea said, arms wrapped around the boy's waist. "Turn us around. I need to know what is happening!"

"We really shouldn't stop, Your Highness," the boy said, breathing hard. "I promised Edghar I would take you as far away as possible–aaaaargh! My ear!"

"Edghar? Am *I* not the Bone Lord of Akrab? I'll let go when you shut up and do as I say," Clea said, squeezing the boy's meaty earlobe. "Don't make me repeat myself."

The boy nudged the undead camel with his heels and made the animal turn, which in turn made Clea release her grip. She leaned to the side, not able to fathom what was happening to her city. The whole thing was surreal. Akrab, one of the greatest city-states in all of Harrah was being demolished by something straight out of a nightmare.

Up until now, she had always been sceptical of the notion that consuming too much God Dust would create an Anchor for an Elder God so they could return to the mortal plane. But witnessing this happening before her eyes left no doubts. It could indeed happen, and it had.

"Hey, that's Marduk." The boy said. "What the hell is he doing?"

"Who?" Clea said. "Where?"

"Up there," the boy pointed. "He's one of the demons Edghar and Varcade brought onboard to . . . You know . . ."

"Kill me? Yes, I'm aware of that."

The boy cleared his throat. "He's climbing up the giant's leg. I don't understand what he's planning to do?"

A couple of moments passed then Clea said, "It looks like this Marduk of yours is—"

"Yup, he's pummelling the giant's gonads. That's what he's doing."

"However crude, it does seem to be working?" Clea said, both hearing and seeing the pained reaction from the Elder God.

"Looks like it. I guess even an Elder God doesn't like being hit in the groin."

The demon kept up his relentless attack, holding on for dear life with one arm and driving up his other fist over and over. Clea winced at the brutal sight. But it ended abruptly when the Taken snatched up the demon and threw him over its shoulder.

The dead rose in droves around Zuba and his mother. The fighting between the demons and the Bone Lord's security forces had littered the streets with bodies, and now the Mad Puppeteer was bringing them all back to do his bidding.

Zuba held his fingers outstretched, sending out close to invisible blue lines that shot out from his fingertips and hooked themselves to the corpses. His arms and fingers danced as he forced the dead to rise again, pulling the strings and controlling them just like a puppeteer which had earned him his nickname.

"I've never seen you control this many at once," Lady Qanah said, looking at all the undead around them. "I didn't think it possible. Not even your father could do this."

Zuba scoffed, his teeth clenched, beads of sweat rolling down his brow. "This is nothing, Mother. I'm far from done. After today, my name will be immortalised." After a moment he added, "And Varcade will like me."

"*Varcade?* Are you risking our lives to impress that buffoon?" Lady Qanah spat.

"He's not a buffoon! He's my best friend. Now be quiet, I need to concentrate."

"I can't believe what I'm hearing," Lady Qanah muttered.

Being a Supreme meant Zuba didn't need God Dust to awaken the magical abilities believed innate in all humans. The Ghul clan (on his father's side) were of the Old Blood. An ancient people that wielded magic like the Elder Gods themselves; some even saying they were actual offspring from the Gods. For Zuba, his magical bloodline had always been a blessing and a curse. His destiny and purpose had been set even before he'd been born. But seeing Varcade, the rogue Educator who had broken free from the shackles enforced on him, had inspired Zuba in a way he didn't know was possible.

"Careful," Lady Qanah said, her milk-white eyes taking in the scene. "Don't exert yourself."

"Stop telling me what to do," Zuba said between clenched teeth. "I'm sick of it."

One by one, the eyes of the undead were illuminated with a violet glow as the magic travelled from Zuba's strings into their bodies. *Just a bit more*, Zuba thought. *We're gonna need big boom booms today.* It was impossible to tell how many corpses Zuba had brought back from death, but it had to be in the hundreds. His father had never gotten close to such a number and seeing his mother's jaw drop at the sight filled Zuba with an evil glee. Finally, Zuba could step out from his father's shadow and cement himself as the artist he truly was.

"It's time," Zuba said, turning his attention to the Elder God wreaking havoc a couple streets down. He created a mental image of the Taken in his mind and the droves of undead climbing all over its body. The army of undead stiffened as the image transferred into their minds.

The corpses began moving towards their target. Their arms and legs twitched; their hands outstretched wanting nothing but grab onto the Elder God. At first their feet dragged, but as the corpses came closer and closer, they picked up their pace and started running. It would have been a horrifying sight if Zuba hadn't been the one controlling them.

The army of undead melted together, turning into a mass of death. The Elder God was too busy swinging its arms and destroying buildings to notice what was coming. Even if it had, it would have been too late. The corpses hurled themselves at the Taken's legs, becoming a swarm of clawing hands and biting teeth. The Elder God lifted its legs, slamming its hands down to rid itself from the attacking force. But it was impossible to get them all, and those undead that weren't crushed and swatted away kept climbing.

Up higher! Zuba ordered mentally. *HIGHER!*

In less than a minute the undead were spread across the Elder God's body. They were on its torso and throat; a few going up so far as the face, while the majority were spread out on its arms and legs. The Taken swung its arms and stomped its feet, frantically trying to get them off but unsuccessfully.

"Now, Zuba!" Lady Qanah screamed. "Do it now!"

Zuba's eyes lit up at the magnificent sight before him. He spread out his arms, lifting them high towards the sky.

Boom.

One by one, the undead began exploding, less than a second between them. The Elder God screeched as the corpses blew up in great blasts all over it. Big chunks of Elder God meat flew in every direction; black blood sprayed and rained down. The Elder God screeched and staggered, its legs now looking like chicken clubs gnawed down to the bones. It fell forward and backward, somehow still fighting to keep its balance. The Taken's left arm suddenly separated from the body, hanging momentarily by its fleshy strings before crashing down on the streets below and blowing up a massive cloud of dirt and dust. The screaming from the Elder God turned into a wheezing and gurgling as large sections of its throat had been blown to pieces. The face, if you could even call it that anymore, was full of holes that one could see through. Its legs gave in, buckling under its own weight. The Elder God toppled into several buildings before finally landing on its back in a resounding crash that sprayed stones and dust.

CHAPTER THIRTY-THREE

Varcade stood by the foot of the dead Elder God. Edghar and Dog Man were next to him, both looking around wide-eyed at the total destruction the battle had caused. There was blood and flesh from the Taken spattered all over, causing a sweet and sicking stench thick in the air. The dust had finally settled, making it possible to both see and breathe. The first sign of dawn broke through the dark sky as the sun's rays slowly lit up the great city.

"Did you see me?! Did you?!" came Zuba's voice as he came running towards them, his gangly arms waving above his head. "It was sensational! Magnificent!"

Varcade smiled. "I did, and I couldn't agree more. You're pretty damn awesome, Zuba," he said, patting the Supreme on his shoulder.

Zuba's eyes instantly teared up, his face turning red. "You really mean that?" he said, his voice cracking. "Like, *really really*?"

"Yes."

"Does this mean we're friends now?"

"Yes, Zuba, we're friends, okay?"

Zuba's eyes lit up like he'd just found a heap of treasure. "I knew it would happen. I *knew* it."

THE CREW

Edghar stepped forward, stretching out his one functioning hand to Zuba. "You saved Akrab. Or at least, what's left of it. If it weren't for you, there'd be nothing left. Thank you."

Zuba cleared his throat. "Does that mean you're not angry about the baby arm anymore?"

Edghar chuckled. "Getting kinda used to it to be honest. I mean, it's still completely useless, but in the scheme of things, I'm still alive. I would most likely be dead if you didn't fix me up."

"That's right," Lady Qanah said, crossing her arms. "My wonderful boy not only saved your life, but also saved this city. Zuba Ghul. You better remember that name and etch it into the history books."

Dog Man suddenly started sniffing the air. "Baaq!"

The marksman came walking towards them. She held her brimmed straw hat and dusted it off before putting it on. "Someone seriously needs to tell me what the fuck just happened here."

That drew a laughter from everyone expect the members of the Ghul clan.

The sweetness of victory did not last long for Varcade, as more and more time passed without Vashi emerging from the ruins. Every sound drew his attention, snapping his head left and right. But his brother was nowhere to be seen. *He can't be dead*, Varcade told himself.

A clickety-clack could be heard, and everyone watched how the Bone Lord and Helmet Head came riding towards them, mounted on the ugly camel. Now that Varcade got a closer look, the animal looked more dead than alive.

Zuba dashed up to the camel and patted its head. "Bogdan! How did you end up here?"

"We kinda borrowed him," Edghar said. "It was the only way we could get back here from the mansion."

"That's fine," Zuba said, scratching the camel under its chin.

Dog Man looked up. "What are you still doing here, Helmet Head? Shouldn't you be gone by now?"

Helmet Head slumped in the saddle. "Is that the thanks I get . . . for everything I've done?"

The Bone Lord unmounted, dusting herself off. She looked at the crew one by one. "So, *this* is the group Edghar brought together to kill me? An interesting bunch, to say the least."

"That'd be us," Varcade said. "Sorry 'bout that by the way. It turned out, we didn't know all the details. I'd blame Edghar for that, to be honest."

Edghar shot Varcade a stern look before he turned to the Bone Lord. "Clea–"

But the Bone Lord silenced him with a wave of her hand. "Not now. We all have a lot to talk about, but this isn't the place or time."

"Don't forget about me," came a guttural and harsh voice. "Marduk lives."

The large demon walked up and grabbed Varcade roughly by the neck. His vest was no more than tattered strips of cloth. His face was covered in dry blood and dust, along with nasty bruises and cuts running down his muscular arms. "Did you see? I crash my fist in balls of bastard. Made them powder."

Varcade hadn't actually seen that, but it was easier to simply go along. "Absolutely. It was great."

Marduk laughed. "It was great. I will not forget this day."

It had been two days since the battle with the Elder God. Since there was no longer the ziggurat to return to, Edghar had suggested they all go to Fish-City's tavern the Golden Coconut and make that their temporary housing. The demon had gladly welcomed them and given them each their own rooms.

Edghar walked down the corridor of the second floor and stopped outside Clea's quarters. He knocked gently and a moment later, she urged him to come inside.

The Bone Lord sat on her bed, combing her long, dark hair.

Seeing her freshly bathed without all the makeup reminded Edghar of when they'd been nothing but children. He'd thought her beautiful then as he did now. However, seeing the shadowed bruises and cuts she had sustained at the hands of Tarkus made Edghar wince.

"How are you feeling?" Edghar said, stepping inside the room and closing the door.

Clea looked up at him before turning her attention back to her hair. "That's a stupid question and you know it. How do you think I feel? How am I supposed to digest all that has happened? How am I supposed to make everything . . ." Her voice broke.

Edghar sank down on one knee before her and gently grabbed her hand. "Hey, easy now."

Clea closed her eyes and took a deep breath before opening them again. "I don't know what to do," she said softly. "I really don't. This is all *too* much. Khanon is dead. Erikz is dead. Even that snake Tarkus is dead. But I needed them all to rule Akrab. I can't do it on my own. I never could."

"You're not alone," Edghar said. "Far from it. I'm here now and I'm not going anywhere." He was silent for a moment before adding, "That is, if we can find it in our hearts to forgive each other."

Clea looked down at him with her deep brown eyes. "You really think we can? I want to, I'd love nothing more. But—"

"We *can*," Edghar said, placing his hand on top of hers. "I *know* we can. Let's put all of this behind us and look towards the future. It won't be as before, but I truly believe that's a good thing. This city needs to change. We both failed Akrab before all of this madness. We need to make things *right*."

Clea smiled and reached down to stroke his cheek. "I've missed you. This part of you that always makes me feel better. It's a gift you have."

"I've missed you too," Edghar said with a smile of his own before standing up. "I have a couple of suggestions on how we can rebuild Akrab. It's not going to be quick, change never is, but the city will be better for it."

"I'd love to hear it," Clea said. When Edghar didn't say anything, Clea added, "Now? You mean right now?"

"Why not? The sooner the better."

Clea laughed. "I guess you have a point."

Edghar went over to the window and looked out at the city that was his home. During this whole ordeal, one thing had become evidently clear, and that was how ignorant he'd been most of his life. Meeting Baaq and Marduk had changed his perspective on things here in Akrab.

How many years have I lived side by side with the demons without even trying to understand what it must be like for them? The awful truth was that he'd never really cared. He'd just figured they'd been happy with a safe place to live in after the First Contact War. But just opening the doors to the city and jamming them into one area clearly wasn't the best way to handle things. It had created a clear divide between humans and demons, and the now existing tension between the two races was a result of this, something Tarkus had used as a crucial tool in his plan.

Edghar walked over to Clea and sat down on the bed next to her. "First thing we need to talk about is the demon population. There's a lot we need to do to fix things, but I think that's where we need to start."

"I'm all ears," Clea said and took his hand. "Let's hear it."

Varcade stepped through the doors of Fish-City's tavern and swallowed a sigh. For the tenth time in five days, his attempts to find his brother Vashi in the ruins of Akrab had wielded no result. The only upside was his body hadn't been found either, meaning there was still a chance he was alive.

Marduk and Baaq sat at a table, and as they noticed him, Marduk wildly gestured for him to join them.

"Still no luck?" Baaq said.

"Nope."

"Your brother strong. I do not think he dead," Marduk said, taking a gulp from his drink. "You will see."

Even though the demon only wanted to cheer him up, in the end it was only empty words. Marduk had no idea if Vashi was alive or not. "Appreciate it," Varcade said, "But let's change the subject. What's been going on with you two?"

Baaq put down her glass. "You haven't heard? Me and this crazy guy are going to be working together from now on."

Varcade hid the surprise he felt. He couldn't imagine what an honourable retired soldier and a revolutionary could possibly do together. These two were like fire and ice trying to hug each other. "What will you do?"

"We're going to be working directly with the demons in Akrab and get them more involved and integrated in the city's affairs," Baaq said. "This thing where we've been living in the same city but not really working together won't be the case anymore. I'm sure there'll be plenty of challenges, but with the Bone Lord and the new Vizier backing us up, I see a bright future."

"New Vizier? Already?" Varcade said. "Who?"

"That'd be me," said Fish-City sinking down in the empty chair next to them. "Can you believe it? The first official demon part of the Akrab regime and advisor to the Bone Lord herself. Not too bad, right? It's about time our voices are heard in this city."

The inner workings of politics bored Varcade, and maybe he was too dumb to even grasp it, but hearing the happiness and pride in both Baaq's and Fish-City's voices still made him glad. These people had become his friends and he wanted the best for them. "Does this mean you'll put your vision of a bloody revolution to rest?"

Marduk nodded. "Yes. I will put my energy into doing good things for my brothers and sisters. No more violence and attacking onions."

Varcade felt a hand on his shoulder. "They are telling you all the news I get it?"

Varcade glanced up at Edghar. The smile on the man's lips could light up a dark room. "Yup. Looks like you guys have a plan."

Edghar nodded. "We do. We'll turn this whole thing into something good. You'll see. Say, do you have a moment?"

"Sure, what's on your mind?"

Edghar leaned in closer and lowered his voice for Varcade's ears only. "Listen, everyone is in a good mood so let's keep what I'm about to say between us, okay? I've been racking my brain over everything that has happened, and have come to the conclusion that Tarkus can't have acted all alone. You don't pull off something this big on your own."

"Huh," Varcade said, stroking his jaw. "So what are you thinking? Who helped him?"

Edghar sucked in a breath. "I don't know. Yet. But I'm going to trace all the steps back and see what I can unearth. I'm telling you, I know it in my gut that I'm right about this."

"Hey, you're the old Spymaster an' all. If you have a hunch then go with it."

"Good. With that said, would you mind sticking around Akrab for a while longer? I might need your help if it turns out I'm right about this."

"Maybe. I have a lot of thoughts swirling around in my head. I need to think about this."

"Hey, take your time. You're welcome to stay as long as you want while you figure things out, even if you decide to leave. Gotta say, I have kinda gotten used to your company, believe it or not." Edghar chuckled.

Varcade cracked a smile of his own. "Likewise."

Someone cleared their throat behind Edghar, and he stepped to the side, revealing Helmet Head. "You're not going to tell him about me?"

Edghar scratched his ear. "Yeah, sure, why not. Helmet–Jasper here is going to be my squire or something."

"Not or *something*. Squire. That's what you promised." Helmet

Head turned his attention to Varcade. "He's gonna teach me how to fight properly, and I get to live in the new ziggurat once they rebuild it."

Varcade laughed. "Not too bad. Not bad all. Good for you. But please do something about that hair of yours, eh? Enough is enough."

"I will, I will," Helmet Head said. "I'm not sure what, though."

"Anything is better than what you've got going on at the moment," Varcade laughed.

"Don't tell me he left already!"

All of them looked to the stairs that Zuba was running down, his gangly knees high in the air as he took two steps down at a time.

"Are we going?" Zuba said, catching his breath. "I didn't miss it, did I?"

"I'm sitting right *here*," Varcade said. "You're literally looking right at me."

"I know, I know," Zuba said. "I just want to make sure you didn't leave without me."

"I'm not going anywhere yet, calm down."

Edghar gave Varcade a surprised look. "Really? You two?"

Varcade shrugged. "I figured why not. I think it's time our Puppeteer here gets to experience more of the world than just being holed up in that dusty old mansion."

"And how does your mother feel about that?" Edghar said to Zuba.

"She's extremely upset with me, but I don't care. She can be as mad as she wants. Wherever Varcade is going, I'm going."

Fish-City stood. "You know what, my friends? I think we all deserve to have a proper feast and celebrate everything we've accomplished. How does that sound? I'll get the kitchen staff started."

"Has anyone seen Dog Man?" Varcade said as Fish-City left the table.

"I think he's outside," Baaq said.

Varcade did indeed find Dog Man standing outside the tavern. He did not seem surprised when Varcade approached him.

"What're you doing out here?" Varcade said, looking around.

"Waitin' for you, kid," the canine said without looking up. "Sure took your time."

"What do you mean?"

Dog Man glanced up at him. "You know exactly what I mean. We talked about this after killing the treasurer. But anything I have to say you already know deep down your heart."

"I really don't—"

"Don't be coy with me, boy. I'm way too old and too tired. If you wanna talk, then talk for real. I'm not like those others inside and you know it."

Varcade sucked in a deep breath then sat down on his haunches. "Fine."

"That's better. So, have you made up your mind?"

"Not yet."

"You know you can't keep runnin' forever."

Varcade nodded, his chin resting on his hands clasped before him. "I know. But I'm not sure now is the time. Going up against the Educator Order? I don't think I'm ready."

"Maybe not. You'll know when it's time. The important thing is that you *know* it needs to happen sooner or later."

"I do." Varcade looked over at Dog Man. "What about you? What will you do?"

How a dog shrugs Varcade didn't know, but that's what the canine did. "I'm staying here. I'm tired and Akrab's nice. I think I could be comfortable here; especially now that I haven't used Dust in several days and it hasn't killed me."

"I like the sound of that." Varcade rose to his feet. "And thank you. I mean it."

Dog Man laughed. "Nothing to thank me for, boy. Let's head inside. I smell something delicious."

Varcade smiled.

EPILOGUE

The moon stood high in the dark sky, sharing its silvery luminance on the city of Akrab. The streets were busy with humans and demons alike, no thoughts of sleep seemingly on their minds. The air was scented with savoury smells of food and drinks.

Vashi found that strange. The night was for sleeping and giving rest to the mind and body. But at the same time, there he stood, a stranger amongst strangers, looking in through the window of the Golden Coconut. He stayed back, careful to not let those inside spot him. It was better this way, he thought, even though it went against everything he'd been taught.

He saw his brother smiling and laughing together with those strange companions of his. Vashi hadn't seen his brother laugh or smile in a long, long time. Maybe when they had been children in the village, but it was hard to say. Vashi's memories from his life before the Educators were getting muddier and muddier as the years passed by.

Vashi knew in his mind what he should do. What he came all the way to Akrab for. But his heart wanted something else. And seeing the happiness on his brother's face made Vashi's decision feel like the *right* one, even though it was wrong. But perhaps, just this time, Vashi would do the wrong thing.

I will see you another day, little brother.

Vashi stepped in amongst the sprawling masses and vanished.

THANK YOU!
A PERSONAL MESSAGE

If you'd allow me, I just want to take a moment and offer my sincerest thanks for reading *The Crew*. You readers are the reason I have dedicated my life to the craft of writing and telling stories. Without you, this path I have chosen in life wouldn't be possible, and I'm not just speaking on my own behalf, but for all the other authors out there as well. In a day and age where there's almost too much entertainment to consume, time becomes more precious than ever, so the fact you wonderful book lovers across the globe decide to give authors like me a shot means more than I can ever express. I can only hope you enjoyed the ride and perhaps even got a few laughs out if. If I succeeded in that with *The Crew*, would you please consider spreading the word and rating and reviewing it on Amazon and Goodreads? It would honestly mean the world to me and I'd be forever grateful.

Best,
Sadir

ACKNOWLEDGMENTS

My lovely Nadja for your unwavering support and believing in my dreams.

My Mom who left everything to give me and my brother a better chance at life. I will never truly comprehend what you had to go through, but know that I love you, and all you had to sacrifice will never be lost on me.

My big brother Samer and his wife Gina for being the best cheerleaders a person can have. I'm glad to have you (and little Alexander) in my corner.

To the American and British Sci-fi & Fantasy community for welcoming this random Swede into the fold and giving me a place to belong. Places like r/Fantasy and the Grimdark Writers & Readers on Facebook were instrumental as I embarked on the journey of becoming an author.

Laura, Kareem, Mike, Jaypash and Anna. You guys are the best. I wish we could hang out more often.

Dyrk Asthon! Thank you for being a wonderful friend and helping me on the road to publication. I seriously can't thank you enough. You rock, brother.

Nick Eames. You're probably not aware, but without a certain conversation we had long ago, *The Crew* would probably never have been written. Thank you, buddy. I definitely owe you a drink or two.

Linn and Daniel! Thank you both for reading early versions of this book and always encouraging me to keep going.

Thank you Love Gunnarson for creating an amazing cover that is more than I could ever have hoped for. You are a master!

Sarah Chorn for being an amazing and brilliant editor to work with, as well as an all-around wonderful person.

Also, I have to give a shoutout to all the regulars at BristolCon! It's always a highlight of the year hanging out with you all.

Lastly, my very own Crew: You all know who you are.

ABOUT THE AUTHOR

SADIR S. SAMIR spent his first years in the Middle East before moving to Sweden. A passion for storytelling manifested early in childhood, and he always knew that would be his guiding light in life growing up. That passion eventually led him to the video game industry where he's been working as a game writer and a producer for over a decade. Now he lives in the medieval city of Uppsala, where he writes tales of the fantastical and bizarre.

www.sadirsamir.com

facebook.com/sadir.samir.1
twitter.com/Sadir_S_Samir

Printed in Great Britain
by Amazon